THE

THIRTEEN

Also by Susie Moloney

Bastion Falls
A Dry Spell
The Dwelling

THE
THIRTEEN

SUSIE MOLONEY

RANDOM HOUSE CANADA

PUBLISHED BY RANDOM HOUSE CANADA

Copyright © 2011 Susie Moloney

www.randomhouse.ca

Random House Canada and colophon are registered trademarks.

This book is a work of fiction. Names, characters, places, and incidents either are the product of the author's imagination or are used fictitiously. Any resemblance to actual persons, living or dead, events, or locales is entirely coincidental.

Library and Archives Canada Cataloguing in Publication

Moloney, Susie
The thirteen / Susie Moloney.

Issued also in electronic format.

ISBN 978-0-679-31381-6

I. Title.

PS8576.O4516T55 2011   C813'.54   C2010-907208-1

Design by Leah Springate

Printed and bound in the United States of America

2 4 6 8 9 7 5 3 1

For Michael, who still bewitches me.

PROLOGUE

CHICK WAS AN OLD-FASHIONED WOMAN. In spite of the hour and circumstances, she was in full battle gear—that was what Bill used to call it. Matching bra and panty set, nothing fancy, but a *good* set; Spanx that were killing her like the old joke; stockings, a full slip, then her dress, her best dress, a dark navy Ralph Lauren with cap sleeves. Her Cartier watch, the pearls Bill gave her on their wedding day, matching earrings and her wedding ring.

She checked her reflection in the mirror, absently working the wedding ring around her finger, something she always did when she was lost in thought. But it was awkward with the bandage on her hand and she stopped. The burn throbbed constantly. She picked up the spray bottle and gave her hair a once-over of lacquer. This she smoothed down. The hair bounced lightly against her scalp with each soft pat, a feeling so pleasant she nearly began to weep again. Instead she leaned closer to the bathroom mirror, and under the cruel light she took a last look at herself. Not too bad. Not too bad for sixty. She was one of the older gals in her group, but she'd bet money no one outside their circle would know it.

—which made her think of the throbbing, painful burned

surface of her palm and Bill saying *give me the keys, darling, don't be silly.* But she wouldn't give them to him. She squeezed the keys in her hand so he couldn't see them. He held his confused smile, unsure of what else to say. Then the sudden, shocking burn in her palm forced her hand open and she dropped the keys, but Bill didn't notice. Bill was under the influence, and it wasn't drink or drugs, but Izzy and he didn't notice her pain, the burned flesh on the key. It was just *thank you, dear, I'll see you tonight,* but of course he didn't see her that night at all—

Chick was still in the mirror; Bill was gone.

She left the bathroom light on and walked through her darkened house. The television, computer, radio—everything was off, and the curtains and blinds were drawn on every window. She used the bathroom light to navigate until she reached the living room, and then she went by memory.

Her shoes were still at the front door, where she'd taken them off after the funeral. They were pretty shoes, favourites. The insoles were cool on her feet when she slipped them on, but she grimaced putting her weight into them. She'd been in heels all day—since nine that morning, when Bradley and Thomas and their wives had arrived from the hotel to pick her up to go to the church. Of course they hadn't wanted to leave her alone, but she'd insisted, telling them that Audra—whom they'd known all their lives—would be with her. But in fact she'd sent Audra away too.

Chick had only sons, no daughters. They would miss her a little bit, but then they would be fine.

Bradley was an EMT. Not quite a doctor, but Chick and Bill were proud of him. He'd been very concerned about her hand. She hadn't let him see it, afraid of the questions he would ask about the key-shaped scar. She'd snapped at him when he'd persisted, and she was sorry now. There had been a time when she would have cut out her own tongue rather than lash out at one of her boys, but it changed when they left home. Bill had filled that void in her heart in a way he hadn't been able to when her sons were little.

Until the previous Sunday, that is, and his horrible crash. What had he seen right before he died? Did he see something in the road? The car had swerved violently off the highway into a tree. He'd been speeding.

Was it an animal in the road? The two-legged kind?

Chick ran a hand up the back of her leg to her knee, smoothing her stockings. Her legs were still good. She didn't need Bill to tell her that, but he always had. Vanity. One of the seven deadly sins. What were the others? *Gluttony, anger, lust, avarice, envy, forsaking all gods except me—* Maybe that one was a Commandment. She couldn't think.

She wobbled a little, feeling the first effects of the four Valiums she'd swallowed with a little supper, just enough to keep the woozies at bay, as the website had said.

The shoes were very expensive, the leather soft as butter and a rich navy, bought to match her dress. Oh, so beautiful. Shoes were one of life's great pleasures. There were really so many: shoes, lunch out, slow and quiet lovemaking in the morning, a glass of wine when you were cooking, fresh laundry, a laugh—

A person didn't need much. Not really. She wished she'd known that sooner.

She made her way to their bedroom, leaving the bathroom light on to guide her.

The bed was made, the coverlet pulled over the pillows. The whole house was clean and tidy, the dishes done and put away, laundry basket empty. She'd watered the plants and washed the kitchen floor, dusted her Hummels and paid what bills there were. She'd done everything she could in the first days after Bill was killed, trying to fill the hours, trying not to be hysterical.

The smell was very strong in the bedroom, unbearable, and there was a bad moment when she felt the smell in her belly and thought the pills she'd painstakingly taken were going to come up. She kept them down by breathing shallowly. She got used to it.

Chick crawled up the bed from the foot until she reached the pillows and allowed herself to drop. She rolled over onto her back, stared up at a black ceiling in a black room and contemplated her exhaustion.

Bill used to like to be tired. It was a silly thing to say, but he used to tell her *there's nothing like sleeping when you're tired, Chick, except drinking when you're thirsty.* The Valiums washed over her with every beat of her heart, thrumming in her ears. It was a pleasant feeling. Downers, the kids called them. It felt . . . smooth.

(but even under the smooth, sweet, soft feel of the pills, her hand still throbbed badly where it was raw and)

Chick felt around under the pillow until she found what she was looking for. Then she reached for the framed photo on the bedside table, of Bill and her on their trip to Mexico two years earlier. She'd debated between this and their wedding photo before settling on the more recent picture, because she realized that she loved him so much more now than when they first were married.

In fact, when they had first been married, she had found him ridiculous too often to admit. He never seemed to do anything right and she despaired of their ever getting anywhere in life. He chewed with his mouth open. Thought he was funnier than he really was.

But their marriage had experienced renaissance after renaissance.

Bill oh god Bill oh god

I am so sorry

The Valium cast a fog over everything, making her movements

sluggish and clumsy. Still she waited a bit, until she was sure that all she ever wanted to do for the rest of her life was

sleep

With her right hand she flipped open the top of the Zippo and, after a weak try, got it lit. She dropped the lighter to the floor of her gas-soaked bedroom and closed her eyes, uninterested in the flames that popped and exploded, focusing instead on the drugged amber glow inside her head. Because she was so afraid of what she might see in the moments before her body died, so afraid of what reckoning there might be—

She did not move from the bed. Not even when the flames swept up from the floor and began their climb over her

surrender your

flesh.

Primarily she felt an exhausted relief.

I give my flesh to you to do with as you please as I please you Father

As the room filled with smoke, the air harsh, her breathing became choked. The hairspray caught and flamed, melting her hair to her head as the fabric of her dress blistered against her flesh, the skin bubbling and puckering in the heat, her scarred hand unfurled like the petals of a flower. Her last breath felt like a sigh.

sorry so sorry my love my Bill

Her last thought was, *That house on the edge of town should burn burn burn*—

She burned, and the fire sounded like screams.

It was a bad night in Haven Woods.

Not long after the first fire trucks arrived at the home of Chick and Bill Henderson (Bill recently deceased), there was more trouble just a couple of blocks over.

Audra Wittmore had been making herself a cup of tea, something soothing, something kind after the unkind day she'd spent with Chick, the two of them in a tight protective (fearful) little hive.

Chick had cried a lot. Not so much when there were people around, but when they were alone. Over Bill, poor old Bill.

It had nearly broken Audra's heart, her good friend so full of self-loathing and remorse. So very broken-hearted.

Audra too had been inconsolable in the first days after Walter died. Had wept. She'd leaned heavily on her own best friend, Isadora Riley—Izzy. Izzy was no longer such a friend. So much could change in ten years.

Walter had died in a crash too. A terrible coincidence.

wasn't it just

Izzy had been at the funeral that afternoon, of course she had. Everyone in the neighbourhood had been there. She'd sat close to the front, with her daughter Marla and the two grandchildren.

Audra had stayed close to Chick, watching always for where Izzy was, keeping the two apart. Except for the receiving line, of course; there was nothing one could do about that. But still she'd stood beside Chick, letting Chick lean into her, holding Chick's arm, the good arm, with the unbandaged hand.

Terrible thing, that burn. Audra had seen it, had bandaged it herself. It was a good two inches long and at least an inch across, the whole thing a sort of T shape.

But it wasn't a T, it was a key. Seared into the flesh of her palm you could make out the letters F-O-R-D. Chick's son the almost-a-doctor had bugged her and bugged her to show it to him. How could she, poor thing?

It didn't bear thinking about. You just couldn't go down that road, or you would never sleep again.

She poured water slowly over the leaves and stared as the brew turned to a rich amber.

Audra's own dear husband had been dead now a very, very long time. She was still lonely for him. At least, she made herself believe that she was lonely for him and not just for anyone at all. Lonely for her family really. Her daughter. Her *granddaughter*, such a pretty little thing, just like her mother had been at that age. She never saw her. Rarely.

Dear Paula.

(dear Paula may you stay away far far away from Haven Woods)

Very briefly she'd had a man-friend. A neighbour, divorced, whose wife had moved away and left him behind in Haven Woods. Gabe, across the lane. He gardened, and when Audra took her dog, Tex, for a walk, she often found herself passing his yard, hoping he was in the garden. They talked about tomatoes and growing seasons and apple pie made from apples from their own trees. They both had real nice ones.

That's just how it goes, no matter how old you are or where you live. It starts with *oh I was just passing by* and then you get a cutting of something and then it grows a little and the giver stops by to see it and then it's coffee on the deck and pretty soon someone's baking something for someone. And then—if you live in Haven Woods—sooner or later Izzy Riley comes over and says with a certain curl of lip: *I see you've made a friend.*

It had gotten as far as apple-tree pie when Izzy came around and she and Audra had their chat about the state of the neighbourhood and how distracting things can be for a woman of a certain age, and was *another* man really a smart thing to do?

Eventually poor Gabe—who was funny and kind and good with the earth—moved away himself. And that was that.

Audra picked up her tea, carried it to the table in the kitchen and sat down. She blew at the steam that still wafted from the cup, and she was just thinking that maybe it hadn't been a good idea for her to leave Chick alone, even though Chick had insisted, begged even

(and Audra had just wanted to go home)

when the first sirens began, far enough away that Audra barely heard them. She had taken a good long sip of the tea before they became so loud she realized they were coming to the neighbourhood. She stood and headed for the front window of the house, where she had a pretty good view.

As she walked, her knees grew sick-weak and her joints suddenly seized up and her eyesight blurred and her heart raced and she was quite sure she was

having a heart attack

and she dropped to the floor like a stone, the teacup flying from her hand, hitting the floor and breaking, the tea splattering against the wall and the curtains over the front window, spreading in a damp smear like blood.

Audra was staring at the ceiling and she was utterly unable to move, but she could see the glow of the fire outside the window even as she heard the spray of water from the huge trucks and the flashing red-white of the emergency lights. .

Then Izzy was standing over her, saying *not feeling well?*

And of course it wasn't a heart attack.

It was a bad night in Haven Woods.

ONE

THE DRUNK AT TABLE EIGHT was shouting something at the dancer. Paula couldn't hear what it was over the music, but from his ugly expression she guessed it wasn't nice. Then he threw something that landed on the stage in front of poor Rachel. A typical Tuesday night at Blondie's.

Paula looked away, pretended not to see. Another asshole in the bar. She hated her job. *Hated.*

"What the fuck?" Andy said from behind the bar. "Go see what's going on."

"He threw something at Rachel," Paula said. She and Andy had a sometimes thing, which she also sometimes hated. Today she could smell his cologne on her hair. Chaps. Right now she didn't like his tone.

"I said go *see*," he snarled, and turned his back to her.

Paula groaned and grabbed her tray, wet with spilled beer, and headed for the fray.

There were only about ten people in the whole bar. It was early, just a couple of hours into her shift. The man had been drunk when she'd got there, obnoxious, loud. She'd picked him out right away. When the first dancer came on, he'd shut up and Paula had hoped that would be it.

"Excuse me, sir," she said. Even as she did she tensed against the inevitable transfer of his anger. His spittle.

Wet-eyed, he tried to focus. Paula had a horrible moment of bar clarity as she imagined this guy stumbling home to his family and picking a fight with his sober, half-awake wife. *Keep your voice down, honey, you'll wake the kids—*

Shut the fuck up—

The man ignored Paula and lurched to his feet, yelling at Rachel to get her fat ass off the stage.

At Rachel's feet was an olive. She must have stepped on it, because it was flattened and the pimento had separated. It must be what the man had thrown at her. Rachel's face was red and her movements were choppy. Choppier than usual. Andy didn't exactly run the A-list on the first shift.

"Sir," Paula repeated firmly, "please take your seat."

An ugly grin began on his mouth and gave up early. "What did you say to me?"

"Could you sit down, please? The dancer's just doing her job."

He was middle-aged—they always were—overweight, wearing a good jacket. Probably from out of town. Maybe his business hadn't gone well. He pointed a fat finger at her. A wedding ring glinted in the stage lights. "And you can shut your fat mouth."

He reeked of gin, usually a pleasant, juniper-bush smell. Not on him.

"C'mon, mister, please?" She tried to smile but she couldn't do it.

"Aren't you just a fucking *crackerjack* bitch . . ."

She stared at him, and for a moment his red-blotched, booze-slackened face disappeared. His eyes were clear and burning on her, his gaze steady. This time he managed his grin, and for an instant Paula felt as if she should duck.

"You should shut your mouth and get your fat ass home," he said, not slurring anymore.

"Excuse me?"

She'd had enough, and turned away. The song was just midway through, the few patrons in the bar every bit as interested in what was going on off the stage as on. She raised her hand to try to signal Andy, and then Rachel screamed.

The drunk had grabbed Rachel's ankle, catching it on a turn, and she fell to the hard stage floor with a terrible thud. Paula heard the air rush out of her.

That was it.

"Let her go!" Paula slapped her tray onto the nearest table. Nickels and quarters jumped wetly in the beery ashtray. It startled the drunk and he twisted his fat head on his fat neck to look at her. His eyes narrowed, whether to focus or to look mean, she wasn't sure.

He was still hanging on to Rachel's ankle. "If I want to watch some old cow take her clothes off I'll stay home with my wife."

Rachel groaned and tried to kick free of his hand. Her cheap strappy sandal came off and dangled sadly from her foot.

"Let go of Rachel and *sit down*—" Paula could feel bile rising in her throat; the smell of him, mixed with beer and sweat, was almost too much. He was her fourth bad drunk of the week and she was done. Fucking done. Her right hand clenched into a fist and she ached to use it. She said it again: "Let go of her."

The drunk made his own fist and raised it. "Gimme a reason."

Paula felt a rush of heat through her body—a tempting heat, a huge desire to lash out, to pound this man's sweaty face. Her eyes closed as she drew her own fist back like a bow—somewhere far away she heard someone gasp and a titter of laughter *hit him kid knock him to the floor*. Then she thought of her daughter,

Rowan. Twelve and at home alone, probably curled up in front of the TV, maybe homework in her lap, waiting for her mom to call on her break. She did not hit him.

She opened her eyes to see the drunk backed up against the stage, hands up, palms out, Rachel sitting up, sobbing and rubbing her ankle, just as Andy got there.

"Back off!" Andy shouted.

Paula's fist was still cocked and she realized Andy was talking to *her*. Her arm dropped to her side. She laughed nervously. "Whoa," was all she could think of to say.

"She was going to fucking hit me," the drunk said.

"Sit down," Andy said to the drunk, who was suddenly innocent *take it easy buddy what kind of joint you running* as if he had never grabbed Rachel, as if he'd never made a fist at Paula.

"Andy—" Paula started. He turned to her angrily and pointed to the back. "Get outta here. Dump your tray and change at the bar."

"I'm not missing a shift for this loser," she protested.

"You're not missing shit, Paula. You're fired."

Her mouth dropped open. He had to be kidding.

"You're kidding."

Andy pointed again to the bar. "Go."

She grabbed her tray and stomped away. Behind her she heard a guffaw. Her stomach got tight and she was momentarily thrown again, this time by fear. She hated herself for it. She set her tray on the bar carefully, and then she lifted the ashtray with her change from the puddle of beer and put that beside the cash.

She was at a loss. She'd stomped out of her fair share of jobs, but she'd never been fired.

"Paula, I'm so goddamn sorry," Rachel said from behind her. Paula turned to find the dancer, an unlit cigarette in her hand, a man's long denim jacket over her costume. Her eye makeup was smeared. "I'm going for a smoke. Bastards. Thanks for trying, Paula. It's a sisterhood, eh?" Rachel popped the cigarette into the corner of her mouth.

She waved Rachel away. "Don't worry about it. Go have your smoke." Rachel stood a second longer, checked over her shoulder for Andy, who was in a firing mood. When she saw him walking very slowly towards them, she scuttled away.

When he was close enough, Paula said, "What the hell, Andy?"

"You were going to hit a customer—what's that shit?"

"I didn't hit him. You're firing me for something I didn't even get to do."

He snorted. "I'm firing you for lots of reasons. That one's just handy."

"What?" she said, too loudly. "No way. No fucking way. I'm on time, I work hard enough. What are you talking about?"

Andy stepped back behind the bar and punched keys on the register. It popped open. He got some bills from under the tray. He held them out to her. They both looked at the money.

"Debbie's hired back," he said.

Debbie who?

"My girlfriend."

Ah. He held out the cash. It was twenties, maybe five of them. A hundred bucks. She laughed softly and shook her head. *Unbelievable.*

"I quit anyway. This place is a dive."

He handed her the money, not looking her in the eye.

Fuck you she wanted to add, but her mouth was too dry. She went into the back and got her jacket and purse. When she came out, he still wouldn't meet her eye. She left by the back door.

She made it as far as the edge of the parking lot before it hit her. She was unemployed. Again.

Worst Tuesday at Blondie's, ever.

—

Normally Paula took a taxi home after her evening shift, using tip money, but tonight she headed for the bus. Who knew when she'd have another job. Streetlamps were the only light on the road. Most of the businesses around there were daytime things, wholesale places and electrical shops that turned off their signs to save a buck. A traffic light half a block away flashed red.

The bus was empty, just her and the driver, who stared straight ahead when Paula got on and put her money in the box. By the time she'd sat down—at the back, where the losers sit—she was in full panic, full pity, full fear mode.

What would she tell Rowan? The truth seemed harsh.

Paula pictured Rowan in her school uniform and decided she couldn't say a thing.

She was twenty-eight years old. She'd just been fired from a bar job. This was not how it was supposed to be. When she'd been a kid back in Haven Woods, bar girl was not on her list of life goals. She couldn't quite remember what had been, but she could remember sitting for hours in a homemade tent with her friends, dreaming about who they would grow up to be.

Not bar girls.

A sisterhood, Rachel had said.

Six hundred in chequing, a hundred and fourteen in her wallet, courtesy of Andy's hush money, and thirty in the coffee can at home. There was a brief moment of regret when she thought about her temper and how hard it was sometimes to keep it down. She had really wanted to clock that drunk

(but I didn't)

She leaned her head against the bus window and watched as industrial turned into downtown, then into residential, across the railroad yard to the wrong side of the tracks. Home.

Every light in the apartment was on, as usual. Paula didn't

mind so much. When she was Rowan's age, she was never left alone, never mind most nights.

She walked through the apartment, flipping lights off as she went until she was in the kitchenette. Supper things were still on the table, a plate scraped clean, knife and fork, a glass with milk slowly drying in the bottom and chopsticks.

Chopsticks.

On the counter beside the sink was a Styrofoam takeout container, empty. She opened the fridge. Two more takeout containers were in there, one with a serving spoon sticking out the top.

A brown bag in the recycling box was from Captain Wu's, the receipt for eighteen dollars, which left twelve dollars in the coffee can.

Paula went to Rowan's door, which was open just a crack, her Ariel nightlight glowing. Rowan still watched *The Little Mermaid* now and then even though she was getting too old.

"Ro?" Paula whispered. She could just make her out under the covers, all limbs and hair. A fierce love rose in her, as familiar as the panic and fear, but better.

She was about to give up and close the door; it was nearly eleven.

"Mom? How come you're home?"

"Ro, did you have takeout?"

"Mmm, yeah. Delivery."

"Where did you get the money?"

"From the emergency can."

"Who said you could use that? That money's for emergencies—"

Rowan sat up and rubbed her eyes. "It *was* an emergency. There was nothing to eat."

Paula groaned. "Rowan! There was tinned soup. Tuna. Leftover casserole from Sunday—I know you don't love it, but we can't just have takeout whenever we freaking want." She was trying to stay calm, but it was hard, thinking of the thirty dollars that had been in the can, reducing their total wealth now to

six hundred in chequing, fourteen in my purse, *twelve* in the can—

"Jeez, I'm *sorry.* I had homework. I didn't feel like cooking." Rowan flopped backwards and closed her eyes.

"Ro—" Paula started.

"I'm *sorry*, Mom. I have to go to sleep. Can't you ground me tomorrow?"

"It's not funny, Ro."

She turned over onto her side and Paula could hear a change in her breathing. Then she spoke again. "I'm sorry. Don't be mad."

Eighteen dollars. What was that? Bread and milk and eggs, maybe the paper.

"I'm not," Paula finally said. "Not really. I love you." She backed out of the room, remembering to leave her daughter's door open just a crack.

In the kitchen she pulled the leftover takeout from the fridge and ate it with the chopsticks, standing up, not tasting it. Her throat was thick, wanting to cry, to freak out.

What was lower than bar waitress? Not too much.

Welfare, she guessed. Rowan's tuition was paid to the end of the year, thanks to her mother, but after that she'd have to go to public school. She didn't even have a car they could live in, although there was a beater for sale across the street. She passed it every day.

She threw the takeout container into the trash, then dropped to the sofa and picked up the remote. She turned on the TV to snow, then noticed a note taped to the back of the remote. She squinted to read it. *You didn't pay cable Mom.*

She flicked off the set and soon she was asleep, dreamless

except for one moment in the middle of the night when she thought she heard her mother calling her to get up. It was *time for—*

It was a beautiful morning, but little of it bled though the frosted glass windows of the second-floor bathroom at St. Mary's Academy for Girls. Rowan was with Nicki and Caleigh. Nicki had stolen a couple of cigarettes from her mother's pack. They were all crowded into the last stall and Nicki was about to light one.

Caleigh had shoved gum in the smoke detectors. It was bright pink against the rest of the gobs of gum, some so ancient they had lost all colour.

Nicki flicked the lighter (also pinched from her mother) and held the flame to the end of the cigarette. It caught and flared briefly, like a firework. Rowan and Caleigh—children of non-smokers—flinched and stepped back a little.

Nicki inhaled and coughed roughly, but not as much as a person might expect. Then she held it out to Caleigh. "Don't just stare at it. Smoke it, dork."

With a glance at Rowan, Caleigh put it in her mouth like a straw. She sucked on it once, then burst into terrible, deep coughs, as if she had lung cancer or something.

Nicki laughed, and patted her hard on the back. *Thump thump thump.* "You baby!" She took the cigarette back. "They keep you skinny. That's why my mom smokes. She says if she quits she'll put on, like, twenty pounds."

Nicki held it out to Rowan. "C'mon."

Rowan shook her head. Caleigh was still sputtering and looked sick.

"I don't think so. It causes cancer."

"Not the first time," Nicki said.

"I don't want to."

Nicki drew on the cigarette herself and blew smoke out like a pro, holding in a cough that made her eyes water. "If you try it I'll let you use my Friis bag for the city trip. My big one." Grade seven and eight French students were going to Montreal for a weekend, to see an opera in French and to eat in French restaurants in order to have an "immersion experience." Sister Claire was taking them. Everyone loved Sister Claire. Rowan would like to *be* Sister Claire, except for the nun part.

Nicki watched her with a half-grin, but Rowan wouldn't meet her eyes. She stared at her feet, then the wall. "No way," she said finally. "I'm not going anyway."

"Really? Why not?" Caleigh said.

"It's lame." It cost five hundred dollars. "I don't want to go."

Nicki grinned slyly. "Can't your mother afford it?"

"That's none of your business, Sickie Nicki," Caleigh said. "Get the money from your dad," she said to Rowan. "That's what I do when my mom won't give me something."

"My dad's dead," Rowan said. "He died in a car wreck when I was a baby. I've never even seen him, except in pictures."

"Wow," said Caleigh. "That's kind of sad. My dad had a heart attack two years ago, but he's okay now." Caleigh looked at Rowan with a new sort of interest.

Nicki played with the cigarette. "Isn't your mom a stripper? They make lots of money, you know. She should totally have the money."

"She's not a stripper, Nic," Rowan said.

"Hey, there's nothing wrong with being a stripper. I think it's cool. I would love to have men staring at me because I'm beautiful," Nicki said.

"They stare at strippers because they're naked, not because they're pretty," Caleigh said. "Is your mom a stripper really?"

"*No!*" Rowan was red-faced. "She works in a bar downtown. But gawd, she's not a stripper."

"But she's poor, right? That's why you're not going on the trip—"

"Fuck off, Nicki." Rowan stared her down.

"Whatever, Wittmore," Nicki said, as she put the cigarette to her mouth for another puff. "If my mom was a stripper I wouldn't lie—" It was as far as she got before Rowan pulled back and smacked her in the face. The cigarette hit the wall, and sparks and ash bounced off the tile.

The smack seemed to echo loudly in the bathroom. Nicki blinked, her mouth dropped open in total surprise, a red mark appearing where Rowan had hit her. There was complete, shocked silence for a split second. Then Caleigh screamed.

"You fucking hit me," Nicki said.

"You have a big mouth," Rowan said, surprised at how her heart was pounding, and also at how good it had felt to hit Nicki's (smug) face.

Then Nicki's chin started to wiggle and her bottom lip practically swallowed her top lip as fat tears plopped out of her eyes onto her pink cheeks. "You fucking hit me, Wittmore! You fucking did so!"

"Shut up, Nicki," Rowan said.

Caleigh put her hands up. "I'm going to—" and then she ran away from them, leaving Nicki and Rowan standing like idiots, staring each other down while the cigarette burned between them on the washroom floor.

That's how it was when Sister Claire came in, Caleigh trailing behind her, and all hell broke loose, shit hit the fan, everybody had a big fat crap sandwich.

Light burned through Paula's eyelids, something wrong about that for sure, but there was something else too, a shoo-fly feeling, an irritation like an itch, pulsing.

She was not in her bedroom. The light was coming at her from the big window at the front of the apartment. Morning light. She was on the sofa in the living room, still in her clothes from the night before. She could smell beer very faintly. From her pants, most likely. *Ugh.*

The phone rang beside her head once more, pulling her completely out of sleep.

"Shit," Paula mumbled, pawed towards the sound of the phone and hit upon the receiver, thumbing the button as much to make it stop as to answer the call.

"Hello?"

"Mrs. Wittmore? This is Candace Fines, principal at St. Mary's Academy—"

"It's Miss," Paula corrected her, her voice froggy.

"Be that as it may . . ." Fines continued, her voice chilly.

Paula listened, anger growing inside her, feeling like the bitter taste of the last straw. She hung up the phone and dragged herself off the sofa and changed her clothes.

Rowan was in deep trouble. In deep shit.

shit shit shit

Rowan was sitting on the wooden bench outside the principal's office when Paula came out. She looked up shyly, but with a tiny bit of the expression Nicki probably had seen right before Rowan clocked her.

The two Wittmore girls stared at each other. Paula kept her expression blank, both because she was unsure how she felt and because she was exhausted. It was only ten thirty in the morning and there had already been a disaster. Mother Teresa would have been exhausted.

"Get your book bag," Paula said. "Do you have anything in

your locker that you'll need?"

Rowan's eyes widened and the trace of defiance disappeared. "Need for what?"

Paula's purse felt as if it weighed twenty pounds. She dropped it to the floor and sat beside her daughter on the bench.

"Need in the next two months. You've been suspended for the rest of term."

Rowan gasped. "Because I hit Nicki?"

Paula nodded. "They have a zero-tolerance violence policy."

"What about the smoking?"

"You were *smoking*?"

Rowan let out a frustrated sigh. "No. Nicki had a cigarette and was trying to make us try it. But I didn't."

"Is that why you hit her?" In truth she was still trying to digest the idea of Rowan hitting anyone. She'd never been what you would call an angelic child, but she'd never been violent. Rowan had always used her words when she was angry.

Rowan shook her head.

"Well, what then?"

Rowan stared at the floor, her hair covering her face, but Paula could still see her through the breaks in the curtain it made. She was frowning.

"Nicki's an asshole."

"Rowan! You're not making this any better for yourself. Tell me why you hit her."

Rowan shook her head and then shrugged. "What did Fines say?"

"She said, 'Nicole and Rowan had a disagreement and Rowan struck Nicole in the face.' And when I asked what the disagreement was about, she suggested I ask you, that it was personal."

She put her hand on Rowan's shoulder. "What was it about, honey?"

"Nicki said you were a stripper."

It was Paula's turn to be speechless. And when she didn't respond, Rowan looked at her, concerned. "You're not, are you?"

"No. *No.* Rowan, you know I'm not. I'm a waitress. Lots of women are waitresses—"

"Not here."

Touché. Paula stood up. "Go get your stuff. I'll meet you out front."

Without discussion they took the long way home, down Cascade Street, past the library and the big Whole Foods that they went to around Christmas time. Neither of them was anxious to get back to the crummy apartment.

For most of the walk they were quiet. Then Paula said, "I'm still surprised you hit her, Ro. You want to talk about it?"

"No."

Paula couldn't help it, and laughed a little. Of course she didn't want to talk about it. Neither did Paula, truthfully. But she had to say something.

She took a breath. "I wish I was a lawyer or a doctor or something great like that, but I got pregnant and had you, and I had to choose. I wanted to be your mother more than I wanted to be a doctor or a lawyer."

It was true, after a fashion. Paula had been lost in those days, heartbroken, angry. She had been only sixteen, practically a child and pregnant with one. Her father had just died. What had surprised her most of all was her mother's solution. At a time when they should have needed each other most, her mother had sent her away, to the same school Rowan was now suspended from. Maybe it had been too much for both of them. Their house had become unbearably sad, grief seeming to echo off every wall.

Paula had been full of secrets that she couldn't share. Sometimes she suspected that her mother knew that. But neither of them said anything then, and they had said nothing since about those days. Bad times, but a long time ago.

Rowan snorted, and that took Paula by surprise. "What?"

"Maybe it would have been better if you'd been doctor or something. Look at us now—we're all broke and crap. We don't even have cable any more."

"Oh, please—"

"Maybe you should have gotten a better job or gone to a better school or something. Instead, now we're stuck and you can't even make it better!"

"First of all, I went to a very good school—the same one you just got booted out of. I don't have to explain my choices to you, Ro."

"Why? Aren't you always asking me what I think about life and telling me to be honest? Well, *are* you a stripper? You could be, right? I mean, you had me and you weren't married or even with a boyfriend—"

"Rowan! What does that have to do with anything?"

"I don't know! I just wish—we were normal. I don't have a dad, I don't have a sister or a brother . . . I don't even have a grandma! All the teachers call you Mrs. Wittmore and I don't tell them you're not married . . . but everybody knows—" Rowan's forehead was sweaty, as it always got when she was upset, and her bangs clung.

"You have a grandmother, Ro. She pays your tuition, remember?"

"But I don't see her," she said, petulantly. "Is she ashamed of me?"

Paula reached out. "Rowan, of course not! She loves you. She's just not . . . that kind of grandmother. Come on, you're upsetting yourself. Let me take your bag—"

She jerked away. "No! I'm going home—you walk too slow!"

"Jesus, Ro—" she said, but Ro was leaving. She'd adjusted her bag on her tiny shoulders and was actually stomping away.

"Do you have your key?" Paula called.

She spun back to face her mother. "Yes, I have my key. Of course I have my key. I always have my key—I'm a latchkey kid!"

"You're not a latchkey kid, Ro. You go to the lunch program."

"I am at night!"

"Rowan, please—"

When Paula got back she found an envelope taped to the apartment door. *Paula Wittmore* was written in pencil on the front in Andy's handwriting.

Paula unstuck the envelope, then let herself into the apartment. She could hear music, a little too loud, coming from Rowan's room. She was grateful not to have to face her. Paula would have to say something about her job situation

(which did not bear thinking about just yet)

and they would have to plan for the days of school Ro would miss. She dropped her purse and tossed her jacket onto the sofa, where the blanket from the night before was still where she had left it. She took the envelope over to the kitchen counter, stuck her finger under the flap and tore it open.

The cheque was for five hundred dollars. Double what she was expecting. There was no note. Guilt money

(and she didn't care)

and she noticed that the message light was blinking on the archaic answering machine.

Paula pressed Play.

"Paula? This is a message for Paula—" and even as she heard the voice, her heart nearly stopped in her chest, and everything else about the day slid off her.

"Dear, it's Izzy Riley, from Haven Woods? I'm sorry to tell you, but your mother has taken ill. She's in the hospital here. I hope you'll come home. I know you and she haven't been so close these past years, but she'd love to see you. And your daughter."

Her mother was ill, badly enough off to be in the hospital in Haven Woods. That crummy little hospital. She and Rowan had been back home to visit only once, and Rowan had gotten so sick they had to go back to the city—there was no way she was taking her baby to the Haven Woods emergency room.

Her mother had come to see them maybe twice since then and actively discouraged any suggestion from Paula that she and Rowan come home.

And now . . . Izzy Riley.

Paula dropped to a chair beside the table and tried to take that in. Last time she'd seen Izzy she'd been standing outside the church after David's funeral. Izzy had turned and looked over her shoulder just as the Wittmores got into their car. A quick glance and then she turned back to talk to someone. That was the last time Paula had laid eyes on a Riley.

Rowan's other grandmother. Not that Izzy knew that.

She would go home. She and Rowan.

Her mother was ill: *Audra* was ill. Old Tex, the dog—he would be sixteen, seventeen? She pondered that, considered that he might be dead. The house would be empty.

Haven Woods, a million miles away from Blondie's, St. Mary's Academy; a million miles away from where she was now.

A million miles away.

TWO

What was I thinking? Izzy Riley was thinking how long the day had been already, wondering *how much longer are these people going to stay?*

It was a full house. Of course it was. It was a monumental occasion, the dispensing of one of their own.

The three oldest of them all, Aggie, Tula and Bella, had grouped together in the corner and were downing wine, shooting shifty-eyed and half-terrified glances to wherever Izzy was in the room, as if she were going to bite them.

If only she could.

They had reason to be looking like frightened dogs; they all did. What Chick had done—Izzy grimaced at the thought of Chick, dead or undead—had upset the balance, and no one knew what would happen next or, more pointedly, to whom it would happen.

But they were all there to see her off. The oldest of them and the youngest, the generation of Izzy's daughter, and of course Izzy herself, the only one of her own generation still standing, now that Chick was dead and Audra was . . . had fallen ill. That was the way to say it: *ill*, ailing. And in deep, deep trouble.

She peered into the sitting room from the kitchen, where she was temporarily hiding, wishing everyone would just go away. She longed to escape to her basement room, where she could figure out the length and breadth of this particular situation and further damn Chick to hell. Audra too.

They were all talking talking talking in the other room, mostly in hushed funereal tones, but she could hear them well enough, and her head pounded. *Ugh.* She would like to strike them all mute. The thought made her smile.

Izzy had done hostess rounds already, once with a nice bottle of wine and then again with coffee. She was in the kitchen now under the guise of putting trays of dainties together. She was visible but mostly inaccessible. Her favourite state.

In front of her on the kitchen counter, beside the tray of stuffed mushrooms someone had brought

(full of cheese and sodium, *ugh*)

was her address book, open to Chick's page. She tapped the edge of the counter with a pen until she caught the eye of her cat, Tansy.

"Up," she demanded. "*Up.*" The cat blinked twice, not wanting to appear eager, and then jumped, landing softly.

"Good girl. Pretty girl." Izzy rubbed the cat's head. From the pocket of her very good suit she produced a tiny treat. She gave it to the cat, who ate it, lovingly, from her fingers. "That's my girl," she whispered, and the cat arched under Izzy's hand.

She picked up the pen and scratched a line through *Margaret Henderson*. She had not liked "Chick" and had never called her old friend that. At one time she'd tried to get Margaret to give up her nickname. She wouldn't.

Yet another good reason for her to be dead.

The line through the name became two, and then absently Izzy scribbled hasty loops over her own handwriting, completely obliterating her old friend's name.

Under Margaret's name and address was more useless information:

Husband Bill.

She drew strokes through that too. Bill was dead too. Just last week. They say that couples who are close in life also die very closely. Chick—stupid stupid stupid—had done her horrible, self-ish deed the day of Bill's funeral. Everyone out there was all *poor thing couldn't live without her Bill.* Gawd, wasn't everyone's husband dead, for chrissakes? Izzy's Roger, Audra's Walter. Aggie's husband had been dead so long Izzy could barely remember if he'd been an Alfred or an Edward. Aggie's husband had been the first to die, and Aggie hadn't torched herself. No, she picked up and went on to a better life.

Audra should have told that to Chick. *You move on.*

"Mother?" Izzy's daughter, Marla, carried a handful of dirty cake plates into the kitchen. Small forks jutted out the sides like porcupines.

"What?"

"Shouldn't you make another appearance? I think Chick's son wants to thank you." She set the plates in the sink with care, but the forks still clattered on the ceramic.

Izzy sighed.

Marla arranged the dishes in the sink. "What's going to happen to Chick's house, do you think? Will they just tear it down?"

"Why on earth would I know that?" Izzy said.

"Lighten up, Mother. You're so angry." Marla looked at her watch. "Well, I have to leave."

"No, you can't go. I need you here. I hate this."

Marla ran a finger around the edge of one of the plates and scooped up a bit of icing. She stared at the frosting on her per-fectly manicured finger. "Timmy has a baseball tryout."

"Don't you have a husband? Why can't he take him?"

"He's making us rich, just the way you taught me a good husband should do. So I'm on baseball duty." Marla scratched behind Tansy's ears.

"Stay a little longer. I really do hate this."

She shrugged. "No, you don't. You like this, having everyone where you can see them."

"But I have something to tell you." Izzy raised her brows invitingly as Marla met her eyes, and for a moment Izzy was struck by how soft Marla's cheek and jaw were, how dewy still. More and more, lately, Izzy noticed such things, getting mushy in her old age. She was fifty. A gorgeous fifty, as she was fond of telling people. Her daughter was prettier than she had ever been, though.

"What?"

"You'll like it."

Marla grabbed for her jacket, a lilac thing that matched her skirt. She had not worn black to the funeral. "Tell me fast, because I'm leaving."

"A good friend of yours is coming home. Her mother is ill." That got Marla's attention, as Izzy knew it would.

Marla's face relaxed into something genuine and she smiled. "Paula?"

"Yes. She's coming back to see Audra."

Marla frowned briefly, considering this, then smiled again. "Really? Well, I can't wait to see her again." She clapped her hands in excitement. "She's never even seen the kids! I'm going to have her over for dinner. This is—"

Izzy grabbed Marla by the arms. She gripped her hard. "We are in the middle of a *dilemma*, Marla. This isn't a reunion of old school chums . . . Do you hear me?" She held her tightly a minute more and then let go. Marla jerked back.

"I know. I just haven't seen her in so long I got carried away." Her eyes narrowed and she shifted her gaze to avoid eye contact with Izzy. "Wait until she finds out her mother isn't really sick."

Izzy moved more dishes from the counter to the sink. She could hear people talking in the main room and she lowered her voice. "Her mother really is sick. She's in big trouble. Don't go spilling the beans to your old friend."

"*Really*, Mother. I have to leave. Tim's tryouts are in half an hour and I have to be there to cheer him on." She slipped the jacket over her shoulders and pulled her hair out from under it, prettily.

"Wish him luck from Grandma," Izzy said. "Paula is bringing her daughter with her."

There was a pause and then Marla laughed softly. "Really." She turned to stare contemplatively at her mother. "You've never met Rowan, have you? That will be interesting . . ." She grinned, the expression incomprehensible to Izzy.

"It will be *necessary*."

Marla's grin disappeared. She opened her mouth, but for a minute the words wouldn't come. Then she said, "I'm sure I don't know what you mean. I have to go, I really do." She picked up her purse, a shade that matched her jacket, and slid it over her shoulder. Just before she went out the door, she shot Izzy a look that was also incomprehensible.

Izzy stood there for a minute after her daughter had gone, then sighed deeply and poked her head into the living room. "Tula, can I have a quick word?"

The old woman looked up from her drink with a nervous expression, then got up out of her chair and made her way around the guests to the kitchen, carrying her wineglass.

Izzy waved her over to the back door. "Get to the hospital. Audra's been alone for hours. Who knows what trouble she might have gotten up to."

"I can't imagine she could get up to much," Tula said.

"Just go. I'll be along shortly."

Tula nodded and plunked her glass on the counter. Red wine sloshed over the edge. Izzy stared at the old lady, disgusted.

"Sorry," Tula said quickly, then grinned. "Glass is half full, eh?"

"It's half empty, Tula. Now go, please."

Tula picked up her purse from a pile of others by the coat rack near the kitchen door, and scuttled out of the house.

Izzy rubbed her forehead. She felt a headache coming on, but she plastered a broad smile on her face—entirely inappropriate for the circumstances—and breezed into the living room, where the guests were subdued, mournful, bereft.

"Who wants another drink?" she said.

Everyone.

THREE

Izzy was tall for a woman, with striking features that had just begun the process of gentle aging. The lines around her mouth and eyes were still soft; she looked elegant, like a woman of a certain age advertising cosmetics. Middle age suited her, as her height suited her. She used both to full advantage whenever necessary.

Standing over Audra's

(poor Audra)

bed, Izzy felt powerful, and very, very healthy. Being in the presence of illness gave her such a feeling of vitality.

Audra's eyes were closed. Izzy leaned over and lay her cool hand on Audra's forehead, tenderly.

"*Poor* Audra," she purred. "Wake up."

The woman's eyelids twitched and Izzy suspected she was faking. But then she opened her eyes. The whites were lightly yellowed, as if from jaundice.

"Hello," Izzy said. "Hate to say it, but you don't look very good."

Audra rolled her eyes away from Izzy and tried to sit up. This appeared to cause her pain, and she dropped back with a groan. Her voice was raspy, like bees and sandpaper, the sounds from a throat not just dry but red and tortured. "What's wrong with me?"

"Well, you're not well, are you? Has something recently happened that made you ill?" But Izzy didn't want to be so sarcastic, at least not yet, so she changed the subject. "You missed Margaret's funeral today—Chick's. I know how close you two were . . . Anyway, it was a beautiful service, blah blah blah."

She sat down on the edge of the bed, not bothering to mitigate her weight. The bed shifted, and Audra with it, eliciting another groan.

"Closed casket, of course, since she was crispy-fried. You know, if you are going to light yourself on fire, I swear, do not use hair-spray first. *Ugh.*"

Izzy had rushed to the funeral home, daubing her eyes with a handkerchief, had insisted on seeing her friend. The kid on duty had finally allowed her a peek

(wasn't he surprised when she ceased her weeping and looked upon the blackened remains of her friend with a sardonic twist of the lips)

Audra clutched her throat. "Get me some water, will you?"

"What the hell were you two thinking?" Izzy said, unable to play the role any longer.

"I didn't have anything to do with Chick's . . . with the—" Audra's eyes puddled with tears. She snuffled thick mucus up her nose. "I don't want to hear—"

Izzy made a face. "You were in cahoots. A little party of two. Bill died anyway, didn't he? And now Chick is dead, and you're . . . ill."

"How long will I be here?"

Izzy got off the bed. "You're a danger to yourself and others, Audra." She went to stand by the window. "You'll be here as long as it takes to fix the mess we're in." The second-floor room faced the mostly deserted parking lot. There was Izzy's car, and Tula's car, and a couple of others close to the park at the far end, where there was a ball diamond. There was no sign of the car she was expecting. Not yet. She tugged the curtains shut.

"Do you remember that time we took the kids to Cranberry Lake for the day? They were . . . what, about six and seven?" She glanced over at Audra, who was staring elsewhere. "Do you remember we went to the playground and that big fat woman with the four fat little children had commandeered all the swings? We waited awhile, waited for those horrible little children to get off at least one of them so our babies could have a turn."

It had been so easy when the kids were little, Izzy thought, and had a painful flash of her and Audra at the picnic tables that day, laughing and drinking coffee from a Thermos. True friends.

"And finally I went over to the woman and spoke to her. And then those kids got off the swings and went and ate the sand out of the sandbox or whatever and we put our little ones on the swings. Do you remember what you said? You said, *Oh, Izzy, you're so bossy.*"

The room was considerably darker with the curtains closed. It was oddly cosy, or at least that was how Izzy felt, remembering old times.

"You said I was bossy and I said, 'People just listen to me.'"

She turned on the bedside lamp.

"Chick didn't listen. And like I said, Bill is still dead. Now she's dead and you're here. And everyone is in very big trouble."

That hung between them for awhile like the patch of light from the lamp.

"But I have good news too," Izzy finally said.

"Izzy, water?" Audra rasped.

There was a pitcher of cold water and a glass beside Audra's bed. Condensation had formed on the outside of the pitcher. She took the plastic off the glass and poured water into it. Ice clinked as it hit the sides. Izzy put the pitcher down.

"I don't know if you're allowed," she said. "You're not well, you know." She picked up the glass and took a couple of dainty sips. "That's very cold. I think it's too cold."

She put the glass back on the table. Audra's eyes followed it.

"We'll let it warm up a little bit."

Audra rolled her eyes and shut them. "I know you're angry. But you need me," she whispered.

"I need numbers, and you're still alive, even if you're . . . indisposed." Izzy flipped on the lamp on the other side of the bed. "You haven't asked me what the good news is."

She leaned in close to Audra and sniffed with interest. "You're not smelling very fresh, sweetie."

"I don't care," Audra said.

"Oh, you will," Izzy insisted. She looked around the room for anything she could use to spruce up the woman in the bed. She opened the cupboard. Audra's street things were hanging neatly there, her white boucle suit, a silk full slip, her handbag. On the floor was a pair of pumps, also white. The outfit she'd worn to Bill's funeral, the day she collapsed. Izzy had ridden in the ambulance with her friend and hung the clothes up herself.

She took the handbag down from the upper shelf and pawed through it until she found a comb, a compact, a mirror and lipstick. "Here we go," she said. She sat again on the bed beside Audra.

"You have to sit up—" and she tugged her friend into position as Audra tried to suppress a gasp. Izzy ran the comb through her hair, tugging lightly at snarls until they came loose.

She leaned over to whisper close to Audra's ear. "Someone very special is coming to Haven Woods today."

"I don't want to see anyone like this. "

"You will. This one is coming *home*."

Audra wasn't listening. Every one of Izzy's ministrations elicited another groan. "How long is this going to go on? What have you done to me?"

Izzy turned the comb under as she got to the ends of Audra's hair. "Me? Only you are to blame for this." She grunted, disgusted. "I have no idea how long. This, I think, is just the beginning. Glory wasn't at the funeral. Would you like to hear why?"

Audra didn't answer. She closed her eyes.

"Lovely, plump Glory. Not plump anymore, of course. Now she's slim, but she's still sticking everything she can into her mouth. What a useless girl . . . but never mind that. Glory called this morning, weeping, as if something had happened to one of her horrible children, but in fact her finger had fallen off."

Izzy stopped yanking the comb through Audra's hair and tossed it on the bed. She got up and crossed the floor to the window again and peeked out. Nothing moved outside.

When she turned back, Audra was watching her, even more anxiously.

"Her finger fell off. On her left hand, I think she said," Izzy continued. "Now that was not my doing. Maybe I tinkered a bit with you out of anger, but this—" she waved her hand over Audra's bed "—was not me either.

She got close to Audra. "*He's* angry with us. And that is your fault. Chick's too, of course, but lucky for her—and I mean that—she's not here."

Audra shook her head. "No. It could be anything. Some trick or error." To Izzy's ears her voice was unpleasantly strained. It sounded . . . guttural.

Izzy picked up the compact and popped it open. She rubbed the pad over the powder and began to pat it on Audra's face. Audra flinched. "Stay still," Izzy commanded, and the woman stilled, her eyes wide, looking into her tormentor's. It was disconcerting, and Izzy couldn't help but pause before she stroked more makeup onto Audra's face.

"Anyway, I have a surprise for you, and since you're not asking, I'll just tell you." She found the lipstick on the bed and rolled it up. The pink tip of it was vaguely obscene. "Smile," she said to Audra. Audra didn't. Izzy applied the lipstick to her pale lips anyway.

"Do you blot?" Izzy tugged a tissue from the box on the table and folded it, holding it to Audra's mouth. Audra turned her head away. Izzy grinned meanly.

"Don't you look pretty," she said. She narrowed her eyes. Audra did not look pretty at all. Izzy pawed around on the bed for the mirror, finding it under a fold of sheet. She fondled it. Should she show Audra herself in the mirror?

"Who's coming?" Audra finally asked.

Izzy smiled. "With your being ill, I thought it prudent to notify your next of kin. Paula's coming home! Isn't that wonderful?"

Audra groaned. "No, Izzy," she said. She tried to wriggle to the edge of the bed, to get up, and it was painful to watch. Her movements were jerky and clearly hurt her.

Izzy put her hand on Audra's shoulder. "Enough. It's too late—she's coming, and her daughter too."

Audra froze, breathing hard from the effort. "No, you can't. Send them home. She's a mother, for crissakes—"

Izzy laughed softly. "A mother. Isn't that how this all started? We're all mothers." She found her purse and fished inside for her own lipstick, found it and put some on. She pressed her lips together. "Autumn Born," it was called. She didn't think she liked it much.

"She's not staying. I won't let her." Audra's voice was a rasp, her face distorted by a mix of anger and fear.

Izzy shrugged. "Numbers, numbers, Audra. We need numbers. Think of Glory and her fat finger falling off and multiply it by what we have left. You included."

"Leave her be."

"Pull yourself together. They'll be here any minute." Izzy went back to her vigil at the window. "Besides, dear, I think Paula's had some trouble in the city. I think she's running home to mother. I think that's just lovely."

She knew Audra couldn't see her smile, but Izzy hoped she could hear it.

Audra had never been a stupid woman

(until recently)

and even as she thought that, a car pulled into the parking lot. It was an old red thing, rusted around the wheel wells.

"Oh my, look at that—a car," Izzy said excitedly. She turned to Audra. "It's them." She turned back to watch a young woman and a girl of about twelve get out of the car. Its doors slammed shut, the sound muffled and distant from the second-floor window. "Oh my," Izzy said. "From the state of their car it looks like they've fallen on hard times. This may be easier than I thought." She clucked her tongue.

"I'll tell them to leave."

Izzy spun around and pointed at Audra. "You'll do no such thing." She flipped open her compact, which was still in her hand. "Do you want to see yourself? What you've done?" She raised the mirror in front of Audra. "Look," she hissed. "See how beautiful you've become."

Audra glanced reluctantly at the mirror, then gasped. Staring back at her was a pair of yellow eyes, the pupils elongated, black and soulless, like a serpent's. She shrieked and covered her face with her hands.

Izzy snapped the compact shut with a scowl. "That's what you get for betraying the sisterhood," she hissed. "Judas. *Judas.*" Then she leaned in very close and said into Audra's ear, "Judas *goat.*"

Audra squealed and clawed at her face with her hands, ran

them down her arms, her sides, eyes frantically searching the room for another reflective surface. There was none.

"Izzy, my god—"

"You don't want that to happen to your pretty daughter, do you? Or her pretty bastard? So shush now." She opened the compact again and fixed her own hair, pinched her cheeks. "Those nasty weird eyes of yours only show in a mirror. Paula won't notice a thing."

Audra whimpered, "She doesn't belong with us."

"Honey, think of it as a fourth for bridge."

Rowan had been dozing the past few miles or so and Paula wasn't sure if she wanted to wake her. The turn signal click-clicked as she took the off-ramp from the highway and followed the curve through a deceptively thin treeline to the road into Haven Woods.

A silly kind of excitement had started to build in her. She'd been gone more or less since she was sixteen and didn't think she'd ever been truly homesick, yet she had butterflies.

Rowan stirred, woken by the car's slowing down. She raised her head and looked groggily out the window.

"Look," Paula said and pointed to a billboard thirty feet high. It showed a happy family in front of a lovely house. WELCOME TO HAVEN WOODS!

Paula turned right, checking off old haunts in her head.

smoking behind the Casey's Lumber sign

watching the boys play football in the big field behind the school

she and Marla walking the perimeter of Haven Woods over and over again the winter they were bored

hanging out the second-floor window of Mrs. Hagen's class at lunch

She was smiling. Thinking of old faces—*Patty, Lonnie*

Sanderson, Pete Kelly—people she hadn't thought of in years. It didn't stop there, of course . . .

David under the bleachers at the
David on the riverbank when
David sweating after ball practice, grinning
still want to kiss me?

His scent stirred in the air of Haven Woods, the river, the bakery, the lime on the ball field—Paula could almost smell him.

"Where's Grandma's house?" Rowan said, sitting up.

Paula pointed a few blocks ahead of them. "That's our street there. Proctor." She grinned. "Everybody lived on Proctor. It's a bay that loops around the whole suburb. But we won't go there yet. We'll go to the hospital first."

Once they had passed the big brick school, Paula found herself slowing to a near crawl, watching for the tall tower of the hospital where the big glowing H was mounted, like a crucifix. When she was a little girl, she'd thought the H was for Haven Woods, not Hospital.

She could just see it through some trees. The trees were taller.

The parking lot snuck up on the right and Paula had to turn suddenly to catch it. It was fine—there was no traffic. She parked and looked up at the building.

Lights were coming on inside hospital rooms, most of them dim, and she imagined the long fluorescent at the head of each bed, doors ajar, panic buttons pinned to pillows. She tried to imagine her mother in one of those beds.

What she remembered instead was the day she was leaving for good, her bags in the hallway by the front door. Her mother pacing.

Why do I have to go away?

The cryptic answer: *I hope you never have to understand.*

And the other memory, at St. Mary's. The two of them setting up her room, putting out photos of the three of them, Dad, Mom and Paula. Happier days. Her mother chattering away. *A very good school . . . best education . . . make something wonderful of your life.*

Going to supper that last night. *Order anything you want, darling.*

Worse things too. Knowing the sisters knew she was pregnant, and maybe the other students too. Paula wouldn't forget those first few lonely days at St. Mary's, avoiding the stares, the tentative welcome. The nuns were kind. *You'll be taken care of here. You'll be safe. It's a very good school.*

Worst of all? Her mother's palpable relief when she left Paula in the dormitory to go home.

I love you very much, Paula. That's why you're here.

(but Mom)

"Is she going to be gross?" Rowan asked when they got to the doors.

Paula smiled. "I hope not." She slid an arm around her daughter and they went inside.

A large woman at the front desk looked up when the doors opened. She stared, blinking behind a pair of glasses that magnified her eyes, then brightened and clapped her hands.

"Paula Wittmore," she said. "I've been expecting you. You remember me, don't you? I'm your mother's friend Tula. Remember?" She lurched out from the behind the desk. "I'm going to take you right up. Your mother is on the second floor, poor thing." She smiled when she said *poor thing*, and didn't stop talking long enough for Paula to respond. "This is your little girl. I forget her name. She looks a little bit like you, but not much." She waved them to the elevator and pressed the button. "You remember me?"

Paula answered, "Yes. Nice to see you again. How are you?"

"Well, you know, if it's not one thing it's another thing." The elevator door opened. "Same old shit." Rowan snorted as they followed Tula into the elevator. Once the doors had closed behind them, Tula went silent as the grave.

Paula held Rowan's hand. At first she thought the girl was going to protest, but she didn't.

The elevator doors opened and Tula ushered them out. "You go ahead. Room 210." She pointed and waited until they were off. The elevator doors closed on her and they were alone.

There was no one in the waiting area and no one in the hall. There were no patients roaming the halls dragging IV poles, and no other visitors. Paula supposed that such a small hospital could be mostly empty sometimes.

A woman came out of a room ahead of them and quietly pulled the door closed behind her. She turned and made eye contact. Paula's mouth opened in surprise, but she didn't speak. Izzy. Tall and still as attractive as Paula remembered. She smiled happily and came towards them, hands outstretched.

"Paula. Paula, darling, it's so wonderful to see you." Izzy took Paula's hands in hers. Paula felt a tiny zap, like static, a reaction from so many years of trying not to think about Izzy Riley, or Haven Woods, or especially Izzy's long-dead son, David.

"Mrs. Riley, it's nice to see you again . . ." Everything else had gone out of her head—what she was supposed to do, why she was there.

"Oh, you're a grown woman, Paula. Call me Izzy." Izzy looked down at Rowan, standing close to Paula. She was a pretty girl, with her mother's hair and face shape. Her eyes were her loveliest feature, large and round, with thick, long lashes, like a boy's. She liked the look of her. "And who have we here?"

"This is my daughter, Rowan."

does she look familiar?

"Aren't you pretty, just like your mom was."

"Thank you," Rowan answered primly. There was a moment of

silence as Paula internally winced at the *was*. Izzy had always been sharp-edged.

To Paula, Izzy said, "Your mother will be so glad to see you."

"What happened? What's wrong with her? I was so flustered I didn't even ask when you called." Paula felt foolish for not knowing. Izzy's face turned sombre.

"Well, she collapsed the night Mrs. Henderson died. Very sad."

"What does the doctor say?"

"Why don't I find him and you can ask him yourself." Like a maître d' she gestured broadly in the direction from which she had just come. "Would you like to see her?"

She led them to the door, where she paused. "Maybe Rowan would like to sit out here with me for a minute or two, just to give you some time alone with your mom." She smiled and again made a large gesture, towards the visitor's lounge at the end of the hall. It seemed a long way away.

Paula looked to Rowan. "Is that okay?"

"I guess," Rowan said, but didn't move. Izzy put her arm around the girl's shoulders and turned her gently.

"There we go, then," she said, her voice unnaturally vital in the quiet corridor. She and Rowan walked down the hall.

Paula smiled reassuringly at her daughter's back, then went in to see her mother, the door snicking softly open and then gently shut.

Hospitals were scary. Rowan had been in a hospital only once in her life (not counting when she was born, since she didn't remember *that*). When she was seven, she had fallen down the last five steps at the apartment they were living in. She had been jumping and missed the stair, fell on her butt and hurt her foot. Her mother acted as if she'd cut her head off. She took her to the hospital and they X-rayed her and she got a lollipop for being brave. It was stupid to think of that now. A lollipop? Seriously lame.

This hospital was way more quiet than that one had been. And even scarier because it was so quiet. Where was everybody? Her grandma's friend sat down on the sofa beside her and stared.

Rowan tried to smile at her, all the while thinking, *It's not polite to stare*. This woman was sort of scary too.

"What are you dear, twelve?"

"Uh-huh." Rowan leaned forward to stare down the hall as best she could, at the door that her mother had disappeared behind.

The woman frowned. "You shouldn't say 'uh-huh.' It's disrespectful. You should say, 'Yes, Mrs. Riley.'"

Rowan blushed. "Um, sorry."

The woman kept staring at Rowan, which made her cheeks bloom hot. She wished her mom would come out. "Um, Mrs. Riley? Were you going to get the doctor for my mom?"

The woman ignored the question. "Mmm," she said instead. "You're a pretty thing. Have you started your period yet?"

Rowan wished she could totally disappear. She stared hard down the hall, willing her mother to come out. She swallowed. She did not answer

(no)

and hoped that *Mrs. Riley* would go away.

She did not.

They sat in silence. Worse, Mrs. Riley put her hand on top of Rowan's head and absently stroked her hair.

And Rowan wished hard

(mom mom mom mom mom)

for her mom to come out and get her.

—

Paula had a single moment of trepidation, but then there she was—her mother, in a hospital gown, in a hospital bed. The two of them locked eyes, alone for the first time in four, maybe five years.

Her mother smiled broadly, sadly. She reached her arms out to Paula.

"Oh, you're really here—," she rasped. The shocking voice caught Paula by surprise.

"You sound terrible!" Paula moved to the bed. She took her mom's hands. "Do you know what's wrong?" It was hard to tell in the dimmed lights how her mother really looked. Her hair was lank and flat to her head, and her eyes had an odd—something—look to them. She was thinner than the last time Paula had seen her, but that could be for any reason at all.

"I'm . . . just, I'm fine, Paula. Really. You didn't have to come."

"Mom—" Her mother's hands were warm in hers. As if she had a fever. "I just wish I'd been here when you got sick. What does the doctor say?"

"Izzy called you?"

Paula nodded.

Audra brightened a little. "Have you brought my beautiful granddaughter?"

Paula smiled. "Yes. She's in the lounge—"

"With Izzy?"

"Mom, don't talk so much, your throat sounds so . . . raw."

Audra's eyes darted around the room, to the door, to the far corner. She shifted stiffly, as if she hurt everywhere. She looked into Paula's eyes, then tugged at her hands, pulling her closer. Paula leaned in.

"I'll whisper," she said, very low.

"Yes, good," Paula answered, in a whisper herself.

"It's not safe for you to be here."

"What?"

"You shouldn't stay—"

"Mom? What do you mean?"

Audra flashed a look at the closed door.

Paula did not get the hint. "We'll stay as long as you need us to—"

Audra shook her head. "No," she croaked.

In the lounge, Mrs. Riley stood up suddenly, startling Rowan. She headed in the direction of her grandmother's room.

Bye, Weirdo.

Izzy stuck her head inside Audra's room. "How are things in here?" The two had their heads together, scheming. She let the door snuff shut behind her.

Audra's eyes narrowed when she saw her, but Paula's were questioning. She wasn't too late, then.

"Paula, dear, you don't want to tire your mother out."

"Of course not. Mrs. Riley, did you find the doctor?"

Izzy smiled sympathetically as she lied. "He's gone for the day. We'll find him tomorrow. Are you going to stay at your mother's?" She bustled to the bed and smoothed Audra's blanket. "I think the key's still where it always is, isn't it, Aud?"

Audra didn't answer, just glared at her old friend.

"I used it myself the day I found your poor mom," Izzy said to Paula. "How're you feeling, Aud? I think I should hustle these girls home."

Audra protested. "No. I want to see Rowan."

"Of course," Paula said.

"Absolutely," Izzy said. "You haven't seen that grandbaby for such a long time. Paula, why don't you go get her?" She leaned in closer to Audra. "We've been chatting out there."

"Izzy—" Audra hadn't let go of Paula's hand.

"What is it, Aud? Can I get you something? Some water?" Izzy took the pitcher from the side table and poured water into a fresh glass, then held it out to her.

Warily Audra took the glass. She drank noisily and Izzy grimaced. It was a little disgusting.

"I'll get Ro," Paula said. She touched her mother's hair briefly and left the room.

Audra held the empty glass out for Izzy to take. She mouthed the words *leave them be*.

Izzy smiled. "It's about numbers, Audra. And bloodlines."

The door opened. Rowan stood there shyly, framed by the light from the hall, her mother behind her.

"And here's your little granddaughter!"

When Rowan's eyes had adjusted to the room's dimness, she saw two faces staring at her, Grandma and Mrs.

(*weirdo*)

Riley.

Something about the way they looked at her kept her rooted to the floor.

"Rowan," her grandmother said, in a terrible raspy voice.

"Hi," she said.

"Come over here, hon. I can't quite jump out of bed right now—" Her grandma smiled, and though her voice was raw, she didn't look very sick, she looked . . . the same.

When she got to the bedside, her grandmother put her hand on Rowan's arm. She was hot. "Oh, it's good to see you, Rowan. You're getting so big—"

"We're going to stay at your house, I think."

Her grandmother nodded. "Yes." She smiled again, and that's

when Ro saw that she *was* sick. Her smiled looked off-centre and forced. "You'll take care of my dog, won't you?"

Ro's eyes lit up. "Sure I will!"

Her grandmother nodded. "Good girl. His name is Old Tex. Paula, will you get my purse out of the cupboard for me?"

"Sure."

As her mom went to the cupboard, Audra leaned towards Rowan and whispered, "I have something for you."

"Grandma, you sound like you have a cold."

Her grandma chuckled weakly and their eyes met, then

(just for a second)

there was an odd reflecting—a flash, like light. Then it was gone. Her mom handed over the handbag and her grandmother took out a small change purse and squeezed it open. From inside she pulled out a key. She held it up. To Paula and Mrs. Riley she said, "This is a secret between me and my granddaughter, ladies, so no listening in." She grinned. Her first real one.

Rowan leaned in eagerly, turning her head so that her ear was close to her grandmother's mouth.

"This key is for a box under my bed. It's a blue box. There's a new collar in there for Tex. It's red and it's . . . decorated. Can you put it on him?"

"Okay," she whispered back. She took the key.

"Old Tex can be your dog while you're in Haven Woods, okay?" her grandma rasped.

Rowan nodded. "Okay," she said again. She put the key in the pocket of her school blazer.

Her grandma sighed and lay back against the pillows, every movement clearly painful.

"Mom," Paula said, "do you want us to sit with you a little longer?"

And then

(*weird weird have you started your period weirdo*)

said, "Well, if you'd like to do that, Paula, I could take Rowan home with me for the night."

Rowan gave her mother a wide-eyed, meaningful stare.

"No, Paula, don't bother. I'm just going to fall asleep here. You two go and settle in at the house," Audra said, and closed her eyes.

Paula put her arm around Rowan. "Okay, I'll come back in the morning. And I'll try and talk to the doctor then."

She kissed her mother and Rowan heard her say, "I'm glad I came. And I'm staying." Her grandmother's eyes opened at that, but it was Rowan she looked at. There was something unsettling in her gaze. Rowan wondered what it was that she and her mom weren't getting.

Just before Izzy closed the door on Audra, she poked her head back inside and cleared her throat delicately until Audra opened her eyes.

"I'll take good care of the girls," Izzy said.

"Leave. Them. Be."

Izzy smiled gently, and with just a touch of the true friend she used to be, said, "It's not just up to me."

FOUR

IT WAS NIGHTTIME IN HAVEN WOODS. Lights had popped on inside living rooms, glowing through freshly hung summer drapes. TV sets were tuned to *CSI* and *House*, the hour-longs of prime time. Streetlamps illuminated roofs and cast a shadow over broad lawns—tidy, green, the sort of lawns that would feel good on bare feet in a month or so. All the cars in the driveways were SUVs and minivans.

Izzy Riley drove courteously behind the junior Wittmores until they reached Audra's dark house. She waited in the car while they found the key under the pot of pansies on the front porch, and then gave them a cheery wave as they stepped inside, glad they could not see the expression on her face. Izzy was weary.

At home she turned out the light she had left burning in the foyer and climbed slowly up the stairs to her bedroom, Tansy at her heels. At one time it had been her and Roger's bedroom, but Roger had been dead about five years. Heart attack

(or something)

Sometimes she missed him, sometimes she didn't.

She stepped out of her shoes, then dropped them into her

closet and stripped to her bra and panties. She put on her robe. The cat jumped on the bed, used to the ritual, and curled up. Tansy would sleep a few hours and then wake to do whatever dirty work cats did in the dark, via the pet door.

It had been a hard day. Margaret's funeral had been difficult. They had been friends for many, many years—good friends—before she started to piss her off, then topped it with a betrayal that got them all in trouble. But it wasn't worth thinking about anymore. The point was to move forward.

Izzy sat at her dressing table and creamed off her makeup. Her skin was very good, very receptive to repair. The girl at the MAC counter had said so. Izzy smiled as she remembered the girl at the MAC counter. A silly, silly bitch.

You look just wonderful for your age, the silly bitch had said.

Izzy had reacted hardly at all to the comment and, in fact, she had bought many more products than she had ever planned to buy, or certainly to use, and had thanked the girl with a nice, wide smile. *Oh, thank you, dear, you've just been such a love.*

The MAC products were sitting on her dressing table. She quite liked the eye pencil.

When Izzy dropped in at the MAC kiosk a week or so later, she asked about the girl and was told that she had quit. For personal reasons.

I'll bet. Taking pains to appear concerned, Izzy gently asked what had happened, and the girl leaned in and whispered, *I'm not supposed to tell but . . . her face, something horrible happened to*—but then the counter manager had come around and she couldn't finish, which was such a shame. But she bet the girl's face was . . . well, *just awful.*

A cup of cold tea she'd forgotten about had formed a skin, but she didn't have the energy to carry it down to the kitchen. There was still a counter and sink full of dishes down there she needed to clean up after the wake . . .

She imagined Audra in her hospital bed, unable to sleep for worry about what Izzy was doing with her precious daughter and her precious daughter's daughter. It would be good for her, that kind of worrying, a proper penance. Marla would call it karma. But that wasn't really what karma was. Karma was a more complicated comeuppance. This was more like Jainism . . . all Audra's doing. Marla wouldn't know about that, nor would that crowd of hers. They weren't readers, those girls.

A book lay invitingly open on the bed: Carol Karlsen's history of New England. She'd only just started it and it hadn't quite grabbed her yet. The good stuff, she suspected, happened around the late 1600s, so to speak.

In the privacy of her bedroom she let herself admit that it had been a difficult day. It was unfathomable, really, that Chick had crawled into bed and lit herself on fire. How was that even possible? How *could* she?

She would have a shower and then take the teacup down to the kitchen and make herself a fresh cup. Sleep, she knew, would be reluctant to come. Memories had been unavoidable all day. They'd been such a close-knit gang once, the whole lot of them. The husbands too. When they'd all been young and the children had been at home

hey Mom, I need five bucks

and they'd spent whole weekends together at each other's houses. Drinks and cards and

what's this scar here, Iz?

backyard barbecues.

When she forced herself to think it through from Margaret's point of view, she guessed she understood it well enough. Margaret was a (foolish) romantic, unfashionably in love with her husband, enough to take a great risk, make a great sacrifice. Audra had got caught in that (foolish) romanticism.

Over the past year things had been changing. She couldn't put her finger on it; it was sort of a constant loose feeling, like a button hanging by a thread, a wobbly heel on a shoe, a pot handle shifting. Their solid group was wiggling and slipping, and that was what was wrong. They had to stick together, they had to maintain. Margaret had broken the rules. It was good, in a way, that she was dead.

Stupid, stupid woman.

a stupid woman gets what she deserves

Her grandmother used to say that all the time. It was all spinning out of control. If she closed her eyes and concentrated she would be able to feel it, as if the very room were spinning, centrifugal force tugging them apart.

Why did Margaret think she was so special? They'd all lost somebody. They'd all had to pay.

She'd been trying to think of the word since the hospital, and it suddenly came to her. *Menarche.* A girl's introduction into womanhood. So powerful, that moment in a girl's life, the transition from useless girl into woman. She smiled, remembering the girl's shocked face when she asked whether she was bleeding yet . . .

The fact that Rowan had not yet entered into menarche was a blessing that would save them all. She wanted to applaud her own cleverness, the serendipity of it all. She would be sure to remind Audra of that.

Izzy stood up then, securely tied the robe around her waist and walked down the hall to the closed door. The door that was always closed, except when she opened it.

It was dark inside David's room, the blinds drawn and the lights off, but she could find every item in the room by memory. She turned the light on anyway. In a cruel, sharp electric gasp, the room laid itself open for her.

It was all as it had been, right down to the forgotten pair of socks at the end of the bed where a sixteen-year-old boy had dropped them. The side table still held a copy of *East of Eden*, the bookmark a dragon slyly watching a tiny knight at his feet *be careful in the company of dragons for you are crunchy and taste good with ketchup*, and four small chunks of agate and a watch, the battery long dead, reading 12:10, whether day or night unknown.

If she opened the closet door there would be his clothes still hanging, and in the dresser, underwear, T-shirts, the many and varied bits and pieces of soccer, baseball, football, basketball uniforms: gold and purple socks, satin shorts in blue with white stripes up the leg, jerseys in electric yellow and green, numbers stencilled onto everything: 11, 15, 67.

The air in the room was bruised with time, filled with a heavy sadness that had once been a sharp, bleeding pain.

Izzy sat on the bed and the springs squeaked. She leaned back and spread herself over it. Closed her eyes. Tried to find him in the room.

Mom you're the best

I'm going to Lonnie's

Mom, I'm late for practice

"I look wonderful for my age," she said into the empty room. The words caught and held in the heavy air, fading slowly. She kept her body still to keep the springs quiet. When she shifted they cried out . . . awful. Like David that day. So she stayed very still, except for two times when she moved just to hear that noise, like a tongue that can't stay out of the rotten tooth.

what's this scar, Iz?

She tucked her hands under his pillow and felt there a soft, worn T-shirt. Without looking she knew what it said. HAVEN WOODS SENIOR BOYS CHAMPS 1997. She tugged out a corner of it and held it under her nose. If she tried very, very hard, she could still smell him.

He smelled like time.

She would dream of him tonight, as she did every now and then. In her dreams he was always as he had been that day, her beautiful golden son, her sun.

The others had lost husbands. She'd lost her *son*. They did not know pain the way she did.

All would soon be made right. The daughters were here, and that would balance things out. Legacy. Blood relatives.

Most important, of course, blood.

FIVE

GLASS WIND CHIMES HUNG from a cord on her grandmother's front porch. The pieces were all different colours, very pretty, and when Rowan pushed, they swung lazily in an arc. Three, four swings and they settled to a stop. When they became still, Rowan pushed them again.

It was weird not to be at school. She tried to just enjoy the fact, but she couldn't help looking at her watch once in awhile and wondering where everyone was. There was a funny feeling attached to it, like the way it felt when you stood at the top of the circle stairs in Convocation Hall and leaned over the rail. You could see all the way down to the lobby, the black railing against the white marble floor spinning and spinning. If you looked too long it felt a little like you might fall. That was sort of how it felt not to be at school

(when you knew you should be)

For instance, they had math at ten, which was second period. Sister Persephone had tufts of hair growing out of her chin that she clearly tried to shave; they would disappear and then reappear looking like someone's dad's five o'clock shadow. Otherwise she was nice. When someone answered a particularly difficult question correctly, she would always say, "Aren't you one of God's special thinkers."

Rowan sighed. She was bored, and totally surprised by the boredom and its accompanying thought: *even school would be better than this.* Her mom had just got back from the hospital and didn't want to say how her grandmother was doing. Rowan had asked if they could *please go somewhere* and Paula barely even looked at her. She said they would walk the dog later. Every now and then Rowan could hear her moving around inside the house.

The weather was beautiful, more summer than spring, and the sun had been shining all morning. That was all there was to look at here. The sky and the porch and the street. Everywhere Ro looked there was a house. There were no buildings, no parking lots, no chain-link fences, no 7-Eleven store, no

(no gang of boys squatting in a tight circle on the steps of the apartment block across the street)

hey little girl c'mere I'll teach ya some school

no city at all. Just houses. All exhaustingly quiet, the people invisible.

Across the street a brown car was parked in the driveway, which sloped upwards towards the house, and so it seemed almost that the car was part of a display. *Check out my car.* Two white cars were parked side by side in the driveways of nearly identical houses just up the street. Those were all the cars.

Except for their second-hand Mazda with the rusted wheel wells, which her mom had bought with her severance cheque from the bar. It too was parked in the driveway on a slight incline. She supposed that, to people in the houses across the street, it looked as if their (piece of shit) car was on display.

check out my pieceofshit

aren't you one of God's special thinkers

Nothing on the street moved. It was dead.

Rowan gave the wind chimes one last swat and then sat down hard on the top step of the porch beside the big, hairy dog. She put her hand on his head and gave him a gentle scratch, and his tail thumped on the wooden floor. *Thump thump thump.* Then it stopped. The dog was good.

His muzzle was flecked with coarse grey (like Sister Persephone's chin hairs) and the tips of his ears were also grey. He smelled. It took him several minutes to get up from his lying-down position, and as he struggled up he grunted like an old man. But it had been love at first sight all the same.

She scratched his head some more, tenderly. The dog thumped his tail some more, but he did not raise his head to look at her. Her mom said he was a mutt, but that he had some collie in him and probably some shepherd, which was why he was so big and hairy. His face was broad and kind and over each eye he had a small patch of black, like eyebrows. This furthered his old-man appearance, and also made him look intelligent, like a cartoon dog who might wear glasses. Another one of God's special thinkers.

She hadn't been able to sleep last night in her mom's old room. Sometime in the middle of the night she'd been woken by a *tap-tap-tap* at the window. She'd tried to sleep through it the way she slept through the sirens and yelling on the streets at home, but it didn't work. Everything else was so *quiet.*

Except for the intermittent *tap-tap-tap.*

Half asleep, she'd gotten up to look. Too tired to really be frightened, she nevertheless felt something just as she pulled the curtain aside to look out

(even though the real threats were not in places like Haven Woods but in gangs of boys who sat on apartment-block steps in the city)

hey little girl c'mere I'll teach you school

A cat was on the porch railing, digging its claws into the wood. It stopped when Ro opened the curtains, and peered at her for a second with its yellow eyes. Then it cleaned a paw and jumped down to where Ro couldn't see it. A cat. It had freaked her out. She'd crawled in with her mother.

"Who's got a cat?" she asked the dog. "Do you have a cat? Are you a good boy?" Tex thumped his tail.

Rowan lay back on the porch, one arm draped across the old dog, her feet on the steps. A little breeze came up from somewhere and the chimes over her head swung and tinkled. The dog stuck out his tongue and licked her hand.

She wished her mother would hurry (*the F-word*) up so they could walk the dog.

From somewhere down the street she heard a car coming, slowly, slowly.

The suburbs were deadly boring. And there were too many cats.

Paula let water run into the kitchen sink over the tiny pile of dishes. A teacup, her and Ro's breakfast things, some cutlery. She didn't have to do them, but wanted the distraction. It was easier to think when she was busy.

She'd gone to visit her mother right after breakfast. She'd tried to talk Ro into going, but her daughter had not slept well. When Paula shook her awake for breakfast, she'd rolled over with a groan, mumbling a sleepy *not yet*. She'd decided to let her sleep. Kid was likely as stressed as she was.

So she'd gone alone, hoping to talk to the doctor and to have a longer, private visit with her mother. It was not to be.

There hadn't been anyone at the reception desk in the lobby, and when she got to the second floor, it was just as deserted as it had been yesterday, except for Tula at the nurses' station. The minute the elevator doors opened, the woman was on her like ugly on an ape. She followed her to her mother's room, jabbering the whole time, barely taking a breath so that Paula could answer her.

She followed her right into her mother's room. "Oh, I just have to take her vitals, you know. Might as well do it now," she'd said and grabbed her mother's arm to take her pulse before Paula could even say hello.

Tula fumbled the blood pressure cuff around her mother's arm—which seemed very thin to Paula—and never took her eyes off them. When she was done, she fussed with the curtains and sheets. When subtle hints didn't work, Paula finally asked Tula if she would please go and find the doctor. She eventually said she would, and on her way out propped the door open.

Paula had made the obvious joke to her mother. "Well, I thought she'd never leave."

But Audra hadn't even smiled. As soon as Tula's footsteps had faded, she'd insisted again, "Paula, you can't stay long in Haven Woods."

She'd protested, said they would stay as long as Audra was in the hospital. But now they could hear the murmur of Tula's voice, probably on the phone at the nurses' station.

Her mother had said, "There isn't time to explain," and "I'm fine, I'll be fine—"

And then Tula was back.

Paula had asked for a few more minutes alone with her mother, her voice as sweet as pie, but Tula had said, "I'm afraid your mother has to rest. Doctor's orders."

"Where is he, then?" Paula had asked, exasperated. "Why can't I talk to him myself? And when is he going to check on my mom?"

But Tula had insisted that he couldn't be reached for the rest of the day, and then she stood there like a statue. So Paula wrote her name and her mother's home phone number on a piece of paper for Tula to give to the doctor when she saw him next. Underlined twice was *I must speak to you.* Tula shoved it in her pocket.

And then her mother had said she did need to rest, and there was nothing for Paula to do but leave. She pecked Audra on the cheek and gave her hand a gentle squeeze and it was over. The visit had lasted less than twenty minutes. She had a firm impression that not only Tula but her mother also had wanted her to leave.

As she'd headed back to her car, she didn't know whether to feel put out or hurt or panicked that everyone was being so evasive. Maybe her mother was more ill than she let on. Terrible words dashed in and out of her head, the stiffness in her mother's joints becoming some kind of paralysis, the drooping eyes and difficulty with speech becoming a stroke. And when she thought of the raspy throat, the worst crossed her mind. *Cancer.*

Paula stuck her hands into the soapy water with a vengeance and fiercely scrubbed dishes that hardly needed it, unable to keep her mind off the fact that something just wasn't right. Not just her mother being ill, but something else altogether.

A car stopped in front of the house, not parking in the driveway behind her mom's

(pieceofshit)

car but just pulling up to the curb. A woman got out; she was wearing big sunglasses, and as she rounded the car to the sidewalk, she pushed them up on her head just like a celebrity. Her hair was long and dark and she wore a little lavender suit. It was like something women wore on TV. Stylish.

She was smiling at Rowan, and though her teeth were blindingly white and really even, there was some quality in the smile

that distracted from her beauty, something that to Rowan looked
. . . *hungry.*

As she came up the walk, the woman's eyes were on Rowan,
the whole time the smile plastered there

(like the smiles on the two church women who sometimes
came to their apartment door on Sundays, smiling just like that
and holding out booklets with titles like *God Misses You* and *Won't
You Come Home to God?*)

The woman stopped at the bottom of the porch steps.

have you found Jebus Mrs. Wittmore?

When she spoke, her voice was musical, warm and rich, like
. . . *barbecue.*

"Well, hel-lo!" The woman actually winked. "You must be
Rowan." A (musical) laugh spilled out of her perfectly pink lips.
"You look just like your mother." The syllables of *your mother* were
drawn out. The woman kept smiling, the smile practically stuck
there, for a full half-minute. It didn't reach her eyes. Briefly those
eyes flicked over Rowan's whole self, from hair to toes, and then
back up to her face.

"You look like . . . your mother," she said again, and finally she
lost the smile.

Rowan didn't know what response she should make to that
sort of declaration, especially said twice. Obviously this woman
wanted her to say something. So finally she said, "Oh." At her feet
Old Tex had begun his lurching rise. Beneath the grunts and groans
Rowan thought she heard him growl. She put her hand on his head
when he was all the way up.

"You're going to be a real beauty," the woman said, the words
tumbling from her pink lips that showed her perfect white teeth,
and this time Tex really did growl, though so quietly probably only
Ro heard it. She scratched behind his ear.

"Rowan. Such a pretty name. Do you know what it means?"

"It's a tree," Rowan said. The dog pushed his head against her hand.

state yer bidness stranger

"That's right!" the woman said.

Weirdo number two. "Um, can I help you?"

"I'm an old friend of your mom's. I was her best friend in school. Her very *best* friend."

"Oh."

The woman continued to smile, the sun glinting off the sunglasses propped on her head.

And?

As if she'd heard Rowan's thought, she purred, "I'm just dying to say hello." She looked up at the house, and just the tiniest hint of a frown wrinkled her otherwise perfect forehead.

Rowan decided she disliked this woman, even if she didn't really know why. "I'll get her. She's just in the kitchen."

"No!" the woman said, and laughed again. "Let me do it." She bent low, swooping like a bird, and scooped up a handful of gravel from beside the walk. It was an oddly elegant gesture. She winked again at Rowan. Taking a couple of steps closer to the house, she made a pretty show of picking out a tiny stone from her palm, lined up and tossed it at the door. It hit the window with a glassy *ping*. She giggled like a kid, and for a second Rowan warmed to her.

There was no response from inside.

Her mother's *best friend* shook her head and picked out another pebble. She tossed it as expertly as the first. It too hit the window. Louder this time.

Rowan started to say, "I'll just get—"

And then the door pushed open and her mother came out in her T-shirt and scruffy jeans, her face screwed into an annoyed frown.

"Rowan, what the heck—"

Rowan pointed at the woman on the sidewalk. "It was her."

Paula looked at the *best friend* completely blankly, and then her head made a shocked dip of recognition.

"Paula Wittmore, as I live and breathe," the woman said, hands on her hips now.

The screen door swung shut behind Paula with a slam. Old Tex jumped and lowered his head. Rowan stroked his neck. *It's okay.*

"Oh, my god!" Paula was off the porch at a run and threw her arms around the dark-haired woman. "Marla! Marla Riley! Look at you! Cripes—it can't be Riley, though? You must be married."

"Married." Marla grinned and wiggled a huge ring on her left hand. "But I'm hyphenated, very chic: Riley-Moore." She pulled Paula into another hug, then held her at arm's length. "I have to take a good look at you."

She did. Rowan saw her mother blush under the scrutiny and she understood why. This time, instead of feeling embarrassed

I heard your mom's a stripper

she wanted to chase the woman away. Beside her on the porch, Old Tex was tense too.

Marla pronounced Paula beautiful. "You're even better looking that when I last saw you!" she said. "When was that, exactly? Hmmm? It has to be about twelve years ago . . ."

Paula shifted awkwardly in her grasp. "Well, we've been home once since then, but Rowan got sick and we didn't stay long enough to see anyone. So it's actually a little longer, I think."

"Mom."

It was clearly an interruption, and two sets of eyes turned questioningly towards the girl. Marla grinned with only one side of her mouth.

"What?"

She swallowed. "We were going to walk Tex, remember?" It

came out more petulant than she'd intended.

Her mother frowned. "Ro, please! This is my old friend Mrs. Riley-Moore. Marla, this is my daughter, Rowan."

"Oh, we introduced ourselves, didn't we, Rowan?" Marla clasped her hands together. "I was so happy when Izzy told me you were here. It's a blast to see you again! I hope you're staying."

The two women were grinning idiotically at each other.

"I don't know how long we're staying, actually. You know my mom's sick?"

Marla's face went sombre for a moment and she nodded. "I heard. My mom was the one who called the ambulance. How is she?"

Paula shrugged. "She just seems . . . sick, I guess. I still haven't talked to the doctor. I tried to find him this morning but apparently he's a ghost."

Marla made a sympathetic noise, then brightened again. "Now that you're back, we have to do it up right. I'm going to reintroduce you to the wonders of Haven. Come to my house on Friday and meet the girls."

Paula smiled gratefully. "Oh, Marla, that sounds great. Can you stay a minute or two now? Cup of coffee?"

"I wish I could. But here's my address." She dug in her purse and brought out a small card. "I'm on Proctor," she said. "By Mom's place. Remember?"

Paula took the card and nodded. "Oh," she said, and glanced back at the porch, where her daughter was pointedly waiting with the dog.

Rowan took the opportunity to hurry things along. "Mom? Are we going?"

Marla tinkled her laugh and put a hand on Paula's arm. "You'd better get going. I know the scene—I have two of my own."

Then the two of them were off again, talking about children, blah blah. Rowan sighed and retreated into the house, taking Tex with her. On their way through the door—her *mu-ther* didn't even notice she was leaving—Old Tex swung his head back for another look. Rowan fantasized that the old guy was broadcasting a warning. *Go home.*

In her mom's old room she parted the curtains just wide enough to peer out at the two of them on the walk. They were still gabbing, gabbing, dark heads bent together like crows

(pecking at something interesting and dead)

She went from the window to the closet, found her school blazer with the St. Mary's crest

(*Semper Vigilans*)

and put it on. She felt a little better. Then she pawed through her school bag and from the bottom fished out her pink plastic crucifix; they had all got one as a prize in the Lives of the Saints spelling bee the week before she got suspended. It was crappy and cheap, and as she pulled it out she hoped the little white Jesus hadn't fallen off.

Jesus was still glued to his cross. Rowan put it in the pocket of her blazer. Then she went into the living room and turned on the television, settling in for the short term at least. A rerun of the *Jerry Springer Show* came on. A big fat lady picked up a chair and threw it across the room at another lady, screaming obscenities that were bleeped out.

She sat watching, sticking her hand into her pocket now and then, keeping track of the cawing and gabbing outside.

Marla was so beautiful now, Paula thought. The awkward teen she had been was entirely erased. Her hair, her eyes—there was no mistaking it was Marla, but it was as though someone had retouched her, narrowing her jawline, lengthening her legs, scooping in her waist.

"I think you'll like the girls I'm hanging out with," Marla said. "You've probably heard of one of them—Joanna Shaw?"

Paula was impressed. Shaw was a popular talk-show host. "She lives here?"

"Yes, and she's a good friend. You know her show is going national next week?"

Paula did know that. "How did you get to know her?"

"Oh, I did a little consulting work for her," she said. "But anyway, I'll invite Joanna and a few of the other girls over, and I promise you'll have fun."

"Well, it'll be nice to see people, whether I know them or not."

"You're home now. Where you belong." Marla put her hand on Paula's arm. It was comforting.

"What about your husband? Will I get to meet him?"

"Oh, he'll be at work. I make sure he works very hard for us." Marla laughed, and Paula felt included in the joke, whether or not she could imagine making a man work hard for her.

Finally Marla said, "I really have to run. Can't wait for Friday." She got her keys out of her purse as Paula walked her to the car. She climbed inside and Paula leaned to look in the open passenger-side window.

"It's so good to see you."

Marla smiled happily. "It'll be like old times. But better—for both of us." And she pulled away from the curb, pushing her sunglasses down over her eyes in a single smooth, elegant gesture. Like a movie star.

Paula reached into her pocket and pulled out Marla's card. It was plain white, with a black border. Very posh.

She looked up at the house, wondering what in hell she would wear, knowing full well that whatever it was, she wasn't going to be able to compete with Marla. She was lost in these thoughts all the way back into the house, where she discovered her daughter curled up with stinky old Tex in front of the TV, so bored she was radiating.

"Okay, okay," she said. "We'll walk the dog!"

Marla was frowning as she drove off. It had been good to see Paula. Weird, and good also, to drive up to that house and see a young girl on the step. For a second it seemed as if Marla had travelled back in time—sixteen, seventeen years back—had shown up at the Wittmores the way she'd done when they were twelve or thirteen. *Hey, Mrs. Wittmore, can Paula come out?* It had been so like that for a moment that she'd been startled.

(that wasn't all—the girl also looked a little like)

Well, she was a copy of Paula as a child. You could see Paula all over her; that was what had startled her. The girl had beautiful eyes. They were not Paula's eyes, though. Paula's eyes could be called catlike and were not her best feature, although she could probably work them a bit more if she wore some makeup.

Of course, the child's eyes could have come from her father.

The first thing she had thought when she saw the girl sitting on the step was *Hey, Mars Bar! Catch!* The words echoed distinctly in her head, though she hadn't heard that voice in years. Too many years

(so what's *that* supposed to mean?)

Marla did not like the direction her thoughts were taking. The reptilian part of her brain shoved them down with a protective instinct so effective that her next thought was *that child looks like Paula—if Paula looked a little better.* "Beautiful" had been a little white lie. In fact, Paula didn't look good. She looked . . . *dishealthy.* That wasn't a word, but it fit. Everything that was wrong in Paula's life was showing: she was too poor and too sad and too lonely. Of course, all of that would change. She was home now. They could be friends again. Everything would be all right.

Three, maybe four long hairs

cheaply dyed, poor thing

clung to the sleeve and shoulder of Marla's suit. She counted them, her eyes darting between the road and the fabric. Four.

She pulled over to the shoulder and parked. The street was deserted, as it usually was in the middle of the day in Haven Woods. People were at work, or sleeping, or doing things with the blinds drawn.

Safety first. Marla dialled her mother's cell. It rang six times before Izzy answered. Marla put on her sunshiny voice. "Hello, Izzy," she said.

"Why won't you call me *Mother*?" Izzy said, exasperated.

Marla reached into her purse and pulled out a small empty Baggie. "It's all set for Friday."

"Oh, good," Izzy said. "That's all right, then."

Cradling her cell between shoulder and ear, Marla got a clothes brush out of the glovebox and slowly, carefully swept each hair off her jacket, picked them off the brush and put them in the Baggie.

"I met the daughter." Marla zipped the bag closed and put the brush back in the glovebox.

"What did you think?"

"She's very . . . young. Clearly bright as a button, though she didn't say much. A little bitchy, I suspect."

"You would know."

Marla held the Baggie with Paula's four long hairs in it. "So why do I feel bad?"

Izzy was firm. "Because you haven't learned the value of sacrifice yet. It comes with age. You'll get used to it."

"Sacrifice." Marla tucked the Baggie into her purse. "I'm sure I don't know what you mean. I'm going home for a run. Where are you?"

"I'm in the car. What have you done with my grandchildren?"

"They're with Esme."

"Oh gawd," Izzy said, disgusted. "She'll have taught them to freebase by now, or to draw dirty pictures."

"Mother, I'm hanging up. And don't use your phone while you're driving; it's dangerous. What if you got into an accident? Then what would I do?"

"I'm hanging up. Bye, dear." The phone went dead.

Marla stared at the phone a moment, her eyes narrowed. Then she texted a message to Izzy. WTCH TH RD *ITCH.

She still had one of the pebbles from the Wittmores' front walk in her pocket. With adolescent vitriol, she flicked it at the dash. It knocked harmlessly against the radio dial and fell to the floor. She thumbed the phone off, put it away in her purse with the Baggie, out of sight. You never knew.

She would stop for Starbucks, she decided. She wanted something sweet. She felt like celebrating. Everything would be all right. The way it used to be. Before Chick went rogue.

Whatever thoughts of Rowan had niggled at her before, they had disappeared. It didn't bear thinking about.

A skinny mocha. That was what she'd have.

SIX

SANDERSON KEYES HAD TREATED himself to a sledgehammer that afternoon, bought at his new hardware store. Nice enough place. Huge. Far. There was nowhere to shop in Haven Woods. To get to the hardware he'd had to drive to a mall twenty minutes away. But he'd get used to it; in the suburbs you drove everywhere. When he'd lived here as a kid, he had a distinct memory of being driven to school, not ten blocks from their old house.

When he got older, he and his buddies—Hop Robson, Butch Wright, Goose Evans—rode their bikes everywhere. Turned them into their recreation too, driving them up ramps, doing wheelies. Sanderson's cobalt blue Specialized had weighed twelve pounds. They'd lived on their bikes, and in the case of his little brother, nearly died. Lonnie, who definitely had the bigger mouth of the two Keyes brothers, had shot it off one summer afternoon, betting he could jump his BMX over the Evans's car. About ten of them had spent hours building a cross between a ramp and hard place. When Lonnie finally worked up the balls to try the jump, he crashed—bad.

Sanderson brought the sledge down hard on the wedge he'd

fitted into the cracked seam in the side of the old brick barbecue. The hammer hit with a flat, solid *crack* and a quarter of the ill-made wall crumbled to the grass in his new backyard. It was going to be a bitch to clean up.

He set the sledge down and worked a few bricks loose by hand, frowning. He was remembering the sound Lonnie had made when he smacked the top of that car, his bike jetting out from under him, sliding off the metal roof, scratching a deep groove in the paint. But the sound! His back and shoulder had hit first, and the crowd of kids gave a collective *oooooh*, thinking, *Cool!* because an accident is just what you hope to see when some kid rides his bike up a homemade ramp and over a neighbour's car. But when Lonnie's head smashed down on the metal roof, the sound was unlike anything Sandy had ever heard—a wet, living sound, the sharp smack as eloquent as an actual word. The worst thing that had ever happened

(but that wasn't quite true)

at the time.

At least until David Riley had his head cut off.

The worst thing until then.

Sandy had jumped up onto Mr. Evans's car and grabbed his brother. In retrospect it was the absolute wrong thing to do, but what did a bunch of asshole kids know about spinal injuries or brain damage? Brain damage was what rubbies got from sniffing glue, and spinal injuries were practically unheard of around there. So he grabbed his little brother, saw the blood, pulled his shirt off and wrapped it around Lonnie's head. *Dipshit*, he'd called him.

stupid dipshit Mom's going to kill us

There had been no permanent damage, except to the rest of the summer. Both of them had to work hard to pay for the damage to Mr. Evans's car. Lonnie because he was a (dipshit) fool and Sanderson because he hadn't stopped him.

The adult Sanderson considered: now that he was back in the

'hood, maybe he should get a bike. And then laughed at himself a little. Maybe he was regressing.

He picked up the sledgehammer again and swung it in an arc through the air, testing the heft. Sweet. He liked a new tool. The head was shiny steel and he could see himself in it if he wanted to look. Which he didn't. He already knew about the dark circles under his eyes and the beer bloat from going out too often with his buddy Lenny, whose break-up theory was *hey, man, the fastest way to get over someone is to get on top of someone else.*

While buying the sledge he'd allowed himself a quick fantasy about what Ted Kimmel, the CKX Weather Specialist—also known as the Big Shit Who Stole My Wife—would sound like as the hammer came down on his skull. Like a watermelon split by a bolt of lightning. In his imagination it was quick, bloodless, not so much violent as cathartic.

Deconstruction of the barbecue would take much of the afternoon. It was a pleasant thought, this idea that the day was laid out for him. He'd panicked briefly that morning when he realized he was pretty much moved into the new place and still had five more days of leave from work.

The new place. *His* new place. Had to get the language right, the therapist said. A hundred and twenty dollars an hour to tell him he shouldn't blame his ex-wife because she had slept with the CKX Weather Specialist (the Big Shit), and to always be sure to *get the language right.*

claim your half, Sanderson

Ripping into the monstrosity in the backyard was the sort of therapy Sanderson could honestly use.

On all fronts except marriage he had done well for himself, getting into home construction and building a company out of dirt and plywood. He was careful and a fair employer, getting and keeping good people by paying well and working hard himself. Sanderson

Homes had developed a reputation for quality. He built houses from the ground up and did major renos, but Sanderson's favourite was restoration. Hence buying this house in Haven Wood.

Built around 1971, it resembled the home in *The Brady Bunch*, with a sloping roof that angled down over the carport and a wide front entrance. It was a tall house and the layout was bi-level: you walked up to the living room and down to the family room. The kitchen and utility room were side by side at the back, and both had exits to a stone patio. The three bedrooms were clustered on the upper level, two smaller bedrooms across from the over-large master. Ensuite bathroom, full second bath. The house still felt a little empty, but he would fill it soon enough. With his own stuff.

He'd been raised in a house much like it, six blocks away. There was a tree in front of his new house, so much like the one in front of the old house, he had an urge to climb it and throw stones at girls as they walked by. *Psych!*

Sanderson leaned the sledgehammer against the barbecue he was halfway through destroying and stood in the sun for a moment. It was a lot of work, but there was no way he could keep the structure, for fear that someone would think he was the one who'd made it. He raised the sledge again and was about to fire it down, when from behind him came a single sharp bark. He looked over his shoulder to see Gusto, paws up on the kitchen's screen door.

"What do you want?" The dog panted happily, barked again. *Come see*. Then his mother was at the door.

She and the dog came out into the yard, Gusto scrambling to get to Sanderson first. The dog jumped up on him and then ran the length of the yard, sick of being cooped up.

"Oh my gawd," Anne Keyes said, looking at the mess that was the former barbecue. "You'll never get that cleaned up." She held a small wrapped box out to him. "I brought you a housewarming present."

He took it. "Is it a ventilation system?"

She laughed. "Something like that." In the corner was a yellow bow. She pulled it off and stuck it on Sanderson's shirt. "There, now you're gift-wrapped for some lucky girl." She pulled the lid off the box and let it drop to the grass. Gusto sniffed it interestedly.

Sanderson peeled away the tissue inside to reveal a square of yarn woven over two crossed sticks. He was confused but grinned at his mother.

"You and Lonnie made them at camp when you were little. I don't remember whose is whose, but they were both the same."

He lifted it out of the box by its yarn hanger. Four concentric squares in white, dark blue, light blue and white surrounded a red and yellow centre, made by the inexpert hand of a boy doing a craft for the first time. "I think it's very nice," he said, touched.

"It's called a God's eye. It repels evil."

"Whoa." He laughed. "I could've used this a year ago."

There was an awkward silence as the dark spectre of the divorce made an appearance. Then it passed.

"You hang them at points of egress—doors, windows, that sort of thing. Where people can see it."

He laughed out loud. "*Egress*? Mom, what did you smoke with your whisky this morning?"

She laughed too. "Just hang it by the front door."

She crouched down to talk to the dog, scratching him under the chin. "What about Gusto? Does my Gusto love that? Does he?"

"You know he's a dog, right?"

She caught Gusto's face in her hands and kissed him on the muzzle. "Be quiet. So far this is my only grandchild."

Her son winced. His brother Lonnie's wife, Terri, was on her third miscarriage, and now Sanderson's marriage had broken up. The dog *was* her only grandchild. It was an old joke, but it had become less funny in the past couple of years.

"Are those hot dogs on the counter for your supper or his?"

"Ma—"

She waggled her finger at him. "Don't use the single life as an excuse to eat badly. I stuck a couple of steaks in your fridge. A few other surprises too."

Touched again, he said, "I have the best mom. Thanks."

His mother gave his cheek a pat. "I'll get going now. I just stopped by to drop that off for you." She looked around the yard. In spite of the heat she wrapped her arms around herself. "I have to admit I don't like coming back to Haven Woods."

"Ma, we used to live here."

"I know. I'm just saying—" She shrugged, smiled. "Don't mind me."

"What?"

"You'll be okay here," she said, very seriously.

"Of course I will." Sanderson was still confused. "Mom, don't worry about me. I'm getting past it all. I really am."

Anne opened her arms and gave her older son a hug. "I'm outta here. Things to do, people to see . . . You take that poor guy for a walk, eh?"

He hugged her back. "I'm on it. See you later."

"Don't forget to hang that up, okay? Indulge your mother, who laboured seventeen hours with you and your big head."

He laughed. Just before she went through the back door, Sanderson saw her give a last nervous glance over her shoulder at the endless row of backyards to the west.

Then Gusto was at his feet, wagging his tail. "You heard her. Let's get your leash. Leash!" Gusto ran towards the house, followed by Sanderson. They were both still figuring things out, but he was a smart dog. He'd have the neighbourhood sussed in a couple of days. The man held the door open and the dog ran in.

In under a minute Gusto was back with his leash in his mouth, tail wagging furiously. Smart dog.

—

Paula walked up the street, east towards the park and the river, trailing Tex and her daughter, who'd moped around the house after she'd been rude to Marla as if Marla was the one who had been out of line. Paula sighed, knowing that her daughter was bored and dreading the weeks ahead without school to keep her occupied. At least she was happy now, tugging the old dog on his leash.

To the west was the rest of Haven Woods, a seemingly endless vista of houses that shifted where the land sloped gently upwards to a vista of roofs, all of them unremarkable shades of green, grey, blue. These familiar streets smelled the same as they had when she was small: of the river and the faint scent of cut grass, and the even fainter aroma of yeast from Dawn's Bakery.

A cat jumped up on a fake wishing well and hunkered down as they passed.

There had been bad things about growing up here. Then horrible things, when David and her dad died within weeks of each other. But those bad things were somehow not what she was remembering now about Haven Woods. Instead she remembered how smooth her life had been back then.

It had all been so easy. It was not like that for Rowan. Never had been, no matter how hard she tried.

"So what do you think of the Cubs' chances for the pennant this year?"

Rowan had been staring at the squares of sidewalk under her feet as she walked, but now she swung her head around and made a face at her mother. "What are you talking about?"

"My dad used to say that to me when I wasn't talking."

"My grandpa?"

"Yeah."

Ro's face was unsmiling. She held Old Tex's leash loosely in her right hand as the dog walked happily beside her.

. *I'm taking Tex home let's change tops*

"What about my dad?"

"What do you mean?"

"Well, was he from here?"

Paula shook her head no.

"But I'm twelve, right? Weren't you still living here twelve years ago? So weren't you pregnant here?"

"Ro!"

"Well, weren't you?"

"I said no."

They stopped at the corner. The only noise was the distant hum of a lawnmower. Suburban Muzak.

"I just want to know about him."

"It was a long time ago."

"Tell me."

With a sigh, Paula said, "You know the story. He died in a car wreck. Before you were born." She reached out and touched her daughter's head. "You have my hair, but you have your dad's eyes." *Dad* was an unfamiliar word between them, and it felt false to say it.

"Was he nice?"

I love you Pauls you're my girlfriend

The tears were years behind her, but thinking about him here in Haven Woods caused a tightening in her chest, sad and bleak. "Yes, he was. Maybe I should get married, huh?" She said it as much to distract herself as Rowan.

"Ew. I don't know. Do you want to?"

Paula snorted. "A boyfriend might be good. And yeah, I think I would like to get married." She thought about Marla's comment about her husband working hard for them. That would be nice.

Very nice.

"That woman who came over—did she really use to be your best friend?"

A car swung lazily around the corner and started moving towards them. It was going no more than ten miles an hour, but they stayed on the curb, waiting for it to pass. If it had been the city Paula would have thrown up her hand and made it stop.

They used to play ball hockey on this street—the boys would— right up until it snowed, a Sears goal net at either end. A car would come along and one of the boys would yell, *Car!* and everyone would move off the street, the goalies carrying the nets on their shoulders.

In the summer they played baseball. The girls would go and watch the boys.

let's go change tops I wanna get some money from my mom

As the car drove slowly by, the female driver leaned slightly forward, grinning madly at them.

Paula stared. "Oh yes," she said to her daughter, "Marla and I were inseparable."

They crossed the road and walked towards the park. Paula thought she could hear the gurgling of the river. More than any other sound

(except maybe the *whoosh* and whistle of something sharp flying through the air)

the sound of the river evoked memories. They'd spent so much of their time there. In the park. All of them, hanging out, sitting at the picnic tables.

(They would sit inside the culvert when it was dry and talk for hours. David did most of the talking—he was one of those people who could find something to say about anything, and sometimes they would hold hands while he talked . . .

He'd grin

I love you Pauls

and later, when they'd already spent too much of their time together, he would reach out, put his hand on her neck and trace it down to her breasts

I love you Pauls

They found everything together.)

"Why did you even leave here, then?"

"Why did I leave Haven Woods?"

"Yeah," Rowan said. "If it was so great and you had friends and everything, why did you go?"

Paula shrugged. "Everyone leaves home sometime."

"Your friend didn't. Grandma didn't."

"Honey, we're here now. Let's just enjoy this. Except for Grandma being sick and the part where you got kicked out of school, we could have a nice time." She grinned at her daughter, wryly, she hoped.

Rowan groaned. "It should have been Nicki who got kicked out."

"Let's just talk about something else and be nice." Paula pointed to the trees ahead of them. "You know, there's a river down there. We used to come here all the time when I was a kid."

Old Tex recognized the park and stopped. He raised his nose and sniffed the air. Rowan squatted and undid the clip on his collar, but Old Tex stayed put. She gave him a little push. "Go!"

The dog looked at her and panted, took a few steps onto the grass and sat down.

"Go play—"

"He's old, Ro. Give him a minute."

The park was empty over to where the river was bordered by tall elms and firs. Play equipment lay abandoned and lonely in the afternoon sun of a work/school day. There were the usual things: monkey bars, two sets of swings, a slide and a broad sandbox that looked untouched. Too big for the slide, Rowan slowly walked over to the big-kid swings. She backed into one and let the wooden plank seat hit her mid-thigh. She backed up until all that was touching the ground were her toes and all she had to do to fly was lift her feet, poetry in motion.

Paula watched. A wave of guilt threatened to overwhelm her. The naturalness of Rowan in this wholesome setting was such a contrast to the places she'd dragged the girl through, each new address a little worse than the last, even though she tried to convince herself that she was improving their lot.

They should have been here all along. With her family.

With *his* family. How different their lives would have been. And across her mind it all flew, like the girl on the swing: If she'd stayed and explained and been able to give all this to her daughter. If her mother had let her stay. She'd been so confused and grief-stricken, and then when she found out she was pregnant, her mother thought it best if she stayed away. Paula figured she'd been ashamed of her, though her mother didn't say so, and Paula had felt so ashamed she never pushed.

Somewhere farther away, a dog barked happily.

Rowan kept her eyes closed as long as she could, opening them only when she started to feel sick. When the vertigo passed, she closed them again—fiercely, her teeth gritted—stuck her legs straight out in front of her on the upswing and threw them underneath her on the way back. Back and forth, like that. She knew her mom was watching her. She deliberately didn't look over at her. She had just decided: except for Tex, she did not like Haven Woods.

On the backswing, leaning way forward, she heard a dog barking, high-pitched and antic.

—

Gusto sprinted out of the trees as soon as he caught the scent of another dog. He ran full bore, small beagle body arcing midair about every twelve steps, the only thing that prevented him from tumbling head over tail across the grass towards Old Tex.

"Gusto!" Sanderson Keyes yelled after him as he beelined for the other dog.

Startled, Paula turned to see the beagle leap through the air at Tex.

"It's okay," the man chasing after him yelled. "It's okay, he's friendly—just a bit starved for company. Gusto!" Gusto was jumping all around and underneath the substantially larger Tex, who for his part was tolerating the younger dog's interest.

Rowan flew off the swing and ran towards the animals, delighted. "Hey, another dog!" She'd seen lots of cats, but until now the only dog had been Tex. She and Paula crouched down and petted the new one. Diplomatically, Gusto divided his time among them all, but he showed a definite preference for Tex.

Sanderson caught up, then bent over, hands on his knees, to catch his breath. "Whew, can't do that like I used to," he said. "Sorry about this. He's been pretty cooped up and he thinks this is a dog park."

"I *love* him!" Rowan buried her face in Gusto's smooth scruff.

Paula laughed and scratched the top of the beagle's head once more, then stood up.

"Paula Wittmore?"

She met the man's eyes, then laughed in recognition. "Sandy Keyes. Oh my god! How are you?"

He took her hand and gave it a half-shake. "You're still here?" he said. "I just moved back."

"Well, welcome home. And no, I don't live here anymore. My daughter and I are home visiting my mom. Sandy, this my daughter, Rowan."

Rowan looked up from the dogs and nodded shyly. She had one hand on Old Tex's head and the other wrapped around Gusto's neck. Dog heaven. "Hi," she said. "I like your dog."

"Nice to meet you, Rowan. It looks as if he likes you too. He's Gusto, for obvious reasons."

"You're the second person from the old days I've run into today," Paula said. "I saw Marla Riley earlier. She looks great." She pointed to the bow attached to his shirt. "You come gift-wrapped?"

He looked down. "My mom. She brought me a housewarming present." He pulled the bow off and then didn't know what to do with it. "It's good to see you. I don't see anybody from the old days, though if Marla still lives here, I'm bound to run into her sometime."

"It's good to see you too, Sandy."

"Sandy? Ha! No one's called me that for awhile. I'm Sanderson now. Running my own construction company and all that." He grinned to show he wasn't full of himself. "What about you? What are you doing these days?"

She thought about lying, then laughed and confessed. "Nothing right now. I'm . . . in transition."

Rowan rolled her eyes discreetly, then got up and ruffled the fur around Old Tex's neck. "C'mon, boy, let's go." She turned to Gusto. "You wanna run? Wanna run?" She galloped backwards. The dogs followed her, Old Tex more out of loyalty than a desire to actually run.

"That your same dog? I remember that dog. He used to come down to the ball field. We used to try to get him to play base." Sanderson laughed. "Riley used to toss him the ball. Long time ago." He looked quickly at Paula. "Sorry. Bad thing to mention. You were an item, you two."

"Long time ago," she said.

Sanderson said, "So, is Rowan your only one?"

She nodded. "And no, to get it over with, I'm not married. You?"

"Was. Just divorced."

"I'm sorry. Kids?"

"No. But don't be sorry—it's all good. Hey, I just had a crazy idea. Why don't you and Rowan come for dinner? My mother dropped off some steaks and stocked my fridge with enough food for an army." He leaned in conspiratorially. "She worries about me."

"I don't know, Sandy," she said. "My mom's not well. She's actually in the hospital here. It's why we came home."

"I'm sorry to hear that, Paula. Can I ask what's wrong?"

"I don't know, actually. I've had some trouble getting in touch with the doctor. She's not saying either. Izzy Riley was the one who called and told me. I'm sure I'll know soon enough."

"Do you want to make it another night?"

Paula stared at the ground a moment, considering. "No, we'd like to come." She met his eye and smiled. "Rowan's been a little bored. I think she'll love the idea of hanging with two dogs."

"Great, we can catch up. You remember Winnie Casper's old house?"

"The one that looks like the Brady Bunch live there?"

"Yes! I bought it and I'm going to restore it. It's great example of early seventies architecture and I'm in love with it. I'll give you a tour of its finer points when you come. About seven o'clock?"

"Sure, we'll be there."

"Bring Old Tex too, okay?"

"Sure."

As Sanderson walked away he whistled for his dog, and Gusto ran to him, chased by Rowan and Tex. Sanderson leaned towards her daughter, saying something she couldn't catch, but from the way Rowan jumped up and down, clapping her hands, she guessed she wouldn't have to talk her into dinner at his place. Their conversation ended with Sandy-Sanderson putting the gift bow on top of Rowan's head.

He turned and gave her a wave, then he and the dog jogged away in the direction of Proctor Street.

SEVEN

WHEN THEY GOT BACK from the park, Paula told Rowan to entertain herself while she made a couple of calls. Rowan fiddled with the TV, but all that was on was that Joanna Shaw show; her mom had said she was a friend of Mrs. Riley-Moore's. She watched without much interest as Joanna Shaw got the audience to yell at a man who didn't pay his child support. Then an ad came on reminding viewers to tune in next week, when the show went national. Rowan clicked it off.

She could hear her mom on the phone in the kitchen. Tex was collapsed on the floor beside her and she reached over and gave him a scratch on his belly. That was when she remembered about the new collar.

Tex followed her to Grandma's bedroom. Her mom's clothes were still in her bag, but she'd put her makeup stuff on the giant bureau against the wall. Rowan got down on all fours and lifted the bedskirt. Under the bed, right in the middle, was a small box. She reached for it and it slid easily towards her on the wood floor. Even though her grandmother had told her to take it, it still felt like sneaking, and she kept one ear on the sound of her mother talking at the other end of the house.

The box had an inlaid decoration on the top. She took the key from her blazer pocket, slipped it into the lock and turned, then lifted the lid. A strong smell hit her and she wrinkled her nose. An old-people smell, like the stuff they put in their drawers and medicine cabinets. Medicine-y.

Tex sniffed the air, then sat on his bum beside her. He whined sadly.

"Do you miss Grandma, Tex? Do you?"

Inside the box were pieces of broken jewellery, a copper penny, a nickel. A teeny-tiny pincushion in the shape of a little pig caught her eye; it had room for only four pins. There were also three small Ziploc bags. One held a sponge, another some powder. The third was empty. Underneath them she found what she assumed was the collar. She lifted it out and held it at eye level. It smelled too.

Her grandmother had wound the whole length of it with red ribbon and had added decorative dots along the ribbon. There were tiny marks that looked like exotic tattoos, circles and stars. Four puffy bits of cotton, evenly spaced, completed the decoration. It was weird, but Rowan liked it.

The dog looked at it and at her.

"You have to wear it. Grandma said," she told him. She put it around his neck and carefully did up the buckle, loosely so it wouldn't hurt him. Then she tilted her head and studied him. "Very handsome for an old bugger."

She undid the old collar and dropped it into the box. Then she closed the lid and slid it back under the bed. Just as her mother came into the room.

"Is that what you're wearing to Sanderson's house?" She pointed at Rowan's school blazer.

Rowan frowned. "Is that what *you're* wearing?" She pointed at the rock T-shirt her mother wore. U2.

"I'm changing, Miss Behaviour."

Rowan got up and patted her leg for the dog to follow her. "Don't change too much or I won't recognize you."

Paula was frustrated. She'd called the hospital and asked Tula for the name of the doctor treating her mother. Tula had stalled, said she wasn't at the desk that had the directory, that he was new to the hospital. She thought his name was Tuck or Tubb or Tucker.

something like that dear—I'll find out and let you know tomorrow

There was no Tuck or Tubb or Tucker in the phone book. So she called every doctor in the area to find the one who was treating her mother. She had to argue with each receptionist even to get them to check

we don't usually give out that information dear

but from what she could figure out, no one in Haven Woods was treating her mother.

So she'd called the hospital and gotten (half-wit) Tula again. Did the woman never go off shift? When Paula explained what she'd done, all Tula could say was, *Well, many of our doctors come from other places. I told you I'd check and let you know tomorrow.* Paula demanded that a doctor—*any* doctor—call her in the morning before she went by to see her mother.

She was still pissed off, and slightly worried, when she pulled off the U2 T-shirt and tossed it on the bed. She caught a look at herself in her mom's dresser mirror. For a moment she panicked. What would she wear?

just a barbecue

She pulled her good blouse from her bag and shook it out. Then she rummaged through her mother's closet and came up with a green jacket to go with the blouse. She put both on and was pleased that the jacket fit her. Then she grabbed her brush and gave her hair a few strokes. It was thick, a striking chestnut, and she was glad that Rowan had inherited it, colour and texture both. Today, however, it was not cooperating. Paula sighed and pulled it smoothly back, fastening it with a large hairclip. She studied herself again. She looked kind of good.

The TV sounded from the living room again and Paula recognized the music from *The Joanna Shaw Show*—not exactly kid-friendly viewing. Shaw favoured the style of commando journalism in which everything is a moral emergency. The issues were usually black-and-white—child abuse bad, long-suffering woman good— and relied on screams of outrage from her audience and Twitter rants delivered in real time that scrolled across the bottom of the screen. It was . . . unwholesome.

On her mother's dresser was a bottle of perfume. With a wry smile and a roll of her eyes she sprayed it into the air and walked through the mist. Just enough. She'd read that in a magazine.

Rowan was sitting in Paula's dad's recliner, which her mother had re-covered in a pattern that matched the sofa. She dangled a foot over the armrest and bounced it, remote in hand, as she stared blankly at the set.

Paula took the remote and shut off the TV. Her daughter, lost in either thought or the program, jerked in surprise. Checking her mother out, she gave her a thumbs-up. "You look like Julia Roberts."

Paula blushed happily.

ha ha

"Get Tex's leash, okay, honey?"

Rowan slid off the chair and held up the leash. She'd been sitting on it.

"Are you really going to wear your school blazer?"

The girl stuck a self-conscious hand into a pocket, looking defensive. "I like my blazer, okay?"

Paula took the leash and hooked it onto Old Tex's collar. Was the collar new? She tugged it away from Tex's neck to see better, and a sudden memory hit her, prompted by the scent of

this smells like mints

tuck it in your pocket, Paula, it's pretty

There were little white cotton pouches stuffed with what felt like straw or herbs

peppermint?

and a red ribbon decorated within an inch of its life.

"What's this?" she said.

"It's Tex's new collar. Grandma told me to put it on him."

"Hmmm," Paula said. "Your grandma has always liked making things. Do you like it? What about the smell?"

"It's okay. I like the smell of dog better," Rowan said.

"Really?"

"Yeah. Especially the smell of Old Tex."

On their way out the door, Paula said, "Do I really look like Julia Roberts?"

This was usually Marla's favourite time of day. The sun was dropping below the horizon and she was finished the shopping, the cooking, the cleaning. She was anticipating baths, books and pyjamas, knowing that in an hour or so the kids would be sound asleep and her time would be all her own.

But tonight there was Coach Crawford.

It had taken her nearly an hour to calm Tim down after practice. He'd *huff-huff-huffed*, unable to speak, only to be overtaken by more sobs. She got him to bend over and breathe, her hand on the back of his head, then held a cool cloth to his forehead and cheeks. *Breathe, honey*, and she'd waited for him to do it. When he still wasn't able to calm down, she had him lie on the sofa with his head in her lap while she rubbed his back.

But he was still upset. It had taken her ages to get him into pyjamas and then into bed, while her poor little Amy stood in the doorway, utterly uncertain about the order of things and needing her order, because Amy was a somewhat unimaginative child.

Is Timmy going to die? she'd asked.

No, honey, of course not. He's just upset is all. It will be okay. You go climb in your bed, doll.

And she had, of course. She always did what she was told. She was the easy one. She was . . . malleable. Her little doll.

Marla could still hear the occasional sob coming from Tim's room. He was crying in his sleep, and she was livid.

Tim hadn't made the baseball team. He had handed her the note, struggling to get the words out: "Mister . . . Crawf— Crawf— Crawford . . ."

She'd read the note while Tim buried his head in her stomach and cried.

> *Dear Mrs. Riley-Moore:*
>
> *Tim's skills are exceptional, but unfortunately he will not be invited to play on the baseball team this year, since he is still too young. We hope that next year he will try out again, when he has reached ten years old. His skills are top-notch and we'll be glad to see him at that time.*
>
> *Yours truly,*
> *B. Crawford, Phys. Ed.*
> *Haven Woods Elementary*

Asshole.

Marla peeked in on her daughter. Amy was on her back looking like a sleeping princess, her hair spread out over the pillow. Her tiny, perfect face was smooth and serene. She would lie like that all night, never moving. Marla knew this because it was always so.

Amy was only six, but so beautiful people stopped them on their rare ventures out of Haven Woods.

oh my god what a beautiful child

Men, women, other children . . . it didn't matter—the girl stopped traffic.

(she was *a doll*

—but that was no fault of hers)

She closed the door and peeked in again on Timmy. He lay curled on his side, his cheeks still stained with tears, his little nose red. His nightlight was shaped like a baseball, and just seeing it inflamed Marla again.

how dare he Crawford the little prick little bastard prick

She'd met the coach on one of her many trips to the school. She volunteered a lot. It was what a mother did, if she could—and Marla could.

Crawford was a stereotype: short but built, with huge biceps and overworked shoulders. His leg muscles were equally defined (she would suspect implants, except she didn't think the little troll made enough money). Marla figured such a man taught grade three because he needed to feel superior, and the best way to do that was to boss around the only people he was certain to be both taller and smarter than (although that was only a matter of time). He was probably jealous of Tim, a natural athlete. That was it.

Marla paced her slowly darkening house, undoing the damage of a day with young children, picking up jackets and shoes, carrying dishes back to the sink. She picked up toys. Barbie, pretty in a party dress, shoes missing; a stuffed dog that had no name that Marla knew; a miniature bow and arrow. And—

And a plastic man who was supposed to be on safari. Jungle Jim was his name. He wore a plastic vest with accessories that attached and detached: a canteen, a net and a tiny toy gun. A little jungle truck, like an SUV, came with him.

Hello.

The truck and Jungle Jim went into Marla's sweater pocket. She started a load of laundry. She turned the lights off in the laundry room, leaving the washer to *whoosh* and purr.

The kitchen, illuminated by the light over the stove, was dim and tidy. And quiet—the dishwasher cycle was complete. Marla would unload it soon.

She stood the toy safari man at the end of the counter. His feet were broad and flat so that he could pose in his safari village with the little plastic cages for a lion, a zebra and a hippo.

Hippos are dangerous animals. More dangerous than sharks, crocodiles or dogs. She and Tim had looked it up on the Internet. More people are killed every year by hippos than by any other animal on earth. Of course the deadliest animal was still the

cougar

She set the truck at the other end of the counter. She bent to eye level and lined it up with the little toy man. The over-muscled, self-important little man.

With an elegant flick of her finger, the car rolled across the counter until it ran full tilt into Jungle Jim. He toppled over, bounced and fell to the floor. If he'd been flesh and blood, there would have been a satisfying *splat*.

Marla stared at the little man, and from her other pocket she pulled the note from school. She opened it and scanned it again. *Won't be invited . . . top-notch skills . . .* Then she dropped it. It floated to the floor, landing on the toy man, covering him completely.

She felt herself relax.

After a moment she looked at her watch. It was just about eight thirty. Doug wouldn't be home for another two hours. He worked so hard.

She picked up the phone and dialled the Wittmores' number, something she had not done in

(how many years had her brother been dead?)

years. Why would she? Audra was her mother's friend. Not so much anymore, of course.

Marla's expression was hopeful and a little yearning. She wanted to talk, to say

Paula ohmigawd I had such a time with my boy tonight I'm so glad you're there I have to say—

She wanted it to be like before.

Paula, Danny Sparks said he liked me but I think he just wants to be—

On the other end the phone rang and rang and rang and rang. No machine picked up. Marla hung up after fourteen rings. Even if she'd dozed off in front of the TV, Paula would have heard fourteen rings. Or her daughter would. Rowan. She wondered where they could be.

Outside it was cloudless and clear.

Marla whistled, a low, sweet sound. In a moment she heard a noise behind her and turned to look. Her cat, Troubles, padded into the kitchen unhurriedly. When he was at her feet, she scooped him up. She held him to her breast just like she'd held Tim earlier, stroked his head and ears and rubbed her finger under his chin. He purred. She didn't much like the cat, but he was her . . . pet. She carried him to the back door, pushed it open and dropped the cat outside.

"Go see what Old Tex is doing." The cat wandered (unhurriedly) towards the front of the house. Marla watched until she couldn't see him anymore.

She was glad Paula was back. It was unfortunate that the circumstances were less than perfect and probably going to get much,
much worse. But in time she hoped Paula would come to see that
there was no other way. All for one and one for all—that sort of
thing.

And Rowan was perfect.

(she knew why too but she didn't think Izzy did)

She considered for a moment whether her kids were really
down for the night. Amy was for sure. And Tim? The little guy was
exhausted and not likely to stir now. She decided they were.

Marla changed her clothes and went for a run.

EIGHT

The backyard still smelled a bit like barbecue sauce and steak, with undernotes of freshly mowed lawn. Through an open window in the house, Paula could hear canned laughter. Rowan had been beside herself with glee when she realized that Sanderson's big-screen TV came with cable.

Sanderson had baked potatoes in the oven and tossed a green salad. He'd even picked up dessert—obviously going for the kid vote—a dozen brightly coloured monster cookies so sweet Paula could hardly finish one. Rowan had ploughed through three.

If he was trying to make friends and influence people, he was certainly making serious headway with Rowan and Old Tex. Paula wasn't sure how she was going to peel her daughter away from the cable television and big cookies or Old Tex from the backyard, where he was now lying half a foot from Gusto. Old friends already.

They talked a little about what he had left behind when he moved to Haven Woods, carefully skirting his divorce. Too soon for that kind of talk. When it got close to her own love life, there were steaks to turn, potatoes to poke, a table to be set.

It was lovely. And *easy.*

After dinner, once Ro was settled in the sparsely furnished living room—a single long, obviously new leather sofa faced the big-screen TV, and that was it *I'm still figuring out what I need," he told them*—she and Sanderson went out into the backyard and collapsed into a couple of folding chairs, the sort you take camping, with a cup holder on the side that fits a beer bottle more easily than a cup of tea.

Sanderson took a long swallow of his beer. "Heaven, on a June day," he said.

"My dad used to say that."

"Mine too. My mom says, 'Fill your boots.' I've never quite figured out what it means. I think it's sorta *do what you want*, you know?"

Paula nodded. "My mother never used to tell me anything directly. She quizzes. When I saw her today, all she wanted to know was who I saw, where did I go . . . when I got to talk to her at all."

"How is she feeling?"

Paula groaned. "Her symptoms are so vague. When I got home from the park, I called every doctor in the book. From what I can tell, no one is treating her at all. The nurse there . . ." She trailed off, not wanting to get into a rant.

"My mom doesn't like that I moved back to the old neighbourhood. She lives over in Lakewood now. Our fierce rivals—remember that? Lakewood Lynxes versus Haven Woods Hitters." The baseball teams.

"Why doesn't she like your moving home? You grew up here."

"I have great memories of Haven Woods, but my mom seems to remember a lot of bad things."

Paula took a drink of her beer and made a noncommittal sound.

(bad things *have* happened here)

"Remember the Chapman house?" Sanderson said. "The guy who killed his family?"

"Sure. We girls used to scare ourselves stiff telling tales about it. Wasn't he supposed to have sacrificed his wife and kid to the devil? Used to give me nightmares. Is that what bothers your mother?"

"I think he just went nuts and killed them. Domestic homicide. But later, the rumour about Satanists practising the *dark arts*"—he deepened his voice comically—"that bothered her."

"Did she think it was true?"

He shrugged. "The guy wrote on the walls: 'He Lives Here' and 'Different god, different rules.' Wasn't that it? He was batshit crazy. Everybody was into weird stuff in the seventies, weren't they? And every generation has their bad murder. In the sixties it was the Manson murders. The seventies was that guy who shot up that McDonald's. What was in the eighties?"

"Glam rock," she said. "May it burn in heck."

He laughed and she was pleased.

Paula took another sip of beer. "So why did you move back?"

"You're going to be sorry you asked." He leaned back in his chair, stretching his legs out in front of him.

"No, I won't. Tell me."

"After college I lived in the city for a long time, got into the scene—you know, the clubs, the music. Girls. Thursday, Friday, Saturday night, all about going out. Hang out with some buddies at Bad Laundry for a beer and a burger. Hit a club or five, crawl home." He laughed self-consciously. "Well, that's what I did for about four years. Clubs, bars, drugs, beer, music, babes."

"It sounds like fun."

"It *was* fun. Good times. Then it turned a corner. Suddenly the same faces telling the same jokes, everybody trying to be hipper than the rest, finding a line—it was so substance-less. Is that a word?"

"Sure."

"And it got to feel a little . . . *Masque of the Red Death*–ish. Do you remember that story? When that guy ran from room to room while everyone was at a party?"

"Yeah, I do remember. I'm impressed we both do."

"It was like that. I kept going into the same room—same faces, same hangover—and after awhile I felt like I was missing everything important. So I married the best candidate: Kelly—my ex-wife now."

He took a long swallow of beer. "We moved to the suburbs. Next on the agenda was a couple of kids, a fence, dog. I wanted it all, you know. Got Gusto about a month after we moved in. A starter baby."

"Sounds perfect. What happened?" Paula asked. "I mean, you don't have to tell me. If you're not comfortable."

He raised his hand. "No, I don't mind. It's not a secret. It might require a fresh beer, though. How's yours?" He stood and held his hand out for her bottle.

"You can bring me one, but this is still pretty good."

Sanderson went inside the house.

It was dark enough that it was a strain to see. There were stacks of flattened boxes just outside the patio doors. In the middle of the yard was a pile of rubble. One side of the old barbecue was still intact and a sledgehammer leaned up against it. It looked as if there might be perennials in the bed along the back fence.

A home in the first stages of rebirth.

Paula was startled when she caught sight of the cat on the fence. It sat very still, the only sign that it was alive at all the steady, rhythmic flipping of its tail. When the patio doors opened, the cat jumped down soundlessly into the yard next door. The dogs hadn't even noticed.

Sanderson passed her a cold beer, still capped. "We got married and moved to the burbs. And I was expecting"—he held out his hands, gesturing to all of Haven Woods—"a neighbourhood, you know?"

She did.

"The place we moved into, Terra Rija, it was so *new* there was no community there. We got to know some of the neighbours— over the back fence type of thing—but there was very little social- izing, even after we joined the club, started golfing. We didn't run into anybody except in the parking lot at Safeway. Remember the backyard parties the Rileys used to throw?"

"Sure, every weekend—"

"Our parents hanging out in the back, drinking beer and cock- tails, while we did whatever we wanted. I remember riding my bike with David Riley, Pete, Lonnie, in the solid dark—had to be mid- night—showing up back at the barbecue and the parents were still at it, laughing. Everybody eating s'mores."

"Do you remember the night we all slept over in the Rileys' family room? There had to be ten of us. We watched movies . . ."

"The original *Friday the 13th*! I remember it scaring my pants off, so to speak . . . I don't think there was any hanky-panky." In the dark Paula blushed.

c'mon no one will notice no one goes into the spare room

"And there was some song we kept singing . . . I think it was Bon Jovi." He tried the chorus. "*I cried and I cried / There were nights that I died for you, baby . . .*"

The song played in her head as if she had heard it just that morning. David—all of them, she guessed, but she only remem- bered him—had sung it in her ear. She'd thought it was the height of romance.

"Our parents just seemed like stealth agents or something, moving behind the scenes, making our lives work but not showing us how to do it ourselves. I was useless for so long in the real world."

"Yeah, you're right. Stealth agents."

"It was like that forever. Right up until David Riley died."

Paula went blank. She was suddenly keenly aware of the chilly air, the sound of the television inside the house, the feel of the cold beer bottle against her thigh.

"You okay? You cold? We can go inside if you like."

She shook her head. "No, this is good. I just . . . haven't thought about that for a long time."

"Oh man. Sorry. You were there that day?"

Paula inhaled the night air, closed her eyes. The beer was sweating against her pants. She took a swallow of her beer. "Yeah."

"So was I." Sanderson picked at the label on his bottle. "Do you know something?"

She turned to him. In profile he was very solid looking, a Marlboro man. "What?"

A slow smile spread on his face. "I had a big crush on you when we were about fifteen, sixteen. Before you left. But you were always with Riley."

"You did not."

"Yeah, I did. You had a red bathing suit with a funny round thing in the middle, and the straps went up around your neck . . . Whaddya call that?"

"A halter?" She thought back; there was a vague memory (fighting against more vivid memories *I wanna change my top*) of the pool and the wobbling, adult feeling in the pit of her stomach when the boys looked at her, how she drank that up, at the same time wishing she could disappear. "I remember that suit," she said.

"So do I. That suit gave me dreams."

Paula cheeks got hot. "Oh, *please* . . . It was a long time ago."

He nodded. "Yup."

She sighed. "The steaks were great. This was really terrific, but

I better get Ro back to the house and to bed."

"I haven't chased you away, have I?"

"No." But she couldn't stay.

"Good. Let's do this again, okay?" He smiled broadly at her and she smiled back and the two them got up.

He towered over her. She looked up, then turned towards the house. Sanderson followed.

Rowan liked Mr. Keyes's house way more than her grandma's. It felt new inside. The walls were just walls; there was nothing on them. He probably had stuff he was going to put up, but he hadn't done it yet and so it seemed . . . new. And it was such a relief to have real TV. She liked his house and him.

She was disappointed when she heard them come in through the patio doors. Already? Her mom probably thought it was time to get her home to bed, and this created a hard stone in her belly. She didn't want to leave. She felt good here.

While they made noises with dishes and things in the kitchen, Rowan went to the table where his phone was. Using a pencil from the cup beside it and a piece of the newspaper that had been on the sofa, she wrote down the number on the phone. His number. 782-3314.

Just in case. Then she took the pink plastic crucifix out of the pocket of her St. Mary's blazer, wrapped the folded paper around it and put the whole thing back in her pocket. It bulged a little bit and she liked that. If she wanted to, she could feel it anytime.

The two of them showed up in the doorway between the kitchen and the living room. Her mom's face was pink and happy. Mr. Keyes's face too. Rowan felt as if she'd missed something.

"Ro, we have to go now," her mother said.

Gusto ran in through their legs, bumping her mom sideways

so that she grabbed at the doorway. Mr. Keyes steadied her with his hand, even though he didn't have to.

cripe

Old Tex followed, limping a little on the hardwood floors. The nails of both dogs sounded loud in the big, empty room. When Old Tex saw Rowan, his tail went up and started swinging back and forth. She crouched and he tucked his head into her arms.

(against her leg when she bent down she could feel the stuff in her pocket and that felt good felt *safe*)

She mumbled dog-love words into his ear. "Hey boy, good dog."

(what's out there boy?)

"Let's go, Ro. It's getting late."

On the front porch Rowan clipped Tex's leash to his collar. Her mom stopped one last time on the porch. "Thanks again, Sandy. That was a wonderful dinner. I hope you'll let me return the favour."

Rowan turned away, rolling her eyes, when her mother started batting her damn eyelashes. On the porch railing was a glass pop bottle full of gunk and feathers. She picked it up. "What is this?" There was a faded ribbon around the neck of the bottle. It was dirty and worn, old.

"What is it?" Paula echoed.

Sanderson took it from Rowan, holding it up so they all could see it. "It's called a witch bottle. It came with the house."

"It's really for witches?" Rowan asked.

"I think it's for good luck or something. A lot of places around here have them."

"Why did you take it down?" Rowan asked.

He pointed to the overhang of the porch roof. They all looked up. Dangling from the single hook was a multicoloured square made of sticks and yarn.

"Oh," Paula said.

"That's a God's eye," Rowan said. "We made them at school."

"My mother practically begged me to hang it up."

"They keep away evil," Rowan said shyly.

He made a ghostly sound, wiggling his fingers at the two of them. Her mom laughed, but standing on the dark porch with the dark neighbourhood still to walk through, Rowan didn't think it was that funny.

"So I have a witch bottle *and* a God's eye to keep me safe," Sandy said. "Lucky me, huh?"

They said good night again, and to Rowan's disbelief, Paula refused his offer of a ride home, even though it was dark as pitch out and people had *witch bottles* on their porches. As one of God's special little thinkers, Rowan thought, *WTF?*

Paula sent Rowan to bed as soon as they got in the house. The girl went with a minimum of complaint, and Paula was grateful for small mercies.

Old Tex's nails clicked on the floor. Paula turned to him, realizing she had forgotten to unclip his leash.

silly me red bathing suit huh imagine that crush on—

She crouched to take it off him, the dog anxious to move away. No sooner had she unclipped him than Old Tex pressed forward, a low growl in his throat, the sound menacing in the dark house.

Rowan!

"Rowan?" Paula called down the hall, but it came out as a whisper. Her cell—where was her cell?

Old Tex turned into the kitchen, still growling. Goosebumps formed up and down her back. She followed the click-clicking nails into the dark . She could hear him growling, but nothing else. Paula swallowed. There was a phone on the wall in the kitchen—gold, the same phone they'd had when she was a girl.

Directly across the lane she could see the yellow glow of Gabe

Newton's bug light. Old Tex stood at the patio door, his nose pressed against the glass, still growling intermittently. He turned his head to Paula and wagged his tail unhappily.

Look.

Paula clapped a hand to her chest, feeling suddenly foolish

—a home invasion in Haven Woods? not after nine—

Obviously a skunk or raccoon had found its way onto the deck and Old Tex wanted out.

"You're not going out there," she said, and flicked on the back porch light.

It wasn't a raccoon or a skunk. It was a cat. It took her a second to realize what it was doing.

The cat's face was buried deep in the belly of something. Tufts of fur were scattered in a tight area around the poor dead thing. A rabbit, a big one. The cat's head bobbed meditatively up and down in the middle of it, purple and black strings of intestine draped on the deck. It raised its head, its white and grey muzzle slick and shiny. It sat back on its haunches and licked its lips. Its tail flicked back and forth. A bit of something hung from its jaw.

Flesh.

She gagged.

It took Paula half an hour to get over her revulsion and go outside. The cat was gone, but the body of the poor wretched creature was still there. She felt a helpless urge to

Help!

call someone—Sanderson—to do it for her. That was out of the question. But she couldn't let Rowan wake up and see that . . . horror . . . on the porch.

Paula got a garbage bag from under the sink, then went out the side door and through the gate into the backyard to get the garden spade. When she was done, she hosed off the spade and the deck as best she could. The cleanup took less than twenty minutes, including hauling the sad thing in the bag to the garbage can. She shoved the lid down hard. She didn't want anything getting in there.

As she stepped over the wet spot on the deck to shoo Tex inside, she had an odd feeling of . . . not strength exactly, but . . . *substance*. It felt good.

And gross. The whole thing had been entirely gross.

NINE

THE NEXT MORNING WHEN Rowan got up, she heard her mother humming. She knew what the humming was about. She wasn't dumb. Her mom had a crush.

She was watching the crap TV, flipping between two shows. One was an old episode of *Bewitched* in which Samantha's cousin Serena turned Darrin into a dog, and the other was the talk show with Joanna Shaw. This episode was about a mother whose daughter had been murdered. The mother figured the son-in-law had done it for sure. Whenever the son-in-law talked, the screen would fill with crime-scene pictures; they had black bars over some of the worst parts, like where her throat had been cut, but you could still see the blood and tell that it was a woman, because of her hands being up around her face. To protect it, Rowan bet. It was really gross. She flipped back to *Bewitched* whenever the crime-scene pictures came up.

Beside her Old Tex slept fitfully, jerking sometimes and growling a little. Rowan put her hand on his head and stroked lightly during the boring parts. The crucifix was still in her pocket, the paper with the phone number wrapped around the base. She touched it absently.

When the show went to commercial, it was almost always to advertise that the *Joanna Shaw Show* was going national on Monday. WHETHER YOU'RE US OR THEM—YOU WATCH JOANNA SHAW! MURDER, MAYHEM, MADNESS—AND THE WEEKLY SERIAL-KILLER UPDATE! STAY ON TOP OF THE BREAKING NEWS MONDAYS—

The cat had been on the windowsill in the night. Rowan had been wakened from a hard sleep by the *tap tap tap* of its paw on the glass. Every time it tapped, the pane rattled a little in its frame. She sat up and looked at the cat, then tried to shoo it away. It sat there and stared at her without moving for a long time, then jumped down.

Rowan wondered a little if she'd dreamed it, especially since she'd already had one bad dream. She was in the school cafeteria, facing a long table with piles and piles of food on it. There were other people there but she couldn't see them. The food was exotic, including whole (gross) pigs, roasted, the way they always show them in cartoons, with their heads and feet still on. They were small, and their skin was blackened and mottled. It was (gross) scary.

Then she noticed that the one in the middle was still alive. Its mouth was opening and closing as if it was trying to eat the pig next to it. She tried to scream to tell someone it wasn't dead and a woman said, *We need them to be alive. And young.* And then she realized it wasn't the school caf but her grandmother's dining room.

Bad, bad dream. Then the cat.

Today she was supposed to go with her mom to see her grandmother. At least it was something to do. Outside of this house.

Paula had slept in. The room seemed oddly dark, then she realized the curtains were closed. Rowan must have closed them. She got out of bed and, first thing, pulled back the curtains to let the light in.

Nice day. She put on the T-shirt from the day before. The green jacket was draped over the chair. She was thinking she might wear it Friday when she went to Marla's.

Bits of the Bon Jovi song were running through her head, and she was humming it when she went into the kitchen. She could hear the television: a woman's voice with an irritating, preachy edge was declaring something, emphasizing every third word or so. Paula could hear only, " . . . *believed . . . killer . . . definitely . . . knives . . .*"

She frowned

what the hell is she watching

then decided to make coffee before she dealt with her daughter. The bottom half of the patio door was smeared where Old Tex had pressed his nose against it in his attempt to get out. Across the outside bottom of the window was a trace of dried . . . something. And the deck was still damp where the sun had yet to hit.

Paula's stomach turned. She thought, *I have to go see my mother today.*

Rowan yelled, "Doorbell!" and Paula was yanked back to normal. She went to answer it.

Paula couldn't immediately place the woman at the door. She was attractive, about her mother's age, and she held a bag.

"Good morning," the woman said. "Sorry to just pop in on you like this. You're Paula?"

Paula nodded.

"I'm Anne Keyes," she said. "Lonnie and Sanderson's mother. Do you remember me at all?"

"Yes, of course," Paula said. "It's been a long time."

"I dropped by Sandy's new place this morning and he mentioned he'd seen you. I haven't seen your mother—the whole crowd, really . . . Izzy, Chick, Aggie . . . well, in years." She trailed off.

"My mother's not well," Paula offered.

"Sandy told me. I hope she's feeling better soon. Do you know what's wrong with her?" Then she added, "You know, I've just heard that Chick Henderson died in a fire. Terrible."

"Yes, just awful." Paula smiled politely and avoided answering the question about her mother. She looked beyond Anne Keyes to the street outside. "Wow, what a great day."

There was just a light wind, the sort of breeze that defines early summer: fragrant and blameless. For a moment Paula was carried away by the simplicity of it. Then she said, "It was so good to see Sandy again. I haven't kept in touch with anyone from Haven Woods—"

Mrs. Keyes all but cut her off. "You haven't? You don't live here anymore?"

Paula shook her head. "Not since I was sixteen. I came back to see my mother."

"Oh well, I'm not here anymore either, so I don't hear much of the gossip. We left Haven Woods as soon as the boys graduated high school." She smiled for the first time with what seemed to be genuine warmth. "Sanderson was so determined to move back here . . ." She shook her head.

Then Mrs. Keyes opened her bag and pulled out a dark green glass pop bottle, the old kind. She laughed. "I brought this over for you. I'm not sure why." She handed it to Paula, who held it up. Inside were leaves and bits of cotton. There was fluid in the bottom that caught the sun.

"A witch bottle?" Paula asked, amused. "Sandy had one on his porch."

"Yes, I'd made this one for him," Mrs. Keyes said. "We used to make them . . . some of the women in the neighbourhood. But I gave him the God's eye instead. You can hang it up, if you like, with the chimes." She looked up at the wind chimes moving lightly in the breeze. "Although traditionally it should be hidden. Do you know the legend?"

Paula shook her head.

Mrs. Keyes took a breath, as if slightly embarrassed. "They're supposed to attract evil spirits and spells. You put a little salt water in the bottom, some earth for grounding, pins or needles, and cotton for purity." She laughed. Paula smiled and raised her eyebrows.

"It was a thing we did, you know." She shrugged. "But anyway, the spell or the evil spirit would be attracted to the bottle—drawn into it—and then be impaled on the needles and drowned and clarified by the salt water. The cotton is supposed to keep it clean or something."

Paula met her eyes with a wry gaze, then looked inside the bottle. She could see a needle sticking up through the clump of earth in the bottom. She swished it, and the liquid it contained shifted the dirt. The cotton was dirty and wet. It was an odd gift. Unsettling.

"Thank you," she said.

"You could just put it behind the post here," Mrs. Keyes said, taking the bottle from Paula and placing it there. She straightened up. "I won't keep you any longer, Paula. It was nice to see you again. I haven't seen you since one of the Rileys' parties, I imagine." She pushed her purse further up on her shoulder, readying herself to leave.

The woman glanced around the porch and at the house. Paula realized she could see some of Sanderson in his mother—she really was quite attractive. Mrs. Keyes reached up and flicked the bottom of the wind chimes. The glass rods tinkled musically. Then she went down the stairs and Paula followed, to walk her to her car, the chimes singing behind them.

Her gold Buick was parked on the street. There was rust around the front wheel wells and a small but noticeable dent in the rear passenger door, the sort that you get hitting something in a parking lot.

"How long are you staying in Haven Woods?" Mrs. Keyes asked. She searched her purse for her car keys.

"I'm not sure," Paula said.

"It's hard to raise a child out here, so far from . . . everything." She found the keys and unlocked the door. She started the car, and Paula was about to head back up the walk when she heard the window roll down. "You know the church closed?" Mrs. Keyes said.

"I hadn't heard," Paula said. "We're not religious."

"Don't rule anything out." Mrs. Keyes smiled at her again, but the worried expression never left her eyes. She rolled her window back up, then waved and drove away down the empty street.

Paula waved back as the car turned the corner. Odd woman.

She noticed as she headed back up the walk that the teal blue porch had been repainted recently. It was fresh and unmarred by scuffs and gouges. Her mother's car was in the driveway: a newish sedan, very nice, expensive. Her mother hardly ever drove, but she had a new car. Mrs. Keyes didn't look to be doing so well. Paula vaguely remembered hearing that her husband had died; maybe he hadn't been as good a provider as Dad had been. She couldn't help but wonder how she and Rowan might be doing if she'd stayed put in Haven Woods. A pretty dream. Paula went inside, glancing at the bottle tucked behind the post. She called Rowan as she slipped into her coat and readied herself for another cryptic visit to her mother. She hoped the nurses had changed shifts.

Izzy ignored the ringing phone for as long as she could, hoping that whoever it was would just give up. Marla or Bridget, maybe Ursula. They were the few she hadn't heard from.

Glory . . . Audra . . . Bella

And worse, Aggie. She could hardly bear to think of her, so she put the thought out of her mind. She'd been fine at Chick's funeral. Then, last night, she had dropped over. Izzy hardly recognized her.

Aggie had been a friend of Izzy's grandmother. When Izzy had moved to Haven Woods, her grandmother had told her to get in touch with Aggie, who'd become a mentor of sorts. She looked to be in her seventies now, maybe mid-sixties. She'd taken care of herself, stayed young. But last night she'd been hunched over, slow, barely able to speak above a whisper. "It's happening to me," was all she had said.

Izzy had moved far beyond Aggie's tutorship, but her decline stung nonetheless. It was all exploding. As though Chick had lit the match to a pack of dynamite.

But it hadn't been a match, it had been a Zippo lighter. The fire department had found it embedded in the drywall across from the bed.

The phone kept ringing and still Izzy stood at the long table in her special room in the basement, listening. In front of her was a wide leather apron, well-worn and stained. It seemed that no matter how clean you thought you'd got something, there was always a bit left on it.

While the phone rang on, Izzy picked up a thin knife and began to drag it rhythmically back and forth over a strop. It made a good sound with every stroke: *throa-k throa-k throa-k.*

It wasn't Audra calling, of course. Or *Chick.* So it would be one of the others. They were all feeling besieged these days. Tula, Aggie, Esme, Glory, Bridget, Ursula, Marla even. And the new ones—Joanna, and the younger one, rescued from obscurity and a life of drugs or some such sob story.

On the tenth ring her voicemail picked up the call and Izzy half-listened because she was busy . . . *throa-k, throa-k, throa-k . . .*

"I know you're there, Izzy," Tula's voice scratched over the phone. "Pick up. Esme's having issues."

Tula lived next door to her daughter Esme. Esme was always having issues. She was a bad seed, that one, who wasted her efforts on foolish pursuits and had made no move to create a proper life for herself. Izzy would not answer.

"I can't take this anymore. Tell me what to do," Tula said. Izzy looked at the clock. It was after ten. Why wasn't she at the hospital?

There was another pause as Tula waited for Izzy to pick up.

(*throa-k*)

Then, with some trepidation, she whispered, "I know you're there. Izzy, there's a boy on Esme's lawn crying blue murder. One of her pickups. The whole neighbourhood can hear. This can't be good. What if his mother shows up?"

Izzy slapped the knife down on the leather apron and picked up the phone. "For crying out loud, Tula."

Tula sucked in her breath. "I think he was there all night. His mother's going to come looking for him soon."

Izzy sighed, exasperated. It was like herding cats. When had everything become so trying, so difficult? Everything had been fine

until stupid stupid Chick

Audra sticking her nose

"There's nothing I can do about this right now. It will all be resolved after the meeting, if everyone will just keep their wits about them," Izzy snapped. "Pull him *inside* or something. Do something yourself. We're not all helpless. Yet."

Tula sniffed uncertainly on the other end. "I thought you would want to know. If his mother comes there'll be hell to pay."

Izzy laughed. What did Tula think they were paying now? Aggie could die of old age before Friday. And as far as she knew, the new girl

the ballerina for crissakes

was finished as a dancer for now.

"Glory lost another finger," Tula said. "She can't eat."

"Glory could stand to lose a few more pounds. Her whole reason for becoming one of us was to be thin. What did she say? *Gloriously thin.*" Izzy closed her eyes against the image. The new generation had it all wrong. They weren't for *family*—that's what was wrong with them. It was supposed to be for the good of the whole; after that was achieved, then you did for yourself. These young ones had it all wrong

(unlike Chick so determined to save the last of hers)

Tula droned on. "Izzy? Are you listening?"

"No. Did you say something useful?"

"I said Bridget gets a terrible screeching sound in her head when she tries to bake. It's loud. And have you seen Aggie?"

Izzy breathed carefully, in through her nose, out through her mouth. The air in her special room was fragrant with the scent of exotic things: bergamot, hawthorn, ginger, lavender.

When the kids had been little, they'd taken them for picnics in the summer. They would spread blankets under the trees. When her blanket was snapped open, scent would fill the air. She'd always stored her linens with lavender. She grew it herself. There had been a time when they all did.

"Oh my god, the boy's started up again. Screeching, 'Esme! Esme!' This has to stop. Someone will call the police. Remember the Symington boy? That's what will happen again."

Izzy frowned and fingered the shaft of her knife. *Nasty.* Nearly made the papers. The neighbours, fortunately, had forgotten ever witnessing anything. Imagine forgetting something like that.

"Why aren't you at the hospital?" On the table four knives were laid out, all but the last one sharp as a razor.

"Because I have to deal with Esme's shit!" Tula screeched, her voice full of panic. When she stopped, Izzy could hear a keening wail in the background. Esme's young suitor.

"I can't help you." Izzy hung up and put the phone down gently on the table beside the knives. She picked up the last one and began again . . . *throa-k throa-k throa-k* . . . a pleasant sound. There was nothing she could do, nothing that she wasn't already doing. He would do what He willed until He stopped.

"I've got business to attend to." She said this to no one. She tried not to think too much about the implements in front of her, the messy business ahead. A woman had to do what a woman had to do. A woman's life was harder than a man's

(and so much more valuable)

and everyone had to make sacrifices. Sometimes literally.

But something her mother used to say—long before any of this—came into her head. *From your lips to God's ears.* But of course, that sentiment was useless to them.

TEN

MARLA WAS APPALLED AT HOW BAD the traffic was in Lakewood. The sister suburb of Haven Woods, it was larger and maybe a touch more cosmopolitan, with a mall and a movie theatre, a couple of restaurants worth going to if you couldn't drag yourself all the way into the city. But the traffic—she didn't know how people could stand it.

Two light sequences passed before she made it through the turn onto Mall Drive. (That was another thing: what Lakewood offered in services it subtracted through lack of originality.) On the seat beside her, Troubles purred; he was sitting up and appeared to be watching their progress through the windshield.

She finally made it into the parking lot of Lakewood Mall, behind a little yellow car that she had tailgated the whole way. It was worse than driving in the city.

The parking lot was in chaos. Stuck behind the yellow car, Marla saw a huge banner strung across the mall facade: LAKEWOOD MALL SPRING BLOWOUT! Four or five cars jostled for position up ahead, pulling out, pulling in, waiting on an empty space. She couldn't go around and she was stuck where she was, so she chilled. It didn't really matter where she parked, or even if she parked, as long as she had a view of the long stretch of road that ran in front of the mall. When the queue in front shifted, she pulled to the left and found a space at the farthest edge of the lot, facing the road. She shut off the car and waited.

Her phone beeped from inside her purse: a text message. She reached over without looking, felt around inside and came up with the phone. The message was from Sharie, the dancer. The new girl. CANT GT MY SHOE ON!! WTZ GNG ON?

Marla didn't respond. She'd had enough. She'd already had calls from Esme and Bridget.

Esme had a boy screaming her name on the lawn. She couldn't make him stop and was scared his mother would show up. Marla had heard the kid in the background: *Essmmee, I love you!* It would have been funny if he hadn't been out on the front lawn. *There's nothing I can do*, she had told Esme.

Bridget had been in tears. She had an order for sixty cupcakes for a wedding shower in the city, but every time she went near the oven, a screech began inside her head. Marla had said the same thing to Bridget: *There's nothing I can do*. Bridget had said, *Talk to your godforsaken mother. Do that.*

Marla wondered half-heartedly if there was anything worth picking up while she was at the mall. The kids always needed things. She would like a pair of sandals to go with a new summer dress she'd bought.

The phone rang. She couldn't turn it off in case it was Izzy, or the school about one of the kids. She looked at the call display— Glory. Marla groaned as the phone continued to ring. Glory was in bad shape.

She had barely said hello when Glory started bawling. Could Marla come over? Please? Please?

Marla felt responsible for Glory . . . somewhat. She'd been her first recruit and she'd been a mistake. Marla's mistake. Glory didn't have the fortitude for this life. "Glory, calm down. I'm out right now. I can't come."

Glory uttered a keening wail like a child denied. Please? *Please?* She couldn't be alone. She was frightened.

With a deep sigh, Marla said, "When I'm done. Okay?"

Glory made her promise.

"I *promise*. Cripes."

She hung up and watched the road. Any minute now. She was excited. Gleeful almost.

On Wednesdays Coach Crawford didn't teach until the afternoon. Most mornings he jogged a circle around Haven Woods before school started, but on his morning off he left his car in the school parking lot, about six big blocks away, and ran over to the mall. Then he ran back. She knew this because she was a runner too, and they'd once had a pleasant conversation about it on the school grounds, both of them in their gear. That was before he ruined her son's life.

Talk to your godforsaken mother. It made her smile just to think about it. *I can't help you* had been a truthful response.

David had been Izzy's favourite, not Marla. She had been a consolation prize at best. Izzy was doing the same thing to Marla's children, favouring her grandson, Tim, over Amy. She'd confronted her mother about it, but Izzy had reacted with surprise that Marla should even think such a thing.

Marla got a pair of small binoculars out of the glovebox and looked down the street in the direction she'd come from, her mind wandering between current troubles and past tragedy, until she saw a small figure about twenty yards from the mall, wearing white shorts and a blue and white striped T-shirt. Haven Woods School colours. The figure jogged closer.

Marla panned along the street from the crosswalk to the light at the far end of the mall, to her right. A black Jeep sat at a red light in the middle lane. She watched the truck as the light turned and the cars moved forward. She followed it with the binoculars until it was about forty feet from the crosswalk.

About ten people were crossing, the lights flashing, everyone heading to the mall. The people moved slowly, women stopping to chat in the middle of the crosswalk, then making their way across together. Marla checked the progress of the runner.

It was indeed Crawford. She tracked him as he swerved gracefully around a mother with a stroller, an older couple, a woman with bags. When he was about four yards from her car, she could see that he was in the zone, zonked with a runner's high, keeping a steady pace.

About twenty feet from the crosswalk he slowed ever so slightly to get around some pedestrians, then picked up his pace towards the crosswalk. She swung her head: the Jeep was moving slowly. The crosswalk was empty. Crawford jogged in place, slapping the button on the post for the crosswalk signal. The lights blinked furiously and the approaching cars slowed, stopped. Except for the black Jeep, which suddenly lurched forward as if the driver had hit the gas instead of the brake and then kept pressing.

Crawford looked up a second too late. As the Jeep ploughed into him, someone screamed. There was pandemonium, and for a moment Marla lost track of the action as a crowd of people swelled away from the path of the truck. Then she caught a glimpse of Crawford, his body curved against the front of Jeep, his face bloodied. Then gone, under the wheels.

The Jeep didn't stop.

People screamed and a boy in a hoodie leapt through the shrubs into the parking lot. The Jeep kept moving. It drove through a pair of women who'd been trapped between a decorative pillar and the road. The pillar went down and the Jeep ploughed over it, bouncing but not stopping. Gore covered the headlights, and a pair of jeans, the tag dangling, from the bumper.

Marla sucked in breath. She dropped the binoculars and fumbled to start the car. The Jeep was headed for the parking lot. Though her windows were closed, Marla could hear crying, screaming. With a hiss, Troubles jumped from the passenger seat into the back.

The engine caught and she backed up fast, narrowly missing a woman running behind her, shrieking. She shot a glance over her shoulder as she gunned out of the lot, and for a split second saw the man inside the Jeep—a young guy, Marla's own age, his face white with panic, his mouth a big O of horror.

The blood drained from her own face, her heart a staccato throb, knuckles white on the steering wheel. She drove past erratically parked cars, trucks, SUVs, abandoned on the road as people jumped out to help the injured. People were lying on the road, on the crosswalk, on the sidewalk. And Crawford: still, his body folded almost in two.

She sped away from the scene, moaning, horrified. It wasn't supposed to happen that way. Only Crawford was supposed to get hit, at the crosswalk. And hurt, not— She hadn't really thought it through, but just him. *Just him.*

Behind her was a cacophony of sirens, so many they threaded in and out of each other like screams. The binoculars rolled off the seat onto the floor when she swerved suddenly to take a side road home. She didn't trust herself

(*what could happen to her?*

what was happening to them!?)

on the busy road.

—

Tula stood unhappily over Audra, who lay supine on the hospital bed. She wrung her hands in indecisive agony.

"Tula, please," Audra croaked. "You're making me nervous. Just show me."

Tula smacked at the little nurse's cap that kept slipping down. Bobby pins stuck out at odd angles and the hair under the cap was dishevelled. Very unprofessional. Of course, she wasn't really a nurse anyway.

Tula bent over to peer into Audra's eyes. She stood up and wrung her hands some more and moaned, "You can't be seen like this. No way, no how."

"Let me see." Audra sat up in the bed, her every move an agony. The pain was in her bones, her joints particularly. They felt tugged on, as if being pulled by an invisible rope. She groaned. "Get the mirror."

"Don't bother me now," Tula snapped. "I'm thinking."

"Paula will be here soon."

"I *know* she's coming," Tula said. She walked to the window and shoved the blinds aside to stare out at the lot. As she turned to come back to the bed, they fell with a flap. "I don't know what to— I should call Izzy."

"Don't call Izzy. Tula, there are sunglasses in my purse." Her words came out thick and wet. The bones in her neck were as sore as the rest, and it hurt her to speak. To hold up her head.

Tula shot her a suspicious look but went to the cupboard and got her purse. She brought it to the bed, dumped it on the blanket. Everything spilled out, including the compact.

Audra reached out a hand. "Mirror."

With a derisive snort, Tula tossed the compact closer to Audra's outstretched hand, then found the sunglasses. "Look fast if you're going to look. I shouldn't even let you see, but I want you to." Audra had never liked Tula.

Audra picked up the compact and flipped it open, raised it painfully to her face. She gasped.

"Isn't that something?"

Her eyes, normally blue, had changed completely. The irises were golden, with tiny flecks of black that only accentuated the elongated black slits that were her pupils. She dropped the compact and squeezed her eyes tight shut.

Tula tsked and grabbed the compact, shovelling it and the rest of Audra's things back into her purse. "You should be better organized. I have this little purse organizer . . . Here, we're going to cover you up. Can't have the family seeing you in such a state. Not yet." She slid the sunglasses over Audra's face and pushed her back on the pillow. "There, that's fine. And don't talk when she's here. We'll tell her your throat is very sore. You sound awful." She closed Audra's purse and put it back in the cupboard, then ran her hand over the bedclothes to smooth them.

"It's only a couple more days and then everything will be fine," Tula said. "Can't let you mess it up, so keep your mouth shut, Judas goat."

Audra did not respond.

When Paula and Rowan arrived, Tula was adjusting Audra's bedding. She looked up when they walked in. "Hullo there," she greeted them.

Paula hardly looked at Tula, her attention on her mother. "Hey, what's with the sunglasses?"

It was Tula who answered. "Her eyes have become a little sensitive to the light, so I'm just keeping her comfortable." She sounded pleased with herself.

Paula was not pleased. "What? Why?" She turned to Rowan. "Honey, why don't you say hi to Grandma and then go wait in the lounge for a minute? I need to talk to her alone."

Rowan rolled her eyes. She looked at her grandmother in the

glasses. "Hi, Grandma," she said.

"Hello," Audra said back, her voice scraping like sandpaper.

"Oh, Mom, your throat—" Paula winced in sympathy.

"Um, I put the new collar on Tex. He likes it." Audra smiled and reached out to her. Rowan took her hand.

"Okay, baby, if you don't mind," Paula nudged.

"Fine, but don't leave me out there forever, *okay*?"

When she was gone, Paula said, "Tula, I need you to call the doctor right now. I will speak to him before I leave today."

Tula's mouth dropped open in indignation. "Sorry, dear, I need to take your mother's vitals. I'll call the doctor later." She pinched her fingers on Audra's wrist and looked at her watch, a large and gaudy fashion item, the sort you pick up for ten dollars in an airport.

"Maybe you could do that after you call the doctor. Could you?" Paula said this as politely and sweetly as she could.

They were both surprised by the ringing of the phone down the hall. No one picked it up. "Shouldn't you get that?"

Tula listened to the phone ring, her nose lifted as if she was sniffing the air like a dog. She shook her head. "I don't think I have to." She started to untangle the tubing from around the base of the blood pressure monitor. The phone rang on.

"What if it's my mother's doctor? I'd like to speak to him," Paula said, as gently as she could manage. She wanted to throttle Tula.

Tula was indecisive for a moment, then dropped her mother's wrist. "*Fine*," she said, and waddled to the door, propping it open with the doorstop. Staring at Paula's mother, she said, "Audra's throat's not right. She shouldn't be speaking. Right?" And then she went to get the phone.

Paula sat on the bed. "I think we're alone now," she joked.

"Yes," Audra rasped, nodding. She coughed rawly.

"You sound awful. You *look* awful. I should get you out of here, take you to Lakewood Hospital even. There's something not right here."

Audra's head turned towards the door and she nodded, croaking out, "City."

"The city? Well . . . that would be difficult. I had a bit of trouble in the city, Mom. I had to leave my job. And Rowan had an issue at school. I'm actually in a bit of a spot." Her cheeks grew red with embarrassment. It was hard to gauge her mother's expression behind the sunglasses. "Then I got Izzy's call about how you weren't well. I have to say that it sort of worked out. But as far as going back to the city, we have nowhere to go."

Audra groaned. "Oh, Paula. Oh dear."

"It's okay. We're here now, and I'll figure it out." When she said it out loud, it felt true. "And I don't want you to worry. First you have to get well."

Audra shook her head fiercely, distressed. "We'll go. Somewhere."

"Mom, I'll look into Lakewood Hospital, but Rowan and I would like to stay at the house—"

Her mother started coughing. Paula reached behind her and propped her up with the pillow. She struggled to continue, shaking her head.

They heard Tula shout, "Not here!" And then a slam. Audra squeezed Paula's hand, harder than Paula would have thought possible, and for a second she wanted to yank away.

"It's okay. Don't talk. I'll tell you what we've been doing. We saw a couple of old friends. Last night we had dinner with Sanderson Keyes. Do you remember him? I went to school with him and his brother. His mother stopped by this morning. She sends her best wishes," Paula said.

Audra managed, "Who else?"

"Of course, Marla heard we were in town. She dropped in.

We're going to her house on Friday—"

Audra squeezed even harder, her lips tight. She pulled Paula close so she could whisper. "Don't. Go. There."

"Mom!"

Audra didn't let go of Paula. Her fingers dug in.

"Promise. Me."

Paula was confused. "Promise what, Mom? It was *Marla*. You know who I mean, don't you? Izzy's daughter. Mom, she's my oldest friend."

Audra shook her head violently, then gasped in pain. She let go of Paula's hand. She wrapped her arms around her chest, awkwardly, as if she couldn't quite control their movement.

Paula rubbed her fingers, staring at her, worried. "Mom, are you all right? You're not well. I'm sorry . . . I'll get Tula—" She got up.

"No," Audra rasped. *"Promise."*

Whatever was wrong with her, Paula thought, was affecting her processing. She wasn't thinking right. And then Tula's footsteps were coming fast down the hall, her great weight in inappropriate shoes, as accurate as a GPS.

"Paula!" her mother said frantically. The sunglasses had slipped low on her nose. Paula gently pushed them back up.

"Okay, Mom, I promise," she said.

Audra relaxed, slumping back on the pillow, just as Tula came into the room.

"There was some kind of accident," she announced. "Bunch of people got hurt and they want to bring some of them here." She tugged her uniform down. "Can't have it, of course. We're completely . . . understaffed." She straightened and adjusted her nurse's cap, pleased with her assessment. "And there's no doctor here," she added, "right now."

She stared closely at Audra, narrowing her eyes. "And how are we doing in here?" She shot a glance at Paula. "Not upsetting the patient, I hope. Her colour doesn't look too good."

She bent over to feel Audra's forehead. "Sweaty. What were you talking about? You're so upset."

"Tula, about that. Did you reach the doctor?"

Tula straightened up and beamed at Paula. "Yes, I did. But he's *unavailable*. I gave him your message and Audra's home number. He'll call you."

"Really. Thank you," Paula said, truly grateful. "When?"

Audra groaned. "Water, Tula. Please."

"Uh, tonight. Or tomorrow. I'm not his secretary," she said. Then, clearly thinking she needed to soften her bluntness, she laughed, a false little chuckle. She stared at Audra.

"*Water.*"

"I'll get it," Paula said.

Tula stopped her. "I will. I'm the nurse." She moved with deliberate slowness to the water pitcher on the side table. She picked up the glass and raised the pitcher, poured. She gently sat on the bed and gave her the glass. "Drink that, Audra."

To Paula, Tula said, "I think you'd better let your mother rest now. You come back tomorrow. Your mother will feel much better."

Paula looked at her mother, then leaned to kiss her cheek. "I'll say goodbye to Rowan for you, and we'll be back tomorrow."

Audra spoke, her voice smoothed a bit by the water : "Paula. Remember? Promise."

"I promise," she said. "Bye, Mom. Get some sleep."

Rowan sat on a plastic chair in the hospital lounge. Except for the ticking of the clock, the floor was quiet. Sometimes she could hear voices coming from her grandmother's room, but not from any other room. She'd peeked in one of the rooms on her way down the hall, opening the door a crack. No one. The bed wasn't even made. All the rooms were empty.

Creepy. Weird.

There was a phone in the lounge, though, and magazines. The magazines were seriously old—Angelina didn't even have kids yet. The phone had a faded note taped to the handset: FOR PATIENT USE ONLY. Ignoring it, she had pulled out the piece of newspaper with Mr. Keyes's number on it and picked up the phone. But she'd put it down again. What would she have said? *Hi, Mr. Keyes. This is Rowan. There's no one in this hospital except my grandma. That's weird, isn't it? Isn't it?*

She settled for reading about Britney's diet. Then a phone had started ringing at the nurses' station, where there were no nurses. No one answered it, of course, until

(another weirdo)

the nurse Tula came down the hall.

Rowan had gone to stand near the lounge doorway so she could hear Tula on the phone. Her voice wasn't exactly quiet, but the call hadn't been very interesting. Just Tula getting upset and telling someone, "Not here! Not here!" and hanging up. Then she had called someone and this time attempted to whisper. Rowan didn't catch it all, just a few things when Tula forgot she was trying to whisper.

She heard: "She's on and on about the doctor."

And: "The kid's with her here."

"I can't stay on the phone. They're alone in there."

When Tula hung up, Rowan scuttled back to the couch and was flipping a magazine when the woman stomped by. She had been talking about them—her and her mom. She wondered about that.

Then her mom came. "Hey, Ro. Sorry I left you so long. Let's go home, honey."

I'll be glad to.

They walked to the elevator. "I don't like it here," Rowan said.

Her mom was distracted and maybe hadn't heard her.

When she heard the elevator doors close, Tula turned to her old friend—her *sister*—and said, "You caused trouble. I know you did."

"She's my daughter. My *granddaughter*."

"Well, I took care of it." Her expression was smug.

Tula stepped to the end of the bed and pulled something out of her pocket. A handkerchief. She brought her hands to chest level and clasped them, the handkerchief between her palms. She looked as though she were about to recite a bit of poetry, or maybe sing a short chorus from a song.

"Tula, don't—"

"I know you made trouble. You have to sleep. Cooperate now." Tula cleared her throat. "I always have trouble remembering this."

"Just give me a pill—" Audra rasped.

Tula stared balefully. "I'm not a *nurse*, Audra." And she began a songlike recitation like nothing you would hear in church or at a theatre. This was suited to darker arenas.

Slowly she raised the handkerchief until it hid her face from Audra's view. The room grew darker still and then—

Nothing. Audra was out.

"Don't let the bedbugs bite." Tula laughed at her own joke.

ELEVEN

MARLA DROVE ALMOST BLINDLY, relying on automatic pilot to get her home, gripping the wheel tightly. Her breath was still coming in gasps, much more than it ever did after a hard run. *What just happened?* It wasn't supposed to happen—not like that.

Not like that.

a broken leg a concussion clavicle shoulder something minor not a—

not what just happened

What just happened?

She couldn't bear to think about it, but the sounds of screaming, the crunch of the Jeep as it hit the guardrail, wouldn't leave her. She wanted very much to call her mother.

(get your godforsaken mother to do something)

Marla was pulling off the highway onto Proctor when she remembered Glory. She'd promised Glory. She was in no state to provide any kind of comfort, to soothe, to coax, to cajole, but she'd promised. She turned west and made her way there.

Glory was waiting on the patio when Marla pulled into the driveway. Her hands were tucked under her arms just as if she were wearing a straitjacket, and her face was puffy from crying. When she saw Marla's car, she jumped and waved her arms in the air, her face twisting with new wails.

"Marla! Marla!" Her hands were loosely wrapped in what looked like Tensor bandages. An end dangled and flapped as she waved.

And she was getting fat again.

"I'm here, Glory. Take it down a notch," Marla said. She squeezed her eyes shut and counted to five, breathing deeply, trying to slow the pounding of her heart. She squared her shoulders and gave her hair a smoothing down. *Ready.* Then she got out of the car.

Glory ran over to paw at her, the bandaged hands clumsy, not so much touching her as . . . *pawing* was the only word for it. She started to sob, then got a grip enough to say, "Oh *gawd*, Marla, I'm so glad you're here. I can't stand to be alone. I had to get the kids off to school, I had to explain what was happening to Mommy—"

"You didn't *tell* them?"

"No! I said I'd bur— bur— burned my hands making cookies. What am I going to do? What?" She held up her bandaged hands in front of Marla. Pink flesh showed between the bandages over the palm of her right hand. The left hand was worse—where the fingers should have been, the bandage was loose.

"Let's go inside," Marla said.

Marla unwrapped Glory's hands, starting with the left. Glory refused to look. "I've seen it," was all she would say. She stared at the ceiling of the kitchen.

Three fingers on the left hand were missing: baby, ring and index. That somehow made it worse, that middle finger sticking up all alone in a permanent obscene gesture, as if from

(Him)

Glory wouldn't look but she couldn't stop talking. "Last night

I was wearing rubber gloves, you know, because I can't let the kids see, and I was putting them in the tub when I could feel—actually *feel*—the baby one coming off. It was like it was *alive*. I had Avis in my hands, was just putting him in the water, and my hand started to feel . . . buzzy. It was vibrating, and then the baby finger— The baby one, it started to wiggle like a worm, Marla, like it was alive. Wiggle, wiggle, wiggle . . . and it wiggled off my hand and into the end of the glove!" She burst into tears again.

Marla grimaced. The flesh where the fingers had been attached was smooth and pinky white, as if they had never existed. As if she'd been born that way.

The kitchen smelled of cooking. The counter was messy, jammed with covered dishes. Every element on the stove held a pot. She could smell soup, spicy baking, fresh bread, roast.

Glory wiped tears off her cheeks with her right hand, which was still mostly covered in bandages. She waved it around the kitchen. "And every time I come back in here, there's more food." She looked helplessly at the counter, the stove. "*I didn't cook it,*" she said. "I just come in and it's *here*. Lasagna, pork roast, mashed potatoes with butter and garlic, cake, cream soups— This morning I got up and there was a *milkshake* on the counter . . . the outside of the glass was frosty . . ." Her face relaxed as she remembered.

"Did you drink it?"

Glory giggled salaciously, then swallowed saliva. "Yeah."

Marla was disgusted. Glory had been her housekeeper for a while. She'd been horribly fat, nothing like now. Then she'd been at least a hundred pounds overweight. One day she'd said to Marla, "Oh, how I would love to be thin like you." That had been a mistake. Glory's priorities were askew.

"Yesterday when I went on the treadmill—you know, to do something about this weight gain—I was walking, walking, and I kind of zoned out a little. When I gave my head a shake to wake it up, there was a plate of eclairs on the table beside the treadmill. *Eclairs.* Chocolate-covered. That's when my thumb fell off. I reached for an eclair and my thumb fell to the floor. Just . . . *plop.*" She looked at Marla with such naked confusion that Marla had to look away.

She took Glory's right hand. "Let's see this one, then."

Glory submitted to Marla's unravelling the bandage.

"You know what else I've eaten?" Glory asked, her voice dipping as if it was a secret. "Last night I ate a macaroni casserole, a kind of stroganoff thing. All by myself. Ben was working late. Somehow I got the kids through that bath with my little finger stuck in the rubber glove." Her voice cracked, but righted itself as she talked about the food. "When I got the kids settled and I came down here, I could smell it. It was still in the oven. I took it out. Burned my hand, look—"

Marla let the bandage drop to the table. On the right palm was a dark pink arc.

"I put the dish on the counter and got a fork and ate the whole thing." Glory licked her lips. "It was so good. I don't make it that good." She laughed uncomfortably. "In fact, I didn't make it at all."

On that hand the middle finger and thumb were missing, the skin as smooth as on the left hand, no sign of anything ever having been there.

"Have you seen Sharie?" Glory asked suddenly. "With her it's her feet . . . or at least her foot. It's not working. She came along after I did, and it's her foot. I was thinking that maybe because we're new, maybe that's why we're getting hit so hard. So *hard,*" she emphasized.

"Sharie's a dancer. I think it's because she's a dancer," Marla said. "Don't you? Doesn't it make more sense?" Sharie's great priority in life was to dance. She didn't have children yet.

What the hell had they been thinking? It was all wrong.

Esme had brought Sharie in. Esme, who had pretended not to care when her baby was born dead. "It's about sacrifice, right? It's all smooth sailing from here." She'd said that to Marla as she lay in the hospital bed, blood still flowing from her empty uterus.

Marla helped Glory find a pair of lady's cotton gloves, not yet worn. They stuffed the empty fingers, and for now at least she looked normal.

"Am I going to die?" Glory suddenly asked.

"I doubt it."

Glory grinned oddly. "But if they keep falling off I won't be able to eat."

Marla left her in the kitchen.

Paula was still distracted when they climbed into the car in the hospital parking lot. After she'd missed for the second time what Rowan was saying, she apologized. She didn't get any better, though, and so the daughter left the mother to her thoughts. The drive was quiet.

Paula couldn't understand what exactly she had promised her mother, what her mother was so upset about. She wasn't thinking straight. Could it be early Alzheimer's, something in her brain? A tumour? It didn't bear thinking about.

Marla was her oldest friend, and the idea that her mother didn't want her to see Marla was . . . wrong. It was a wrong idea. So something had to be wrong with her mother's brain.

For so many years Marla had been Paula's best friend. Two little girls, playing in Paula's room, Marla's room, after school, on weekends. Paula had known her practically all her life. They fitted together, the two girls. Marla had been chubby and Paula had been quiet, awkward and shy. By junior high they had begun to grow out of their old ways, and though Marla didn't suddenly get small

(unlike now)

she was smart and funny and commanding. Paula had stayed quiet but had grown pretty. Paula had spent so much time with Marla that Izzy would introduce her as "our adopted daughter, Paula."

hey Paula don't you have another home?

Then it had become the three of them: Marla, Paula and David. They had been thrown together so often. David, two years older than Marla and Paula, had been a reluctant playmate when they were little. Then he became like a brother and teased her as much as he did his sister. Then later, when they were teenagers, he became something else.

The sun was pouring into the car, streams of midday light, the sort of light she remembered from childhood. When it had been easy. *Why did I come back here?* She could remember crying with her mother the night she told her she was pregnant, could remember the two of them crying

don't tell your father

But no matter what her mother said or how it looked at the time, she had loved David Riley. And he'd loved her too.

David was a guy everybody loved. He was nice to people, even people shunned in the adolescent pecking order. David would stop the outcasts in the hall at school and ask, "What's up?" High-five them. "Hey, you coming to the game Saturday?" Nobody bugged him about it.

He was good-looking in an unflashy way, and talented. He played baseball, basketball and football, not just on the school teams but in the community leagues as well. On weekends you would find him on the b-ball court in front of the school, the ball field at Haven Woods Park, throwing the football to his dad or his friends in the Rileys' backyard.

It had only been a matter of time for her and David. She

remembered when it started. The three of them, Paula, Marla and David, had been at the park just after the less predictable days of spring had passed and the warm weather had become reliable. The ground was starting to dry out and they'd gone to look at the river. It moved so fast in the spring, turning into something fierce and exciting, while the rest of the year it was just a nothing strip of slow-moving creek. Since just about every year somebody died in the water, they weren't supposed to set foot in the park until the river had dropped, so there was an element of fear to their being there.

They were tossing stones, trying to hit the rock that jutted out of the water near the far bank. David's frequent hits echoed, while the girls' rocks generally fell short. Marla got bored and wandered farther along the bank, away from them. Then it was just David and Paula.

Paula still had a handful of pebbles, but she'd stopped throwing them; the water was moving so fast she could hardly hear the *plop* when one missed the big rock. She'd begun instead to drop them at her feet and press them into the soft earth with the toe of her running shoe.

It had gotten so quiet on the bank, just the sound of the water rushing. She could feel him looking at her, the way she sometimes looked at him—sideways, fascinated, from under lashes, under bangs. She felt suddenly very aware of herself, of her movements, how warm the little stones were in her palm. She couldn't seem to move; she was stuck there, the ground at her feet littered with pebbles.

"Pauls?"

"Uh-huh?" She hadn't been able to raise her eyes to his face, pretending hard that nothing was going on. She kept her chin tucked in, staring into the mud, at the beiges and browns and pinks of the pebbles against the rich black earth.

"Pauls," he said again.

Eventually she had to raise her face to him. "What?"

"Um, I don't know," he said. "Do you want to—"

She didn't even nod, in fact hardly reacted at all, but he leaned in and kissed her on the mouth. They stood there, the cool, wet smell of earth around them, his mouth on her mouth, for a long time. His lips were so warm, so soft, tasting like the air warming up, tasting like light diffused through cluttered trees.

That was when it had started. She and David.

Paula turned the poky little car onto her mother's street and wondered if that was why she had come back, if she'd hoped to find just a bit of that *good* here. Of course, David was dead. It would be like wishing for a ghost.

She didn't turn into her mother's driveway but instead drove slowly past. She and Rowan turned their heads and looked at the house as they went by. A cat was sitting on the porch. What she wanted was to touch a piece of that history, to revisit it as best she could, even if only remotely. She wanted to see Marla.

"Hey," Rowan said quietly.

"I don't feel like going home just yet. Do you mind if we go see my friend?"

"Which friend?"

"Marla," Paula said.

Rowan shrugged. "I guess."

Paula reached out and squeezed the girl's knee. She was so skinny under her jeans. "We don't have to stay long."

Rowan gave her the side-eye and sighed.

Paula followed the road when it curved, nearly to the end.

Marla sat at the table in her tidy kitchen, her head down on folded arms. Her cell was off, but there had been six messages on her home phone's voicemail when she'd walked in. She didn't bother to look at the numbers; she knew who they would be and she couldn't face another crisis. She had her own to figure out.

She would have liked to go for a run, burn off the feelings, but she couldn't move. She couldn't even think of running, not with that image in her head: Crawford's body in his jogging clothes wrapped around the front of the Jeep, the Jeep not stopping, not even pausing. The most awful feeling, uncomfortable and clinging, was taking root in her thoughts. It was . . . unusual.

Marla was a pragmatic woman—every mother is. There were things that had to be done when you cared for others, and you just did them. It was not pleasant to pull a sliver or a piece of glass from a screaming child's foot, but you did what you had to do. It wasn't nice to say no, to spank, to deny your husband sex if he was misbehaving. But a woman runs her world her own way, and to the benefit of everyone.

She'd made lots of hard choices for her family over the years, but no one had ever been really hurt. Not really. Not until now. Marla's face crumpled. *All those people.*

It had been rash choice, a bad choice, but made for the right reasons. A mother wants to protect her child from pain, from suffering. Marla hadn't meant for anything like this to happen. She hadn't meant it.

Tim had been born with a hole in his heart. A tiny little opening, invisible to Marla even when the doctor had shown her pictures of it. It had seemed the most inconsequential thing—so small. "He'll always need extra care," the doctors had said.

They took him home from the hospital, she and Doug, and just . . . looked after him. She panicked often, watching him run, watching him fall. *Is something going to happen now? Now? Now?* She would watch him for signs of strain, for flushing, sweating, clammy flesh.

There came a day when the two of them were in the park, Marla heavy with Amy, and she was sitting on the park bench looking at her fat

(no, not fat yet, but getting there—still chubby then, but you could see the jowls of the fat kid, the fat teenager, the fat man, right there in his face)

looking at her chubby son playing by himself in the sandbox while four other boys ran around the big field with a soccer ball. It broke her heart that she was embarrassed to be his mother

(but she was when his shirt crept up over his belly, exposing soft white flesh)

So she took matters into her own hands and changed him. Wasn't that the whole point? Wasn't that why the women—her mother, Audra, Aggie, Tula, Bella—wasn't that why they had become what they had become: to make the lives of their families, their children, better?

She'd made his heart beat strong and steady, made his body firm and ready. Made him good at sports. Like her brother David had been—golden. That was the way Marla had always imagined her son would be: a re-creation of the brother she'd lost. Izzy had said as much in the hospital as the two of them, in a rare genuine mother-daughter moment, cooed over the newborn Tim. "Just like Uncle David," Izzy had said.

When her daughter, Amy, needed glasses and was as chubby as Tim had been, Marla was less reluctant. She fixed her daughter too. Now her son was good at sports, her husband was a good provider and her daughter was a living doll.

Paula, now a stranger to Haven Woods, had no idea what Marla was capable of doing, what any of them could do. She wouldn't understand. Paula had been gone too long.

Sent away by her own mother

(and don't we all know why)

Of course, Marla understood now. But thirteen years ago she hadn't understood why Izzy had allowed Audra to send Paula away. Izzy hadn't sent Marla away, likely hadn't even considered it. Izzy had dragged Marla into the life kicking and screaming.

Marla realized that she was terribly conflicted over Paula's coming back to Haven Woods. She wanted her back. She hadn't had a good friend—a real friend—since she'd left. Esme had sort of filled that gap in her life, but Esme had changed. The life had changed her. She was so into it.

Marla had felt genuine delight at seeing Paula again, but now she felt completely torn between wanting the old days back, when she and Paula were best friends, and needing what Paula could do for the women of Haven Woods. She also realized, darkly, that she was envious of Paula's clean hands and her life far, far away from Izzy and Haven Woods.

The phone rang. Marla raised her head and stared in its direction. She didn't want to talk. There was a whole list in her head of people she didn't want to speak to, but to distract herself, to *keep busy,* she walked over to check the call display. It was Izzy. She snatched it up in mid-ring.

"Mom?" she said, her voice cracking.

"I need you to do something, Marla," Izzy said.

"Mom? Something awful happened. I don't know what to do about it."

"Something awful's happening every minute of the day right now, dear. I need you to do something important. Where's Doug? Is he available?"

"He's at work. Mom, there was an accident—"

"Is Tim all right? What's happened?"

Marla stiffened. Typical that Izzy would leap to thoughts of her grandson, not her granddaughter.

"The children are fine," she said pointedly. "But . . . Tim's baseball coach—he was killed today. He was run over. But more than just him . . . there was a crowd. It was a mistake. I meant only for—"

"What did you have to do with it? Marla, hurry up and finish your story. I need you to do something."

"I only wanted Tim's coach to be hurt, not killed. I didn't mean for anyone else to be hurt at all. But something went wrong, and—"

"Oh, Marla, this is not the time to be doing anything like that." Izzy—unflappable Izzy—groaned. "But there's nothing you can do about it now. Tell me about it later. Right now I need you to get Doug to make a call, do you hear me? Doug has to call Paula."

As Izzy was talking, Marla heard a car pulling into her driveway. She carried the cordless to the window and peered out.

"Mother," she interrupted. "Paula's just pulling into the driveway."

"That's good. When she leaves, you deal with Doug, all right?" And she went over it all one more time. Marla listened, nodding but not speaking, taking instructions from her mother.

Status quo.

They settled down in the kitchen and Marla made tea. From a container in the fridge she got out some yellow cake and set squares of it on a plate. She put some for Rowan on a pretty tray with a matching mug, just for her, and settled her in the family room.

"You make yourself at home, Rowan," Marla told her. She pointed out the Wii controller and the television remote and promised not to keep her mother too long.

Paula looked around the kitchen, thinking that it felt odd to be in grownup Marla's house. She kept looking for things that reminded her of her old friend, the one she remembered. And then she noticed a photograph on the wall in a corner. She got out of the chair to look at it. There they were, the three of them, Paula, Marla and David, in the Riley backyard, their arms linked. David was in the middle. Marla's long hair was crimped and she wore clunky Doc Martens. Paula had overalls on. They were laughing. In the background was the Riley house with its blue roof.

Not the red roof yet.

Paula figured she was about fifteen in the picture, Marla the same; David would have been seventeen. That same summer. She couldn't remember the picture being taken, but looking at it she could smell cut grass, hot blacktop, the wet scent of roses just blooming.

Then Marla was beside her, close enough that her breath touched Paula's cheek. "It was that last summer," she whispered. "It was developed after he died."

She couldn't peel her eyes from it. "A long time ago," Paula offered.

Marla nodded. "Everything was different after that. Your dad died. You left town. I was stuck here with Izzy."

Paula turned suddenly, with a guilty look.

"Rowan's in the family room," Marla said, her voice soft. "Do you ever think about that day?"

She didn't have to elaborate. There was only one day. Paula nodded, and her eyes filled with tears.

"C'mon," Marla said, with warmth. "Let's sit. Tell me what's going on."

So Paula did. She told her about living in a crummy apartment and Rowan getting suspended from school, losing her job and being broke. She told her about the man shouting at Rachel onstage; she told her about Rowan ordering Chinese with twelve dollars of the emergency money in the jar. She stopped only when her embarrassment finally eclipsed the cathartic feeling of spilling her guts, stopping just short of telling Marla that her own mother didn't seem to want her in town, but that she had nowhere else to go. And of course she stopped before telling her biggest secret—whose daughter Rowan was—though sometimes she suspected that if anyone knew, it would be Marla. She and David had been so close.

Marla put her hand on Paula's arm. Her expression was compassionate.

"Guess I haven't had anyone to really talk to in awhile." Paula stared at the floor.

"I'm glad it was me," Marla said. "I've . . . missed the old days. Things were so simple, weren't they?"

"They were. It's strange to be back. My mother . . ." She trailed off.

"Your mom will get better."

Paula nodded. "I know she's sick, but she's acting so oddly. I don't know what to think. The hospital here is hopeless too. I'm thinking of moving her, to Lakewood maybe. Whatever is wrong with her, I think it's affecting her mind. She doesn't seem to be thinking straight."

Marla answered carefully, "Shouldn't you talk to her doctor?"

"I'm having trouble getting his attention, actually."

"Well, you know doctors. They're so busy. He'll call." She poured a little more tea into their mugs and pushed the cake closer to Paula. "You're home, where you should have stayed. You'll stay now. Have a piece of cake."

Paula took a piece and popped the bite-sized perfect thing in her mouth. It was delicious.

actually

"I don't think I can stay in Haven Woods long," she said. It was lemon cake, delightfully tangy. There was a slight aftertaste that wasn't unpleasant, although she couldn't place it. It made her mouth water. Her head felt light, as though she hadn't eaten all day.

"Drink your tea," Marla said. "It's getting cold."

Marla's hand was on her arm. Paula took a long sip of tea. She blinked. She looked at her friend.

Marla held her gaze. "Sure you can stay," she said in measured tones. "You'll be happy here. You can have everything you want."

Paula shook her head, and then it just came out. "Audra doesn't want me to stay," she said. *Audra?* "My mother," she corrected. The word felt heavy, like a pebble dropping out of her mouth to the floor.

"Mmm," Marla said. "I think she does. Audra does want you to stay. She wants you to stay forever. You and Rowan." Her voice was soothing.

"Yes."

"And on Friday you'll come to my house and meet my friends."

Marla's face was unlined and serene. Paula couldn't stop staring at it.

Marla nudged her mug towards her. "And have another piece of cake. I made it myself."

Paula took another long sip. She picked up a piece of the cake and looked at it.

"We're a very special group. You can be with us. You can have everything you want. Just as we do."

Marla nodded and Paula put the cake in her mouth. There was a sensation of its being almost too lemony, but it was even more delicious the second time.

"Well, you'll stay until Friday at least. After that everything will be wonderful. I promise. You believe me, don't you? And you'll bring Rowan."

Paula nodded and swallowed the cake. "Yes," she repeated.

Marla smiled. "Good."

—

They were in the car driving home.

"Mom? Are you okay?"

Paula turned her head and met her daughter's eyes. For a split second she was entirely lost. Then, quickly, her eyes were back on the road. *Was she?*

"I'm okay," she said. Her throat was dry, as though she hadn't spoken in a long time. Must have been the cake. Although the cake had been delicious, moist.

She followed the road back to her mother's house. When she caught sight of it up ahead, it looked nice. Comforting.

"Did you have some of that cake?" Paula asked.

Rowan shook her head. "I tried it but it tasted funny. I think it was old. Why did we have to stay there so long? You said it was going to be short."

Paula glanced at the clock on the dashboard. It was after three. They had been at Marla's for three hours. It seemed impossible.

Marla was feeling a little bit better. She was about to call Doug at work, thinking, *Might as well get the rest of it done*, when she heard something outside. It was a persistent and irritating *foom-pf foom-pf foom-pf*, the sound both familiar and unfamiliar, like something out of context, just under her radar, leaking up every now and then to drive her mad.

foom-pf

The phone rang. Marla picked it up. A little dried glue was clinging to her hand, and she peeled it away. "Hello?"

"Mrs. Riley-Moore? This is Mrs. Mackie from Haven Woods School."

"Yes?"

foom-pf foom-pf

"We've had some upsetting news. There's been an accident: our gym teacher, Mr. Crawford, has been killed. Is Tim at home with you? He was upset. We're all very upset; it's been a very trying—"

"Home?"

foom-pf

Frowning, Marla walked into the mudroom, the phone still at her ear. The sound was clearer, louder there

FOOM-PF FOOM-PF

and she pushed open the screen door.

Tim was in the driveway, bouncing a basketball off the garage door. *FOOM-PF.* It hit the asphalt and he caught it expertly, bounced it once and tossed it into the hoop over the garage door. It swooshed through the net and hit the garage door and bounced on the asphalt and Tim caught it expertly. She had a sick feeling in her stomach.

"Mrs. Riley-Moore?"

"Yes, he's here," Marla said.

"That's fine, then—" Marla thumbed the phone off, even though the voice on the other end kept going.

Tim was so intent on the basketball he didn't hear the screen door open.

"What are you doing home?"

Her child, her firstborn, her beautiful damaged boy, stopped dead in mid-layup and turned his head towards her, his body unyielding in its perfect form. "Mr. Crawford's dead," he said. He turned back to his work. The ball went up in a perfect arc, hit the backboard and swirled again through the netting.

"Are you upset about that, honey? You know you should be in school."

The boy seemed not to hear her. Every move he made was deliberate and concentrated and perfect.

"I can be on the baseball team now," he said, catching the ball. He turned to look at her. His mouth stretched slowly into a long grin. "Good, right?"

FOOM-PF

The phone, still in her hand, rang again. It was the school calling back. The secretary, irritated, said she hadn't finished. Amy was not feeling well. Could Marla come and get her?

"Of course," she said.

Before she left, Marla took a piece of leftover cake and a bit of earth from her backyard and put them together in a jar. She shook up the jar and then put it in a bottom cupboard. She did this hastily though, because she needed to go get Amy.

Outside, Tim was still bouncing the basketball over and over against the garage. She poured a sports drink into a go-bottle and took it to him. His face was flushed and sweat had gathered along his hairline. He was concentrating. He didn't say a word to her. She made him drink it.

Her boy was not right. Something was not right with him. He had drunk it—that was something. But it was unravelling. Everything.

In the car she focused on Amy and hoped it was a cold or the flu. Hoped that the girl had vomited or something, in the throes of some normal childhood virus. But she didn't think so.

She thought maybe it was her turn.

In the space of a half-hour her mixed feelings about Paula had sorted themselves out. They needed her. Marla's children were now at stake.

And they needed Rowan especially. She allowed herself to think *the girl the girl* who would save them all, and afterwards Paula would come around to their way of thinking. She would have to. They had all made sacrifices.

And Marla had never had a choice. Friday couldn't come fast enough.

TWELVE

A LONG DRIVE LAY AHEAD OF IZZY, and at the end of it, a horrible task. On the floor of the passenger side of the car was her leather apron, rolled and tied tightly. On the tight curves of the highway, if she listened carefully, she would hear the clinking of the heavy business inside. She did not listen. In her life, it didn't pay.

Of all the women in Haven Woods, Izzy alone would have understood Paula's life in the city. The slum where Paula and her daughter lived was a world away from Haven Woods, but it was not very far from where Izzy had started out. Her neighbourhood had been Borwin Street. An ugly name.

Borwin Street was no place to be raising two kids. The streetlights were burned out routinely. Most of their block was populated with people like them, poor people just trying to do their best, raise their kids without killing them. All night long you could hear wandering drunks, shouted obscenities, howling fights, police sirens.

That was after Roger's car wreck. He'd lost his job—however lame it had been in the first place, it had kept them housed and fed—and then they couldn't pay the rent on their decent apartment. They'd had to move to the bad neighbourhood. Roger healed slowly. Isadora—she'd been Isadora then, not Izzy—had worked for a time at a restaurant a few blocks from their place, then lost that job after the boss made a pass at her and she turned him down. She cried. For minimum wage.

For a while she had another waitressing job, but it was two bus rides and a good long walk from home. She was spending all her time on buses, leaving before the kids were up, getting home just before they went to bed, exhausted and smelling like beer and french fries. Roger couldn't manage two preschoolers, either.

Missing everything. The children growing up.

Marla was whatever she was: an unhappy child, alternately quiet or overbold, a couple of years younger than David. But David! He was her pride. Tall even at five, talented, handsome. The kind of child who would succeed. He'd been—they'd both been—her reason for listening to the old woman.

Even when Izzy was little, her grandmother had been crazy, at least according to her mother. Someone to stay away from. She'd occupied the back bedroom in whatever house her parents were living in. Izzy's mother had brought her from Haven Woods to live with them after the old woman went mad. At least that was how her mother explained it. There had been an incident—a feud with a neighbour, dead animals on his doorstep, some kind of final blow-up—that ended with Izzy's mom physically removing her grand-mother from her own house and sticking her in a mental hospital. When she was released, they brought her home to their place and locked her in the back bedroom, watching her all the time.

Grandma's crazy don't talk to her don't go in there stay away

Izzy had a vague memory of her mother and father moving her grandmother's things into the tiny room, and a more vivid memory of them in the backyard, burning what was left from her house in a big oil drum, the smoke black, the flames brilliant colours.

Of course Izzy knew all about it now. She knew who the old woman had been, knew what she'd been.

Izzy's parents had been poor their whole life. Sometimes during those very bad days, Izzy would look at her parents and feel horrified that she was looking at her own future—Roger unemployed, her working a shit job, the two kids growing up with no opportunities.

When Izzy was very little, her grandmother would eat with the family, but her mother was ever watchful, watching the old woman for . . . something, and chastising her when she saw it. But Izzy had been a smart child, and she picked up on the things that were said. When they came to visit, her aunts would talk. Izzy was supposed to be sleeping, would feign sleep, on the sofa while the woman chattered like crows in the kitchen. She heard things.

Secrets. Pieces of impossible secrets. For most of her life, until things got so very, very terrible, she hadn't believed them. The talk of women raised in a different world, who saw spirits and omens in tea leaves. Who used nearly unintelligible words—*damon*, *hexe*, *ubel*. They didn't live in the real world, where evil was a glassy-eyed girl with a knife in her pocket looking for money, where evil was a fat man on the corner getting the girl stoned in return for nasty work.

Ubel indeed.

Then came the Chapman murders.

It had been summer, one of those hot, hot, sticky days that make things like murder and violence seem possible, the kind of heat that tastes like copper, like blood. It was big news and it got around fast; even in those days before Twitter and Facebook, everyone seemed to know.

Izzy first heard about it on her break. One of the women showing up for a later shift told everyone. "A man went crazy and killed his family," she said, clearly excited to be breaking the news. "Just outside the city. In Haven Woods."

Where her grandmother had lived. Izzy had been there before her grandmother went nuts and had to be pulled out of her house screaming, with the neighbours watching, the old man next door yelling, *"Jedza, Jedza!"* She wondered where exactly in Haven Woods it had happened.

For days it was all over the radio and the papers. It wasn't just the murder—in their neighbourhood people were killed fairly regularly—it was a *bad* murder. A man named Martin Chapman, thirty-seven years old, had gone crazy. He stabbed his wife twenty-three times and drowned his eight-year-old son in the bathtub; then he shot himself in the head. Those were the official details. But rumours spread, and in time they became accepted as fact.

He'd killed the boy first, people said, and laid his dead, wet, naked body on the dining room table. He'd placed the dead boy's head on a pillow, his arms spread, his legs open. And then he had plunged a large kitchen knife into his chest.

When his wife came home, he killed her in the dining room. Then he cut her throat and hung her body from a ceiling beam, over the boy. In her blood he wrote on the wall

HE LIVES HERE

No details were given about who "He" was, but people guessed. In the days following the murder, neighbours, friends of the family, families of the children the boy went to school with were interviewed. Or they wrote letters to the editor. Or they just talked and talked and talked.

The day before the killings, Chapman had told people there was something in his house. That the house wasn't just a house but a place where lines intersected. The Chapmans had lived there less than a year. It had been a steal of a deal, it was said, having been empty for a very long time.

It was an awful murder.

When Izzy got off work the day she heard about the murders, Sears came and took away her washing machine. The repo guy had had his own details to add.

"Yeah, he stabbed his old lady fifty times or something and drowned the kid, shot himself in the face. You know what I heard? I heard she was banging some guy in the bedroom and he drowned the kid to mess her up," the Sears guy had told her as he dolly-wheeled her washing machine into the front yard where the neighbours could see.

"Sorry about hauling your washer away like this. It's the shits being hard up."

"It's all right."

A month later, two streets over from where Izzy and Roger and their children lived, a woman was strangled to death by her drug-addicted son and left to be eaten by her two Rottweilers. That was awful too. It made page six.

Izzy's exit came up and she pulled onto a road bordered on both sides by chain-link fence. Behind the chain-link was a maze of filthy, blackened concrete, an abandoned warehouse that had been stripped of every usable piece of material until all that was left was the pillars and the fence. Every ten feet or so a metal sign was bolted to the fence. KEEP OUT. OVERHEAD DANGER. PRIVATE PROPERTY. TRESPASSERS WILL BE REMOVED.

If you watched for awhile you could see people slinking around in there. Mostly they hid.

She drove past it, past another warehouse, then another. The deeper she got into the city, the bolder the people became, standing out on the street drinking from paper bags, smoking little pipes, vomiting on the sidewalk. As she drove slowly by, a man repeatedly smacked a sad, hunched woman, who stumbled with each blow but never fell. Everyone looked up as her car went by, but few stared. Nobody cared. Not anymore.

She watched the streets carefully for what she was looking for. When she spotted what she needed, she pulled in and parked at the end of an alley behind a set of large blue Dumpsters. Her car was not invisible, but it was not particularly noticeable either. It would not be stolen, that was certain. It would likely be taken for the car of someone best not messed with

(how true—they had no idea)

like a drug dealer, a gang leader. Still, there was always the possibility of graffiti, baseball bats, rocks, *anger*. It was best to hide the car, so she did.

She worried less about herself.

Mountains of dark green garbage bags were piled around the Dumpsters. She picked her way around them and over the other detritus of the alley—the rats, the shit, the used condoms, the dropped needles—to the street. Partway down the block the vomiting man had collapsed to the pavement, his head hunched down between his legs. He seemed to be asleep. It looked like sleep.

She slipped out of the alley, walking with determination and authority. It was the only way to walk in a neighbourhood like this.

The old woman, her grandmother, had been excited by the murders too. She sat at the kitchen table in her daughter's house, clipping articles. The pile of them grew. Usually she rarely went out, and then only in the company of her daughter, but every morning in the days after the murders, she asked permission to go out and buy all the papers. As long as she asked calmly, her daughter said it was okay.

She concentrated.

Izzy's mother would babysit Marla and David when Roger had a doctor's appointment or physiotherapy and Izzy had to work. She'd haul herself into her parents' house, exhausted after her shift, and the kids would be lying on their bellies on the bare floor watching television. The old woman would be at the table or in her room with the door open.

Izzy's mother's vigilance had grown laxer, and sometimes the old woman would talk to Isadora or make the *spitz* at her—put her fat fingers in her mouth, get them wet with saliva and flick it in Izzy's direction.

protect you from getting vain

Sometimes she'd whisper a comment about the other women in their family—the aunts, Izzy's mother.

a stupid woman gets what she asks for

She would eye Izzy up and down.

a smart woman—a smart woman gets more

She thought Izzy was a smart woman. And she wasn't wrong.

A half-block up the sidewalk, in the dull light of a broken street-lamp, the filthy man was still bent over, retching. Izzy crossed the street, her shoes hardly making a sound on the asphalt, and stepped around a puddle of something vile, perhaps from the puking fellow, the smell of it lost in a plethora of odours from the neighbourhood.

Across the road was a short brownstone with wide concrete steps. There another man sat, his shoulders hunched, hair thin and dirty, eyes sunken with need. He gaped at her with an ingratiating half-smile. Beside him was a dog that looked about the same.

She stopped in front of the steps. The man looked her over.

"Nice dog," she said.

It was so easy. Which was why she'd chosen this neighbour-hood. She knew the neighbourhood. If she got up on the step and stood behind that disgusting, egg-sucking little wreck of a man and raised herself on her tippy-toes, she would be able to see the kids' first school.

She led the dog away on a brand-new leash, purchased yester-day for just this purpose.

The man who had been vomiting now stood at the entrance to the alley where Izzy had parked the car, watching her with yellowed eyes. He was wearing a ball cap, the bill filthy from a million fingers, coated in god-knows-what, rubbing the brim when . . . What? When a lady went by? When his brain itched from thinking something up?

There was a week's worth of growth on his face and something clung to his chin, something he'd tossed up probably. He was dis-gusting. Izzy smiled at him.

"Is that your dog?" he said, and grinned. His teeth were yellow too, and he was missing one, a dark hole visible when he talked. "That's not your dog. I know whose dog that is. It ain't your dog. You got money though?"

Still smiling, Izzy leaned closer to the man. The stink of puke wafted off him, but she'd smelled worse in her time. She pointed to a place between his wet, weaselly eyes. "What's that on your head?" she asked softly, deliberately, slowly, so that the words came out as if separated by beats.

The man blinked and stepped back, unused as he was to dis-cussion. "What?"

"Right there. Between your eyes. Here—" She stepped close enough to touch, pressing her index finger hard against the man's waxy flesh.

He blinked twice more and stepped away from her, nearly stumbling. His hands flew up to his face and he swiped at the place she'd touched. "Wha— wha—?"

He knocked his ball cap off. It hit the filthy sidewalk and rolled so that the underside of the bill could be seen. Brown stains that Izzy recognized as blood formed oval smears.

He jumped around, swiping his hands at his face, making little surprised, alarmed noises. "Yi-yi-yi! Oh, git it, *git it*—"

Izzy smiled again. "Good luck with that," she said. And she led the dog on its pretty red leash away from the man, who was now bouncing and jumping around like a lizard on a hotplate.

"Ain't your dog, ain't your dog!" the man shouted after her, banging his head on the bricks of the building, screaming like an unhappy, unwell child.

Izzy closed the trunk lid gently and got into the car with a heaviness in her chest, in her legs, in her heart maybe. She started the car, the sound of it barely discernible, the engine so quiet and perfectly made. It was a miracle, that car. Maybe *miracle* was the wrong word. The wrong god. At every turn on her way out of the city, she could hear the lurch and thud from inside the trunk.

She remembered thinking how odd it was that the Chapman murders had happened in Haven Woods, her grandmother's old stomping grounds. There had been a photo in the newspaper of the place. A two-storey house, white with dark trim. Ordinary, except for the crime that had taken place inside.

The other thing her grandmother used to say to her, along with "Are you a stupid woman?" and "A smart woman gets what she deserves," was "Are you tired of your poor, poor life? You poor, poor woman."

are you a smart or stupid woman?

At first Izzy would simply placate her—"I'm smart, Grandma. I'm smart." But after awhile she began to really listen.

are you tired of your poor, poor life?

She was.

And then one night she got to her parents' place late. There was no one there but the old woman. The kids had gone out for McDonald's with her mom and dad. The old woman had been waiting for her.

are you tired of your life yet?

Izzy pulled off the highway into a restaurant parking lot, making sure to park towards the back of the lot with the trunk facing the open field. She bought a double cheeseburger and a water and took it back to the car. She popped the trunk; it opened on silent hydraulic hinges.

The dog, panting, looked up at her, blinking painfully in the light. He was scrawny and dirty, but he wagged his tail when he saw her and drooled at the scent of the burger.

"I brought you something," Izzy said. The dog rose awkwardly on his skinny legs, cramped and sore from the trip. She screwed the lid off the water bottle, poured some into a cup and held it while he lapped manically. She unwrapped the burger and held it out to him. "Here."

The dog gobbled it as if he was starving. It occurred to Izzy that he probably was. After he had burrowed into the very fabric of the trunk floor in search of every crumb, he went back to the water in the paper cup. His nose was too large to get at the last few drops, so Izzy tilted the cup and held it for him.

Her expression was troubled, serious. "I'm not a bad person . . ."

The dog wagged his tail slavishly.

And she really wasn't cruel. She was dedicated. That was all it was—she wanted to do the right thing for her children. Wasn't that what mothers were supposed to do? Any means necessary. If that was true in war, why not in child rearing?

She wasn't mean. She could get very irritated, and perhaps on occasion that had turned ugly, but everyone was guilty sometimes. The girl at the MAC counter—that might have been a little mean. Well, *c'est la vie*. Izzy was only human. Human-ish.

The dog looked up at her, his watery eyes limpid and subservient, his whole posture pathetic. Wagging his tail carefully, he came closer and licked her hand. She yanked it away. "I'm not really a dog person," she said, and closed the trunk.

She got into the car and drove. About halfway to where she was going, she turned off the AC and rolled down her window. Warm, scented air whirled through the car. This time of year always reminded her of David.

Izzy rested her elbow on the edge of the open window and sped down the highway, trying her best to think of good things. But it was too hard, even for Izzy. All she could smell was dog.

That day she came home late to the house, empty except for the old woman, her grandmother was standing at the door as if waiting for her.

He's back she said cryptically. It sounded like *bek*. Her face was animated, not with pleasure but with excitement. She hooked her finger at Izzy.

Come in here she said. Her gaze bore into Izzy's with such confidence there was almost a transfer between the two of them.

The old woman said, *Do you know that house where the man killed them?*

As the last word dropped, she knew which house the old woman meant. *Yes*, Izzy had said. *I know the house.*

Good. You know this house.

Everyone does, Izzy said.

The old woman grinned at her. She pulled open the top drawer of her bureau, and even though she was barely tall enough to see inside, she reached in and pulled out something wrapped in cloth. *Come here girl, and I'll open you up. And you'll go. A stupid woman settles. You're not a stupid woman.*

And when Izzy came close, she cut her with the knife, underneath her left breast. A small slit that hardly even bled at first.

"This," her grandmother said, "will let him in. And then you'll have everything you've ever wanted."

It wasn't late when Izzy got back to Haven Woods. And it was odd, and funny at the same time, that she was happy to leave the city behind, happy to be back with just one more odious task in front of her, and then home.

Just one more thing. Ritual sacrifice. Necessary—like dishes, tidying, laundry. All odious in their own way.

THIRTEEN

ROWAN HAD FALLEN ASLEEP on the couch. She woke up with a sore tummy. It hurt really low down, sort of like when you have to go to the bathroom, but different. Tighter. It felt hot. She wanted her mom.

Paula was having a nap. She'd been acting tired and weird ever since they got back from her friend's house. She'd made Rowan something to eat and then lain down on the bed. Rowan checked the clock. Her mom had been sleeping ever since and it was almost seven.

Rowan watched TV and tried to eat, but her stomach was aching too much. The PB&J sandwich and glass of milk were still in front of her on the coffee table, half eaten. She needed a Bromo.

When they were living in the crappy house before the crappy apartment, her mom had a job at Walgreens, the overnight shift. It was the scariest of her jobs because she didn't get home until just before Rowan had to get up for school, so Rowan had to spend all night by herself in that creaky house. She got a lot of stomach aches that year. Her mom would bring home Bromo from the drug-store. Whenever she got a stomach ache, her mom would tell her to take half a cup of Bromo and burp it up.

As far as she knew, Bromo was a popular product. She'd seen a bottle of it in the janitor's room at school once. Maybe her grandmother had some. Her mom was still sleeping and Ro didn't want to wake her, so she turned off the television and went snooping.

The bathroom was enormous, not at all like the bathrooms Rowan was used to. The tub was oversized, sloped at one end and had feet, like something out of a magazine. The medicine chest was just as old-fashioned, with a tiny latch midway up the mirrored door.

She wasn't supposed to go into someone else's medicine cabinet, of course. That much she understood. She knew all about taking medicines and how if you took the wrong thing you could end up thinking you could fly and jump off a building or something. Her mom had told her lots of times never to take a pill someone else gave her or to go into someone else's private things. But this was her grandmother's house. Surely the medicine cabinet wasn't off limits . . .

The cramping feeling in her stomach was worse, if anything. Rowan undid the latch and opened the door. There were five shallow shelves, each lined with pretty blue paper. And there were all kinds of pill bottles in different colours: brown, green, blue. It was hard to see what was in them. She took down one of the bigger jars, blue, like the Bromo at home. It was capped with a piece of cork that looked hand-cut. She shook it. Something clunked inside.

She wiggled the cork out and peered inside. The smell hit her first. It wasn't unpleasant; in fact it smelled a little like a holiday or something. Christmas. Ro brought the bottle closer to her nose and breathed in the nutty smell. It was much stronger up close, and for just a moment Rowan sort of . . . swooned.

She closed her eyes and lowered the bottle. Her nose and eyes stung and then her head got light and her limbs went kind of loose, as if she was about to fall asleep. She sat down hard on the toilet, which jolted her into alertness.

But just before she went down, she thought she had heard voices, maybe singing

just me and you

I love you

then they were gone. But the voices had shot through her head like bullets from a gun.

Rowan put the jar back. She twisted more bottles around, looking for labels. A few of them were prescription drugs with long, unintelligible names, some of the labels so old they were faded. Her grandmother had obviously reused the bottles. Others had no labels at all or the labels had been peeled off, sticky grey glue remaining. Most of the bottles were half filled and the contents looked like . . . grass or something.

She turned another little bottle so she could read what it said.

DANG GUI HUA GOA
   1985 take with

The one next to it was so worn she couldn't read the date, but the rest of the label said

GRACIE KIMBOL
   for blood disorder
   100 c to be taken after dark

and the next said

JUDY KEEL
   may cause bleeding
   take with 1988

Bromo looked like salt or sugar. You put it in a glass of water. It fizzed. She wished her mom would wake up.

There was no Bromo in the medicine cabinet. Or anything like it. She crouched down in front of the vanity and opened the door. Typical under-the-sink things, the same stuff they had in their bathroom at home: a package of TP, some toilet-bowl cleaner, a bottle of glass cleaner. There were also some zippered bags, like makeup bags. A couple of them were pretty big and could hold all manner of

(secret treasure)

Bromos and potions and things to make her feel better.

She opened the one closest to her, a pretty bag with circles inside circles of blue and white and lighter blue. Inside was a collection of scissors and files and little tools that she guessed were for manicures. She zippered it and put it back. Behind it was a paper bag with the logo of a drugstore. She reached for that.

Hair. It was a bag of hair.

"Ew," she said, but she was actually intrigued. A smaller plastic bag rested on top of the hair. She gingerly fished it out. It took her a moment to figure out what it was, then she dropped it back in disgust.

Fingernail clippings. Why was her grandma saving them? She rolled the bag up and stuck it back in the vanity, deeper than it had been. Disgusting. Gross.

She touched one of the bigger cosmetic bags—even more curious now—intending to see what could possibly be in that one. But when she picked it up, something moved inside.

Startled, she dropped it, falling backwards. She hit her shoulder on the side of the tub, but hardly noticed. She jumped up and slammed the cupboard shut with her foot. There was nothing like Bromo in there.

In the hallway she heard the dog's nails clicking on the wood floor. He stopped just outside the bathroom door, whining low in his throat. *Grmmmm.*

"It's okay," she said to Old Tex. "I hardly touched it. It's okay. It's okay."

Rowan slammed the medicine chest door shut and stood up. *Old lady stuff,* she told herself. *Weird old lady stuff.*

As she was leaving the bathroom, bending to give Tex a pat, the phone rang in the kitchen. And then her mother was up, running for it.

Paula picked up and listened for a moment without really hearing the voice on the other end. Her head was foggy with unspent sleep, but when the word *doctor* penetrated her haze, she came wide awake.

"You're my mother's doctor? I'm so glad you've called." She could barely keep the annoyance out of her voice. At least he'd called. "Can you tell me what's wrong with her?"

The doctor cleared his throat. "I can tell you that we are doing some . . . tests. Your mother is suffering from . . . exhaustion. And she's stiff in the joints. There's also evidence of some . . . deficiencies."

Paula frowned. "What kind of deficiencies? Like vitamins? Is her joint pain arthritis, something like that? What's wrong with her exactly?"

There was an odd cadence to his speech, and she wondered if he stuttered. It was disconcerting. "I won't know very much until the tests are done. We're doing them . . . soon."

"Right. What kind of tests? Are they painful or difficult? Should I be there?"

"Um," he said. There was a long pause before he spoke again, and Paula felt her anger rising. Then he said, "I think it's best that you let us do the tests before you visit again. Okay?"

Okay? "How long?" she asked.

There was another long pause and she half expected to hear papers shuffling on the other end, as though he were checking schedules, finding dates, times, but there was nothing, just dead air.

"After Friday. You can visit after again on Saturday morning."

That seemed a long time for tests. But whatever had to be done had to be done. It was just a couple of days. "All right," she said. "If it's necessary, I'll wait. Can you tell her that you spoke to me and that I send my love?"

"Sure," the doctor said and hung up. It was so abrupt that Paula stood there holding the phone, waiting for something else to happen, until the dial tone sounded. She replaced the handset on the cradle and stood there thinking.

Paula didn't have a lot of experience with hospitals or doctors, but it felt to her as if the whole conversation had been off somehow, and she was unsatisfied. But it was only a couple of days.

Then she realized that she hadn't even got his name. She'd missed it. If he'd said it at all.

Doug Moore hung up the phone and looked to his wife for approval. Marla was smiling. "Very good, dear. Thank you."

He nodded, his expression flat.

"You can go back to work now. Do you have to go back to work?"

He nodded again.

She put her hand on his cheek. "Good. You go back to work and you can forget all about this. Forget all about this . . ." As she said it she stroked her hand across his face. He closed his eyes and she took her hand away.

"Are you going back to work, honey?" she asked again, her tone suddenly bright.

"Yeah," he said. "I still have a couple of contracts to go over. I just came home to get my— my—" He frowned.

"—file folder in the den," she finished for him. "Should I get that for you?"

"Thanks, Marl. And jeez, I wouldn't mind a sandwich or something. Do you mind?" He opened the fridge and peeked inside.

"You can pick something up on the way back to work," she said and went and got a file for him. Any file would do.

After Doug left, Marla went into Amy's bedroom to check on her. She was lying on top of the bedcovers, stiff as a board, staring at the ceiling.

"Amy?"

The child didn't move. Her little chest rose and fell with her breath, but she was otherwise still.

"Honey, Mommy's right here. I'm right here."

Outside there was the steady *foom-pf* of the basketball through the hoop.

It was all about her babies now. She had to protect her babies. But a persistent thought kept popping into her head. *What have we done?*

What have we done?

FOURTEEN

Izzy was parked outside the Chapman house, waiting for dark. She ached for darkness, wanted only to hide under black skies. She had ill work ahead of her and no desire to see it performed.

The foliage, once scrubby and sparse, had grown thick and wild around the house. The drive had grown over too, and a broad patch of brown grass ran up the middle, mixed with thistles and stinkweed. Twenty years of tire marks had compressed the earth, turned it grey. In spite of the (mostly abandoned) farmland around her, there was no greenery here, just blank, empty fields.

At the foot of the drive was the fading post that bore the house number: 362. Someone had long ago scratched over it with a key or a knife. It could barely be made out now. The house stood alone at the edge of Haven Woods.

It would be dark soon.

The thumping from the trunk had stopped. The car was still. Since the house was close to the river, she should have been able to hear spring peepers and crickets, but the yard was silent, as though nothing living could possibly stay for long.

It didn't matter how often she came here or how fated her connection, every time she was filled with fear. Izzy, who inspired her own kind of fear in her women, sat in the car with the windows rolled up and watched fretfully, knowing that the random, uncontrolled evil that permeated the very boards of the house, and the earth around it, could turn on her as easily as it gave. Even with her gift of flesh today, she was in arrears, and it could all turn.

The house looked different now. The yellow crime-scene tape was long gone. The windows were broken, rocks thrown by teenagers on a dare.

But a girl never forgets her first time.

Do you know that house? her grandmother had asked her. She had taken a knife from her drawer in the bedroom and pressed it to Izzy's side, under her left breast. The slice was fast and clean. Izzy had gasped and stumbled back with the impact, placing her hand there, covering it. The wound began to bleed through her fingers.

I was there her grandmother said, beaming at her. *Before this. Long time ago, your mother dragged me away.* The old woman's mind was wandering, her expression faraway for a minute. *Things fell apart. We weren't strong.*

She pushed the bedroom door closed behind Izzy. The room was illuminated only by the brown light coming from a dirty bulb under a dirty lampshade in the corner. Izzy pressed back against the door.

Her grandmother raised the knife, not as a threat but to emphasize. *You must have thirteen. At all times.*
women
find them yourself
She put the knife back into the bureau and took out a photograph, held it out to Izzy. *My sisters.* She pointed a frail finger at a

smiling woman with dark hair. *This is Aggie. Find Aggie. She's still there, waiting. Find her, and she'll be your first.*

You'll have everything you ever wanted the old woman said again. Then she reached out and put her finger to the bloody wound in Izzy's side. She held it up.

He will want flesh. Do everything He asks and you'll have everything. You hear?

After that she'd been sent to the Chapman house, dragging a heavy bag that made a wet sound when it banged against her leg. What was inside the bag was unthinkable, killed by her grandmother as an offering to Him. Next time Izzy would have to do her own killing.

everything you've ever wanted

The wound under her breast ached, burned, where the knife had penetrated. At first it hadn't hurt at all. When the old woman sliced between her ribs, she'd been afraid that she had cried out and her mother would come rushing in.

you crazy stupid old woman get back get away from her

But her parents and the kids hadn't come back yet. When Izzy left the bedroom, the rest of the house was still empty, dark, the television off.

Once she'd seen her mother wale on her grandmother with the cord from the iron. Because the old woman had struggled her way into the kitchen and blown something ground up and fragrant towards her mother's tea.

don't you dare pull that bullshit

If Izzy's mother had come home at that moment . . . But she hadn't, and Izzy had left her parent's home that night to do dark things.

The wound, she was sure, had seeped blood through her blouse. Soon it would work its way through her coat. She'd driven like that through the city, all the way to Haven Woods, to the house, the dead thing in the bag on the floor in front of the passenger seat. She went up the walk to knock on the door, the bag in her hand heavy, awful. She was terrified but

everything you've ever wanted

she was doing as she'd been told.

The door opened as she was climbing the front steps. A perfectly ordinary but very large hand, fingers spread, pushed it wide. She stopped on the middle step and looked up, her heart pounding so loudly under her coat she was sure he could hear it.

In the doorway of the Chapman house stood a large, large man, with hands like catcher's mitts. His jaw was square and shaded with the beginning of a beard. She could hardly see his eyes; his overhanging brow shaded them.

This is a threshold he said to her sternly. *You have to ask your way in.*

May I come in? she asked. She hadn't said, as her brothers might have, *I'm coming in, eh?* or *Whatta ya want? I'm coming in.* It was polite, the way she said it. And saying it that way made what she carried in the bag seem that much more of an offering. Made her feel brave.

The big man grinned broadly. She saw that his teeth were very white, and that two at either side, just inside the cheek, were sharp, like a wolf's.

He stepped back and, with loaded gallantry, threw his arm open to gesture her inside. *Mi casa es su casa* he said. She didn't know what he meant, and he'd laughed.

Once inside she felt the heat of the place, unpleasant, like a fever. She held the offering in front of her, away from her, like a shield.

She followed the man deeper into the house until he said *Stop* and she did. It was dark and her eyes hadn't adjusted to it; she could see nothing, just the faintest outline of his head against a window. He lit a match, and the shock of it made her gasp.

He said *I smell you*. The blood had seeped out of her, soaked through her blouse and coat. She could smell it too. Blood dripped at her feet. From the bag.

He said, *Look*.

He shifted the light, and on the floor she saw a woman, on her back, arms akimbo, legs spread, skirt pushed up over her knees. The centre of her was black with something, the same something that spread out around her body, all the way to his shoes. The woman's eyes were open, staring up.

It was not Mrs. Chapman. It was someone else.

Izzy jammed her hand over her mouth so she wouldn't scream. The man chuckled softly.

And behind you he said. She didn't want to look, but her head turned of its own accord. There was Martin Chapman. She recognized him. And near him, his wife. The bullet they said he'd put between his eyes had obliterated much of his face. What remained was a single eyeball, and even that was halved.

A sob escaped her lips. *They're not really here* she said.

He ignored her. *I like to keep my work about me*, he said. *It's beautiful work. You'll come to see that.*

Izzy pressed her eyes tightly shut. The wound in her side was aching and she could feel a trickle of blood running down into the waistband of her skirt. She kept her eyes shut because when she opened them, she could sense others moving in the shadows beyond the light from the match.

The man snapped his fingers and the light rose to near the ceiling, illuminating everything.

Look at me. He was now sitting cross-legged on the floor in front of her, smiling pleasantly. *What have you brought me?* He held out his hands eagerly.

Izzy reached inside the bag, ignoring the sounds that had begun behind her. Wet sounds, the strangled sounds of dying breath.

The thing inside the bag was cold. She curled her fingers around it and pulled it out. No different than a piece of liver from the market, no different than the steaks she would barbecue after all this was over. Cold.

She pulled out the heavy thing and held it out to him, her neck straight. *I brought flesh* she said.

He took it from her.

Now you he said. *You must give me you.*

Her skirt was pushed up around her waist, her blouse torn down the front. Blood smeared her stomach from where his hands had been on her, where his fingers had dragged from her open wound across her breasts. The beast had mounted her.

There was nowhere for her to look. Her head was pressed against the dirty floor. If she opened her eyes she would see the woman, whose head had twisted so that the staring eyes were looking right at her. The dead man just to the right of the woman was watching them unsmilingly, teardrops of blood dripping steadily from his chin. If she looked the other way she'd see the child perched on the edge of the stair rail, his arms wrapped around his naked legs, also watching.

She kept her eyes squeezed shut and tried not to feel.

The thing that had penetrated her, it might have been a tail.

Afterwards he bent his head to where her grandmother had cut her. His cold, sharp tongue poked inside the wound, making her squirm with a kind of pain-slash-ecstasy that she bore with blank stoicism. His lips made a seal around the wound even as his tongue penetrated it, he had suckled from her. The sound of it filled the room.

Long fingers were curled around her thigh, nails pressing and releasing with every pull on the wound. It reminded her of when she'd breastfed

(David)

the children.

Her vagina was slick with his offal and her own blood.

It's always a woman who pays the old woman had told her. *Because in our way we are gods.*

This is my mark he said when he lifted his head. His breath smelled like her blood.

you're not a stupid woman Isadora

This is my mark. She felt scored where he'd touched her—everywhere, but especially in the wound under her breast, where he'd left a trail of something caustic that burned like acid.

There will be a reckoning the thing said. The words came out of his mouth wet and heavy. *When this reckoning happens, you will know and you will get down on your knees and thank me.*

Yes she said.

You must keep your number. Do you understand? You will keep your thirteen about you and you will stay close and true to me. To this place.

She nodded. *This place. Thirteen,* she repeated for him, like a child.

Thirteen women at all times. There would be gifts for their sacrifices

(everything you want)

Sometimes He would take. He told her so.

Do you love your daughter? he had asked when he was slaked and panting his cold breath into her ear. He pinched her nipple between his thumb and forefinger and twisted it painfully but thoughtlessly, as though rolling a grape between his fingers. No more than that.

Yes, she'd said. But she was thinking of David.

Do you love your son?

Yes, she did, it was true. Even the sound, the thought of his name soothed her. In the worst times it was he who—

And who do you choose?

Without hesitation she said, *My son,*

(I choose David above all David above everything)

her voice shrill with just the beginnings of panic—and something else, of course, something ancient, a protective thread that shot rapidly through her centre. Too late she asked,

(it was later she would realize she'd asked too late—choose David for what?)

reckoning

When the thing left her, it bore no resemblance to who had answered the door, to the large, handsome man who had told her she had to ask her way in. The thing that had crawled atop her, that had plunged into her with pain and ice, had doubled in size. It had the head of an animal and the eyes of goat, slit like a reptile's.

Before it disappeared it grabbed the naked child's hand, yanking him up in the air like a doll. "You are mine, as this is mine—"

As it left, it repeated *Thirteen.*

And everything changed.

Sometimes it was easy to forget that any of it had happened, especially after the old woman died. Death had shut those knowing eyes that grinned and smiled at Izzy even as she cackled happily and spit out her non sequiturs. Once she'd even said, *how's your cunt feeling, Isadora? Is it stuffed full of money yet?*

And by then, of course, it was, so to speak. The very day after her visit to the Chapman house, Roger got a job, a good job. Within weeks he'd been promoted twice. Suddenly there was money.

Her parents' neighbours hardly missed their

(*flesh*)

puppy.

It was easy to forget. To start anew.

They soon moved to Haven Woods. Izzy found Aggie, who already bore the mark. It was easy enough to recruit the others.

Izzy cut them herself and spread her blood over their wounds, making them all one, sisters. Whatever the beast was, He had kept his promise. Her life grew exponentially better. They had everything she wanted: a good life for her children, a good life for *her*. The city was left far behind.

Haven Woods became Izzy's as she adapted it to her needs and to the needs of her sisters and their families. The church closed. The hospital had fewer and fewer patients—no one got sick, doctors didn't stay.

All had been forgotten about that time. By her.

Until He took David.

It was getting very dark and Izzy knew she had to get moving. Outside the car, things crept close and bumped against the glossy tan exterior. Shadows seemed to be moving just outside her peripheral vision, darting away if she turned to look. She didn't look, didn't need to. She had a good idea what she would see.

An odious task. No different than the dishes, the last load of laundry, wiping someone's bloodied nose.

Izzy leaned forward and pulled the lever that popped the trunk. With a hollow snap it opened about two inches and stayed there.

Outside, the night was alive. Something dark darted past the car and there were sounds that might be . . . nothing, might be just the night, might be voices. Bits of things being said, only theoretically human, like the drone of a radio far away. There was another bump against the passenger side and the sound of something dragging along the car. Then it was gone.

She fished around on the floor for her leather apron, then opened the door and got out.

As if a drop of oil had been added to a dish of water, the shadows and shapes, the forms in the dark, spread out and away from her. Briefly she saw the outline of what might have been a woman, a flash of breast in the moonlight, a shimmer of hair. A hint of weeping permeated the air over her head.

Even in the moonlight, the dark seemed to follow her like a large shadow. She lifted the trunk lid. Inside the dog, clearly terrified, looked up at her with sunken eyes. He whimpered piteously as he jerked himself to his feet, awkwardly, painfully, from his cramped position.

Izzy put her hand on his head, both to keep him from jumping out and to soothe him. "It won't hurt," she said.

From somewhere around her there was murmured discussion, voices

(what might have been voices)

that disagreed, agreed, wanted to *see*.

From her bag she pulled a container and a small handkerchief. She poured from the one onto the other, and when the reek hit her nose she held her breath. It wouldn't do to pass out, not here.

"It won't hurt," she repeated to the dog. She felt sorry, but from a distance. For the dog and for herself. Especially for herself, because of all the people who wouldn't understand.

She stroked the dog's head, so little flesh between fur and skull that she might well have been petting him long after he was dead. He looked up at her with knowing eyes. He didn't fight when she pressed the sodden cloth to his snout and held it there.

In less than a minute his skinny body collapsed to the floor of the trunk, still breathing

(that was important)

but still as the night. Some other night. Somewhere other than this place.

Around her there was more discussion, fogged laughter, muffled delight. And maybe she heard

dead dead dead

It was hard to tell because the wind had picked up. As she lifted her offering out of the trunk, dropped it to the ground and dragged it to the porch of the legendary, boarded-up house, that breeze ruffled her hair with mock affection and whispered in her ears. Hollow sounds, like music from a seashell.

She laid the dog on the porch and dropped to her knees. She unrolled the leather apron and took out the large, well-honed knife. It caught moonlight and flashed—of course it did. She raised it above her head and brought it down on the poor thing's throat. Blood sprayed against the door. Izzy didn't notice her tears falling into the blood

(because it reminded her, as it always did, as everything always did, of David and how he'd fallen and how it had sounded and looked and the blood)

The blood formed a puddle on the porch floor, where it slipped towards the door.

"Please," she said. "I bring you death."

The things in the yard, which didn't dare come to the porch, fell silent. She could hear the blood gurgle as it emptied from the dog.

"Tomorrow we have thirteen," she said.

The porch door opened.

The large man stood there, grinning.

Please she thought.

"What else do you offer me?"

Izzy hesitated, and in that quick second of reluctance she felt the old wound under her breast suddenly shoot with pain. But still a million images ran through her brain.

"A child," she said. "I will bring you a little girl."

He held the door wide and with a hand swept the air mockingly, gallantly, for her to pass. "*Mi casa*," he said. "*Su casa*."

She dragged the dying dog behind her.

Afterwards she made it back to the car, but no farther. She slept, even as the voices around her quieted and dawn broke. Even in that place.

FIFTEEN

ROWAN HADN'T SAID ANYTHING about her stomach ache to her mom. It would have been hard to explain, given that she was eating her second piece of French toast slathered in butter and syrup. But the pain hadn't gone away; it had settled into a kind of ache that she couldn't put her finger on. She didn't feel like throwing up. She didn't have to go to the bathroom. It just sort of *hurt* down there. A dull throb in her lower half, sometimes poking into her back. She was starting to get used to it. Maybe later she would ask her mom for an Aspirin. That helped headaches, so maybe it would help this ache.

Old Tex was sitting at her feet. She'd discreetly fed him some of her French toast when her mom was at the stove making her another piece—"You must be in a growth spurt"—and he was still licking syrup off his snout when his head shot up and he started getting awkwardly to his feet, tail wagging.

From the porch they heard, "Hello in there," followed by a friendly bark.

Rowan started to say, "I think that's Mr. Keyes," but her mom was already on her feet and she and Old Tex were on their way to the door. *Jeez*, she thought, with a twelve-year-old's embarrassment, *anxious much?*

She ate the last square of French toast on her plate, then went to the door too. Her mom was leashing up Old Tex. The two dogs were wagging and panting at each other, and Gusto was tugging on his leash to get close enough for a sniff at Old Tex.

"Hey, Rowan," Mr. Keyes said. "You feel like a walk with the boys?"

"Yes!" She grabbed her blazer from the hook by the door.

Her mother frowned. "It might be too warm for the blazer, honey."

Rowan took Old Tex's leash from her hand and shook her head. "I need to wear it," she said, and patted the pocket quickly, feeling reassured by the lump. She tugged on Old Tex's leash. "Let's go, old man!"

Mr. Keyes laughed. And they all went for a walk.

Tap tap tap

In her dreams, Izzy Riley squirmed in the seat of her car. *No. Not ready. Don't come for me.*

tap tap tap

Her lovely face screwed into a grimace and she turned away from the sound. Inside her head was the image of the thing in the house, malevolent, hungry, and her heart

tap tap tap

pounded in fear. It reached a paw out to her. *It is time?*

She groaned and slowly opened her eyes. Facing her through the windshield was a cat, a single paw on the glass. Tansy. When she saw Izzy's eyes open, she dropped her paw and sat there, tail flickering. Beyond the cat was the Chapman house, in daylight. It stared at her with its second-storey windows. Izzy looked at the cat. The cat stared back, at least benevolently. Her friend.

She rolled the window down. "I'm awake," she told Tansy. "Get inside." The cat delicately dropped off the hood of the car and jumped easily through the driver's-side window. She landed on Izzy's lap. She was purring. She rubbed up against Izzy, who brought her hands to the cat's head and stroked. *Good girl.*

Tansy accepted the petting and then stepped elegantly over to the passenger seat and curled up. Her tail moved above her like a thought before wrapping around her body. Izzy started the car.

As she drove she reached for her cellphone on the dash and turned it on. Twenty-seven messages. She would pass for now.

It was Thursday. Everyone had to hold on for one more day. She looked at the house receding in the rear-view mirror.

Ego sum vestra serva. I am your servant. For better or for worse.

In the end it would be worse. She knew that now.

At the end of the lane she turned right to drive along the river. The road eventually angled away and met with Proctor, the street that circled Haven Woods. It was a pretty drive, with the trees lining the river and the houses so neat and new. It never betrayed the monstrosity that she'd left behind.

She must have slept deeply, but she was tired. The skirt of her suit was grimy from picking up the dirty dog, and a cat's paw print lay dead centre above the hem. She pulled down the sun visor and quickly peered into the mirror. Her hair was a mess, her makeup worn off.

As she flipped the visor back up, she saw people walking towards her, with dogs. She squinted. Smiled.

Paula was still here. And the girl.

Izzy gave thanks. *Ego sum vestra serva.*

She broadened her smile and slowed as she approached them. Through her open window she waved for them to stop. They did, five sets of eyes staring at her like deer in headlights, as she pulled the car alongside.

"Hello there, Paula," she said, but she was looking at the girl. The child's expression was grave and suspicious. *Good for you.* She was holding the leash of Audra's stupid, ancient dog. The thing should be dead already. She'd once bought her friend a cat, but it had disappeared, run off or something. Izzy suspected the dog.

"Hello, Rowan," she said. The girl raised her hand in semi-greeting.

"Hi, Mrs.— Izzy," Paula said, with some warmth. She smiled.

The man with her smiled too. He was attractive, and somehow familiar.

"And who's this?" Izzy asked, and saw Paula redden.

"Sanderson Keyes, this is Izzy Riley. Sanderson grew up in Haven Woods," she said awkwardly, not wanting to bring up the obvious. "We grew up together," she added, as a clue.

Izzy's face sobered, her smile slipping.

hey Lonnie and

"Not Lonnie Keyes's brother?"

He nodded. "Yeah, that's right. I was a friend of David's," he said, without Paula's awkwardness.

She reset her smile. "I remember. And your mother too. She was never happy here, was she."

Sanderson was noncommittal but polite. "I do think she's been happier since she moved away."

Izzy returned her gaze to Rowan. It was remarkable how much the child looked like Paula. It was like seeing her as a child again

(and the blood that ran through her was lovely alumna blood)

"How are you enjoying your mother's old hometown, Rowan?"

Rowan shrugged and Izzy frowned. *Rude.* She tried to stare the child down, but the girl turned her attention to the dog, stroking him. The dog had dropped his head and was glaring at Izzy, his upper lip curled.

Back off, dog. She grinned to show her teeth.

"Rowan, answer Mrs. Riley," Paula said firmly.

"It's good," Rowan said, without looking up from the dog. "What's wrong, boy?"

Izzy chuckled, her laugh a tinkle. "I have Tansy in the car. He must smell her." At the sound of her name, the cat on the seat beside Izzy raised her head and got up in a stretch. The stretch ended as she placed her front paws on the dash and peered out through the windscreen at them all.

"A co-pilot." Sanderson Keyes laughed. "Gusto sticks his head out the window. He's useless as a navigator."

Izzy looked at Gusto. *Another dog.* A beagle, if she wasn't mistaken. Just what the neighbourhood needed.

Rowan tugged on Old Tex's leash and brought him closer to her, pulling his head into her stomach. She muttered to the dog, "It's okay."

Something was peeking out through the fur on his throat. Izzy squinted to see what it was. "Old Tex seems quite taken with you, dear. It's nice to have an animal friend, isn't it?"

Hearing her voice directed at the girl, the dog turned his head abruptly once again. The thing around his neck was red.

"What's he wearing there?" she asked.

Rowan reached down and touched it. "New collar," she said. "My grandma made it for him."

Izzy's eyebrows went up. "Really? How crafty of her." Inside she could feel a slight panic. "Can I see? Audra is always making lovely things . . . And where are you all headed so early?" She put her arm out the window and waggled her fingers for the girl to bring the dog closer.

"We're just walking the dogs," Paula replied. "We might take

Rowan to the river. We've gone near, but we haven't gone down to the banks yet."

Rowan stayed where she was. Izzy waggled her fingers again and looked sternly at the girl, her face a mother's face, commanding. Rowan stepped towards the car, tugging on the leash. Old Tex took a couple of steps too and then dug in, baring his teeth. He barked, angrily, loudly.

"Oh my," Izzy said.

Paula was on him. "*Tex!*" The dog looked up at her reproachfully, his teeth still bared, but clearly not at her. "Stop!"

He ducked his head and stopped growling, but he would not cave in to Izzy. Gusto watched his new friend carefully for some sign.

"It's the cat, I'm sure," Izzy said. "That's all right. Nice doggy." Tansy, serene, never took her eyes off Old Tex.

"Sorry, Izzy," Paula said.

"Oh, no worries. I'd better get a move on. It was nice to see you, Paula. You and this darling here"—she indicated Rowan—"are coming to Marla's tomorrow evening, right?"

"Yes, we're looking forward to it."

Rowan looked sharply at her mother and shook her head, barely perceptibly.

The rebellious child. Their saviour.

"Well, enjoy yourself this morning. It sure is a lovely day." Izzy put the car in gear, called a friendly goodbye out the window and drove off. She checked the mirror, watching the five move on. Only the dog looked back at her.

Izzy's smile was completely gone. The dog. The dog was a problem.

She pulled over to the side of the road, opened the door and got out. She bent over and looked at Tansy, sitting up on the passenger seat. "Get rid of that dog," she said.

The cat gave a stretch and picked her way over the seat, then jumped down to the road. She flicked her tail goodbye and ran into the trees towards the river.

Audra struggled to clear the fog from her brain. Whatever Tula had done to make her sleep before she left, it hadn't been painful. It may have been an act of kindness, but she doubted it. Tula did not have the imagination for kindness.

She did know that Paula hadn't come to visit today. The hospital was silent as the grave. Tula was noticeably absent too. But for how long?

When she'd woken, she'd tried to call for Tula, though her throat was parched, her tongue fat with dehydration. She'd opened her mouth to call and—

the sound that came out of her was that of an animal. She could guess which one.

Judas goat

On her arms was a spattering of coarse hairs, white and long. It might not be noticeable to others yet, but if it got any thicker . . .

She had no idea how far this would go. Misplaced, unbidden pieces of thought ran through the space between her ears where cognition used to be. Snippets of songs, conversations she'd had years before, headlines. Oddly placed and terribly distracting. She had to concentrate. She had to act.

Paula hadn't come to see her yet and she had no way of knowing why. Had she left town, or had something happened to her or Rowan? Had she simply forgotten to come? That was unlikely.

She had to do something before Tula came back. She wriggled up to a sitting position and looked around the room.

Under other circumstances she would have been confident they would not do the *sabbat* without her, but they were desperate. There

were things you could invoke. She was sure Izzy had thought of something. Or one of the new bunch. The young ones were a clever lot.

No, it all hinged on Paula. She was the thirteenth.

That couldn't happen. She wouldn't let it.

Audra looked around the room for something, anything, to
enchant. There was the closet with her things in it. She went over
the items that might be in her purse: makeup, shopping list, pen—
Aren't you glad you use Dial? Don't you wish—

Pen. *Pen.* Audra struggled to get the thought back. Pen and
notebook. Keys? No, she'd given them to Paula. There was a safety
pin stuck in the lining of the bag for emergencies, there was her
chequebook, her wallet.

The heart monitor was still in the corner. There was the table
beside her

(what was in the drawer?)

on which stood the water jug, some plastic cups, the vase and
flowers Paula and Rowan had brought her.

Audra closed her eyes. Her heart was pounding; she was
breathless and losing focus again. She let her head fall back against
the pillow and listened. There was nothing to hear. She was still
alone on the floor.

There was nothing in the room to work with.

She looked at the flowers, a cheap bunch from the grocery
store—more sweet for that, somehow. Rowan had walked in with
them, but had Paula held them?

Mom, smell

She thought Rowan had taken them from Paula and put them
in the vase, the vase procured by Tula. Izzy had been there.

(had Paula held them?)

She tried to remember. Rowan hadn't come in right away. Paula
was holding the flowers. She'd buried her face in them, then held
them out

smell, Mom

They would have to do.

The vase was about four feet from where she lay, maybe a little less. Audra's joints felt so unyielding. She felt confined in unfamiliar flesh that was sprouting stiff little hairs up and down her arms

(and who knew where else her chest was itching even if she didn't want to think about it)

There was no help for it. She leaned forward and tried to shift herself along on her bottom, moving an inch at a time. Her leg joints were as rigid as her arms; only her neck seemed fluid. She led with her neck and got her body as close to the edge of the bed as she could. She leaned, but the vase was just out of reach. A fading daisy dangled; she swiped at it with a heavy and unwieldy hand and caught it, toppling the vase. Water spilled across the tabletop.

Startled, she yelped, but managed to grab a handful of the flowers, a mash of daisies, carnations and baby's breath. A single fern clung to the tangle of stems, and she snatched it with her other hand.

Audra clutched the flowers. She called every name she could remember, the sounds coming out of her mouth guttural, animal, unintelligible. But, she hoped, *they* would know what she meant. Amid the stray memories and other mental intrusions, she began her chant, each syllable a pain and a relief, her heart broken yet full.

A simple command, delivered to her daughter amid chaos. She had no idea if the message would get through: *Go home. Leave. Don't stay. Leave. Go home.* And so on and on, as long as Audra could stand it.

The worst thing they ran into along the riverbank was a large deadfall they had to navigate. Erosion and time had set the tree on an angle and then, probably after a heavy rain, the whole thing had

pulled up and fallen forward. The roots had left a hole in the erod-
ing bank, thick ropy tendrils spreading out at the end of the tree
in a spray. Even then, some still clung to the earth, buried deep.

The dogs solved the problem with the least amount of fuss.
Gusto followed Old Tex's lead when he jumped arthritically into the
water and paddled slowly around to the other side of the tree. Paula
worried whether Old Tex would make it back to the shore, but
Sanderson pointed out that swimming was probably easier on his
old bones than trotting along the cement sidewalks he was used to.

Rowan ignored her mother's shouted advice and easily bounded
through the mess of sharp branches and heavy limbs to the other
side, where the dogs were.

"Don't get too far out of sight," Paula called to her.

"Can you make it?" Sanderson asked from close behind.

"I'm okay."

"Take your time."

Paula shinnied up onto the trunk, then looked over her shoulder and realized that her ass was in his direct line of sight. He
grinned at her and she laughed, a belly laugh that felt good, and
a little fluttery too. Butterflies.

Paula scrambled over and jumped down without incident, and
Sanderson followed. Rowan had run far ahead with the dogs.
Sanderson grabbed her arm lightly when he landed, as if to balance himself. She looked up, his face only inches from hers. His
hand slid to her hand and he held it loosely.

"Hey," he said softly. He smelled clean.

"Hey."

He looked at her for a long moment, a half-smile on his face.
She thought he might kiss her and wondered how she would feel
about that.

He didn't kiss her.

She slipped ahead of him and they picked their way past debris from the spring thaw, sticks and rocks, cinderblocks tied with ropes that went nowhere. A small wildflower poked out of the mud, all by itself. She started to grin; it was a perfect little reminder of—

She was about to say something to Sanderson about the flower, the way it stuck up so prettily through the muck, but just as she opened her mouth, a single word screamed inside her head

LEAVE

Startled, she gasped. She turned to Sanderson. "Did you say something?"

"Not yet. Is there something you want me to say?"

She half smiled and shook her head. "Never mind."

She stood rooted to the spot. The flower seemed to be begging her to do something, so she reached out for it. It was a little, daisy-like thing. She knew the name: brown-eyed Su—

GO HOME

This time the voice was loud, forceful and close. Automatically she looked ahead to where the riverbank curved into the park. There was no one there. Even as she looked, a numbness came over her neck and shoulders. Her head felt suddenly heavy.

"I have to leave," she said. It came out automatically.

"But we just got here." Sanderson was beside her now, a narrow strip of grassy bank between them and the water. The water made a pleasant sound, not fast at all, but lapping like a gentle brook in a movie.

"Haven Woods," she said. "I have to leave Haven Woods."

"Why?" He put his hand on the smallest part of her back. It gave her a shock, like static electricity. She was very aware of his hand.

"Uh . . . there are lots of reasons," she tried.

"You can tell me," he said. "I've been divorced. If it's money— Hell, Paula, I've been in every imaginable kind of financial trouble. It won't shock me . . ."

It was hard to think when he was beside her like this. She shook her head. "It's not that. I wish it was that." She did. "My mother doesn't want me to stay."

"Are you sure? I mean, is she—" The question hung in the air.

Rowan's voice floated back to them. She was talking to the dogs, her voice deeper for Old Tex, higher for the younger dog.

"—in her right mind?" Paula finished the question for him. She shrugged. The little flower bent in a gust of wind, bounced back and then bobbed again.

leave go leave go

"Yeah. You said she wasn't well."

Paula couldn't tear her eyes away from the daisy.

He turned her towards him. "Hey, look at me for a second."

She pulled her eyes reluctantly away from

leave go don't

"She really wants you to go?" His eyes were blue; she hadn't noticed that before.

"We have this history, you know? We've had a difficult relation-ship. Estranged. Since I . . . was a teenager."

He turned her around and nudged her forward along the path. "My feet are getting wet," he said.

She barely heard him but moved with the press of his hand on her back.

"I remember you just disappeared back then. Did she kick you out?"

"It wasn't exactly like that." Paula's cheeks burned at the thought of what rumours there might have been, and she hoped he wasn't looking at her. His hand was still lightly against her back. They both seemed to be moving very carefully, so as not to disturb it.

She took a deep breath. "Do you remember when I left? Do you remember that year?"

"Of course," he said. "It was just after David Riley's accident.

I had nightmares about that for months."

"Yes," she said quickly. "David Riley, and my dad too. They both died that year. A few weeks apart. It was a horrible time. My mom and I just wandered around the house like ghosts. My dad was everything to her, to me too."

Sanderson lifted the hand from her back, wrapped it gently around her neck under her hair and gave a reassuring squeeze. It felt so wonderful that she thought she could stop talking then, and maybe never talk again about anything.

"You poor kid," he said.

Hardly a kid anymore. "It was so *awful*, all of it. Every day some new kind of pain. I don't know what you know about David and me"—she faltered, and caught her breath for a moment."But he was my boyfriend. And my dad—I was close to my dad. And they both died. Just like that. I—I don't think I could even talk the week after it all happened. I just remember staying in my room, coming out at night to wander through the house. We didn't put the lights on. My mother wouldn't answer the door. Not even when it was Izzy Riley, who of course was going through her own hell.

"Anyway, maybe my mom couldn't stand it. One day she told me that she had decided to send me away to school. That she thought I needed to get away."

"Maybe you did," Sanderson said gently.

She shrugged. "Maybe I did."

They walked for awhile, the bank less soggy when they came out from under the shadow of the trees to where the sun was able to break through.

"Anyway, I went away to school and I guess she didn't want me home again. I only came back once, when Rowan was really little. When we saw her at all, she came to the city."

"And you never talked about why you were sent away?"

"My guess is, she couldn't stand to have me around without my dad there. Maybe she blamed me."

"Paula—"

"I'd asked him to bring me something from the bakery. His car went off the road just before he got there. Maybe if I hadn't asked him to stop—"

Sanderson turned her around again, to face him. "You can't do that. Accidents happen all the time. It's horrible, it's awful, but it wasn't because of you. Right?" His eyes held hers. His hands on her shoulders were warm.

Up ahead, Rowan came running into view waving a long stick, the dogs following her and barking. They broke eye contact and turned to watch her where she had stopped at the edge of the bank. She waved at them with the stick, smiling broadly, the two attentive dogs at her feet. They waved back.

Paula finally said, "She sent me away because I was pregnant. I think she was ashamed."

Beside her, Sanderson was silent.

"So Rowan and my mom have never been close." Her mouth opened and she might have added something, but Rowan squealed. They both looked up to see Gusto launch himself into the air trying to reach the stick, which Rowan was holding just out of range.

Paula let go of a breath she didn't know she'd been holding, and Sanderson turned her back towards him again. She felt shaky and frightened about having revealed the biggest secret of her life. The only secret that mattered.

He leaned down and kissed her. "Please don't leave," he said.

Rowan watched Mr. Keyes kiss her mom. She was a little bit pissed off

(jealous)

but mostly what she felt was a kind of dread. If her mom started up with a man they would be stuck here forever. But, on the other hand, it's not like this was Andy. Andy had been a Number One Creepoid. Her mom didn't have great luck with guys. Her own father, for instance. Where was he? Dead.

Mr. Keyes, of course, was alive, and Ro actually liked him. He made her feel . . . normal. He was a normal guy. The kind of guy you could complain to about crappy things at school, and he would say dad things like *well, you just ignore those girls. They have nothing good to say.* Or, if you wanted to go on a ski trip to Quebec, the kind of guy who would say, *you betcha! here's the money.*

Normal. But a normal guy who had just bought a house in the neighbourhood might want to stay here. A normal guy might want his *girlfriend* to stay here. And the thought of staying here made Rowan's stomach hurt worse.

She wrestled the stick out of Old Tex's mouth—which wasn't too hard—and both dogs danced around her, eyes never leaving the stick. She'd deked them out a couple of times, but they were no longer falling for that. They knew she was about to throw it into the water. Finally she did, and both dogs plunged in, their paws working furiously as they raced to get to it. They looked funny and she laughed, forgetting for a minute that her stomach was sore and her back kind of hurt. She'd thrown that stick pretty far, though.

aren't you God's special thrower

The dogs chased the stick more than halfway across the river, Gusto closing in first. Old Tex was off to the right of him, paddling almost as furiously. Gusto snapped at the stick, which was still a foot or more ahead of him. He barked. He swam and snapped and snapped again and then he got it, water splashing all around him.

"Good dog!" she called out.

Old Tex seemed to pause in the water, staring at the far bank as Gusto headed back to Rowan. Tex did not. He started to swim to the other side.

"Tex!" Rowan called.

The dog threw her a look over his shoulder. *I'm heading over there.*

Gusto hesitated, turning around to watch Old Tex.

"Hey, Tex!" Rowan yelled. "C'mon back, boy!"

But by then Tex had reached the far bank. He pulled himself up with more vigour than he'd shown for awhile. He sloshed and clumped his way to the treeline and then he sat down facing Rowan, panting.

"C'mon back, boy!"

He wagged his tail. Barked once, assertively. Then his head drooped and she could almost hear him whine.

What?

Gusto swam back to Rowan, never letting go of the stick. He made it up the bank easily and dropped it at her feet. She touched the top of his head. "Good dog," she said. He wagged happily. They both watched Tex.

Old Tex whined and snapped as if at a fly in the air. He looked up unhappily and then dropped his head between his paws. Gusto and Rowan watched their friend. Gusto barked at him. *Better over here.*

"Tex, you *come*!" Rowan called.

Tex wagged his tail cautiously. He stood up and stepped closer to the water, then sat back down again. He wagged. She could almost hear his whine. *Please?*

Gusto panted and went down to the waterline on their side. He barked at his friend. *Come back.*

Tex went to the river's edge and put a foot in the water, then withdrew it. He sat down again. He whined, and this time Rowan really heard him. *You come here. You come to me.*

Rowan took a step towards him. The water lapped over the toe of her running shoe. It looked cool and refreshing, in spite of the muddy colour. She bet it was lovely in there.

Old Tex stuck a foot in the water again and barked hard.

The lap of the water was a gentle drumbeat

swoosh swoosh swoosh

and she was so hot. Beneath her blazer she could feel sweat on her back, under her arms. She hadn't been swimming yet this year. She put her foot in the water, sneaker and all. *Mom's going to kill me.*

Behind her, barely audible, came the pitter-pat of small animal feet. Gusto growled softly. She turned her head just a little, not wanting to lose sight of the water for too long, and saw a cat standing behind them. It stared unblinkingly at her, just watching. Gusto lowered his head and growled at it, not softly at all this time.

She'd seen this cat before. She turned back to the river, and Old Tex barked madly as she waded in up to her knees, the water so cool and refreshing on her legs that she almost wanted to cry

so soothing it would wash over her tummy and all the pains would go bye bye bye bye

as she took another step deeper—

Old Tex went insane, bouncing around on the far shore, barking and whining. He put both front feet in the water, then backed away, turning in circles of frustration—

—and she walked in up to her waist, holding up the bottom of her blazer, not liking the idea of the piece of paper in her pocket getting wet

no!

oh that doesn't matter

no!

Gusto barked and barked and barked—

Someone yanked at her from behind, screaming her name.

As if something had snapped, Tex was released into the water, launching a good two feet into the air and landing with a spectacular splash. He swam as fast as he could back to their side of the river.

"What the hell were you thinking?" her mother said, getting the wet girl out of her soggy shoes and socks, then pulling off her blazer and shaking it. "I paid two hundred dollars for this, and you're going *swimming* in it? You're lucky you were holding it up, boy oh boy—"

"I'm sorry," Rowan said, and she was. "I don't know what happened. I just wanted to . . . go swimming." She burst into confused tears.

Her mother, equally confused, hugged her tightly for a minute, which got them both wet.

By the time Paula had let her go, Old Tex was licking her bare feet in mute apology, as if he were the one who had gotten her in trouble. Her jeans clung wetly to her legs. Foul brown muck from the river clung to her everywhere the water had touched. She smelled faintly of rotting leaves.

Gusto came bursting back through the trees towards them, with Sanderson trailing.

"I got him. He was chasing a cat," he said. He winked at Rowan. "Going for a swim, huh?"

She shrugged unhappily, embarrassed by her tears, glad Mr. Keyes hadn't seen them. He patted her on the head and she managed a grin.

He turned to her mother. "Everything okay?"

Paula held out the blazer. "I think so. Except I guess I should take Rowan swimming more often." Her voice was a little sharp.

"You okay, really?" Sanderson asked Rowan.

"I'm okay."

"She's okay," Sanderson said. He put his hand on Paula's

shoulder. Paula looked up at him and nodded, smiling a little. They said nothing.

Old Tex nudged his head under Rowan's hand. She looked down at him. His big brown eyes were sad. She patted him gently. *'S okay, boy.* She leaned to rest her face against his snout, and he licked her cheek, whining in his throat. *Sorry, so sorry, so*

hot hot hot hot

Paula handed Rowan her blazer and picked up the wet socks and sneakers. "Good thing it's warm enough for you to walk home barefoot."

"Mom . . . I'm sorry." Rowan looked up at Paula with such a pathetic expression that Paula softened. "I don't why I was going into the water. I was . . ." She faltered, the reason sounding so foolish now. "I was hot," she finished.

Paula put a hand on her daughter's head and stroked her hair as she shook her own head. As always, indecision was creeping up on her. Should she make an issue of things or let it go? Parenting 101. The class she had skipped. "Let's go," she said.

The three of them, with the two dogs straggling tiredly, made their way up the steep bank to the park. Rowan carried her blazer in one hand and held Old Tex's leash in the other. Tex was walking slowly, head down.

Paula's thoughts strayed to her mother, who was having those tests. She wondered if she should show up at the hospital anyway.

daisy brown-eyed Susan smell them

The idea repelled her, like a nasty odour. Sanderson must have heard her sigh.

"Gusto and I will walk you home," he said. And then he put his arm around her shoulders and she sank into him, and it felt better than anything had in a long time.

SIXTEEN

As they headed slowly back to her mother's house, there seemed to be flowers everywhere Paula looked. Front yards were bright with purple, pink, white and blue annuals, and pots over-flowed from their perches on front steps and porches. Foliage and bloom spilled out of quaintly overturned kegs, poked out of the earth around bird baths, under trees, beside picket fences.

leave . . . go

She turned her head away from them—they seemed insistent, not beautiful. Behind her she could hear the *pat pat* of Rowan's bare feet on the sidewalk. When the house came in view, Sanderson put his hand on her back again, gently, and that tore her mind away from the

go home

colours and faint scent of the flowers. She was grateful. Her head was starting to hurt.

He walked them all the way up the front walk to the door. Gusto too, following Tex onto the porch, where the dogs sat and waited, panting, in the shade. Rowan, her jeans still wet, plopped herself down on the top step.

"You're not planning to take off just yet, are you?" Sanderson was staring at Paula.

"I don't know. No. Maybe. But not before Saturday at least. Rowan and I are going to that thing at Marla's."

"Aw, Mom!" Rowan protested. "Why do I have to go?"

"Rowan, you're going to come, and don't fuss about it. Go inside and get out of your wet things." She held out the shoes and socks. "Take these with you."

Rowan grabbed them and pulled open the screen door. The inside door was unlocked, the way it always was in Haven Woods. She tossed her footwear into the hall, then reached down and unhooked Tex from his leash. With a glance at the other dog, Old Tex followed her inside. Gusto flopped to the porch floor with a whine.

Sanderson laughed. "I think Gusto's in love."

Paula laughed too, and Sanderson leaned over and kissed her. All thoughts of flowers and Marla went away. She put her hand on his chest and could feel his heartbeat through his shirt. His arms went around her and he pulled her close.

They kissed until they were breathless, but Sanderson didn't let go of her when they stopped. "Come to dinner tomorrow, before you go to Marla's, okay?"

She nodded. "Wow, making out on the front porch. What will the neighbours say?" She disentangled herself gently.

"Just like a couple of kids." He kissed her on the forehead. "I'd better go."

Halfway down the walk with Gusto, he turned and said, "And hey, why don't you let Rowan stay with me while you go to the party? There won't be anyone there her age and you know she'll probably be miserable. I'll make us all pizza and then she and I can watch the tube."

She smiled at him. "The way to a woman's heart is through

her kid, you know."

He winked. "I'm a smart guy, Paula."

She raised her hand in a wave and watched him as he walked away.

Rowan had dropped her wet things on the bathroom floor and was already in dry clothes and back in the living room in front of the television. The TV was on, but Rowan was curled up in a ball on her side, eyes only half open.

"You okay?"

"My stomach hurts."

Her mother made a sympathetic noise.

"When are we going back to the city?"

"I'm not sure, Rowan. Soon, but not tonight."

"What about Mr. Keyes?"

"What about Mr. Keyes? What do you mean?"

"Isn't he your boyfriend?"

She laughed. "No, what makes you think that?"

"But you like him."

Her face softened. "Yeah, I do. Do you like him?"

"Yup," Rowan said simply, and closed her eyes. Paula reached over the back of the sofa and ran her hand over her daughter's pretty hair.

"A nap will help your stomach," she said. "Do you want me to get some Bromo?"

"No, Mom, I'll be okay. I'm just really tired," Rowan said, her eyes still shut.

On her way out of the living room Paula noticed a vase of silk flowers she hadn't taken note of before. She reached out and felt the petals, and even though she knew they were fake, she bent over and put her face into them, breathing deep.

smell, Mom

—

Paula stood in her mother's bedroom, picking up clothes and folding them, repacking her bag. They would go back to the city on Saturday, she guessed. A week was a normal visit when someone was in the hospital, and her mother had Izzy, after all, and her other friends.

go . . . leave

The thought seemed to permeate her whole being. The room felt over-scented, even though there were no flowers in it. It must be the perfumes on her mother's dressing table, but why hadn't she noticed the smell before? Or how many flower images her mother had surrounded herself with? The curtains and matching bedspread were a pretty, old-fashioned chintz, with large peonies and roses in pinks and lavenders. Pretty, but overwhelming.

She tried to concentrate on what she had left where, in the room, in the house. She packed everything she wouldn't need again, setting aside a few things to wash, including the blouse she'd worn to Sanderson's the night they had the barbecue.

Kissing.

Paula dropped to the bed. The kissing, the worrying about her mother, being back in Haven Woods—her resistance was gone. In a way she'd never allowed herself, she let memories of that terrible day that had started everything overtake her. The day David was killed.

She and Marla had gone to the ball field to watch the boys play. It had been hot, the kind of heat where you can't walk barefoot on concrete. Everyone was thinking about ice cream and ice-cold Cokes and jumping into the pool.

Let's change tops.

They'd given up pretty quickly on watching the game, since the boys hardly acknowledged the girls, preferring to hit ground balls to each other, one after another, so fast it was impossible to catch them all. They scored based on how many you caught. David had been in the field. He'd looked over once after catching a fast one hit by Lonnie, or Pete, she couldn't remember which, and held it aloft for Paula to see. She'd grinned stupidly, clapping. She had a secret she hadn't told him yet, and the secret had been keeping her up at night. The secret would turn into Rowan, but on that day she still wasn't sure. If they got a minute alone that night, though, she would tell him what she suspected, and they would be scared and wait for her period together.

(she wanted to remember)

She'd looked over her shoulder as they were leaving the park and he was watching her go, and they smiled at each other. Maybe he even winked. She wanted to remember it that way, because it was their last private moment.

Let's change tops.

It had been Patty who wanted to go to Paula's and put on different tops. It had been a summer of clothes and boys. Marla and Patty were boy-crazy. The three of them spent hours doing things to each other's hair, trying on each other's clothes, putting on makeup. It could take them two hours to get ready to walk to the park and the river. At the time it didn't seem foolish; it seemed crucial.

So they went to Paula's and they all tried on her new hoodie and then they traded clothes with each other. The boys caught up with them when they were leaving Paula's. They ran up behind the girls, trying to scare them. Marla and Patty screamed prettily, jerked around and yelled (prettily) at the boys, the kind of flirting understood only by teenagers. Then they walked six abreast on the road, talking idly of summer things, who had won the game, who the boys were playing next week, the inner tube Pete had found floating in the river. It was a perfectly ordinary day and they were all going to the Rileys because the Rileys were getting a new roof and they could check it out.

They were talking and laughing, everything so normal that Paula even forgot about her secret for awhile, content just to have David walking beside her, his hand occasionally brushing against hers.

Some of the parents were already at the Rileys watching the roof go up, and they would probably hang out there for the rest of the day, having a few drinks, passing the time. Before Paula had left the house that day, her mother said, *we'll be at the Rileys if you need us, dear.*

It had been like a lot of afternoons and evenings. The whole day had been like a lot of summer days.

Until David died.

Paula rolled over on the bed, not ready yet. It had been years since she'd thought that day all the way through. There had been a time when she couldn't stop thinking about it, about the sound of the moment that had changed her life. Like a sabre rattling. Then *swoosh*—

Haven Woods was thick with memories waiting to be exorcised. She had no idea how to do that.

At the hospital, Audra lay very still on the bed. Tula had picked up the flowers and stuck them in the garbage can by the door, had mopped up the water from the vase, moving so painfully that Audra had felt sorry for her. For a moment or two.

Tula's arthritis was in full bloom, like the flowers. She'd held her hands up—they'd turned into claws—and screeched at her, "This is your fault!" Even Tula's walk was laboured, her hard breathing all about pain.

Pain.

Tula had stomped out and down the hall, still muttering how it had been *all your fault*. Now Audra lay nearly paralyzed with panic and grief. She was completely helpless. Her body was betraying her. Her voice was useless. The only thing she could hope for was that, like everything else, this state of being would also begin to fall apart.

Tula had been right about one thing. It *was* her fault.

That day at the Rileys, it was supposed to be her husband, Walter, who died.

Walter had a good job at a company that processed film for photography studios all over the world. He'd started out in the plant, but fairly quickly—he was a smart man with a university education—he'd moved into administration. After Paula was born they needed a bigger house and wanted something outside the city where there were trees and parks, where it was safe and lovely. The suburbs. They found it in Haven Woods.

Audra had first met Izzy in the park, both of them with their little girls. It was late summer, those days just before school starts, when kids and mothers are restless and trying to find new things to do. Audra had noticed Izzy and her children around the neighbourhood—you couldn't miss seeing the neighbours in a place so tiny—but she hadn't had an opportunity to say hello until that moment in the park.

Their girls were about the same age, about eight: Izzy's Marla, a chubby, dark-haired beauty, and her Paula, with her thicker, wilder chestnut hair. Circumstance sometimes dictates who your friends will be, and it was inevitable that they and their daughters would became friends. Marla and Paula were two peas in a pod because of age and circumstance. And so were Izzy and Audra.

Izzy back then had been fun. She was vivacious, said outrageous things and was very sociable. She talked about how lucky they were to live in such a great community. They had everything they wanted. Didn't they?

It was as if Izzy knew that Audra was keeping a secret. And she did have a secret by then.

When had it started? Walter would come home complaining that his commute from the city was a killer. He would have a drink to unwind. One would turn into two. Two into four. She could see it happening, but it was such an easy thing to ignore. He would fall asleep in front of the TV—*poor thing he works so hard*. He would trip on his way upstairs to bed—*I have to get that carpet nailed down properly*. He would forget things, stay late in the city, arriving home in terrible condition. He slurred over the phone. He missed work. He got drunk at a company function, was the life of the party—then got demoted.

At first she had begged him to stop. Then she refused to go to social events with him. It didn't matter. By the time Paula was seven he was a full-fledged alcoholic, and there wasn't one peaceful day in their marriage. Not that they fought. Audra was one to hold it in. She would give him the cold shoulder, turn away from him in bed.

Izzy would say to her on particularly quiet days, *If you could have anything you wanted, anything in the world, what would it be?*

She would say a diamond ring, a Dior gown, a Mercedes. She didn't mean those things; she would say them because they were expected. In fact her needs were simple. A good life for her daughter. A husband who wasn't a drunk.

One bad, too quiet day she had told Izzy about waking up to find Walter sprawled on the lawn. About the long nights when he didn't come home and she didn't know where he was. How he would drink in front of Paula, who was probably too young to

understand, but to Audra, who'd grown up with serene, conserva-
tive parents, it was tantamount to running naked through the
streets. Grown people simply didn't do that.

She had wept. And Izzy had said again, *What if you could have
everything you wanted?* She wanted that.

What was involved in getting everything she wanted took some
explaining, some finessing on Izzy's part. In the end Audra agreed,
if not wholeheartedly, then in deed.

a sacrifice is required

He requires flesh

In the dark of night, when the knife slits you near your heart
and all around you whisper the voices of another world, there is
little room for disagreement. She had nodded yes and entered that
world, holding on to Izzy's promises. In that dark night it had all
seemed like a pretend thing. Like becoming blood sisters, a thing
she'd done with her best friend under a tree with a sharp pin when
she had been a little girl. Blood sisters.

Your husband or your child Izzy had told her.

In the dark, in a whisper, while blood from her wound soaked
into her sweater. She'd hesitated. But ultimately, what does a
mother say?

Walter

It was over for Audra, she understood that now. She had only one
thing to do before she succumbed to her bloody sins.

The place under her left breast throbbed, as it did whenever
sabbat was close. The wound did not open or bleed, but it *recalled.*
Her mark.

The claiming could come at any time, Izzy had told her. But
Izzy had also grinned and said that nothing had happened to her
yet. *Maybe nothing will happen. Maybe our allegiance is enough.*

And afterwards Walter stopped drinking. He got his position back. He was promoted. Life was good. Paula grew, as did the Riley children. They were happy. Very happy. She had *everything she wanted*

After her own blood was spilled, Audra had met Aggie, Izzy's first recruit. Together the three of them brought in Tula, Bella, Chick and others, faces that sometimes changed, sometimes through tragedy. They had tried to find thirteen, but it was harder than it seemed. And easy to forget why. There was always a normal veneer to what they did—got together and drank coffee, talked about their children, food, their husbands.

How many had they been during the summer of Walter and David? Twelve? She couldn't think. It was easy to let the days pass, to not think of hard times, when things were good. So good. There was time enough for more to come, they had thought. Audra had thought.

Not so.

Izzy fussed and worried during those days. She and Audra had been so close then, something the years had erased, and the group of them, the things they did, had eroded their friendship too. But back then it had been the two of them at the centre of things.

We must make good on our promises Izzy had told her one day. *We must make a sacrifice.*

Audra remembered laughing at that. It was so dramatic. Izzy's expression had changed to one of wonder and then she smiled.

Do you know why Aggie is a widow?

Because her husband died? He'd drowned.

Izzy nodded.

Funny. Audra hadn't known Aggie's husband. Just that he was dead.

We were nine then. Now we are twelve.

What about—Audra hadn't been able to remember the name

of the new woman. She hadn't been with them for very long after that.

She tried now to remember what had become of her. What the woman's name had been.

Izzy had shaken her head. *She's not been made one of us. She's being cultivated.*

The word, said like that, sounded like metal, tasted like copper. Cultivated.

We'll have to do something now Izzy had said. She reached out to Audra, patted her arm. *We can kill two birds with one stone.*

Then the Rileys ordered their new roof and Izzy called Audra and invited them to watch.

Three weeks earlier, Walter had started drinking again. She knew now that it was supposed to have been Walter that day in the Rileys' backyard.

Walter had become a sacrifice anyway, not long after David died. They had grieved together, she and Izzy, over their losses. But Izzy felt that losing a husband was not like losing a son. She talked crazily. She said she had brought Marla into the fold, and that made it thirteen. With thirteen it would be all right for awhile. Izzy hadn't been herself those days. Who could blame her? Her son was dead. But then she began speaking of Paula. That one day they would have to

(*cultivate*)

bring Paula in. So Audra sent Paula away and never let her come back.

She stayed in Haven Woods, though, because she didn't know how not to. Chick had been stronger. When she wanted to break away, she had confided in Audra. They were both going to do it.

What had been the first thing Audra said when they talked about getting away? *We can go to Paula's.*

It was Audra who had set this in motion. Her fault. She had

to conserve her energy, gather her strength. One last thing to do. She was a mother. And a grandmother.

Izzy had dropped into the big chair in the living room when she arrived home and just sat there. She had napped a little, she thought. But now she was smoking a cigarette. Of course it was a vile habit, but sometimes she just did it. It was the least of her sins.

She flicked her ashes into a saucer. There hadn't been an ashtray in the house since Roger died. He had smoked cigars. She'd liked the smell.

She was still wearing her soiled suit. She kept telling herself she would get up and change, but not yet. The skirt was ruined. She drew smoke into her lungs and contemplated it. It was garbage. What a shame, it was a good suit. She'd spent a lot on it, but she had others. She had lots of clothes. Lots of things.

She'd been thinking about Audra. Beside her on the little occasional table that she'd had for nearly twenty years, that had survived when so many other things hadn't, was her phone. It blinked with unheard messages: *green, black, green, black*. She'd scrolled through the calls—the usual roster. Esme, Marla, Tula, Bella, Bridget, the superstar-in-waiting Joanna Shaw, Glory. Even Ursula had called, and that was almost unheard of. They were terrified of her. She had only to look askance at Glory and she would wet her pants. *Ugh*, but fun. And funny.

She pressed Play, half listening.

Esme had got her boy-thing back into her house. She was trying to snap him out of it. Wasn't working. She was panicking. For Esme, that involved screeching and demanding that Izzy *do* something.

Bridget was crying, and Izzy could hardly understand what she was saying. She couldn't work, had a project, blah blah . . .

Tula's arthritis was very bad. That didn't surprise Izzy. Arthritis was how Izzy had brought her in. Sad story: the poor thing couldn't get a twist tie around a bag of peaches at the supermarket. Izzy had said, *How would you like to be free of that pain forever?* Such good intentions.

With Bella it was her eyes. Her degenerative eye disease was back. She couldn't find the glasses she hadn't worn in seven years. She too was crying. Could Izzy help?

Sharie, the new girl, the one who hoped to be a professional dancer, had not called. She had asked Glory to call for her. Glory sounded stoned, or maybe drunk. Her voice tilted in and out of the receiver, far away, then close. She giggled at intervals, and Izzy could hear her chewing. *Sharie can't reach Marla. She says her leg is the size of an elephant's.*

Bella had called twice. The second time was about Aggie. Poor Aggie, who was aging rapidly. Izzy wondered how old the woman really was. She had been an old, old woman when she found her, at her grandmother's suggestion. Was she 110? Older even? Aggie, of all of them, had known best what she was getting into.

She didn't listen to every message. They would all be the same, a litany of trauma and fear. They should have thought things through, and they hadn't. Now they were suffering. She was doing her best for them, as if they were her children. She supposed they were her children. Without Izzy they would not be who they were now. Because of her sacrifices. She had, after all, given up her

(only begotten)

son for them. For this—for the cigarette, the twenty-year-old table, the high ceilings in her living room, the silver, the china, the good and comfortable life she led.

(she was not a stupid woman)

Why did she feel so defeated? All the crackerjack work she'd done to put things to rights, the night she'd had, and she was feeling defeated. It was unconscionable.

Izzy butted out the cigarette and leaned her head back against the chair. It was still light out.

She had given a son to Him—her only begotten—and a daughter too. If she didn't keep things as they were, it had all been for naught.

She had given her daughter. Audra, for her sins, could give hers.

The night David was killed, Izzy had woken up, even though the doctor had given her pills that promised relief—however temporary—from her grief. She'd sat there in the dark, smoking cigarettes as she was doing now, but then it was in the dark bedroom. Roger was sleeping beside her, dead to the world. If only. He'd been given a shot by their family doctor at the time, Dr. Deedes. Funny the things you remember. Deedes. Dark Deedes.

She'd asked him for pills so she could minister to herself. She wanted to control her oblivion. She had said, *I don't like needles. Please, Dr. Deedes, give me some pills. I promise I'll—* Of course he hadn't wanted to do that. Mothers who lose children should not be given enough sedatives to kill themselves, especially not in the first hours after, when reason and logic are subjugated by pain and emotion. But in the end he did.

You're a strong woman he told her.

She was. And she wasn't stupid. That had been proven.

But then—

She'd been awake in the dark and it had been time to go. She'd put her robe on. What time had was it? It had been after midnight by then, surely. Hours after the ambulance had left, hours since the house had emptied of people. Audra had stayed, but she'd sent that worthless-bastard-drunk-waste-of-space home to drink on his own.

It should have been his turn.

On bare feet she slipped through the house, out the back door and into the yard, where the blood of her son had soaked into the earth. She relished the cool, sticky feel of it

(him)

on her soles. Of course she wept. Maybe through all of it.

And because it was required, she fell to her knees. To give thanks. For her life, the one she had asked for and received. And paid for that afternoon. She fell and prayed.

Laus aliis qui audiunt meam causam

(praise be to others who hear my plea)

(praise be)

As it had been told to her when she received His mark, she prayed. *Laus aliis qui audiunt meam causam*

there will be a reckoning

I will require flesh

this is my mark

She'd fallen on her knees and, in the great abyss of grief and pain, she did what was expected of her, she gave praise to her Maker, to Him. She pulled off her robe and, naked to the moon, swayed in the grip of an ecstatic pain so deep she did not hear anything until—

Mom?

The timing, she suspected in retrospect, had been bad. She was mourning her son, and was presented with her daughter had appeared. She'd jerked her head around, to see saw the girl's stricken face. At that moment, *daughter* was a sound and a word that felt like spit in her mouth. Like a hag, a harridan, she'd leapt to her feet with a shriek and a wail. She'd gone to the girl and had yanked her forward, pressing her to her knees.

On your knees— She pushed her with great force to the soiled grass, still wet with her brother's blood. *On your knees you will thank the Father for your life. Say it!*

Marla sobbed, as much with fear and surprise—Izzy had never been physical with them—as natural grief for her brother. *Mom! What are you doing? Why are you acting like this?*

Izzy had reached out and, with a single jerk, pulled her daughter's night gown from her body. The girl had knelt before her, naked except for cotton underpants, her breasts white against the night.

Marla was a woman. Izzy needed thirteen.

Izzy knocked the back of her head hard, pushing it forward until her chin touched her chest. *Bow your head and give thanks for your life—*

Mom!

Do it!

The girl tried to do as Izzy asked, said through heartrending sobs, *Thank you, God, for—*

Izzy forced her head up.

Marla looked into her mother's grieving, fierce, reddened eyes.

Not that god she said, and held her daughter's gaze until there was a stillness. Then Izzy bowed her head again, and Marla did too, without being asked.

They prayed.

Izzy had given a son and a daughter. Audra could give her share.

It was late. She butted out her cigarette and went to have a shower.

SEVENTEEN

ONE TIME WHEN ROWAN was at school, she'd had a terrible feeling in the morning, as if she'd forgotten something. It had started when she woke up and had kept hanging on through her first class. It was like forgetting something important, such as the house key or her backpack. She couldn't shake it.

Then, in second period social studies, Sister Aurelia gave them a surprise quiz. The minute the paper landed on her desk, she felt relief inside, a complete *Ah, that's what it was.* She'd guessed it. That night she'd told her mom about guessing. Her mom had said that kind of guess was called "women's intuition." Men get it too, but women tend to put more stock in feelings than men do.

Rowan had a woman's intuition now. She had a strong feeling that this place was the creeps.

She'd woken in the night to go to the bathroom. Old Tex had followed her as always, but this time when she was done, he wasn't outside the bathroom door. She guessed he'd just gone back to bed on the floor in her grandma's room, but when she left the bathroom, she heard him growling. She'd found him at the front window, up on his hind legs, front paws resting on the sill, growling at something outside. Rowan hadn't wanted to look, but she did. On the porch railing were, like, a hundred cats. Well, six really. There were six cats outside, staring into the house. What was it made of, tuna? It was too weird.

She had a feeling that if she googled Haven Woods she would get "World's Creepiest Place," and the images would be of spiders crawling up your pant leg, things under your bed and . . . cats.

Her blazer was still hanging by the front door where her mom had put it when they'd come home. Rowan put it on. She felt as if she could smell the river clinging to it, and for a second she thought she could hear

cool cool soothing

the sound of water, lapping against the shore rocks

clop clop

She didn't know what to make of her trip into the river. At first she'd wanted to rescue Tex, but then it was something else. It was as if she was making herself go into the water; there had been a feeling that she wanted to *be* water. Just thinking about it creeped her out

(everything here creeped her out)

and she stuck her hand into her pocket. Her fingers closed around the crucifix and the piece of newspaper with Mr. Keyes's phone number. She wished she could phone Mr. Keyes. But what could she say? *Um, Mr. Keyes, I know you like my mom. Would you come and get us and TAKE US HOME?*

Her mom was in the laundry room. Rowan could hear the water pouring into the washer drum. Earlier her mom had been humming. She thought she knew why.

She sure would like a string or a chain to hang the little crucifix on.

She listened. Her mom still humming. While she was doing laundry. When she did laundry at home, she was cranky all day.

There was a desk at the far end of the living room. She knew she shouldn't snoop, but she told herself she wasn't snooping—she was looking for something to hang her cross from. She pulled the top drawer open. Blank paper, pens, a pencil. A notebook. She picked it up and flipped through it. It looked like recipes. She put it back.

There were four drawers along the right side of the desk. The top one wouldn't open. *Aha.* She knew how to fix that, because the sisters' desks at school were exactly the same. You had to open the bottom drawer first and then the top one would open. She quietly pulled open the bottom drawer, taking it slowly, listening for sounds from the laundry room. All she heard was the beep of the dryer, a load finishing.

The drawer at the bottom was messy, a jumble of things. She dug around a little and her fingers brushed against something rough and thin. She pulled it out. It was a length of brown twine, the kind you use on a package. There was quite a lot of it.

"Bingo," she whispered. It was thin enough to slip through the small hole at the top of her crucifix. Now she could wear it like a necklace.

She started to paw through the mess to see if there was anything really interesting. A small envelope was jammed against the side of the drawer. She grabbed it and opened it up. There were photos. She flipped through them. Her grandma with the ever-weird Mrs. Riley, her grandma with the creepy nurse from the hospital, except that she wasn't a nurse in the photos, just a chubby old lady with a death grip on her grandma's waist. They were smiling. In the pile of photos she found one with Joanna Shaw and Marla. Why would her grandma be friends with a woman her daughter's age? But it looked like she was.

She rubbed her hand over her lower belly and made a face. It was still achy, though it felt more like a bathroom thing today than it had before. It felt . . . full.

At the bottom of the pile of photos was a really old one. The three women in it were young. She recognized her grandmother and Mrs. Riley, but not the other one. They were holding up drinks as if they were toasting. There were other people in the background not looking at the camera. A full house. A party. Two girls, younger than Ro, were playing with Barbie dolls. The one looking up at the camera was surely her mom.

They all looked so happy. That was how her mom had grown up, she guessed, with a crowd of laughing people and a bunch of food on the table. One of those Barbie dolls was a special edition, the kind they make once a year. Barbie as a fairy princess.

The table was the one in the room behind her, so the photo had been taken here, at her grandmother's house. She turned around and looked. She could not imagine happy, laughing faces in this room, not now.

A younger Rowan had sometimes wanted a Barbie just like that, or something else special. The answer was always the same: they couldn't afford it.

(maybe sometimes she wanted a smiling, laughing life with lots of people around too)

Everything was always too expensive. Or *where would we put it?* Like the time Rowan wanted a trampoline, a bike. Envy screeched inside her head. *No fair! No fair!*

(her mom was a loser stripper who worked in a bar)

As soon as the ugly thought materialized, Rowan felt instantly bad. Her cheeks burned with embarrassment. Her mom could say the same thing

(no fair no fair)

because her friends here had husbands and dogs and cats and family, and they didn't. Her mom had spent her time taking care of Rowan instead of getting those other things.

Sometimes a girl in the higher grades at Rowan's school got pregnant, and it was always a big fat deal. Everyone talked trash about her for awhile and then no one thought about her at all, except a little slut talk came up. *Remember that girl? OMG.*

Her mom had gone to the same school, which was why Rowan was there at all. Her grandmother must have thought it was a pretty good school, because she'd paid for both of them to go there. Or maybe she just wanted them both to stay far away. Maybe now her grandmother wanted them back.

Rowan suddenly felt like crying. She tossed the pictures into the drawer without putting them back in the envelope and shut the drawer with her foot. She sat down on the floor with a thump. Old Tex, lounging by the TV, put his head up when he heard her hit the deck and shambled to his feet and came over. He stuck his nose under her hand. *'S okay.*

She slipped the string through the crucifix loop and tied the ends together. Then she put it in her pocket, feeling a little guilty that she'd snooped, feeling as if the string would give her away.

Her mom probably really missed those parties and friends. She buried her face in the dog's neck fur. And her dog. Now there was Mr. Keyes. Everything her mom probably wanted was right here. The house was a nice house, she had to admit that. It was big and there was a yard. You could walk to the park without passing hoodlums and garbage. Everything looked nice.

In Creepyville. Obviously it was only Rowan who saw it that way.

Paula had dumped a basket of laundry on the bed and was folding. She was thinking about the unsatisfying conversation with her mother's doctor. She'd done her bit and not visited, but now she thought she should go in. The tests would be done and maybe her mother would be feeling better. Maybe she would be ready to come back to the house; maybe she would want Paula and Rowan to stay awhile and help out. Maybe she would say, *Oh, Paula, I've been so confused. I'm so glad you're here. Please stay.*

Maybe pigs would fly.

Part of her was ready to get out of the place on Saturday, as she'd said, but if she was honest, her heart ached at the thought not just of leaving Haven Woods but of returning to what, exactly? Another crappy job, another crummy apartment, probably a new school for Rowan to adapt to—

And then Rowan walked in.

"Mom?" She had her blazer on.

Paula frowned. "Honey, do you really have to wear that jacket?"

The girl obstinately put her hands in the pockets. Paula shrugged.

Their bags were side by side on the floor. Rowan sat on the bed next to the piles of folded towels and sheets, then pointed to the bags. "Are we going home?"

"I guess we are," Paula said.

"To where?"

"Why don't you let me worry about that, Ro."

"Does Grandma hate you because you had me?"

Paula grabbed her by the shoulders so she could look right into her daughter's eyes. "Don't ever say such a thing. Grandma loves you. *I* love you." She pulled her into her belly and held her fiercely close.

"Would it have been better if you'd never had me?"

"Oh, Rowan! Of course not! You're my daughter, and my life would be *awful* without you. Why would you say such a thing?" Paula squeezed her as if she could transfer her feelings to her daughter.

"If you want to live here, I will," Rowan said, and the sincerity nearly broke Paula's heart. She let her go and the two of them sat down on the bed.

"I don't think we could afford to live here unless we stayed with Grandma. And I don't know if that's really what she wants. She's lived alone a long time, you know. It would be hard to have two new people in your house."

"But do you *wish* you lived here?"

Paula laughed. "I wish I could give you a neighbourhood to live in just like this one. I wish I could give you the kind of childhood I had. We were always safe and warm and loved—" She put her hand on Rowan's head. "You're loved, Rowan. Very much."

Rowan looked away from her mother. For a minute she debated inside her head whether she should tell her what she really thought and risk hurting her feelings. She couldn't imagine that Haven Woods had ever been a good place. Ever since Old Tex had nearly drowned them both at the river, Rowan had noticed that even the air here had a strange feel to it. Or smell. Like when Darcy Peak peed on the floor at school—Darcy had taken the short bus, the kids would say—and the janitor cleaned it up with bleach. You could still smell pee under the bleach. It was like that.

There were too many cats and hardly any dogs. That wasn't normal. And the hospital was empty. Even if everyone here was really healthy, where were the old people? People who had to get tests? Broken arms, sprained ankles, heart attacks?

But she couldn't say these things to her mother, couldn't even put them into words that wouldn't sound like she was complaining. She couldn't say, *this place is weird, Mom. WTF?* And mostly she couldn't hurt her mother's feelings. Paula wanted Rowan to like Haven Woods, although it went deeper than that, she knew. And it was more confused, as if she wanted Rowan to *want* to like Haven Woods. It was all making her brain freeze.

Very thoughtfully she said, "I guess this place is different now from when you were a kid." It seemed the perfect compromise, and Rowan, had she felt better, would have felt proud of the remark.

"What do you mean?" Paula said, ruining it.

A wave of cramping hit Rowan and she groaned a little. She lay back on the bed and clutched her stomach. "I don't know."

"Your stomach still sore?

She nodded.

"I think there's been too much change for you. I think it's stress." She got up just as the phone started to ring. "I'll grab you a Tums, honey. You chew them, okay?"

Rowan nodded and Paula went to answer the phone.

It was Sanderson. Paula carried the phone back into the bedroom with her, grinning. She said to Rowan, "What do you want on your pizza?"

The girl gamely got up from the bed and yelled, "Pepperoni!"

Paula relayed this, minus the volume, and hung up. "He's taking Gusto out for a walk and then he's going to come and get us."

Mother and daughter were both happy in their own ways.

"Been a while since we've had pizza, huh?"

"I like his house," Rowan said simply.

When they got there, Sanderson hung Gusto's leash on a hook by the door and kicked his sandals off. The dogs ran to the water dish and began lapping. Rowan rushed into the living room and threw herself on the sofa, calling out that she was going to watch *real* TV for a change. Paula and Sanderson had to laugh as they headed for the kitchen.

"Now that you've had a few weeks back in Haven Woods, how do you think you're settling in?"

"Getting there," he said, "and I love the house itself. Though something weird happened the other night. It sounds stupid—"

"Then I can't wait to hear."

He held up a finger. "Let me get supper started first." He went to the stove and turned the oven dial. A huge bread maker sat on the opposite counter. He peered in.

"Forty-five minutes to pizza dough—gotta love home cooking."

Paula laughed. "So what happened?"

"I think I had peeping Tom." He laughed. "Or a peeping tomcat, anyway. Actually, I think it was a female."

Paula looked at him, a question in her eyes, as he pulled a beer out of the fridge and offered it to her. She took it, he grabbed one for himself and the two of them went into the backyard. Though the chairs from the other night were still on the lawn, they stood and looked out over the fence at the roofs of the other houses.

"A peeping cat? Really?"

"Yeah. Last night, actually. I was already asleep when I heard Gusto going nuts at the front door. Barking as if Manson—or Chapman, if you prefer a local reference—was coming up the walk with a hatchet."

As if he knew he was being talked about, Gusto appeared at the kitchen door with Old Tex behind him, both dogs panting happily, water dripping from their snouts. Paula let them out.

"So what was he barking at?"

"I'm getting to that. First I yell at Gusto to shut up, shut up—it was 3 a.m., and I didn't want to make enemies of my new neighbours—but he doesn't stop, and that's not like him. By the time I get to the door, he's bouncing around like he wants out, like he's got the trots or something. I look out the window and there's a cat out there, sitting midway up the walk, flicking its tail—"

Paula's mind skittered to the cat she'd caught on the deck after she'd been to Sanderson's the first time. The blood. *Horrible.* She shivered.

"What did you do?"

"I laughed. 'Settle down, dog,' you know. Like this is the first cat he's seen? Still, there really are a lot of cats in this 'hood."

Paula nodded.

"So I'm trying to calm Gusto down. I give him a rub, and when I look out again, there are three cats sitting there. So I open the front door and scan the yard, and that's when I see a fourth cat, in the shadow under the tree. And they're just staring at me. All I've got on is my underwear. Remember how hot it was last night?"

"Must have been quite a pair of underwear," she said. "What did you do?"

He sipped his beer. "I said, 'Shoo!'"

"Did they?"

"Not at first," he said. His smile disappeared. "They just kept staring at me. Then the one under the tree turned and walked out of the yard. When she got to the sidewalk, the others turned to follow. I've never known cats to group together like that. Have you?"

"Never. Hey, how do you know they were females?"

He shrugged. "They sure were checking me out in my underwear."

Paula laughed hard enough to get beer up her nose. It hurt, which seemed somehow funnier. Sanderson laughed too.

Rowan was lying on the sofa in Mr. Keyes's living room, absorbed in a rerun of *Friends.* She was happy. Her mom came in and sat on the couch.

"Hey, Ro, you okay in here on your own?"

Rowan sat up. "What are you guys doing outside?"

Paula put her hand on her daughter's forehead. It was not warm. "Just gabbing. Do you want to come out too?"

Rowan shook her head and gestured at the TV. "It's the one with the monkey."

Paula laughed. Everything sounded funny to her right now.

"I don't want to go to Marla's with you." Rowan said.

Behind them in the kitchen there was a brief clanging, and then the oven door opened and closed.

"Rowan, she's expecting us both."

"But I don't feel good," Rowan protested, not sounding sick in any way. Paula gave her a look. "I really don't. Maybe I have to go to the bathroom."

Paula felt gently under her daughter's jaw for lumps. Then she felt her forehead again.

"Feel it with your lips," Rowan said.

Smiling, Paula leaned over her daughter and pressed her lips against her forehead. "Hmmm," she said. "Do you have a head-ache? Should I take you back to Grandma's?"

Rowan shook her head. "No, but I better not go to Marla's. They might catch something. Can't I stay here with Mr. Keyes?"

"You like him?"

"Uh-huh. Don't you?"

Paula gave her a hug. "Okay, you can stay—he already offered."

Rowan threw her arms up over her head and fell back against the sofa. "Yay." She yawned. "I think I'm really tired," she mumbled.

Friends went to commercial. The spot was for Joanna Shaw's new program. Paula watched for a minute, and as she did, Rowan's eyes closed, her face quickly slackening. Paula waited a bit, but Rowan had really fallen asleep. Just like that. Paula got up care-fully and left on tiptoe.

—

Sanderson had tried not to eavesdrop but he had heard enough. He's heard that Rowan liked him, and it sounded as if her mother did too. As he cut up pieces of pepperoni for the pizza, he couldn't keep the grin off his face.

He rolled out the dough. Pepperoni and sausage, with some veggies thrown on to make Mom happy. Just in case Paula left Rowan with him, there was a horror movie he'd picked up that morning at the grocery store. And he always had Gusto and Old Tex as backup. They loved him. He was a dog person.

By the time Paula came into the kitchen, the pizza was rolled out, sauced up and covered with fixings. Sanderson slid it into the oven and set the timer.

"Is everything okay?"

"Yeah. She fell asleep." Paula shook her head in amazement. "That never happens. I've worked a lot of weird hours, and she'd always wait up or wake up when I got home. I hope she's not coming down with something."

"Nights and evenings, huh? Hard."

She shrugged. "What can I say? I'm in demand."

"Now that doesn't surprise me."

She looked at the floor and laughed softly, a lovely sound. Sanderson had the strongest impulse to reach out and palm the top of her head, to bury his fingers in her hair and pull her to him. She looked up and saw his expression. Her cheeks went red, her mouth opened a little in surprise.

The house was silent, the air suddenly too warm. From the oven.

"How long for the pizza?" she said. Once the words were out of her mouth, she couldn't remember what she'd asked. *Is it raining? Have you ever been to Greece?*

"Long time," he said, in the same tone. "Twenty minutes, give or take. I'm not exactly Chef Boyardee."

"Ha. I think he makes pasta."

"See?"

"Rowan's excited about having pizza. The food's been pretty basic the past few days," Paula said.

"She's a great kid. You did a good job, Paula. It couldn't have been easy."

She shrugged modestly. "She is a great kid. A good sport too. But . . . she really doesn't want to come with me tonight. I guess an evening with a bunch a women talking doesn't appeal to her the way television does."

"I meant it when I said she can stay here with me and the dogs. If you're okay with that."

"I wasn't fishing."

"I know. But this would give us a chance to hang out. Would she be comfortable with that?"

"Well, she likes your house. She said so."

"She's welcome to stay. Just leave me Marla's number in case she starts breaking stuff or stealing my beer."

Paula suddenly became aware of her hands and arms; they seemed to be dangling, impossibly weak, from her shoulders. And she couldn't find a safe place for her eyes, so she stared at the stove.

Then there he was, his hands on her arms, his face close to hers. As his lips touched hers, her spine became butter. She felt it melt until she was pressed against him, her breasts wanting to defect from her body, become part of his. This struck her as funny, and she smiled under his kiss.

He pulled back and looked at her. "Is this okay?" he asked.

She nodded, put her arms around his neck and pressed into him for a heartbeat or three. Then she let go and stepped back.

He reached out to take her hand. "Lemme give you the rest of the ten-cent tour."

"Okay."

"You've seen the kitchen," he said, and led her up the stairs.

He pointed out the mouldings around the ceilings, the old-style pedestal sink in the bathroom, the impossibly deep-set windows at the end of the hall and in the spare bedrooms. One of those bedrooms would be his home office, he explained; inside she saw a desk and chair, the desk covered in papers and files.

"You're a busy man," she said.

"I am. Business is good. I've got lots of jobs to get back to next week." His voice held a trace of pride. He turned to indicate the room across from the office.

"And this is the master bedroom. There's a little ensuite in the back. Being a bachelor and all, it's very messy, so you can't see it."

Paula laughed and pressed by him. "Now I have to see it." She went through the bedroom, which was tidy for a man living alone, and peeked into the bathroom. He was right, it was messy. He followed her in.

"Ew. Wet towel on the floor—"

"A quick shower before I came to get you. Didn't want to offend my guests."

"The soap dish is full of water. The soap'll bleed away if you're not careful, you know."

"Yeah, the place needs a woman's touch."

"A cleaning woman's touch," Paula said, smiling and wrinkling her nose. She stepped back into the bedroom and looked around. "It's not bad, though. The house is great, Sandy."

He smiled back and reached out, touched her hair. "Thanks for coming for dinner. Can we call this a date?"

She raised her eyebrows, trying to keep it light. "With my kid in tow?"

"Yes," he said.

"Okay."

And he kissed her again. It was long and lingering and full of promise. She kissed him back, the same way. It might have gone on forever if Rowan hadn't called out.

"Mom? Mr. Keyes?"

One of the dogs barked.

"Coming, honey!" she called back. They grinned stupidly at each other.

In the last few minutes before the pizza was ready, they played a game Sanderson knew called Spelling Major. You picked a word and changed one letter to make another word, for as long as you could go. When they ran out of real options, they made them up.

The pizza turned out great, for all of Sanderson's modesty about his cooking. Paula had a single piece and then noticed the time. "God, I still have to change." She saw Rowan roll her eyes at Sanderson, and that tickled her. *This is what life could be like.*

"Pizza is the most important meal of the day," Sanderson said sagely.

"A day without pizza is like a day without sunshine," Rowan added, her mouth full of it.

Paula laughed. "I had a piece. Anyway, I'm sure there will be lots of food at the party." She turned to Sanderson. "I don't think I'll stay too late. Maybe I'll even make it back before the end of the movie."

"Sounds great. Don't worry about us. We have stalwart dogs to protect us."

"Good to know. Ro, walk me to the door, hon."

Tex padded after them.

As she was slipping on her shoes, Paula said, "You're sure you'll be okay?"

"Mom," said Rowan, "stop worrying."

Paula pulled a piece of paper out of her jeans pocket and pressed it into her daughter's hand. "This is Marla's phone number and the address. If you need me you can call or come and get me, whatever you want. You're really sure?"

Rowan appeared to consider this deeply for a moment, her eyes on the floor. Then she looked at her mother. "We like him. All of us."

"Yes," Paula said, "we do."

"It feels . . . safe here," Rowan said, indicating the house with a wave of her hand.

Paula embraced her daughter as if embracing the world. As she let her go, Rowan mock-protesting the tightness of the squeeze, something dark crossed her memory for a moment

whoosh

then was gone.

"I won't stay late, okay?" She kissed her daughter on the forehead and went off to change for the party.

EIGHTEEN

PAULA LET THE HOT WATER flow over her. It hit her face and rolled down her cheeks, off her chin onto her chest, warming her breasts. She knew she had to hurry, that she'd stayed too long at Sanderson's, but a barely remembered sensuousness had overtaken her and she didn't feel inclined to shake it off. After she turned the water off, she dried herself carefully with the fluffiest of her mother's towels. She strolled to the bedroom instead of walked, she dipped instead of bent, she sighed rather than breathed.

She thought, *Could I love him?* It was an idea that seemed impossible, since she had really just met him. They'd had only a few days . . . *and*, she thought, *a time, a place.* The place being Haven Woods and the time being summer

(the crack of ball on bat)

As Paula dressed, body and soul floated together in some dreamy state, and she couldn't help it. It was as if she had to let go of one thing to get the other. She rolled pantyhose up her legs and pulled on her skirt. She sat in her bra on the edge of her mother's bed amid the same smells—soap and clean and bleach and

(worse)

grass being cut and copper and asphalt

crack . . . hiss . . . the whoosh of something shiny through the
air

I have a secret

bad nasty hard scary beautiful secret

She was just sixteen that year.

Her mother had said that morning, "Your dad wants to watch them fix the Rileys' roof. We'll be there all day."

They might not have gone back except that everyone's parents were at the Rileys.' If the boys had kept playing ball, if they'd all gone to the pool, if the girls hadn't gotten bored at the ball field . . . That thought still had the power to alarm her. In the years since David had died she'd gone over scenario after scenario: what if she'd not been there?

(what if what if)

The girls had followed the boys to where they were playing on the ball diamond, and they had left when the boys seemed more interested in the game than in them. She wondered some-times if everything would have been different if they'd stayed put. If the girls had sat on the bleachers and waited for them, they might all have gone for ice cream afterwards or wandered over to the store for slushies. If they had just watched instead of getting bored and leaving, it might all have turned out another way.

(if if if a butterfly beats its wings in California there's a hur-ricane in—)

It was funny but the names were burned into her memory, even after all these years: Terry, Danny and Pete, Jake, Lonnie Keyes. She and Marla, with Patty, Jake's sister. Lisa Evans had been at the park too, but she had left later. Paula's mind had been occu-pied with feeling scared and maybe mad at David, at least a little bit from the night before.

The night before, they'd gone down to the river, just the two of them, and Paula had tried to talk to him about her *secret*, but he had Roman Hands and Russian Fingers, as they used to say. Her mouth had gotten dry and she had forgotten everything in the rush of feeling. They were only human, after all.

C'mon Pauls, just this once.

Of course it hadn't been just this once, but she knew, even if he didn't, that it wasn't like he could get her pregnant again. So she hadn't told him. And the next day she'd been hanging out at the ball park and maybe she was a little quiet and maybe Marla had at least noticed, because one of them said, *let's go try on tops* and they left.

The girls had gone the long way back to Paula's, walking up Proctor to Princess Treats Ice Cream and buying Tiger Tigers, talking about school and boys and Pete and David and Danny, the three cutest boys.

That morning, when Paula was leaving the house, Audra had told her, *We're going to the Rileys. Your dad wants to watch them fix the roof. We'll be there all day. Take your key.*

They went from the ice-cream store to Paula's and they raided her closet, trying on all her clothes and finally trading tops with each other. Paula put on shorts—funny how she could remember them so well. They were blue calico short-shorts. Her prettiest pair, the cotton soft and the cut hugging her curves in a perfect and promising way

(and she knew in the back of her mind that her days with those shorts were numbered)

She knew in the back of her mind that her days were numbered, period, an unacknowledged thought, but there nonetheless all the time. She had slipped the shorts on over still-slim hips with a kind of knowing. But everything changed in that instant. She felt the swell of change pressing against the waistband, the panic that came with it, and suddenly she wanted to go back to the ball park where the boys were and pretend she was just an ordinary sixteen-year-old girl—not pregnant, not scared.

Let's go to my house and get some money Marla had said when they left the house. Paula took the key from around her neck and locked the door, and the three of them headed down the street, so pretty and young. She couldn't remember why Marla had wanted money. They were only halfway to the Rileys' when the boys caught up with them. Everything got louder, the roughhousing and their sheer physical presence changing the dynamic.

What did they talk about? Everybody was reading Stephen King that summer; Paula couldn't remember which book. *Oh, I'm not going to. That's too scary* Marla had said. They wondered whether anybody was going to the beach on the weekend and said how they couldn't wait until Pete or David got his licence so they could drive around Haven Woods.

Lazy things, little nothings. They had been so bored and content. A perfect summer day.

But that wasn't exactly true. She and her mom had been fighting for most of that year, at first just once in awhile, taking care afterwards to be extra civil with each other, and then later not bothering to be civil, and not bothering to fight in private either. There were slammed doors, broken plates, and tears from both of them. She blamed her mom, since her mom was fighting with her dad too, not the way she and Paula fought, but using great long silences of disapproval. Her dad would disappear into the spare room for whole evenings, drinking, while her mother slammed pots and cupboards in the kitchen. Briefly, she remembered, in the weeks before that horrible day, they had all seemed to wear out and a state of uneasy unnatural truce had ruled.

(*your dad wants to watch them fix the roof*)

When they got to the Rileys, they wandered into the backyard among the adults, who were standing in loose clutches around the patio, wove around the mothers and the dads, the boys slouching and punching each other, the girls watching the boys from under eyelashes and bangs. In her mind that afternoon in the yard existed as a complete scene: Pete standing there, his hand still in his glove, his glove tucked under his left arm, leaning a little, his freckled cheeks plumped in a grin. Danny slouching, not laughing but serious, as he always was. Jake had just grabbed Lonnie by the head and had him bent over

noogie

and they were laughing. Sandy's jeans dusty on the bum from the sandbags, most of their gloves scattered on the grass . . . David—

David standing beside his dad alongside Paula's dad, Walter, all three of them looking up, of course. At the roof.

(*your dad wants to watch them fix the roof*)

Audra was on the patio with Izzy, smoking as if she were in the movies, her torso tilted back, her hips thrust forward, her arms crossed to prop up the hand that held the cigarette.

All those impressions that had lasted so long—for years—were of just a second in time. The girls

wanna go back to the

on the grass with Audra and Chick. Above it all, three strangers, men, stood on the roof, a machine whirring, gnawing into something above.

Marla had turned to her mother *can I have five dollars?*—and about halfway through she turned back and looked over her shoulder, tossing them a smile—*We're going to*—

Paula still didn't know what she had been about to say. *Stay for dinner? Go to the movies?* Because her dad had called out, the words lost but the timbre one of alarm. All of it adding up to the same thing—*No!*

In that moment, twelve sets of eyes turned first to the three of them standing there: Mr. Riley, David and Paula's dad. Mr. Riley, his mouth wide open, a twist in his lips, was screaming by the time they all looked over.

From the roof, in a split second—so fast Jake still had Lonnie in an embrace, so fast Audra was watching without expression, so fast Izzy had just turned her head—something came gliding down, a flash of red that matched the trim on the house and went very nicely with the ochre stone patio. It came down in a perfect inverted arc, almost invisible, so thin and fine was the aluminum sheet they were cutting on the roof. It came sliding, gliding down in the direction of the three men.

Towards David.

David! Izzy had screamed, knocking over the little patio table and the drink that had been on it. *No! Not David! David—*

But it was David. The perfect arc had been aiming for him the entire time. It came down from the roof in a graceful swoop and cut his head right off.

Paula stuck her fists into her eyes and rubbed hard. Her nose was red and hot from crying, but her tears felt like a betrayal, crying over a boy who had been dead more than twelve years. What had been the last thing he'd said to her. *Aw, c'mon, Pauls?* Had that been it? Or could she say that his last words to her had been spoken with his hand, when he'd touched the small of her back just before they got to the Rileys'? Not territorial, not possessive, just as usual.

Then he'd run on ahead. His hand had slid off her back, leaving his fingers behind to move more slowly, like water swooning off the beach after the wave has already receded. *That* was the last thing he'd said.

Sanderson had touched her in exactly that spot, the place where if she tried she could still conjure up the feeling of David's hands, his slow release of her. Sanderson's hands had been there not an hour before, holding her tightly to him. A man, not a boy.

The same place.

(I love you David and I love our daughter)

Paula wiped the tears from her eyes and her cheeks. She stood up and pulled on her blouse, then went into the bathroom and did her makeup. Carefully.

Somewhere between brushing her hair and finding a pair of her mother's shoes that fit, she stumbled forward into the rest of her life. She realized that she finally wanted to move on from that terrible day when everything had stalled inside her. She wanted to make a real life for herself and for Rowan. She wanted to make it right. She would start by telling all of them tonight about Rowan.

David's child.

For a moment she wondered why Izzy had never guessed. Who else could have gotten Paula pregnant? But maybe she'd been so shocked by her loss she'd never even thought. Had never sat there counting on her fingers. Had never seen, even when she met Rowan at the hospital, that the girl had her son's eyes. How could anyone be so blind?

Izzy brushed her hair back from her forehead until it was so slick and flat she looked bald. Her hair, left undyed, would be white. That would never happen though. She was simply too vain. She put the comb down. In the mirror her expression was stern and there were circles under her eyes. Of course there were.

Fresh clothes were laid out on the bed. She dropped her robe and pulled on underpants. She kept her eyes down; she didn't want to see any more. At that moment, if she had looked up she would have seen herself in the glass of the window. She didn't need to look at herself to remember who she was and what she would see if she looked. Izzy put her hand on her belly and slowly dragged it up under her breast. Her left breast. Near her heart, of course.

Her finger went immediately to the scar, a puckered pink half-moon with a small twist in the corner where it had torn—He, or it, had torn it—twenty years earlier and healed off-kilter. If you tilted your head sideways it looked like a half-hearted grin. The scar was as pink as if it were new, but otherwise there was no indication that it had been recently reopened. Except for a lingering smell and a slight throb, which always happened on the *sabbat*. To them all.

Izzy slid a T-shirt, soft and white and expensive, over her bare breasts, and the scar disappeared. But like a tongue that teases a sore tooth, she couldn't help but touch it again. It would never truly heal or go away—that was part of the deal. And she thought of it that way, as a wound.

She pulled her jeans on, every movement slow even though she needed to hurry. They would bring Paula and the girl to the Chapman place, and she had to be there waiting for them. After she had slipped on her flats, she glanced once at her reflection. She looked like a well-to-do woman, climbing the hill to middle age but still lovely, going out to play cards, to have coffee, to meet with her book club. If anyone saw her, that would be what they would think.

No one would. See her.

On her way down the hall she paused and opened the door to David's room. She stuck her head in and breathed deeply, holding the air in her lungs so that whatever of him was left inside there, whatever air he might have breathed out that still remained, was now inside her. It helped, but not much. She closed the door and went downstairs into the kitchen.

The leather apron with the knives was on the counter where

she'd left it. She put on an apron over her clean clothes and ran water into the sink. She cleaned the blood off the bigger knife, carefully, because the edge was still razor sharp. She dried it with a tea towel, the one that matched the washcloth. Ivy danced across the hem. The set was understated, elegant; that was how she liked things. Izzy ran the ball of her thumb over the edge of the blade, frowning. There was a small nick from where, she suspected, it had hit bone.

She got the stone out of the drawer by the sink and began to run the knife over it. She had to take the knives with her. Not for the girl. The thing in the house would take her for his master. The knives were for anyone who tried to stop it from happening.

She rolled the newly sharpened blade into the pouch and tied the thong around it tightly. At the Chapman house, by now her previous offering would have been consumed. The thing was waiting grudgingly for his main course.

The Murder House, the kids used to call it. It was apt.

But not long now and all would be set to rights. They would be thirteen. The Father would be appeased. Everyone had to make sacrifices. Hers had been the greatest.

One more, very necessary chore. Izzy went out the front door into the cool of the evening and stood on Proctor Street. She turned slowly, raising her arms as she did. She was careful to cast her eyes over every house as she turned. She sing-songed, "Early to bed, late to rise, hear no evil, see no evil, see that you do. No trouble for me, no trouble for you." She dragged out the last syllable of the spell until her magic covered the whole of Haven Woods. Then she stopped.

As she lowered her arms, the lights went out in the houses, one after another. The neighbourhood went dark with sleep.

—

Tim was quiet, finally asleep, still dressed and on top of the covers. He was curled around the basketball, his arms cradling it like a baby, his sweet face twisted into an expression of concentration: his game face. She draped a blanket over him and the ball. Even in the dark room he looked too pale.

Marla left his door slightly open and went to her daughter's room. Amy too was sleeping, or appeared to be. The night light was enough to illuminate her peaceful face

(please just sleeping)

and she sat on the bed and put her hand on Amy's head. Her hair was silky and warm. She was lying on her back on top of the blankets, exactly as Marla had left her. She had tried to put her pyjamas on, but Amy's limbs were stiff and uncooperative, and she had been reluctant to force them in what had felt like an unnatural direction

(she remembered all too well what happened when you tried to bend your doll's arm the wrong way)

She eased the covers out from under her daughter and tucked her in, pulling the blankets up to her chest. The girl's breathing was smooth and easy. She kissed her forehead. *Mommy's pretty doll.*

Her heart ached. This was her doing.

Doug was in his office downstairs, oblivious to the drama. If she went into the office she'd find him working, hunched over paperwork at his desk, his forehead wrinkled, muttering to himself.

if you're going to marry such trash the least he can do is make something of himself

Doug had been a happy-go-lucky man whom she loved, and so, as her mother said, she had made him better. Just as she'd made her slightly chubby, definitely normal children better. What had she done?

She could hear the others moving about in the living room. Esme had arrived first, then Glory with Sharie, Joanna, Bridget and Ursula. When Paula got here, she would have to join them. But now she climbed the stairs again to her daughter's bedroom, stretched out beside her little girl and watched her sleep.

(please just sleep)

Marla's very pretty house was at the top of a broad lawn, lushly green in the evening light. A ring of shrubs surrounded it that seemed to march around to the back. All was still. Pastoral. There was a flutter at the curtains as Paula approached, and she raised her hand in a self-conscious wave.

She felt self-conscious, watched even, as she made her way around to the side of the house, where she opened the screen door and knocked. Why was her silly heart pounding? This was just a night out with Marla's "girls." How bad could they be? Especially considering that lately her girls had been strippers

(it's a sisterhood ha ha)

There was no answer, so she knocked again and then finally pulled open the door. She poked her head in. "Marla?"

No answer.

"Marla?" she called again, when she reached the hall.

A big woman suddenly loomed towards her. She grinned, her teeth so white Paula could hardly concentrate on the rest of her face. "Hel-*lo*," she said, her voice almost flirtatious.

"Hi," Paula answered. "I'm Paula—"

When the light from the kitchen doorway hit her, Paula saw that she was beautiful. She was dressed in black and her hair was dark and fashionably short. She thrust her hand at Paula. "I'm Esme." Her grip was strong, her flesh very warm. "Marla's still with the children, so I'm playing hostess," she explained, dragging out the final syllable with élan.

Paula smiled, shyly, because she couldn't help herself. And

all she could think of to say in response was "Oh."

"You have to come in and meet the rest of the girls. We've been waiting on you." She glanced over Paula's shoulder. "Where's your daughter? We thought she was coming with you."

"Rowan," Paula said. "I'm afraid she isn't feeling well."

"*Really*? Does Marla know?"

Paula shook her head. "Not yet. I'm sorry," she added, feeling oddly compelled to apologize. The woman was still holding her hand, and she tugged her farther down the hall.

"Well, come on in. Everyone is expecting you."

The drapes were drawn in the candlelit living room. The flames flickered in mirrors and crystal vases, even the chandelier on the ceiling. It was beautiful, and she couldn't help but let out a little gasp. "This is so pretty," she said.

"It *is* beautiful," Esme said. "We all have beautiful homes. Do you have a beautiful home, Paula?"

What is with this woman? Paula thought.

The others were clustered at the far end of the room. The first to turn towards the new arrival strode slowly over to Paula, holding out her hand. "Bridget," she said. "And you're Paula." She shook her hand and then let it drop. Just as Esme had, she looked beyond Paula. "And where's this little girl I've heard so much about?" Not a hair was astray, and she was very pretty.

Esme said pointedly, "She didn't bring her."

"Why not?" Bridget demanded.

Paula was at a loss, so she chuckled. "Don't worry, I'll bring her next time. She had a bit of an upset stomach so I left her with a friend."

The other women had now gathered closely around her.

"Which friend?" Esme's voice was loud.

"Um, he's new to the neighbourhood. I'm sure you don't know him."

They were all lovely, and every one of them was in black. The fashion standard in Haven Woods, apparently. Paula felt underdressed.

A plumpish redhead wearing—were those really old-fashioned lady gloves? Wasn't that some sort of fashion crime?—spoke up next. "We'll just have to go get her." The others giggled. "I'm Glory. I used to be really fat. Want to see?"

Before Paula could respond she pulled out an old Polaroid and thrust it at her. The woman in the photo had to weigh at least three hundred pounds. She was standing at a stove, a huge smile on her face, a wooden spoon in her hand. "My God," Paula said, "that can't be you."

"It is," Glory said brightly. She took the picture back and tucked it away as she looked Paula over. "Wouldn't you like to lose a little weight?"

"Excuse me?"

Glory laughed, all tinkly. "Oh, I'm just saying. There are always things we want to change about ourselves, aren't there? What would you change?"

Paula had a sudden memory of kissing Sanderson in the kitchen

you're so beautiful

"I don't know. I guess I'd have to think about it."

"Well, I suspect you would like a beautiful house," Bridget said. They all laughed.

"Yes," Paula said, because it seemed like the right answer.

There were so many of them. Ursula was Bridget's sister and they worked together. There was Glory, who used to be fat. Sharie was a dancer, though her poor leg was swollen and wrapped in bandages, looking huge against the tiny, fit rest of her body. On closer viewing, Esme was wearing a nearly see-through top and no bra. And, as Marla had promised, the famous Joanna Shaw was there. Paula felt shy meeting her—she had just seen her on TV—

but Joanna's eyes were distant and her words were quiet, completely unlike her television personality.

When the introductions were finished, Bridget led Paula to the sofa, putting her in the middle between her and Esme. The other women settled themselves across from them in a selection of love-seats and overstuffed armchairs. It felt strange to be the centre of attention.

A buffet of treats was spread on a side table, but no one was eating. Or drinking. What kind of a girls' night was this? She didn't feel it was right to ask, although a glass of wine would have been good to take the edge off.

She gestured to Joanna and grinned. "I just saw you on television. You sure got here fast."

"It's taped in the afternoon," Joanna said gravely.

"Oh, of course."

"I'm sure you're a big fan of Joanna's. We all are." Esme reached over and gave Joanna's knee a squeeze. The woman hardly reacted except to smile wanly. "She got to the big time with a little help from her friends, right? Right?"

Joanna nodded at Esme, her expression unchanging.

"We could all use a little help sometimes, isn't that true?" Esme stressed.

"Tell us, Paula," Bridget said, "what do you want out of life?"

Paula laughed—it was such a bald question. The room was silent, waiting for her answer. She wondered where Marla was. She wished she would appear. "I would have to think about that too," she said.

"Come on, Paula," Esme butted in. "We all want the same things, don't we? A beautiful home, a good man, the best for our families. Isn't that what you want too?"

"Right now all I want is a drink. I would love a glass of wine," Paula said finally.

Bridget turned to her sister. "Good idea. Ursula, get her a drink. Get us all one."

Without speaking, Ursula got up.

"You must want a husband," Esme said.

"I want all of that. I—" Paula faltered. They were too close to her. They were paying too much attention. They were too lovely. She felt as if the joke was on her, that at any moment Marla was going to jump out. *Ha ha ha ha, gotcha, Paula!*

"You could have it all," Esme said, seriously. "You could have everything you want."

"I got thin," Glory said.

"I'm a dancer," Sharie said, but she was looking at her leg.

"And I have a very successful business," Bridget said. "Maybe you've heard of it—Bridget Bakes?"

"Oh goodness, yes!" Paula said. They were beyond Paula's budget, but she'd seen them often: exhaustively beautiful things, tiny cakes iced to perfection, decorated with real flowers. She was impressed, and it showed on her face.

"I get laid whenever I want," Esme volunteered, and laughed hard, and everyone joined in.

Paula laughed uncomfortably. *This is a really strange party*, she thought. "You're all very lucky," she said.

"We've had help. Everyone needs a little help now and then, don't you think?" Bridget put her hand on Paula's arm.

"Yes, I think that's true." A silence fell, and Paula let it ride uncomfortably for a moment. Then she said, "Does Marla know I'm here?"

Ursula came in with a tray of wineglasses, already filled. "Here we are," she said quietly, and handed glasses to everyone. Paula was last. "And for you, Paula."

"Thank you." She took the glass. Everyone stared.

"To new friends." Bridget raised her glass and the others followed suit.

Paula raised hers too and took a tiny sip. She wasn't really a wine drinker, but she could tell this white wasn't so good. It was bitter and sweet at the same time; she tried not to grimace.

The others took similarly genteel sips, echoing, "To new friends."

Esme leaned in close. "Now where did you say your daughter was?"

Paula took another sip of wine. *Where's Marla?*

NINETEEN

PIZZA CRUSTS AND PLATES smeared with tomato sauce sat on the low table in the TV room. A half-drunk glass of pop and a just-opened beer sweated on the tabletop. Rowan burped daintily into her hand.

"Oops. Sorry," she said.

Mr. Keyes held up a DVD. "I've got a classic for us to watch. Not too scary, in deference to your mom, but good just the same." He held out the package. On the cover a sleeping man lay on his side while something green and slimy hovered above him.

"*Invasion of the Body Snatchers.* The 1978 version. You're going to love it."

Rowan smiled and nodded and hoped it wasn't in black-and-white.

He poked the Open button, and when the tray slid out he put the DVD in the machine. It closed smoothly. He found the right remote and pressed buttons and clicked menus.

The dogs were lying on the floor in front of the sofa. Gusto had his head down between his paws, but Old Tex was watching the front door. Now and then Gusto would raise his head too, and he whined sometimes, looking at Old Tex. But then he would return to the floor with a sigh. Old Tex never varied his pose. Rowan knew, because she was watching him.

"Mr. Keyes? Where's my blazer?" she asked suddenly. "I want to put it on."

He turned, remote still pointed at the screen. "I don't know. Maybe your mom hung it in the front closet."

"Right." As Rowan got up, music poured into the room from several sources, surprising her.

"Surround sound." Mr. Keyes grinned.

"Cool," she said and went looking for her jacket.

Sanderson pressed the fast-forward button through the ads at the beginning of the disc and paused at the trailers. He grimaced and rubbed his face; a slight headache was coming on. Rowan had complained about a stomach ache—maybe they were all coming down with something.

"I paused it," he called to her.

Her blazer was hanging in the closet as Mr. Keyes had said. Rowan slipped it on and put her hand in the pocket. The piece of paper with his number was still there, folded, maybe illegible now after her trip into the water, but even if she couldn't read it, it was a talisman of some kind. She left it in her pocket.

She dug out the makeshift necklace and hung it around her neck, the twine rough against her skin. The little Jesus on his cross looked a bit like the pictures of ovaries they showed in sex-ed class, but she knew who it was supposed to be, and that made her feel safe. School-safe and something-else-safe. Safer.

She was tucking the cross under her T-shirt just as a terrible cramp hit her right in the . . . ovaries . . . She clutched her middle, groaning.

From the TV room she heard Mr. Keyes call, "Rowan? Are you all right?"

"I'm okay. Stubbed my toe. I'll be right there." She stood up, grimacing, and made her way to the bathroom. A couple of times she touched her shirt where the crucifix hung beneath it.

In the bathroom Rowan pulled her jeans down and sat on the toilet, absolutely uncertain about what her body was trying to tell her. Another wave of cramping hit her. She peed, then sat a minute more wishing for *something* to happen, even diarrhea, so she could feel better and go watch the stupid movie. She wiped herself, glanced down—

Oh. My. God.

The tissue, and her underpants, were stained with blood. She made a face. *Gross.* Then slowly she realized, *I beat Caleigh and Patty!* She had her *period*.

"Holy crap. Wow." She sat there on the toilet and thought of ways she could tell Patty (that bitch), phrasing it nonchalantly to seem like such a pain and a bore, just a thing that women got. Women. *So yeah, I was at this* guy's *house and totally got my rag—*

It occurred to her that she *was* at some guy's house, and she *had* totally got her rag on. She blushed, realizing that she had no way to deal with it. She looked around the bathroom, half hoping God or someone like Him had placed a Kotex dispenser

(I will never make fun again)

in there like the one in the second-floor washroom at St. Mary's. She leaned over and opened the door to the cupboard under the sink

(just for second thinking about the warm, *breathing* bags under her grandmother's sink)

but there was just a four-pack of toilet paper and a rusty can of Ajax, probably left by the people who used to live there.

"*Mr. Keyes!*" she finally shouted through the door. "I need my mother!"

Sanderson was looking through the cupboard in the kitchen,

where he thought he'd put the Aspirin, when he heard Rowan calling. He ran to the bathroom and stood outside the door.

"What's wrong, Rowan?"

"I need my mother."

"She's at Marla's by now. Can I help?"

"Can you phone her? I've got the number in my jacket pocket. I need her right now."

"Okay, okay. Where's your jacket?"

There was a pause. "In here."

Sanderson laughed in spite of the pain in his head. "Should I come in?"

"No! Wait, I'll shove it under the door."

While he waited he thought, *Maybe diarrhea*, and then he thought, *Poor kid, she's just at that age when these things are really embarrassing.*

Just at that age.

As the little piece of paper came wiggling under the door, he started to put two and two together. He grimaced with embarrassment for her. And himself.

He bent down to grab the note. "Rowan, I'm on it. I'll get your mom. It's all going to be okay. Is there anything—Do you have—"

"I want my *mom!*"

"Absolutely. Hang tight, kiddo." He ran for the cordless on the counter in the kitchen, grabbed it and thumbed the on button. He punched in the number on the paper and put the phone to his ear.

The pause had come off on the DVD player and he could hear the trailers starting. He headed for the living room, phone to his ear, found the remote and paused the movie again.

The phone wasn't yet ringing at the other end. He shut it off and turned it back on, but now he wasn't getting a signal. He stuffed the handset onto the charger base and went searching for his cell, calling out, "Rowan, the battery is dead. I'm just going to find my cell, okay?"

He took the stairs two at a time and did a quick scan of the bedroom, spotting it on the table beside the bed. He flipped the phone open. No signal, even though he was upstairs and the signal was usually stronger there. He walked down the hall with it, watching for bars. At the end of the hall he got one.

Sanderson dialled Marla's number. Even with his head pounding and a little girl trapped in his bathroom, what he was thinking was, *I'm going to fall in love with Paula.*

After four rings, someone picked up. "Hello, who is this?" a woman's voice asked.

"Hi, is this Marla? Marla, this is Sanderson Keyes. I'm Paula Wittmore's—" Paula Wittmore's what? *Friend.*

He was about to say it when she spoke. "This isn't Marla. And Paula isn't here. She's been—" The line crackled, the signal breaking up. "—detai—can't—"

"The connection is bad," he yelled. "Where's Paula?"

He waited, but there was only crackling on the line. "Paula?"

"—not here—"

"Where is she?" he shouted again. There was static and then what sounded like a laugh. The phone beeped twice. He checked the bars; the display blinked SIGNAL DROPPED, SIGNAL DROPPED. Disgusted, he shut the phone and stood indecisively for a minute. Then he ran to the stairs, taking the first one on the fly.

There was a second when it passed through his mind, *Stairs are slippery. Why did I use the glossy varnish?* Then he pitched forward, all two hundred pounds of him barrelling down, his ankle striking the edge of the step and sliding off at an angle. The crack was so loud, so alarming, that even as he screamed in pain he knew exactly what had happened.

The phone went flying out of his hand, disappearing into space.

There was a pregnant moment of silence after Sanderson hit the landing at the bottom of the stairs, the wind knocked out of him. The dogs came running, a frantic Gusto getting in his face. Sanderson had to push him away, but he and Old Tex continued to hover like a couple of old ladies. It would almost be comical, except for the pain. And then he remembered Rowan in the bathroom. *Oh God, where is Paula?*

At the moment Sanderson Keyes broke his ankle, Paula was being poured a second glass of wine by Ursula, who seemed to be the waitress for the evening. Thinking of her in those terms made Paula grin, and she wondered a little at herself. *Why so easily amused?* She did feel funny. Was wine more potent than beer? It had not improved the evening.

Joanna was leaning close, explaining how she had got where she was. "When you're a little girl, you think you're going to grow up to be someone. We all think we're going to be *someone*, you know? And I was, in a limited way. I was . . . someone. But you want more. You always want more, right?"

Paula had a feeling that her version of *more* would be different from Joanna Shaw's. But she nodded.

Joanna said, "Exactly. So you do what you have to do. You find a *way*." This seemed to be the point she wanted to make, because then she leaned back against the sofa where Bridget had been sitting—where had Bridget gone?—and said nothing more.

"What our resident celebrity means," Esme added, "is that we want what we want. And we do what we have to do to get it. Do you understand, Paula?"

She felt as if she was the target of a hard sell of some kind. Like when a vacuum cleaner salesman comes to your door and won't leave until you agree, "Yes, I like my house to be clean." She tried to focus on the question, but the sound of the women's voices was all she could take in.

"Where did you say your girl was?" Bridget asked.

"Sanderson's." To say the name was pleasing to her. *Sanderson.* It felt nice to say it, to think it. She repeated it in her head. She wondered if she was drunk.

"I would do anything for my children," Glory said. Esme looked sharply at her.

"Of course," Paula agreed.

"Children aren't everything," Esme said.

"I have a little brother," Sharie offered. No one responded.

Ursula poured more wine. "You're the waitress tonight," Paula said, smiling gently at her. "I was a waitress. In a bar. A terrible bar." She cupped her mouth with a hand and whispered confidentially, "A stripper bar." The women tittered.

"What would you give to never have to work in a stripper bar again?" Bridget asked.

"It's not so bad," she said. Defensively this time.

Bridget smiled winningly at her. "But if you don't want to do it, you don't have to. You can join us."

Paula picked up the wineglass that Ursula had refilled and held it to her lips. Then she thought better of it and set it down. She was feeling . . . funny. She'd been drunk a time or two in her life, and this was like it, but different. Her body felt tired, loose. Her tongue seemed too big for her mouth. But she didn't have a *drunk* feeling.

"Drink up," Esme said. "Who is this Sanderson? Is he your boyfriend?"

Sanderson. She smiled in spite of herself. "No," she said, embarrassed, her face flushed. From wine.

"Oooh, yes he is, I bet," Sharie said. "I like a guy at dance class. He's very tall. I like tall men. Is your boyfriend tall?"

Esme snapped, "Nobody cares, child."

Sharie shut up.

"So where does he live?" Esme pressed. "Near your mom's?"

"Esme, we were talking about Paula," Bridget said, shooting her a look. Paula saw it. *These women are strange*, she thought again. The conversations were hard to follow.

"She's going to join us," Bridget said. She squeezed in between Paula and the glassy-eyed Joanna. Joanna shifted lazily, but didn't get up.

"Join you?" Paula said.

"You can have everything you've ever wanted," Bridget said. "It's simple, really. Don't you want your life to be perfect?"

Paula thought, *What do I have to buy?* But she said, "Where is Marla? I should go, but I would like to say hello to her before I do."

"Don't go," Ursula said, with force.

"I'm here, Paula. Please don't go yet."

She turned and there was Marla, silhouetted in the candlelight. She too wore black. She looked slender and perfect, her hair falling softly over her shoulders. She came close and took Paula's hands in hers. "I was with my children. They're not feeling well, but I suspect they'll feel better soon." There were dark rings under her eyes.

"Are you all right?"

"I'm fine. I'm sorry for my absence. I'm so glad you came." It sounded rote. Like something you'd say to a stranger. It occurred to Paula that she *was* a stranger, and then, out of nowhere, she remembered that she had something to tell.

"I've got something I want to talk to you about," she said to Marla. But there were too many eyes looking at her. She couldn't do it now.

"I want to hear it," Marla said.

Esme got up so Marla could sit beside her girlhood friend.

"Paula, my children are sick."

"I'm sorry to hear that. Rowan didn't feel well tonight—"

Marla cut her off. "Can you help me with my children?"

"Of course," Paula said, confused. "What can I do?"

"All you have to do is join us."

The room fell dead silent. Marla was still holding Paula's hands. It was uncomfortable, but it was Marla, so she didn't pull away.

"Your poor mother has been sick too," Marla said. "And Bridget and Ursula have had business problems. You haven't met Aggie, yet, but she's an old, old woman now and she'll die if you don't help us. Even Sharie—her leg has swelled right up, like a melon." Sharie held her leg out awkwardly. It looked painful.

"It's bad times for us right now." Marla pressed Paula's fingers, ready to say her next bit, but instead she sighed. Her eyes dropped from Paula's and she turned away.

Esme said, "Marla?"

"Be quiet for a moment," Marla said. "I'm thinking." She looked around the room. "Where's Rowan? Is she watching TV?"

"Rowan isn't here," Glory deadpanned from a chair.

Marla looked at Paula. "You didn't bring her?"

Paula shook her head. "She wasn't feeling well. What's this about my mother? What does she have to do with this?"

"Oh," Marla said. She seemed to ponder that.

"My mother, Marla. What about her?"

Esme poked Marla in the side. "Quit thinking so much. Find out where Rowan is, and let's get on with things."

Marla turned back to Paula and opened her mouth to speak, but nothing came out. She closed it again.

"What's going on, Mars?" Paula said.

As if the childhood nickname had upset her, Marla let go of Paula's hands and shook her head.

Esme groaned. "Marla, get out of the way."

Marla stood. To the room she said, "I'm sorry, I'm just so tired. The kids haven't been . . . right." She tried to smile.

Esme sat down where Marla had been. "Paula, all you have to do is join us. We're like a club. A women's club. It's no big deal. You simply join and then you'll have everything you want. Everyone will be fine. Your mother will be fine. Just nod."

Paula was watching Marla, who was backing away from them all. "Mars? Are you okay?"

"Paula, you've got to concentrate," Esme butted in. "We know all about your life in the city—it's shit. Room for improvement! We're proposing that you join us as we are, and then your life will be better. Okay? Done. There, now let's get going." She stood, yanking Paula to her feet. Paula squealed at the suddenness of it. So did several of the women.

"Join you in what? What *are* you?" Her thoughts felt fat and sluggish.

"Honey, it rhymes with *bitch*," Esme said. There were surprised snickers from the others.

"Huh?" Paula was trapped between Esme, the sofa and the table.

"Well, what rhymes with *bitch*? Let's see." Esme pretended to ponder this as she held Paula upright. "Ditch. Kitsch. Pitch." She grinned with those unnaturally white teeth. "Rich. Switch. What else, Paula?"

Paula's mind was too slow for this. She shook her head.

Glory yelled, "Witch!"

Everyone erupted into laughter. Paula looked around at Marla, who wasn't laughing.

"Witch?" she said, uncomprehendingly.

Esme nodded. "That's right—witch. It's no big deal. You don't have to grow a wart or anything. You just have to come with us."

"And tell us where we can pick up the kid," Bridget said, close to Paula's ear.

Esme patted her on the back and then smoothed Paula's hair off her shoulder. "It'll be great. You'll love it. Your hair will be thicker, your skin so clear and smooth."

Bridget grinned. "You'll tan without burning, and your whites will be whiter without bleach."

Esme slipped a hand under Paula's jacket and ran it delicately over her too-soft belly. "This will go away. And your mother's punishment will be over. Don't you want that?"

"What has this got to do with my mother?" Paula tried to shift away, but Esme wrapped her arms around her in a tight embrace. Bridget grabbed her hands.

"Let me go, guys."

"Sorry, we can't," Bridget said. "I'm afraid we need you."

"Need me for what?"

"Honey, we *need* you. You're an alumna—"

"What?"

"Ever heard that expression 'blood is thicker than water'? Audra's one of us. You're Audra's daughter, and that makes you an alumna. Blood—it counts for a lot with Him."

The others nodded.

"Your mother's being punished. If you cooperate with us she'll be well again. We all will. Be a good sport, Paula. We're running out of time," Bridget said.

"My mother's one of—" She couldn't finish the sentence. Her head was spinning from the wine and the nonsense. It *had* to be nonsense.

"She is," Esme said. "She's. A. Witch."

"My mother is not a witch!" The sentence sounded crazy coming out of her mouth.

"We need that little girl." Ursula waggled a finger in Paula's face. "You could have saved us a lot of trouble if you'd just brought her with you. She was *expected*. Now we have to go through a whole rigmarole to find her."

"Marla? What's going on?" Paula's voice rose in panic.

"Paula, I'm . . . sorry," her friend said. "My children are . . . in trouble. You knew me before. Before I was—"

"Stop fussing," Bridget said firmly.

Glory moved in and grabbed Paula by the upper arm. "Another finger coming loose," she said to no one in particular.

"Marla!" Paula was pleading now.

"*Crackerjack*," Marla said, in a deep voice not her own. A man's voice. The man from Blondie's. Paula screamed.

"Remember? *Crackerjack*," Marla said sadly, in the same voice. Then in her own voice, "Paula, you knew me before I was . . . evil."

"All right, all right," Esme said impatiently. "Stop making this like a crime movie where everyone explains everything in the final scene. I *hate* that. Let's go." She yanked on Paula and Paula stumbled after her.

"They do that on *CSI* too," Joanna volunteered.

"We have to get moving." Bridget was looking at her watch.

"Road trip!" Sharie shouted, clapping her hands together. "Paula, thank you so much! Auditions are next week—I'll get my leg back!"

Paula dug her feet in and yelled, "Let me go!" She tried to pull her hands away from Bridget's, who held fast.

Glory's weirdly gloved hands wrapped tighter around Paula's right arm, pulling it down. "Don't!" she screamed. "My fingers are falling off!"

"Okay, wait. This is stupid. Somebody just *do* something to her." Bridget said.

Paula tried to jam her elbow into Glory, but she was holding back, still unable to accept that this was happening. Her rational mind just couldn't believe it.

The women looked at Marla. Esme said, "Do something. You're the best at this."

Marla shook her head. "I can't."

"You have to, Mar," Esme said.

Marla shook her head again.

"You fucking crone, get on it!"

Paula couldn't believe her ears. *Crone? Rhymes with witch.* She said it out loud. "You're really witches?"

Esme grinned. "You're catching on. Practically one of us. Here's a tidbit for you. You know what I hate?" she said, getting in close to Paula's face. "I hate when they add a 'k' to *magic*. New Age bullshit—I hate that."

Paula laughed. "You really think you're witches? That's hysterical. C'mon, you guys, joke's over. What is this, really?"

Esme ignored her. "Marla, come on. Now she's insulting us."

"What are you going to do, burn a candle and tell me my fortune? This is ridiculous. Let me go. I have to get my daughter."

"We know where she is," Joanna said with menace. "We really do. You had a barbecue there the other night." Suddenly she sounded the way she did on TV. "We've been watching you. And we'll be seeing her soon." She turned to Bridget. "Someone has to text Izzy, tell her what's going on. Who's going to get the girl? I go fucking *national* in a week!"

Paula's eyes grew round and the next laugh died in her chest. Her mother? Rowan? What did they want with Rowan? "This has gone far enough," she said.

"You're being selfish," Glory hissed. "Think of your mother! Don't you think she wants to go back to the way she was? This would do it—"

"Leave her out of this!" Paula yelled. "And stay away from

Rowan! Marla . . ."

"Marla, come on, fix her up here," Joanna said.

Marla slowly came towards Paula, who struggled futilely against the women holding her fast. The look of betrayal on her face stopped Marla in her tracks.

"My husband won't stop working. My children—" she choked. "My children . . . Paula, maybe I'll do this badly too," she whispered. She put her hands on either side of Paula's face and said, "I'm sorry, but my babies—"

"Marla, don't."

She held Paula's face still and looked into her eyes, compelling Paula to look back. The heat from her hands was penetrating. Soothing.

soothing

"Paula, see me. Look at me." Marla held her hand in front of Paula's face, her fingers pointed downwards. She wriggled them, as supple as worms. Then she said, "You. Are. Weak."

Paula swooned, the energy draining from her muscles, her legs collapsing under her, her head lolling. The women stumbled under her weight.

"Ew, she's a heavy one," Bridget sneered.

crackerjack bitch

witch

crackerjack witches

before I was evil

Wind tunnelled through Paula's head, spinning everything in it together. Far away someone said *call Bella and get them on the kid.*

Paula tried to scream, but what came out of her, exhausted and breathless, was "Rowan. Don't. Not Ro—"

"Let's get her to my car," Esme said. "We're running late."

TWENTY

Rowan had heard the nasty crack of bone, the *thud* of Mr. Keyes hitting the landing, the air whooshing out of him. Now it was quiet, and she hoped

(hoped)

that he wasn't dead. Or unconscious.

"Mr. Keyes?"

No answer.

Rowan kept listening for Mr. Keyes as her embarrassment struggled with her need to help him. She took the toilet paper off the holder and rolled it around and around her hand and wrist, making it look as much like the pads on TV as possible. The wad she ended up with was too fat but it was long, and she thought that might be a good idea. She cleaned herself up as well as she could and then stuffed the makeshift pad between her legs and pulled her panties and jeans up over the whole thing. It felt strange and uncomfortable.

Sanderson heard Rowan call him, heard the water running, heard her call him again. As if from a great distance—he was entirely preoccupied with his ankle. He bit his lip and struggled to a sitting position, trying to keep his foot still. But it shifted, and the pain was a snakebite, a fire bomb. He rested his foot on the stair while he caught his breath. It was broken, he was sure of it. He leaned forward and eased his pant leg up. Even through his sock he could see the swelling.

Gusto wouldn't stop fussing around him. "Gusto, sit."

The beagle briefly dropped his ass to the floor, just to be obedient, then was back up and nudging Sanderson.

He heard Rowan calling, "Mr. Keyes? Are you okay?"

"I'm on the landing," he managed, and suddenly she was there.

Her hands flew to her face. "Oh jeez! Mr. Keyes, did you break your leg?"

"My ankle. Rowan, you're going to have to get help."

She nodded, her face grave.

"The landline is fuck— Sorry." He grimaced in pain. "The phone's out. And I can't get a signal with the cell. You're going to have to go the neighbours, okay? But first help me take a look at what I've done here."

At his instruction, Rowan peeled the sock off his foot, Sanderson gritting his teeth. "God, Mr. Keyes, that looks awful."

There was no bone showing through, but the ankle was twice its normal size and already turning a very wrong shade of indigo.

"I'll go get some ice."

In the kitchen he could hear her opening his mostly empty freezer. Thank heavens, he'd bought a bag of ice, just in case Paula wanted a real drink and not a beer. She came back, carrying a tea towel full of cubes. "Did you get my mom?"

"She wasn't at Marla's. The line was so bad I couldn't tell what the woman was saying. Do you know Izzy Riley?"

"*Ugh*. Yes, my grandma's friend."

"Before the line died, all I got was her name. Sorry, kiddo . . ."

"It's okay. I'm okay. We have to get you to the hospital first."

Sanderson gingerly held the ice to his ankle. Its weight hurt so much his eyes watered. He needed a cast and some antibiotics for sure. He had to get to the hospital. Those were facts. But something else was wrong. It might be stupid to feel so sure, but inside him was a sense of terrible urgency. He just knew something was wrong with Paula. They

(he)

had to find her.

"Rowan, go to the neighbours and call 911. Then call your mom, okay? Find out where she is."

She nodded briskly. "I'll be right back."

The girl ran out the front door, the dogs following her. The door bounced once in the frame.

The house was suddenly silent. His ankle was throbbing and the pain went all the way up to his knee. He tried to move his leg. It shrieked agony, so he stopped. *Shit.*

Sanderson spotted his cell on the floor about six feet from where he sat. The screen was dark but the green light indicated the power was still on. Useless. Even if he stretched as far as he could, it would just be out of reach.

There was no sound from outside, no rush of neighbours through the door, no sirens in the distance. There was something uncomfortable about the silence.

To hell with being helpless. Sanderson leaned and leaned, stretching in the direction of the phone, until he fell over—*shit, that hurt*—stretching in the direction of the phone.

"Ahhhhhhrrrrrrrr—"

With the ends of his fingers he could just touch the casing. Pausing to breathe, he then used his good foot to push himself away from the bottom step. He got two fingers around the phone, and then his thumb, and he had it.

He propped himself up on one elbow, ignoring the drumbeat of misery in his lower leg. He closed the phone and opened it again. There was a full set of bars.

Redial. The phone rang and rang on the other end. He hung up. He checked the bars—still full—and punched in 911. The phone lost its connection. "Fuck!" What was going on?

Rowan ran to front door of the house next door and knocked hard. What could she say that would create the maximum amount of urgency? *My mom's friend broke his ankle—*

My mom's friend is having a heart attack—

is dying—

My friend—my Daddy is badly hurt—

No one came. Rowan knocked again and then rang the bell for good measure. Still no one answered. Gusto was sitting on the step beside her, but Old Tex was on the sidewalk. She wondered if someone was looking out and was afraid of the dogs.

"Go home!" she loud-whispered. "Go!" Old Tex turned reluctantly and went as far as the tree in front of Mr. Keyes's house, where he sat down. Gusto looked up at her, but then went to sit beside his friend.

She waited a few seconds more, then gave up and cut across the front yards to the house on the other side of Mr. Keyes's, where she repeated her actions. No one answered there either, even when Rowan pulled open the screen door and knocked hard on the inside one. Surely that would wake someone up if they were at home in bed. No luck.

So she went to the house next to that one and saw that it was dark inside too. Just for a second she thought, *Everyone's dead*, before she pulled herself together. Big deal—a bunch of the neighbours were at some football game or something, Bingo night, some stupid art thing like they had at St. Mary's every year and hundreds of people came and it raised tons of money for blind people or something.

Rowan turned around to face the street. As if ticking off items on a list she looked at every house in viewing distance, one after another, *tick tick tick*. And every single house was dark. Deserted.

Frustration welled up in her and she clenched her fists and yelled, "I hate this place!" It echoed impotently up the street . . . *this place . . . this place.*

Her hand went to her neck and she felt for her stupid cheap plastic Jesus on the candy-pink crucifix and she couldn't help it; she wrapped her fingers around it and prayed. "Holy Mary, mother of God, pray for us sinners now and at the hour of our—"

That's when a car turned onto the street, driving slowly, the lights bouncing.

Rowan waved her arms in the air. "Stop! Stop!" she yelled.

The car slowed down and stopped in the middle of the street. A city girl from way back, Rowan didn't get close to it.

A woman rolled down the front passenger window. "What is it, dear? Are you all right?"

She shook her head. "No, my friend is hurt. He needs an ambulance—" she gestured to Sanderson's house. "And I have to find my mother. She's at her friend's house. I have the street number . . ." She dug around inside her pocket. "Do you have a cell that I can use? The phone's not working and none of the neighbours are home." Rowan's face twisted up and she gulped air for a minute to ward away tears.

"There, there. Oh dear. Oh my. We don't have a cellphone— we're old ladies. Let us take you where you need to go. Would that be all right?" She opened the car door and struggled to get out. A tiny, round lady, leaning on a cane. Rowan could smell the woman's perfume, which reminded her of the scent worn by the grandmothers who came to St. Mary's on blind-people benefit night.

Gusto and Old Tex moved to flank her. Old Tex put his head down and growled, and then he barked. It echoed up the empty street and sounded so *loud*.

"Shhh, Tex," Rowan said. "Go home."

"That's okay, he's just worried for you. Animals are very sensitive and you're obviously upset. You poor thing."

Rowan swayed in the old lady's direction. "I'm not supposed to go with strangers."

"Of course you're not," she said. "Let me introduce myself. My name is Aggie. If you peek in the car, that's Bella driving. And in the back is our good friend Tula."

Tula ducked her head as Rowan bent to see her.

"Hey, I know you," she said. "You're the nurse from the hospital."

The driver waved, smiling kindly. "You poor dear," she said, leaning towards the passenger side window. "Come on and we'll take you where you need to go." Three old ladies. Not exactly serial killers. She didn't like Tula, not one bit, but she was in a spot. And really, what was Tula? Not exactly a monster

(but creepy)

Aggie opened the back door and Tula shifted over to make room for Rowan. Still the girl hesitated.

Aggie said gently, "Your friend needs a doctor?"

Rowan decided she had no choice. She got into the back seat. "He broke his ankle. Can you take me to a phone? I need to call an ambulance." And then she burst into relieved tears.

Aggie clucked in sympathy and under her breath said, "Poor thing, poor thing."

The car door was shut with a bang and Aggie got back into the front seat. They drove away. The dogs barked and chased the car.

"I should have put the dogs inside," Rowan said tearfully. No one responded. She wiped her face on the sleeve of her blazer, embarrassed that she'd let go like that. Tula nudged a Kleenex into her hand. She took it gratefully and wiped her eyes and then her nose with it.

In the front the driver, Bella pulled a soft pack of cigarettes off the dash and shook one out, putting it in her mouth. She pressed in the lighter.

"Oh jeez, the car is going to smell like smoke, Bella—"

"Just shut up. It already reeks of perfume. That's terrible stuff." The lighter popped and Bella lit her cigarette. Smoke filled the car.

At the end of the block the car turned onto a side street. They were going very slowly.

"Izzy—" Bella muttered under her breath to Aggie, gesturing to something in the old woman's lap.

Aggie put her glasses on. From the front seat came the distinct and familiar sound of a cell dialling. *Pink pink pink.*

"Do you actually have a cellphone?" Rowan asked, leaning forward. "If you do, we can just call an ambulance for Mr. Keyes and we can call my mom. She's—"

"There's no phone, dear," Bella said. "Sit back, it's not safe." She took the veiny hand with the cigarette off the wheel to wave her back.

Pink pink pink pink

Aggie leaned in closer to Bella and muttered low, "Are we going right to Chapman?"

Bella looked in the rear-view mirror before answering. Rowan kept her expression blank. Bella nodded.

Aggie cursed. "Shit, I can't see a thing. My eyes are 110 years old. These glasses are shit." She pulled them off her face.

These old ladies curse a lot, Rowan thought.

"Use mine," Bella said. "They're stronger. The case is in my purse."

"Did you say Izzy?" Rowan asked. "Mr. Keyes said my mom

might be at Izzy's. Do you know her? She's Marla's mom. Do you know Marla?"

Tula looked at her sideways.

"Hey," Rowan said, "you know Izzy. You've been taking care of my grandmother. At the hospital. Remember me?"

Tula's only response was to give her a quick pat on the leg. Then she winced. "Ow, my hands, my poor hands," she said.

"Can you shut up about it, Tu?" the driver said.

Rowan persisted. "You're her nurse—"

Bella said, "Shush, dear, you're upsetting yourself."

Something in the atmosphere of the car had changed. Bella stared straight ahead at the road, smoke from her cigarette curling up into the fabric ceiling. Aggie kept a smile painted on, her head turned partway towards the back seat.

"My mom might be at Izzy's," Rowan offered again. No one said anything. Bella smoked. They were nearly at the end of the side street. Rowan didn't know where she was now.

"What's Chapman? Is that where Izzy is?" Still no reaction.

There was a light of some sort up ahead, bright and artificial, from a gas station or store front. "I should get out. I can call from that store up there."

Bella cleared her throat. "Dear, you should put your seatbelt on. It's not safe, or legal. Strap her in, Tula."

With a warning snort, Tula leaned to reach around her. "You be a good girl now."

Rowan put her hand up to block Tula. "I'll just get out—"

Tula grabbed Rowan and shook her. "You cooperate or I'll pinch you!"

"Hey, don't!"

Just then they slowed for the stop sign. Tula got hold of the belt and yanked it, catching Rowan on the chin with the clasp. Rowan hollered.

Bella waved a fat, wrinkled arm at them, her cigarette dangling out the side of her mouth like a cartoon gangster. "That's enough! If I have to stop this car—"

But the car *was* stopped. Rowan, scared out of her wits, screamed once more, "Let me go!" She grabbed the handle of the door and it opened, swinging wide. She jumped out. As Tula shrieked angrily, Rowan ran. She ducked low and darted between the houses, each of them dark as pitch and silent as the grave.

Bella and Tula chased her as far as the second yard, but by then the girl was so far ahead it was ridiculous to keep trying. They hobbled back to the car, panting all the way.

"Shit," Bella said. "Aggie just texted Izzy that we had her."

"Well, we did. Shit," Tula repeated.

Through the car window Aggie said, "Where's she going to go? The boyfriend's hurt and she's got no idea where her mother is. We'll wait outside the boyfriend's place."

The women got back in the car.

"I hate kids," Tula said.

TWENTY-ONE

Sanderson had been calling for Rowan every few minutes, but neither she nor the dogs had come back. He'd messed up, he knew it. Something was wrong, and he shouldn't have sent her out there on her own. He couldn't wait—he had to find her.

He tucked the useless phone into the breast pocket of his shirt. Then, steeling himself against what he knew would be terrible pain, he scooched slowly around so he could back towards the front hall closet, using his elbows to pull himself along the floor. Despite his efforts to keep the whole leg steady, his foot bounced with the first pull, flopping towards the floor. He shrieked and broke out in a cold sweat. He couldn't look—to look was to feel sick. It was the kind of break that would require a lot of care. And no movement.

He groaned and gasped and tried to breathe through his mouth without any more screaming, and he managed to pull himself a couple more feet along the hall floor.

Tucked into the closet was a box of things he hadn't gotten around to unpacking yet. The tall box had once contained aluminum tracking for industrial lighting. Inside it was a badminton net with adjustable poles, his golf shoes, a lacrosse racket, two tennis rackets—a Yonex and a lesser wooden racket he'd had since college—and a set of ski poles. Also a hockey stick, a CCM Vector. It would make a decent crutch, he hoped.

He worked himself across the floor, concentrating on how Paula had looked as she'd turned to meet his eyes before she left, her face so vulnerable.

When they were gone, Marla went to the back door and listened to the quiet. She did not turn on the outside light. The neighbourhood was dark. She would have to go soon, do her part for the greater good. The greater evil.

It was probably too late to help herself. Or Paula.

But there was Rowan. David's child.

isn't that right Pauls isn't that who she is

Her mother didn't realize it, Marla was sure of that. Not even Izzy could be so cruel as to ignore that fact, to have such designs on the offspring of her favourite child.

Marla had suspected, had wondered, but not seriously. She'd thought that if David had got Paula pregnant, Paula surely would have told her. The realization that she hadn't was at least as painful as knowing what she had just done to Paula and her daughter. Her niece. *Why didn't you tell me?*

What had she done?

When she'd seen Paula again, here in Haven Woods, she'd realized how much she'd missed having a real friend. The girlfriends she'd made since Paula had left had at best been recruits, even if they hadn't begun that way. As she'd watched them embrace the faith with such passion and gusto, eating up their opportunities no matter how blood-soaked they were, the friendships had changed. And not into sisterhood either, despite the cant.

Of course, now she was more blood-soaked than most. All because she'd used her power, her persuasion, to help her mother—a woman who had done her utmost to make Marla feel second best all her life. Now Marla had no way to stop it, and a trail of blood followed her everywhere. The stupid coach, all those people at the mall, now her

(niece, blood of her blood)

she couldn't quite bring herself to say it out loud.

But maybe there was something she could do to make it right. And if she was successful, maybe her own children—her blood—would be spared.

Father, forgive me, for I am sin.

Doug was lying with his head on his papers, eyes closed, the lines and circles around them invisible in the low light. He looked like his old self when he slept

(if he slept)

She whispered, "I have to go out, darling. The kids are in bed. I won't be too long."

Next Marla went to the room at the end of the basement where no one ever went but her—a housewife's room. There was built-in shelving along the walls, nearly full of the usual pickles/relish/homemade jam. She reached behind the canned peaches and retrieved a small brown bag. Without looking inside she carried it back upstairs.

Once again the phone was ringing. It rang and rang and rang, until finally she gave up and answered. She didn't recognize the man's voice at the other end of the line, but she knew the tone. Worry. Soul-sucking worry.

"She's not here," she broke in. "They're taking her to the Chapman house. It's best you stay away. Watch out for that little girl. This is no place for a little girl." She hung up.

Then Marla went out into the night. She pushed herself into

a light jog, then faster. As she ran along the road she saw tiny shapes dart out of hiding, falling in silently behind her. She didn't care. It felt good to run.

Sanderson stared down at his phone in disbelief. The Chapman house?

Now that he was upright, the hockey stick jammed underneath his armpit, his ankle throbbed and throbbed. But all thoughts of hospital had vanished from his head. He had to find Rowan first. Then to hell with what Marla said, he was going to go get Paula out of the Chapman house.

He hobbled out the door, not bothering to try to shut it behind him. The street was very quiet, as if everyone on the block had gone out for evening. Maybe they had. Or maybe they were inside, hiding because they were afraid.

His car was in the driveway where he'd left it what seemed like months ago. The keys jingled, bouncing against the stick as he limped to the driver's-side door.

He would find them both, make it right. Rescue them. From what, exactly, he didn't know, but there sure as hell was something going on. *Save the female* is an ancient male imperative, a guy thing, but in this case it seemed more than that. An imperative of unknown origin.

The car started. He had to use his left foot on the accelerator, resting his injured leg on the hump in the middle. It was awkward for a minute, but he adjusted. Cars are also a guy thing.

The hospital lights loomed just ahead of her. There was no one in there except Audra; Marla knew this for a fact. The lights were on a timer, to keep up the pretence.

Behind her grew a sound like rain on the sidewalk, dozens of cat feet, padding on the road, coming from behind trees, mailboxes, shrubs, fences. So far that was all they had done—follow her.

She pushed through the front doors, ignoring the small, elegantly lettered sign on the desk at reception: VISITING HOURS ARE OVER. THANK YOU FOR CARING ENOUGH TO STOP BY. SEE YOU TOMORROW! Marla hit the elevator button to take her to the second floor. The doors opened almost instantly and she stepped inside. Just before she did, she glanced back through the glass front wall of the hospital. Staring at her was a row of cats. Twelve or fourteen of them. Beyond them there would be more. The elevator door shut.

On the second floor, Marla passed room after empty room, beds perfectly made, cheery yellow blankets pulled taut over snow white three-hundred-thread-count, private-hospital-grade sheets, half lit by the soft glow of bedside lamps. It was eerie.

A single door near the end of the corridor was closed. She pushed it open and gave a gasp. She couldn't help it. Audra lay on her side, spine curled, knees up. Her arms stuck straight out from her shoulders, wrists and fingers stiff.

The older woman's eyes opened and moved in their sockets, and Marla gasped again.

"Oh god, what have we done to you?"

Audra's speech was even more garbled from the spell. "Maarrrl—"

"Audra, your eyes, *your eyes*—"

"Iiss it Friid-aaay?"

"Yes."

Audra closed her eyes and seemed to sleep. There was an unhealthy heat in the room, and Marla could smell her, a pungent animal scent.

"Are you an animal?"

"Iiimm a Juu-daass goat," Audra said, those horrible eyes opening to meet Marla's. "Chick," she said. It sounded like *shik*, or *shit*.
She repeated it. "Chick."

Marla nodded; she got it. Just the sort of thing that would have
seemed clever at the time. But it couldn't have been Izzy. Izzy would
never have done this. It had to have been . . . something else.

"Are you in pain?" she asked, and then regretted it. From the
woman's posture and voice, it was obvious that she was.

Still, Audra shook her head slightly. "Inn heeere," she said, and
looked down, her reptilian eyes focusing on her chest. Her heart.

"I want to help you. And Rowan, and Paula if we can. But we
don't have very much time."

Audra met Marla's eyes once more and Marla fought the urge
to look away.

"I think I can set you free, at least for a little while. Maybe
long enough."

Marla took both of Audra's stiffened hands in hers and held
them tightly, until she could feel the heat of their bodies joining.
The goat smell was distracting. But that was not entirely a bad
thing, because Marla was scared.

Audra closed her eyes and said, "Doo waad yoouu caann." But
by then Marla was concentrating on calling up larger forces.

"*Humilis oro ut recreaturus sitis feminam vestram . . .*"

Audra began to shudder. Her eyes flew open as if she had been
startled by some great noise. They widened until a white circle
surrounded her slitted pupils.

"Restore this creature, your woman, to her bloom, in Your name
to undo that which has been done . . ."

A moan started from inside Audra, like a growl in her stomach, and rose up and out her throat. An awakening—an angry one.
Her body seemed to vibrate. Her spine uncurled and she grew
longer, her legs stretching out, straightening, her feet lengthening.

The fingers of her right hand, still held in Marla's, flexed, the hard edges of her fingernails scraping painfully against the inside of Marla's palm.

Marla felt as if a hot wire was cutting through her core, but she hung on to Audra with everything she had. She hoped that this wasn't a mistake, that her children wouldn't suffer any repercussions, because it was too late to stop now.

Audra's head went back, her mouth stretched open and she *shrieked*. It was an unholy sound. Her eyes glowed briefly gold, the whites turning pink and then red. Her skin became shiny and sleek from whatever power was thrumming through her body.

Marla felt the hot wire turning back on her, and she groaned too, not sure how much longer she could hold on.

The woman on the bed sat up abruptly and yanked her hands away. "No!"

And everything stopped. The hot wire inside Marla popped, the wretched fire in her hands, the fear—all disappeared.

Audra blinked a few times. "Dry," she croaked.

Marla looked around the room. There was a covered container on the table in the corner. She went and got it, pulled the lid off. The smell was horrible. She shook her head at Audra.

"Clothes—"

All Audra had on was a short-sleeved nightgown. Her arms no longer looked frail and skinny; she seemed to have gained ten pounds.

"Okay," Marla said. She checked the cupboard, which was empty. A hanger swung lazily with the motion of the door opening. "They must have taken your things."

Audra slid off the bed tentatively. She let out another groan, this time a relieved one. Her feet were bare. Marla looked in the bottom of the cupboard and under the bed, but there were no shoes either.

"How much time do I have?"

"I don't know," Marla said. "It could be forever. Or until we get to the door."

"We better get going then," Audra said.

The hall was as empty as it had been before.

"Is Paula at the house? And . . . Rowan?" Audra said.

Marla shook her head. "I don't know where Rowan is. They were going to find her. Paula didn't bring her. Did you do that?"

"No."

"They took Paula to the Chapman place, but it's Rowan they need now. Sanderson Keyes called me just as I was leaving. I told him to keep Rowan with him." She choked up.

"Marla?"

"My babies . . . my husband. They're in terrible shape. I don't know what will happen to them after this—" She started to cry in a way she hadn't for years. Like Izzy, she thought she'd lost the ability.

Audra put her hand on Marla's back. "If I can fix it I will. I'm going to Izzy first, though, okay?"

Marla nodded.

The two of them walked down the hall, Marla's footsteps echoing impotently, Audra's bare feet not making a sound. When they came out of the elevator into the lobby, about two hundred cats sat looking in at them, tails flicking.

Rowan crouched behind a shrub, her heart pounding so hard she was afraid the old ladies would hear it. She had no idea where she was. Except that it was someone's backyard.

She touched the plastic Jesus around her neck, making sure it was still there. And that it was still *that*. She wished it was a cellphone. Everyone had a cell, except her.

It was dark, although this particular backyard had motion detectors, so the light had come on when she ran from the lane to the bush. It had since gone off again, but it was a problem. If she moved, the light would come on again.

As far as she could tell, they had driven her around two corners and down four or five blocks. But she wasn't exactly sure which direction she'd gone when she ran from the car. Rowan took a deep breath and let it out slowly. She closed her eyes and in her head went all the way back to when the car had stopped in front of Mr. Keyes's house.

After about five minutes she stood up and walked straight out front to the street, ignoring the light when the motion detector turned it on. She was in the zone.

Sanderson drove slowly, eyes shifting from side to side, looking for any sign of anything. He did not call out the window. For some reason he thought it was best to stay quiet. He was alone on the road.

Rowan . . .

He willed the girl to show herself.

TWENTY-TWO

"SHE'S TOO DAMN HEAVY!" Paula heard Glory say from outside the vehicle. She was in the back seat of someone's minivan. She could smell the faint whiff of sour milk, the familiar odours of a family car. Other than that, she had no idea where she was.

She remembered her friend Marla coming at her, muttering incantations, and that she'd collapsed, hadn't been able to move a muscle, had passed out. Testing carefully, she realized her limbs could move again a little.

She heard someone yell, "Bring Paula."

Both feet had pins and needles—unpleasant, but wholly welcome. Whatever Marla had done to her, she'd made a poor job of it, maybe for Paula's sake. Maybe that's what she'd meant when she'd whispered that she was trying to be on Paula's side.

A seatbelt buckle dug into her lower back. She could see very little of the outside, just sky and stars. A single streetlight somewhere behind the car cast some light into the interior. She didn't know where they were, but they wanted her out of the van—that much was clear.

She'd taken a self-defence course in the city because of all those late nights she'd had to make her way home alone. Her mind flitted through what she'd been taught, but the only thing that came back was the second-location theory. The course instructor—big, intimidating, male—had stressed that no matter what, if kidnapped, you must do everything in your power to prevent your kidnapper from taking you to a second location. The second location was where they killed you. Ted Bundy had kidnapped girls from all kinds of public places, but he killed them all at the next stop.

Paula had to stay in the van.

Glory's voice again: "I don't think I can use my left arm . . . I think it's about to come off. When is Izzy getting here? I'm getting nervous about this . . ."

The fingers of Paula's left hand grazed the carpet on the floor. She could feel the rough nap on her knuckles. The van rocked slightly as Glory leaned against it.

Outside, she figured, were the ones who had held her: Esme, Glory and Bridget. She had no idea if anyone else was with them, wherever they were parked. It had to be somewhere private, because the girls felt okay about shouting out their business to one another. They seemed to be waiting for Izzy. Why David's mom? Why Izzy? Clearly she was key.

Logic suggested that time was crucial. Likely she had only minutes before one of them opened that door and pulled her outside to face whatever fate awaited her. The pins and needles had progressed up her legs and arms and by now had almost disappeared. Her chest felt heavy and full, as if she had heartburn, and her scalp was still numb. She flexed her ankles and was surprised to find that they felt normal.

She made fists, then pressed one hand down on the floor of the van, putting a little muscle into it. That was too much, and she released the pressure, gasping. But the act had sent blood into her arm so that when she tried it again, she was able to raise herself a little.

She relaxed, resting her hand on the carpet a moment. Then she felt around, hoping there would be something on the floor she could use. Under the driver's seat her fingers closed around something and she pulled it towards her. It was a doll, a Barbie knockoff, made of very hard, inflexible plastic, its legs sticking straight out. She supposed it was better than nothing, and she held on to it.

She concentrated on listening for other cars, conversation, the sound of her daughter's voice, hoping she would not hear it. *Not Rowan.*

The door handle clicked and Paula tensed, uncertain what to do with the makeshift weapon in her hand. A goddamn Barbie doll? But she didn't have time or the presence of mind to react except in the most primal way when the door opened.

It was Glory, who excused herself and whispered to Paula, as if she were interrupting a nap, "Sorry, just going to grab my purse. I think I left an Oreo in there—"

She leaned in, giving Paula just enough time to jerk herself up before fear could stop her. She swung the doll as hard as she could and made sudden, hard contact. There was a terrible wet, tearing sound and Glory staggered back out of the van, clutching the side of her face. Her mouth opened and a gasp came out—*uuuhh*. Paula jammed her hand against her own mouth to keep from screaming out loud. The doll's legs had plunged right into Glory's eye.

Blood soaked into Glory's glove, dripping down as her good eye stared, shocked, at Paula. Then she staggered and fell forward heavily onto Paula's legs, hovering a moment until gravity pulled her large body to the ground.

Paula scrambled out of the van. She stared at Glory sprawled on the grass, her mouth open in horror, then looked at the doll in her hand. It was covered in blood to the knees. *Murder-Weapon Barbie.* She flung it to the ground and it landed beside Glory. Then she tore her eyes away and looked around at where she was.

The van was in a yard, about fifty feet from a house. She could hear voices rising and falling. No one had reacted to what had just happened. What *had* just happened? Had she killed Glory? *Now what?*

For the first fifteen or so seconds, the building she was staring at was just a house. Then, with a terrible clarity, she realized—

He Lives Here

It was the Chapman house.

She had to get away.

Glory was lying very still, and Paula begged in her mind, *Don't be dead*. Then the woman shifted and moaned, clutching her eye, and that made Paula move, fast. She leaped into the driver's seat. The keys were not in the ignition. She pawed around in the console recess. Gum, candy, a couple of pens, a tiny dinosaur, some fuses. She popped open the glovebox, taking care to stay low and quiet

(oh please oh please oh please)

In the glovebox: papers, operating manual, gloves, sunglasses

(oh please come on)

Paula flipped down the visor over the driver's seat and the keys fell, hitting her on the head and dropping into her lap. She fished them out from between her legs, hands shaking, and jabbed them at the ignition . . . missing, missing, missing . . . then the key slid in, she turned it and the motor roared into life.

A voice called out, "Hey!"

Paula flipped the headlights on, threw the van into reverse and backed up past the moaning body on the drive. Just as she was pulling onto the road, she looked into the rear-view and saw

I swear

people in the windows—dark silhouettes

(a child for certain)

even as three women ran screaming down the front steps as she drove madly out of view.

—

Marla and Audra looked out at the cats.

"There's Tansy," Marla said.

Izzy's golden-eyed familiar sat perched above the others on the concrete base of a tall streetlamp. The cats now covered the entire wide walkway. Tails flicked lazily, contemplatively, and their eyes never left the women's faces.

"Do you think they'll do something?" Marla said.

Audra didn't answer. She stood, blinking slowly, her arms wrapped around her waist, listing a little.

"Audra?" Marla put her arm out, steadying her.

"I'm all right, dear. Just a little unsteady on my feet—"

"I'm sorry," Marla said. "I didn't know what else to do."

Audra trembled ever so slightly in her nightclothes. Marla put both arms around her and rubbed her back. She was chilled, in spite of the warm night.

"I should have put a stop to all of this years ago. And it's certainly time now." Audra touched a cold hand to Marla's cheek and smiled. "You did the right thing. Thank you." Carefully she pushed open the door.

They were greeted by a steady vibrating thrum. Purring.

The two women exchanged looks, then stepped out into the gathering of cats. They kept to the concrete sidewalk, moving carefully, avoiding tails. The cats got out of the way elegantly, unhurriedly, heads high. But after the women passed they snapped unholy looks at them, eyes iridescent in the halogen lights.

The street in the front of the hospital was quiet, deserted. It was probably after nine.

"Everyone sleeps," Audra said, pointlessly.

Marla nodded.

They walked towards Proctor Street, going slowly, Marla

worried about Audra's bare feet. The cats followed, keeping their distance. At the corner the road split. One way led to the Chapman house, at the edge of Haven Woods, and the other to where Marla lived. All around them the purring of the cats bounced off the expensive house fronts, the asphalt.

"I have to go home," Marla said apologetically. "I have to stay out of it now."

Audra slipped her arm out of Marla's. "I know," she said. "You've done enough." Her hands were still quite cold, but the process of becoming whatever it had been had halted. She looked frightening, nonetheless, with her golden eyes and coarse, wild hair.

I'm sorry, Marla thought.

"Go now. I have a long walk."

Marla looked behind them, around them at the cats, which were sitting idly.

"I don't think they'll hurt me," Audra said to reassure her. "I think if they were going to, they would have by now, don't you?"

"I guess . . ."

"You have to go to your family. I'll be all right." Audra swayed, but only very slightly.

Marla turned away, breaking into a run. Audra watched until she was halfway down the block, then took the first step towards her own fate.

As she walked, the cats followed behind her, edging closer and closer.

Rowan wanted her mother. Very badly. She would not cry, though, not yet.

She thought she recognized the street she was on. When she got to her grandmother's house, she'd use the phone to call her mom. And an ambulance. And the police, if she had to.

She touched her plastic Jesus and ran across the street, watching for signs of life and seeing none. She snuck down the narrow path between the houses and into another backyard, climbing the fence, then hopping down into the neighbouring yard. She crept along the side of that house, and there, not ten doors away, was her grandmother's.

She broke into a jog. She just wanted to get somewhere safe.

Sweat beaded Sanderson's forehead as the car lurched and jerked. Using his left foot on the pedals, he was driving like a teenager behind the wheel for the very first time. He'd propped up his broken ankle as best he could, but every time the car hit a bump or jerked forward, pain shot up his leg all the way to the hip. Everything was on fire. But he couldn't give up—he had to find Rowan.

He scanned the streets, which were dark and silent. He tried to see between bushes and behind trees. He resisted the idea of sticking his head out the window and calling for her; he still had a feeling that was a bad idea. He did a loop up the block and then went back the way he had come, scoping the other side of the street. He willed her to appear. *Rowan . . .*

Sanderson turned onto the next block, heading for Paula's mom's place. For all he knew Rowan had a key and might have gone back there to use the phone.

It struck him that it was completely weird for the streets to be this deserted, for all the houses to be dark. No doubt economical and ecological, but spooky as all hell.

Twice Rowan thought she heard something behind her, but when she spun around to look, forgetting all about being careful and quiet, there was no one behind her. But that didn't mean there wasn't someone, or something, following her. It didn't mean she could let her guard down. What it meant was

(just go)

Her running shoes made almost no sound on the sidewalk, so she could keep track of other noises. And she did. A rustle of leaves, the wind blowing litter, a rattle in someone's throat—

"Rowan?"

She jumped out of her skin, letting out a squeal. She looked behind her. The sidewalk was empty. She swung to look at the houses on either side of the street, but their windows were still dark, their yards full of shadows.

"Rowan, *dear*," the voice said, and then out of the shadows came the woman from before. The woman Bella.

Rowan backed away. "No—"

"Don't be afraid," Bella said. "I'm all on my own; it's just you and me. I've come to keep you safe."

The woman's voice was soothing. There was a halo of light around her head from the streetlamp behind her. It was . . . peaceful. The girl paused for just a second.

"Rowan, you're all alone out here. I'll take you to your mother. You want to see your mother, don't you?"

"Yes," Rowan admitted. And took a step in Bella's direction.

As she did, her mind did a funny thing. Into it popped an old memory from her neighbourhood in the city, of the boys who sat on the steps across the street, jeering at her when she walked to school

c'mere little girl I'll teach ya

Once, feeling bold, she had started to answer back. A passerby had wagged his finger at her and said, *stay away from those boys they're no good.*

(*no*) *good*

"No!" Rowan said. She stepped back and jammed her fists into her eyes and rubbed. The woman's voice seemed to be coming from inside her own head.

"I'm not going to hurt you. I want to take you to your mother. She's at a special place, the Chapman House. With friends. It's not far . . ."

no good for you

Bella put her hands out and Rowan felt her body leaning towards her. *How nice it would be to just*

(give in)

no good for

She turned and ran. Light reflected off the pavement where it was shiny from hundreds of cars driving over it every day, fathers and husbands going to work, children being driven to school, mothers and wives driving to their own work, to school, to the grocery store, the hospital, the dry cleaners.

The woman ran after her, but not very fast because she was old. "Stop, stop! You have to come with me! Oh, stop, stop, stop!" She was running out of air. "Rowan . . . you damn little bitch! We already have . . . your mother. If you ever want . . . to see her again . . . you . . . have . . . to . . . come . . ." The woman stopped, hunched over, gasping for air, her hand waving as if asking Rowan to *Stop, just stop* out of plain courtesy.

Rowan did. She turned to face her and shouted, "What? What did you say about my mother?"

Bella straightened up as best she could, still gasping for air. "I'm sorry, Rowan . . . but we have . . . your mother."

"Why?" she asked. "Why do you have her?"

"We need her, Rowan. Just like we need you. Do you know who you are?"

The woman took one step towards Rowan and then another. "You're very important. You're the granddaughter of someone very important. A blood alumna. Do you know what an alumna is?"

Rowan tried to think. They were always talking about alumnae at school. Was an alumna someone who had been to school?

"You and your mother can be of great service to many people, and to me too," she said. "I'm sorry I tried to trick you. Will you come?" She held her hand out in a gesture of friendship or supplication.

"What's my mom an alumna of?"

The woman's eyes narrowed and she looked jolly for a moment, as if she had something wonderful to tell. "Well, she's an alumna because of your grandmother, basically. Your grandmother is one of us."

"One of who?"

"She's a witch. We all are—your grandmother, Izzy, me, my friends. Do you believe me? Does that frighten you, Rowan? Or are you a brave girl?" Bella took a few more steps forward.

All at once Rowan did believe it. It explained a lot of weird stuff. She also figured that if she wanted to find her mother, she had no choice. "You'll take me to my mom, no tricks?"

"Yes."

"Okay, I'll come—"

Just then a car turned the corner and its headlights fell on them, causing both to throw shielding arms over their eyes. Then Rowan squealed, this time with delight, as she realized whose car was sputtering and jerking towards them. She waved frantically for the driver to stop.

And then someone yanked her off her feet. She wriggled and twisted to see who had grabbed her. Then she shrieked.

"There'll be none of that," said Tula, as Mr. Keyes gunned the engine and came barrelling at the three of them.

TWENTY-THREE

Izzy paced back and forth inside the Chapman house. On the floor beside her was a large stain, gone brown with time. Blood. Impossible to tell from what. There were fresher stains on the long slab of beechwood table that dominated the room. Her recent offering. The rest of the dog sacrifice, however, was gone. Where no one would have ventured to guess; no one would want to try. Not even Izzy.

She'd been pacing nearly an hour. She could not stop, gripped as she was by a nearly uncontrollable rage. At times she couldn't contain it and would simply howl her anger, terrifying the women who had stayed outside. They would venture as far as the porch, but they were definitely too afraid to come in. She would like to believe they were afraid of her. But they were just afraid.

Her hair was wild around her head; she looked fierce and uncontained. The women should be afraid. This was their doing and they would pay—all of them. If Paula wasn't found. If the girl didn't come. If. If. If. This was what happened if you didn't take care of every little thing yourself.

When she'd arrived, there had been something akin to hope

inside her. In a few hours their *sabbat* would be complete and they would once more be as they were, though humbled by their recent experiences

(and they would be humbled by the power they saw)

But instead there was no Paula, and worse, no *girl*. The girl had been promised. Even without their thirteen, they might survive a little longer if they offered the girl.

When Izzy got there, Glory had been sitting bleeding on the porch steps, moaning and clutching her moronic fat face—oh, my eye, my eye. The rest all spoke on top of each other, trying to explain what had gone wrong. Which was everything.

Once Izzy had made sense of the catastrophe, rage had over-taken her and she'd lashed out. At Glory, an easy target

(so annoying and pathetic the kind of person you just want to smack)

letting all that fury pour through her fingers in the moaning woman's direction. Flames born of years of rage and frustration had zapped out of her fingers and hit Glory dead on. Glory became airborne. Then she fell, hard, onto the roof of the Chapman place, rolled to land on top of the porch and tumbled down the steps into the dirt. Not a sound had come out of her except for a

(pathetic)

oof, oof, oof as she hit each step.

The rest of them had gasped and backed away, Bridget edging right into the house, then yelping in horror when she had realized where she was and quickly covering her mouth lest she squeal again. She jumped back onto the porch fast.

Glory's fall had sobered Izzy, put a brief lid on her anger

(and she was sorry truly sorry in a deep part of herself that saw less and less light over the years)

She had to think. And so she made them speak one at a time. Made them explain.

They had brought Paula here but she had gotten away. They said it was all Marla's fault—her spell had worn off before they were ready. And it was Paula's fault that they didn't have the girl. Paula hadn't brought the girl to Marla's.

Fault. How little that mattered. If they couldn't face Izzy's anger, how would they deal with real wrath, the wrath of ages and time and endless power. Which is what they'd all be facing, very soon, if the girl didn't come.

Bella, Tula and Aggie were getting the girl. That was what the text had said. *When the girl comes, the mother will follow.*

Izzy had caught an exchange of looks between Joanna Shaw and Esme, a conspiracy of escape. *Try it*, she had thought. The house would not let anyone go this time.

And now, behind her, the house was awakening. It seemed to breathe, and in each exhalation was the smell of death and ash. The Father was coming.

If the girl didn't show up, . . . all hell would break loose.

Really.

Audra's progress was slow. And she was afraid. Still, she had already passed Princess Ice Cream, which was closed and dark as if it were the end of the season. She was now trudging along beside the ball park, a wide, empty space beyond which were trees. If she got as far as the end of the ball field, she would be able to see the single streetlight above the trees near the Chapman house.

For the past half-mile, every so often five or, six, or so cats at a time would surge past her, sometimes close enough that she could feel the flick of a tail on her leg—making her keenly aware of how much of her flesh was exposed.

About fifty or so were now in front of her as she walked. So

far they hadn't tried to stop her, but she could tell they were growing impatient.

Tansy had made sure her presence was felt. She was never far
out of Audra's sight, never lost in the sea of rolling fur and muscle.
And now the cat stopped and turned to look at Audra. *I know.* The
stare was so penetrating, Audra wanted to look away. She didn't.
Her time for looking away had passed.

Audra was walking inside a thickening mass of cats, which
began to stop in front of her, slowing her progress. They crouched,
haunches tucked under, ears back, tails flicking with menace. She
stepped over them, around them. Carefully, slowly.

How had she ever fallen in so far? Why, after Walter died and
she thought she'd got Paula to safety, had she stayed on here? She
could have packed up, left, gone far away, or even just to the city
where Paula and Rowan lived. She could have. The thing was, it
had been at first easier, then safer, to stay near Izzy. In the beginning she'd been foolish. At the end, a coward.

After Izzy said to her, so many years ago, *What if you could
have everything you've ever wanted?* she'd grabbed Audra by the
arms and said, *Tonight you'll have a dream about me. Listen to it,
okay?*

Audra had laughed. *Iz—*

Izzy had shaken her. It wasn't a joke. *I'll come to you in your
dreams. Do as I ask. For our friendship.*

Izzy, you're scaring me—

Promise. Promise.

And that night she had dreamed of Izzy. At least, Izzy was there
too. And a man who was handsome and powerful and offering her
the world she wanted.

After Walter was taken, she'd been strong enough to try to save
her daughter. But not herself. Weak. Afraid. And that was why it
had come to this.

In front of her all the cats had now stopped, a small calico so suddenly that Audra nearly stepped on it. Their backs were hunched and they were so close together, to look over them was like gazing at the surface of a lake or a wheat field lightly stirred by the wind. Audra guessed that fifty cats now held her there, slyly checking her out, some directly facing her, others at an angle, their eyes glassy and hollow.

That night in the dream, her friend Izzy had walked across a bare wooden floor, smooth from legions of feet, centuries of use, the brush that had scrubbed it bristly and harsh, the water cold. Her steps echoed in the cavernous room, the walls so much vague space beyond.

Audra had held out her arms to her friend. *Izzy, you came!*

But Izzy's expression had been so different from her usual spirited one. *I've come to make you an offer. It will change your life. You will have everything you've ever wanted. All you must do is declare yourself His . . .* On her shoulder was Tansy, little more than a kitten then, purring, rubbing herself against Izzy's cheek.

Izzy it's just as you said. You're in my dream! And even as she was wondering at this, the space behind her friend had begun to move; shadows seemed to writhe and dance and swoon.

There are many with me. All come to see you! Give yourself to Him . . .

Izzy's hands had been behind her back. When she brought them forward, one held a knife, the large carving knife from Audra's own kitchen. She pointed it at Audra's chest. *It hurts only a moment and His loyalty is yours forever. But you must belong to him to wear His mark.*

Then everything seemed to happen at once, not with dreamy, sleep-weary speed but in real time.

Say yes.

She had had a sudden image of everything she'd ever wanted

—embarrassing things: plates of cakes, a room full of dolls, wild sexual abandon a hundred different ways; a future for her daughter filled with love and money; child things mingled with adult things; silly good easy impossible wondrous profane—all of it seemed to appear to her in a minute or less, along with a voice speaking with such authority

be mine and all you want

and in the last few seconds, before she had had time to acquiesce or protest, the ultimate vision of what she wanted was a vision of herself, standing there as she was, wanting everything not for her husband or her daughter, but for herself, the very image of a greedy spoiled child. Her wanting was hugely profound and intense and wholly personal.

The size of her wanting inspired joy in the thing she could not see.

Izzy had come close and closer, and Audra said, *Who is He? Who?*

Without answering, Izzy very deliberately pierced Audra's side with the kitchen knife, not deeply, but it surprised her, as did the pain. When she looked down, Izzy pulled the knife out, and then came a gush, a small waterfall of blood. In shock she looked at Izzy, and Izzy opened her arms wide to show Audra that she too bled. *Sisters*, she said.

In the morning, after a restless night filled with dreams, Audra had found the knife in the sink. Startled, she checked under her left breast, and there was the wound, healed over but still pink. When she thought about it, when *sabbat* approached, it ached, then bled—a new kind of cycle.

But from that point on, her life had been different, and easier. At least until she had blood on her hands. David's blood, and Walter's. Over the years it had felt as if the blood were growing thicker and ranker, and she began to wish for an end. But from the moment when she and Chick had begun trying to resist the bloodlust, to stop paying the endless bills, to when Chick had taken her own life, to this moment now, as she stood stock still in an ocean of menace, she'd known it would come to this. She could die on this road, never having made things right. But she had to try, for Paula and for Rowan.

At her ankle, finally, came teeth, sharp and hot. Audra put her head back and howled in pain and sorrow. She yanked her foot away, and the cats reacted as one. They rose up and leaped upon her with unholy shrieks. The sheer weight of them drove her to her knees. She landed on one of them, and the cat retaliated with a slash to her midsection. Then she went all the way down.

With fists and feet she tried to fend them off, but they were everywhere. Beneath the writhing, wailing, lusting tide, she screamed and wept and called out for Walter, for Paula, for Rowan, whom she'd only wanted to protect. So intense was the attack, she didn't hear her rescuers at first, just realized that the weight on her chest had lessened. Then the cat calls seemed to change in tenor, and she sensed they were retreating.

She opened her eyes, her hands held to her face, and between her bloody fingers she saw a ruff of dark fur

(a huge cat)

that was shaking something in its mouth, hard. Then another creature jumped on its back, and as it turned to snap, she saw her—

"Tex!" Her dog. Her Old Tex. He shook the cat until it was limp and then tossed it away, only to snap at another and another, his jaws clamping down on whatever moved close enough. Another dog was with him, a beagle she didn't know, and it was fighting just as hard, its fur dotted with red-pink blood.

Audra struggled to her feet, pulling her tattered nightgown around herself as best she could. Cats were running towards the trees that flanked the river, running up the street. Some lay on the road, their bodies rent and still.

Old Tex limped over to her, his snout red with cat. He snuck his head under her hand and whimpered. She knelt close to him. "*Good dog*. You poor thing, look at you—" Tears poured out of her as she pressed her face against his and repeated, "Good dog, good dog . . ."

The beagle panted nearby, a youngster, barely more than a pup. There was a cruel slash above his left eye, and he had to keep blinking the blood away. "Here boy," she said. The dog came, and she stroked his head gratefully.

Then she straightened. She hurt everywhere, yet now she felt she was destined to do this one thing before she

(died)

stopped.

"I have to go," she said to the dogs.

Audra limped towards the Chapman house, its streetlight glowing like a beacon. Behind her the dogs followed, Old Tex moving slowly, as if also in great pain.

TWENTY-FOUR

PAULA WAS DRIVING TOO FAST, the tires squealing in the darkness and silence as she careened around corners. The noise they made was as scary as a voice screaming after her.

(Glory?)

Her head swung from one side of the street to the other, looking into doorways, windows, porches, seeing huddled figures, the flash of eyes. Her panic escalated. She had to get to Sanderson's, she had to find Rowan and get her mother out of that hospital and get them all out of Haven Woods.

Those women were crazy. And dangerous.

(but witches?)

The neighbourhood was familiar to her from childhood, but so much had changed. So many of the old houses had been torn down and new, monstrous houses had replaced them. Yards she had cut through from one friend's house to another's had been swallowed up by square footage.

She *was* driving too fast. She passed Good, Pacific. After Pacific came Williams, which she almost missed. She took the corner so fast the van leaned onto two wheels. Paula screamed and swung the steering wheel too far in the other direction. The tires slid on gravel, all traction gone, and she plowed into a telephone pole. Glass, plastic and metal sang together in a squeal of destruction. The crash released the airbag, which pushed her back against the seat with a hard slap.

The front end was wrapped around the pole. The grill had split and pieces had flown in all directions. The van settled with a hiss. Groggy, Paula reached around the deflating airbag and automatically turned the key, shutting off the motor. Then she tried to start it again.

Click.

Paula rested her head against the bag for a minute, then pushed the door open as far as it would go. She squeezed out and fell to the ground, landing hard on her knee. Then she lurched up and forward, leaving the van behind. Her head throbbed and her chest felt bruised; the airbag must have hit her harder than she thought.

She scanned her surroundings. If she cut through the backyard in front of her, Sanderson's was just two houses away. She staggered into a jog, her knee screaming, and just barely held back calling out for him.

She lifted herself painfully over Sanderson's fence and fell into the yard. The lights were on in the kitchen and she thought she could hear the television. She sobbed, the fear and panic of the past hours bubbling up and out of her. She made it to the door, and finding it locked, she banged on it.

"Sanderson! Rowan! It's me—"

She gave them no time to respond before going through the side gate to the front of the house, still calling. "Rowan? Ro? It's Mom!"

The front door was wide open. Through it she could hear the television, too loud. Her heart pounding painfully, she went inside.

The house smelled of pepperoni and tomato sauce, and through the archway she could see the empty pizza pan on the stovetop.

"Rowan?" she called, and then louder, "*Rowan!*"

The house was empty.

And then she thought, *No dogs.* She let go of her panicked breath and almost grinned. They'd taken the dogs out for a walk. If she waited she would see them any minute now. She just had to relax. She leaned out to shut the screen door—*men are just forgetful that way lots of them go out leave the TV on, the door open*—and noticed the empty driveway.

No car. They'd left in a hurry

(to walk the dogs)

Now the fear and panic rose in her twofold. She realized then that it was all horribly, horribly wrong and that something very bad was going on in Haven Woods. And that it really could be

(witches)

Paula ran out into the street, ignoring the shooting pain in her knee. She headed for her mother's place, hoping that was where they would go. She hoped to god

(to God)

that Sanderson was taking care of her child.

I'm coming Rowan. Mom's coming.

Sanderson lay on the horn as he caught sight of them in the headlights.

"Holy shit!" he yelled, and stamped his foot down hard on the brake, sliding forward in his seat, which jammed his right leg into the dash. The pain was so intense it blocked out every other thought in his head. He let out a howl and his left foot slipped off the brake.

He looked up to see the women scattering, one stumbling to the right, the other two trying to get out of his way in the other direction. He jabbed the pedal again and the brakes squealed, the car shuddering as it slowed. The two women on the left seemed to be struggling, and suddenly one of them broke away—a girl. She ran towards the car and his heart jumped with relief. It was Rowan.

Then his clumsy left foot slipped again, hitting the gas pedal hard. The older women, frozen like animals mesmerized by the dazzle of the lights, didn't move. They stood with their hands still reaching out towards the girl, mouths hanging open in shock. He jabbed at the brake again, too hard: the back end slewed and the car went into a spin. It seemed to him that everyone was screaming at once: Rowan, the women and he himself. It was a weird parody of a musical number—the same note, the same tone.

The car's back end swung uselessly as he braked, then caught and jerked to a standstill. Sanderson felt as if he were still moving. He shook his head, orienting himself, the pain no longer isolated in his ankle but a bodily thing, a *wrong* thing. Sirens in his head, alarms from his body—*stop stop stop*. He gritted his teeth and tried to lift his right foot to ease it some.

"Mr. Keyes!" came the scream from outside the car. "Mr. *Keyes*—" Rowan cried again, and then he heard the other voices, and none of them was yelling for help.

"Come back, girl!" the old ladies yelled in unison.

"Is everyone okay?" he called out the window.

The motor was still running, his left foot still on the brake. He punched it into Park and the car settled with a lurch. He twisted as much as he could in the seat, hung his head out the window and yelled again, "Is everyone okay?"

Then Rowan was at the passenger door, yanking it open, jumping inside. Her face was tear-stained, her eyes so wide they were like beads in white circles. *"Drive away drive away drive—They have my mom—"* She tugged and pulled at the door.

"Ro— Rowan, calm down. What's going on—"

And then one of the old women was at his window, and she was a vision of madness. Her hands were curled into claws and she thrust them at his face. "*A posse adesse . . .*"

Rowan screamed and leaned over him, accidentally hitting his right foot. He howled, but Rowan, oblivious to his agony, was intent on rolling up the window, batting at the woman's hands. "Drive away, Mr. Keyes, drive away!"

The old woman at the window bared her teeth. They could hear her through the glass, still chanting, "*Addo mentos los betrose, addo mentos los betrose . . .*"

Sanderson's eyes watered madly as he tried to gain control of the pain. Sweat poured down his sides; he couldn't sort out which stimulus was which, what he should do. Through the blur of tears he saw the woman fold her claws into a fist and then point her index finger at his eyes. She poked at the air once, twice, three times—and suddenly his eyes were burning as if acid had been thrown at them. He screamed and screamed, clawing at his face.

Outside the window the old woman said, "Give me the girl."

Then Rowan was across his body and he felt himself being shoved aside. He tried to help by moving over, but the pain made him cry out more loudly.

"Mr. Keyes, I'm going to drive. Help me drive—"

She got the car into Drive, lurched forward and stopped, lurched forward again. Then they were moving fast, interrupted by occasional jerks as Rowan shifted her foot between the brake and the gas. He could hear the foreign-sounding threats fading behind them.

Sanderson pushed the button on the glovebox. It flopped open and he felt around for the bottle of water he kept in there for emergencies. He opened it and upended the bottle over his face. The water poured into his eyes, offering instant relief.

"Say a prayer over it," Rowan said.

The car lurched and jerked. He exhaled great gulps of air and swished more water over his eyes.

"Holy Father, bless this car and all its occupants—" Rowan was hiccupping now and then with sobs.

"What the hell is going on?" he managed to say.

"Do you know where Mr. Chapman lives?"

"Huh? Chapman? The murderer?"

The girl groaned with fear. "That makes sense. Do you know where the house is? We have to go there."

Sanderson put the bottle up to his lips and poured the remainder into his mouth. "It's at the end of town. But, good God, why? Why would we go there?"

"Because they're witches and they've got my mom."

TWENTY-FIVE

OLD TEX WAS BREATHING HARD behind her, and the other dog, the one she didn't know, was whining. The dogs made Audra feel safer, but she wasn't sure if they would make it. She was barely making it herself.

Such a terrible house. Such a terrible history. Audra, of course, knew it well. They all did. She was nearly at the gate before she realized that she was bleeding from her secret, ancient wound. The mark under her left breast was opening and closing, beating. Breathing. Eating. Bleeding.

The air was electric. She could feel it. Him.

He was coming, and she was so afraid.

The porch light was off and the front rooms of her mother's house were dark. Paula figured that meant they couldn't be there, unless they were hiding, and that thought was enough to make her run.

Her car was in the driveway. She couldn't see Sanderson's anywhere

(could have parked in the lane)

and there were no lights on at the back of the house either (maybe they're waiting in the kitchen)

She made her way slowly up the steps, battered and exhausted but powered by a strange panicked energy. Her footsteps on the porch conjured up such a raw image of childhood

hi Mom I'm home going to Marla's what's for supper did you see Dad

that she very nearly collapsed.

Paula pulled open the screen door and turned the knob. Locked. Her heart sank. She banged on the door. *Let me in.*

"They're all gone," said a voice behind her. Paula swung around, a scream just escaping her. An older woman stood at the bottom of the porch steps.

"You scared me," Paula said.

The old woman *tsk-tsk*ed softly, gently, so kindly that Paula felt her body sag in gratitude. "I'm sorry, dear, I didn't mean to frighten you. I'm an old friend of your mother's. Don't you recognize me?" She smiled sweetly.

Paula squinted, tried to make her out. She could hardly see her features with the streetlight behind her, shining through her hair like a halo. "No, I don't," she said.

"That's all right." The woman took a step up towards the porch. "You're looking for your little girl, aren't you?"

"Yes." Paula's bottom lip quivered like a child's.

The woman took another step up.

"I don't know where she is . . ."

"They've taken her. I know just where—"

"They took her?" Paula felt oddly sleepy, as if the events of the past couple of hours were catching up to her. "The . . . women?" She couldn't bring herself to say the word. *Witch*. It was something from a movie. Not real.

"She's in a sacred place. A very powerful place." The woman

took another step up. Paula closed her eyes, wanting only to listen to her voice. "Where He lives . . . the Chapman house. Do you know it?" Her tone was so soothing.

"Witches," Paula mumbled.

The woman whispered, "*Somnus et tranquillitas . . .*" and Paula almost swooned. She grabbed the door handle to steady herself.

"Where is . . . my . . . daughter . . ." It did not come out as a question. She struggled to remember what she was doing. *Rowan.* Rowan.

"We'll go there together and then you will see your daughter. She's important to us."

Rowan. Paula just wanted to let go.

The woman took the next-to-last step up the porch stairs and whispered again, "*Somnus et tranquillitas . . .*" Then suddenly she screeched as though she'd been burned. "What have you *got*?!"

She backed up, stumbling down the stairs. Paula jerked awake. The woman continued to back away, practically hissing at her, "What have you got there? What have you got? What *evil* do you hold?"

Paula's eyes fell on the bottle that Sanderson's mother had hidden behind the post. The witch bottle. Her eyes widened and she stared at the woman. This was one too.

The woman had turned her face partly away, as if Paula were a strong light, and the glow from the streetlight revealed her features. She was sunken and old as the ages. Her eyes were yellowed where they should have been white and her pupils were so large there was no other colour. Her skin was thin and papery, her nose hooked, lips thin—a dollar-store witch's mask.

"Get it away from me, you stupid little bitch!" she screamed. "The bottle, the *bottle!*" The woman wailed like a mourner, covering her face and weeping. Paula ran down the stairs and past her to the car. Inside, she slammed her hand down on the door-lock button. There was a hard, satisfying *clunk* from all four doors. She flipped down the visor. The keys fell into her lap—it was a Haven Woods thing

(thank God for bad habits)

The old woman pounded on the window. She grabbed at the door handle and pulled, to no effect. "Let me in, let me in. I'll take you to her. I said, *let me in!* I'll peel your face from your skull, you little bitch—"

The car started on the second try and Paula screeched out of the driveway.

The suburbs are all about driving.

The Chapman house was humming with something alive, if not actual life. Light poured out of the windows, coming from no source at all. It looked natural, as if the sun had risen inside and was now pouring out.

The women on the porch stayed where they were. All of them had been inside many times. They knew the house's history, of course, but after awhile they had ceased to think about it. The house had become just another stop in their roster of chores, not very much different from the post office, the dry cleaner, the grocery store. But tonight, what it was and what it had been was unavoidable. And the women—the sisters—stood just outside of the circle of light.

Terrified.

Izzy had seen them out there on the porch, whispering, but it was Esme whose eye she caught. She knew a guilty look when she saw one. She could see what was afoot, could tell by Esme's expression that she was thinking about walking away. Betrayal.

Just try it.

Izzy sent her a glare so fierce that it forced Esme to her knees, the heat and sudden pain in her chest too much to bear. She gasped for air, collapsed, unable to breathe; her vision dulled and her thought function went cottony, as if she were suffering from a hangover.

How dare you, Izzy mouthed.

On her knees, Esme bowed her head in obeisance to whomever it was who required it, her voice a mumble amid the drone of the unseen from the house.

Soon after, Bridget brought an offering. By then Izzy had stopped pacing and had dropped to the stairs in exhaustion, her head down, her hands clasped in dark prayer. Bridget stood in the doorway of the house and called to her.

She gasped when Izzy looked up. Izzy grinned, knowing how she must look, herself feeling the slackness of her skin as though the flesh had melted away, the way her eyes were wide and round yet sunken. Her mouth moved so awkwardly there seemed little correlation with what she was saying.

"What do you want from me?"

Bridget held out a bag. "It's from Glory . . . all of us, really . . ."

Izzy eyeballed it: a plain kitchen-waste bag, the contents small and dark through the translucent white plastic. Probably from someone's glovebox, a refuse bag for coffee cups and McDonald's containers.

"What is it?"

Bridget opened the bag and, with a grimace, reached inside and pulled out a finger. The last of Glory's complement of lost digits.

Izzy laughed, the sound muffled, a silent movie laugh. "Bring it here," she said, still grinning. A dare.

Bridget shook her head. *No.*

Izzy was astonished. Really, how could she say no? *Why* would she? *He has given you everything you asked for, everything you wanted.*

Bridget just stared.

You don't honour Him.

Bridget held the bag out from her body as if it were electric. Clearly she longed to put it down, to get it away from her.

"That is what will kill us all," Izzy said, scolding.

Bridget finally set the bag down just inside the doorway, such a meagre gift that the bag looked almost flat. Then the contents began to move inside the plastic. Bridget stared, horrified.

"He doesn't like it," Izzy had said, disgusted. "He wants the child he was promised—"

Behind her a man appeared, staring cruelly, his shirtfront covered in blood, a hatchet dangling from his left hand. It was not Chapman—Bridget had seen enough photos of the man to know that. She backed out the door, half stumbling, wanting to scream but, to her credit, not giving in.

Izzy laughed. "He'll take it all from you—whatever He promised—because you are all *bad daughters*."

Bad sisters.

Whether they left or not was no longer a concern. It was all over. They would pay one way or another, if they stayed or if they left. There was little hope for salvation now.

Not salvation. Izzy stopped herself. *Salvation* was not the word. That was a different god.

She heard Joanna scream. There were things in the yard, made bold by the air of evil that was gathering, no longer held at bay by other forces. They'd sensed an overtaking and had come to taste the agony.

The house filled itself, drinking whatever poisons were in the air and casting them as walking shadows. Around her she heard breathing, rattling, hissing, the screams of the damned and the occasional voice raised in prayer to Him.

Through it all Izzy sat and waited. For the girl.

The girl could still make it right.

—

Marla held Amy in her arms, one arm supporting her back and the other under her legs. It was a comforting position, except that Amy's body was so stiff. Her legs stuck straight out and would not fold over her mother's arm. Under Marla's right breast she could feel her daughter's heart beating. It was soft, but it was there.

She carried the girl into the den, where Doug had collapsed over his papers. She laid her on the leather sofa, which cracked in an unfriendly way. Marla had chosen that sofa for its masculine qualities, not considering how unpleasant it would be to sit on.

Tim was heavier to carry, but she wanted them all to be together. As she staggered towards the den she tried to think of the last time she'd weighed either of them. It was funny how such things got away from you during the course of regular busy days. She always had so much to do.

He moaned, "Mom . . ." on the way down the stairs.

"Just a minute more, honey," she said encouragingly. "Two more steps. Two more steps and then we're all done—"

"Ma . . ."

At last she managed to lay him down beside his sister. Then they were all there

(*crackle crackle crackle* if they got out of this that sofa was going to the Salvation Army)

She lit candles and placed them strategically by her beloveds. With each candle she mumbled her choices, her sorrows, her apologies, her repentance.

She doubted she would make it out of this mess. But they might.

When the candles were all lit, Marla sat amid them and began her plea. To other gods. Other God. It began, "I am the spider. I am the rat. I have been in bad holes . . ."

—

They were all in dark holes. Izzy knew Joanna had probably lost her show. She'd seen her dipping into her pocket again and again, sniffing at whatever potion she had stashed there. *Too late*. She knew that Esme ached in her loins, a horrible, hollow ache that would never now be filled. Boys were her weakness and she had never controlled it. Bridget was greedy. Sharie, the youngest, the dancer, was simply stupid.

Their bad choices had undermined them. The elders—and she included herself in the indictment—had allowed their children to run wild, to have whatever they wanted without check. Oddly, Izzy realized that only Marla had consistently maintained her priorities. It came as a revelation to her. Her daughter had been all she had hoped she would be. A good mother, a good daughter . . .

And then it occurred to her that Marla wasn't there. Her head shot up. She had not come. Her daughter had forsaken Him. Had she?

Marla—the least of her ambitions. It shook her. And a wave of regret swept over her, almost visceral. Her daughter. Her daughter.

Not her choice. *David*, she'd said, without hesitation.

(oh no)

It was all so far gone. Over, really. Wasn't it? Yet in her heart she hoped for something else. Still

(and still for David she could not shake David so long dead)

The heat was unbearable. But the girl was coming now; she could feel her somewhere close.

It was marvellous. They could all be saved.

Izzy put a finger in her mouth. Her teeth were becoming loose. She'd always been vain about her teeth.

She bowed her head. *"Laus aliis qui audiunt meam causam . . ."*

Still.

TWENTY-SIX

SANDERSON, HIS EYES CLOSED against the pain, could not believe what was happening. The world had gone crazy. What had that old woman done to him? What did Rowan mean? He hurt so much he wanted to give up. But they had to find Paula . . .

"Rowan, we have to go back to your grandmother's, or to my house. Your mom will—"

"My *mom* is with those women. They're all witches, even my grandma. They're going to do something bad to her." She sat up as tall as she could, defiant, clutching the steering wheel hard. The car seemed to veer of its own accord from side to side, no matter how hard she tried to keep it steady. But she was doing well. Considering.

Mr. Keyes, however, was fading. He just couldn't take this in. He was leaning his head against the window and he was very pale. His ankle and foot were grotesquely swollen, the skin shiny and the toes like fat little sausages. She knew she should take him to the hospital

(although part of her was quite willing to skip that part, the hospital where nurses were *witches*) but she had to get to her mother. She wanted her mother so badly, badly enough that she couldn't feel how brave she was being. She didn't know it, of course, but it was the same feeling that sends mothers into burning buildings.

She could see the glow in the sky and knew it was where she had to go. It was the only light in the neighbourhood.

"There it is," she said. He opened his eyes to slits and looked at the strange light. Even as they stared, a kind of reverse aurora borealis was taking place, dark shapes blending and changing, merging and breaking in the sky over the house, faces appearing and disappearing, each of them a mask of agony.

"Christ!" Mr Keyes gasped, and shut his eyes again.

Rowan pressed down on the gas, biting her lower lip. She wanted nothing more than to feel the crucifix through her shirt, but she dared not take a hand off the wheel.

And then they were upon the place. It was surrounded by feral ivy. Through gaps in the ivy she could see an abandoned car, a pile of tires, a burn barrel.

Rowan slowed down, and as she did, the gate opened wide for her. The headlights picked up the shapes of women, standing around as if they were waiting for her.

"See," she said, sighing. "I told you it was witches."

Mr. Keyes seemed to have passed out. She wished she could too.

She drove in through the open gates. On either side of the car *things* slithered and sneaked.

The house seemed to rise up and stretch itself when the car came through the gate. Whatever was spewing from whatever portal now filled the air inside with the darkest of spirits.

Izzy picked her way towards the door. The floor had begun to seep. Wet, viscous, with unidentifiable bits of flesh, hair, bone spread over every surface. The smell was beyond horrible, but she didn't notice. For the past two hours she had used too much of her energy keeping it all at bay, begging her dark god to honour her loyalty, her love, her *worship* . . .

But she was growing weak. She stepped through the blood and waste of a thousand years towards the door. Towards the girl. To rescue them all and return things to where they had been. Where they should be.

You did not die for nothing, my darling David. Mommy promises.

Mr. Keyes stirred, looked around. Shuddered.

"I'm getting my mom," Rowan said.

He let out a loud groan and reached for her. "No—"

He missed, and Rowan opened the car door. But she couldn't get out. A dozen eyes were on her, and she was sure some of them weren't human. A small thing—maybe a man, maybe a boy—stood ten feet from the car, its head misshapen and bulbous, patches of hair missing. It carried something in a bag that was trying to get out, and something else wriggled near its foot: a tail, slick and pink like a rat's. The man-boy thing smiled at her pleasantly. It had a mouthful of perfect teeth.

She squeezed her eyes tight and then opened them again. It was gone.

Mr Keyes reached out for her again, catching the back of her jacket.

"No!" he said again, and yanked.

She pulled away. "Sorry, Mr. Keyes. I've got to find my mom." She got out of the car, telling herself, *Just don't look.*

From the front door Izzy saw the girl coming. She gathered the last of her strength. In her sweetest voice, made all the more sweet by genuine longing, she called out, "Rowan! Oh, goodness, you're here! Come here, darling! Come to—

come to Mommy

At the sound of her mother's voice, Rowan began to run.

From the back pocket of her jeans, Izzy drew the knife. She stood at the doorway with arms spread wide, a smile on her lips, her head tilted kindly.

"Darling," she said.

Rowan ran without reservation towards her mother, who held open her arms for her to jump into. She was so relieved, so happy to see her, that she was laughing and crying all at once. "Mom, Mom, Mommy—" she cried, her eyes never leaving her mother's face. And then

(no?)

she saw her mother's expression seem to waver, the way the road will on a sunny day, up ahead on the highway.

And she slowed so suddenly she nearly tripped, and then her mother's face seemed to briefly

(no)

split in the centre and spread apart. Rowan screamed, and her hands flew to her face even as her momentum carried her forward. She hit the hard earth with an *ooompf!* and lay there, face first in the dirt, for a moment completely birdy.

No matter. Izzy dropped the Paula charade but kept the voice, since the girl couldn't see her now. This was all very exhausting.

Sweat ran down Sanderson's face. He didn't dare look at his leg, but he could feel his calf straining at his pant leg. He couldn't think about that now. He had to get Rowan out of there.

Gritting his teeth, he lurched upright, trying not to listen to the hum of whatever was outside the car. It sounded like voices, but not real ones. The kind you imagine in nightmares.

He moved just inches at a time. But he was moving.

Rowan coughed as she caught her breath, then struggled to her feet. Her hands were scraped and she'd torn her jeans at the knee.

"Hello, Rowan," said her mother.

But Rowan was staring at someone else.

"Do you like magic?" Izzy asked. She held up a knife, not with menace or threat, but like a mom coming to the door hollering for everyone to come in for supper. Sunday roast.

I'll carve

Audra was almost at the gate. She paused for a moment to catch her breath and search inside herself for any reserves of stamina she might have left. There was very little, but some.

Suddenly there was a car behind her, tires spinning on the gravel road. She turned and looked into its headlights. Gusto barked. The car slammed to a stop and the door opened.

"Mom?"

Paula jogged over to her and the two of them stood there in the blinding headlights. "My God, Mom, what are you doing here? We have to get you back to the hospital."

Paula tried to pull her to her car. With the last of her strength, Audra resisted. "No. Listen, please. I made a terrible mistake. I loved you and your dad very much, but I owed my debt."

"What are you talking about? I have to get you to the hospital. Rowan is missing; I have to find her. God, Mom, I just ran away from here. It's dangerous! They've all gone crazy—"

Audra kept talking, insistent. "It was supposed to be your father that day at the Rileys'. I never meant for anything to happen to

David. I thought I was securing your future—"

"Mom, now is not the time—"

"Then He took your father anyway. I'm so sorry. Paula, I tried to protect you. You and Rowan."

Paula had stopped tugging on her arm. Her expression was confused, alarmed. She stepped back now. "Mom . . . is she here?"

Both of them turned to look at the house. The second-floor windows were eyes. The front door was a black maw, lit with fire, shapes dancing. There was something seductive about it, a scent, a music of its own.

"It's a portal," Audra said. "I have to stop this."

Izzy grabbed the girl by her jacket and pulled her forward. Rowan resisted, then screamed loudly, shrilly, as only a twelve-year-old girl can scream.

Izzy stopped and shook her head impatiently. "That's enough!"

"Where is my mother? For real!"

Izzy yanked at the girl again, using only one hand because the other was full of knife. "Be a good girl now. Don't you like magic? Everyone likes magic. Come with me and I'll show you some goddamn magic." Then she realized what she'd said and she laughed.

"Help!" Rowan screamed.

With an irritated groan, Izzy raised the girl up off her feet. Something odd vibrated through her arm. There was a special weight to the girl, a forceful weight, a productive weight. It confused her, derailed her. The knife dangled from her hand as she puzzled over the meaning of the force.

Just as Rowan cried out, Sanderson managed to push open the passenger-side door. A thing, hardly human, grotesquely moulded, peered at him and said uneasily, in a surprisingly suburban, motherly tone, "You can't go in there. You can't get the girl—"

Its hand reached over and grabbed Sanderson's ankle. He threw his head back to howl in pain, the world around him growing fuzzy. He felt as if he was about to faint, when suddenly the hand was removed. He opened his eyes to see the creature being pulled away from him, its face a picture of surprise, almost comical. What the hell?

And a fierce and nearly unrecognizable

(Tex)

wrestling the thing to the ground. The dog buried its face in the creature's throat and Gusto leapt into the fray, tugging on the thing's arm.

The creature fought back, wrapped its arms around Old Tex's neck and yanked hard. Gusto leapt around them, barking, dashing in to nip at the creature and jumping out of reach in an age-old dance.

"Good dogs," he managed. "Keep it busy." Fishing his hockey stick out of the car, he jammed it under his arm. Then he started limping after Rowan.

The disgusting thing's force waned with every snap of their jaws. Eventually Tex and Gusto snapped at air; the creature dissipating, fading, and gone.

Gusto leapt about in triumph, not noticing at first that Tex could not. The old dog sat down heavily instead, then lay down on his side, his chest rising and falling in gasps. Gusto sniffed around him, licked his face, whined.

Gusto stood watch over the old dog, snapping and growling when things from the shadows came close. Old Tex lay still.

The house glowed orange-red, like fire, although Paula could not see much beyond the open doorway. The air was so loaded with heat and fury that for a heartbeat she was paralyzed with fear. Above them the hydro line snapped and hissed with a life of its own; she could smell the sharp odour of burning wire. The line buzzed, a robotic purr, like a cat before it leaps.

Then her mother rushed forward. Izzy was standing in the doorway of the Chapman house, Rowan dangling from one arm. Paula screamed, a mother's wail of anguish.

"Izzy, *stop!*" Audra yelled. Izzy looked up and saw her, and then a small, sad smile crossed her lips.

But Izzy was lost. She shook Rowan, and the girl groaned and pried at her captor's arm, nearly scratching holes in it. Something was wrong.

The girl shouted for her mother, and there was Paula in the yard. Izzy thought, *Too little, too late.*

late

Then she realized what the weight, the *substance* of the girl meant. She howled at the moon. "You're bleeding!" she shrieked. *"You bleed!"*

The girl bit down hard on Izzy's shoulder through the thin fabric of the expensive T-shirt and Izzy screamed, but it was not because of the bite, but because she was so angry, so tired of black luck. She gave a mighty heave on the girl, all the strength in her coming from elsewhere, not from her old, skinny body.

"I'm using you anyway! You're His! I *promised*—" And she pulled Rowan with her into the ugly dark maw of the Chapman house.

The earth under Paula shifted and rose as if it was waiting to trip her, to eat her up. She fell twice, picking herself up only to have a creature jump in front of her and speak, in horrible tones, YOU ARE NOT INVITED IN.

It wrestled with something it held in its arms. and Paula saw that it was a piglet, eyeless, with a misshapen jaw that showed all its teeth.

Her mother walked up the porch steps, unimpeded.

"Mother!" It was a cry of betrayal, despair. Shame.

Izzy half carried, half dragged the child to the altar. The Master's works faded in and out in the flickering light, the damned and the forgotten. The reek was incredible.

Rowan screamed and squirmed in her arms.

Izzy threw her on the wooden table. Rowan's head knocked hard against it, rendering her briefly, thankfully silent. Izzy held her down with one powerful hand and with the other raised the knife above her head. She began her words of offering.

Behind her, Audra said, "She is David's child."

Izzy stopped in mid-breath, the name bouncing around in her brain.

Then Audra was right beside her. She put her hand on Izzy's back, and Izzy was surprised to realize that she could still feel human.

"Izzy," Audra said, "Rowan is David's child. She is your granddaughter."

Rowan could hear everything. When the woman's hand let up on her chest, she curled into a protective ball. She dared not open her eyes. All around the table there were . . . *creatures*.

"Mom, mom, mom, mom, mom . . ." she chanted under her breath.

Izzy turned to Audra. "No."

Audra nodded. "Yes. I was afraid to tell you. She's my grand-daughter too."

"Why wouldn't you tell me something like that, Audra?

Something that could have—"

Izzy looked down at the girl on the table, curled up and now sobbing. Her heart went out to her. She bent over and pried the girl's hands off her face.

"My David . . ." she said. "David and Paula . . ."

Izzy put a gentle hand on the girl's cheek and whispered her name. The girl's face was frozen in terror.

"My Rowan . . ." she said.

Paula ran into the dark house. It was crowded with bodies and shadows and shapes so horrible there was no way to register them. She simply held her arms out in front of her and pushed her way through, bellowing for her daughter. "Rowan! *Rowan!*"

"Mom? Mommy?"

Paula pressed forward, the slime and stink and wretchedness jostling and pushing her back.

Izzy and Audra locked eyes.

"You knew," Izzy said.

"I couldn't tell you. I couldn't let this become their life," Audra said. "Blood . . ." She offered no other explanation.

For a moment Izzy looked ready to nod, to agree with her old friend, and then she didn't. "My son was everything, and taken from me. It was supposed to be *your* sacrifice, it was supposed to be Walter. And you took my grandchild from me. David's child. How could you?"

Audra reached out to touch her friend. As she did, the house began to shake, and an excited, frightened murmur went quickly through the crowd of shapes.

he comes

he comes

Paula stumbled forward even as the house danced around her, the floor rising and falling like a funhouse ride. As if it were breathing. She pushed her way past a huge thing covered in hair and smelling of earth. There, suddenly, was her mother. And Izzy.

"*Mom!*" From between the two women came a set of small arms, hands stretched out to her. Paula ran for her daughter, the shaking, shifting floor tossing her towards the altar.

"Paula, get the child out!" Audra yelled.

Paula gathered her daughter in her arms. The house creaked and screamed around them, the voices rose into something unworldly, unholy.

"No!" screamed Izzy. She grabbed Rowan by the hair and the girl shrieked.

Audra wrapped herself around Izzy and said, clearly and loudly, "Paula, take her away from here."

Paula yanked her daughter free. She held her like a baby and carried her through the stumbling, reeling, jubilant crowd.

he comes he comes

She ducked her head low and, like a battering ram, she pushed headlong through the mass of writhing, twisting evil as they celebrated the advent of their unholy Father.

"No!" Izzy screamed and tried to go after them.

"Let them go," Audra shouted over the din into Izzy's ear. "It's our turn."

The house shook with energy. It was blazing hot, and the women were suddenly deeply terrified. Audra pulled them both onto the altar nonetheless.

"Let him take us," she said. "It will end."

Izzy stared at her. Both of them were bleeding from their wounds; the blood had a coppery menstrual smell to it, but repellent, rotten. She collapsed into Audra's arms and they clung to each other on the altar. The house began its disintegration. The roof cracked and shook.

"They'll blame us, you know," Izzy said to Audra. "They always blame the mother."

And then a great shaking rent open a wound in the earth, black and dark and endless.

Sanderson saw what he never thought he would, Paula running towards the car, half carrying, half dragging Rowan, refusing to let go of her.

She yanked open the door and jammed the two of them inside, just as something leapt at them. They screamed in unison, then they heard the a familiar bark.

Gusto.

Sanderson looked around quickly for Old Tex— he might even have said, *where's Old Tex, hey boy, huh?* Old Tex was lying on the ground, completely still.

"Wait!" he called. He hobbled over to the dog. Behind them the whole house was burning. He awkwardly heaved Tex up and hauled him to the car. Paula opened the back door and Sanderson lay the dog across her and Rowan's laps.

"He's hardly breathing," Paula said.

Rowan moaned and buried her face in his side.

"He saved me." Sanderson ran his hand over Tex's fur. "Good dog." And again, fiercely, "*Good* dog." Gusto jumped in after his friend.

Sanderson got into the driver's seat, breathing hard, and lifted his broken ankle out of the way. The pain was beyond pain. He backed up the car awkwardly and drove through the gate, bouncing it open with the grille. Then he pulled onto the gravel road and hightailed it.

Sanderson took a last glance in the rear-view mirror as Paula and Rowan looked out the back window. The burning house was falling into itself. They were silent for a moment. Paula kept watching over her shoulder, but Rowan covered her face with her hands.

Finally Paula rolled up the window, the screams from beyond the grave too much for her. "Get us to Princess Ice Cream and then I'll drive," she said.

When they got there, Sanderson pulled off the road and turned to look in the back seat. Paula and Rowan were stroking Old Tex. "He's gone," Paula said.

Sanderson nodded. Rowan started to cry.

"I'm going to drive," Paula said to Rowan. She sat her daughter up and wiped away her tears. "You loved him and he loved you," she said. "We'll take him with us, away from here, okay?"

Rowan nodded and laid her hand on Old Tex's head.

Paula helped Sanderson out of the driver's seat; he leaned on her as he hobbled around to the other side. When he'd got himself in, she took off her jacket, bunched it up and, carefully as she could, put it under his foot. Muttering mother words, words of comfort.

Love words.

As they drove away she said to Sanderson, "You rescued us."

"No, I didn't."

"Yes, you did."

"No. It was Rowan. I just wanted to watch a movie."

"I wish we had," Rowan said. No one laughed.

They passed the sign on the road near the highway, all three of them looked.

THANK YOU FOR YOUR VISIT! WE'LL MISS YOU!

"Are we going home?" Rowan asked.

"Yeah," Paula said. She took the exit ramp.

EPILOGUE

PAULA PULLED ON THE EMERGENCY brake and it snapped into place with a solid clunk. Lots of things were solid now.

"Just a sec," she said and got out the driver's side. The minivan was new and she was still learning its ways. The side door tended to stick, and she braced for the big yank. Through the window she saw Sanderson laughing. She blushed and pulled the door open.

"You looked like you were about to tackle Everest. You stick your tongue out when you concentrate. Did you know that?" He reached down in front of him and picked up his crutch.

"I thought you liked my tongue," she said.

"Eww," came Rowan's voice from the front. "You guys are gross."

"All right, all right," Paula said and got out of the way so Sanderson could manoeuvre himself out of the van.

Rowan jumped out of the front passenger seat, saying, "Can I let the dogs out?" Before Paula could answer, the back of the van was open and two very happy animals jumped to the ground. The puppy, a Shepherd-Lab cross, bounced around in a circle while Gusto wagged his tail indulgently. They had taken to each other nicely. Surprisingly nicely. Rowan snapped leads onto both collars. The puppy nipped at her fingers, and she waved a pointer at his nose.

Rowan ducked down to their level and let the dogs lick her face. Paula didn't like that much, but she let it happen anyway. The dogs made Rowan happy. And whatever helped to erase the events of that night in June was fine with her.

Sanderson put weight on his good foot and planted the crutch. He'd just had another surgery on his ankle, but the doctor thought this would be the last. He would probably have a slight limp forever, but it was ultimately going to be fine. Everything was ultimately going to be fine.

"Okay," Paula said, as Sanderson successfully negotiated the curb. "Let's go to the dog park!"

"*Dog park*," Rowan said to the dogs. They pulled her forward, dragging her to the entrance. She and the dogs ran through the gate and it slammed shut behind them. Rowan bent over and unsnapped Gusto's leash. She rubbed his head and scratched under his chin. In an indulgent parental voice, she said firmly, "Now, you watch your little brother, and I mean it."

Gusto seemed to understand. He sat while the girl unleashed the puppy, who then nearly upended her. She laughed and rubbed his tiny, perfect little body with both hands and snuggled his face into hers. "Oh, you're such a good boy, such a good, good boy, aren't you—"

And then a voice behind her said, "What a nice little dog. Can I pet him?"

Rowan had to squint because the sun was in her eyes. "Sure," she said.

The old woman put her hand on the dog's small head. "He's a precious. How old is he?" The puppy was being oddly placid, wagging and wiggling but not running off. Gusto came closer, to get his share maybe.

"Almost three months."

"What's his name?" the woman asked.

"Tex."

"Oh, that's a good name for a dog."

"Thank you," Rowan said politely. She didn't know at all what the old woman meant.

The woman petted the puppy and the puppy wagged his tail happily.

When Paula saw the woman talking to Rowan, Sanderson put his hand on her back. "It's okay," he said. "We're not in Haven Woods. This is beautiful, boring Goodview. Right?"

"Okay," she said. They started walking again and she resisted the temptation to tell him to hurry up. "Hey, Rowan, you have to let those dogs run!" she called.

The old woman and Rowan looked up at the sound of Paula's voice.

The woman took her hands off the dog's ruff and gave him one last scratch behind his ear. The puppy leaned into it. "Your mother's right. You run off now, Old Tex."

"Hey," Rowan said, "how did you know his—"

And then Paula was there and she put her hand out for the woman to shake. "Hello," she said, her smile a little brittle. "I'm Paula. This is my daughter. And you are?"

"She's a good girl."

"Thank you," Paula said. Sanderson came up behind her and regarded the stranger carefully.

The old woman took a deep breath and let it out, smiling. "It's so nice here. Close to home," she said. "And I had better get there."

She nodded to Sanderson, meeting his eyes, and he smiled back slowly. For a moment he felt something tug at him.

"Goodbye," she said. She took a good long look at Paula, her expression wistful. "You have a lovely family."

"Thank you."

"You'll have a nice life," she told Paula. "You have someone watching over you, I think."

Sanderson and Rowan moved off as Rowan threw a ball for Gusto. The old woman stood there as if reluctant to go. Paula thought that her eyes were kindly, a pretty blue. The woman suddenly leaned close, putting her hand delicately on Paula's stomach. "You're going to have a boy," she whispered.

Paula was too surprised even to gasp.

The woman turned away from her then and waved. "Goodbye, Rowan. You take good care of that dog, now!"

"I will," Rowan called back as she tugged at the ball in Gusto's mouth. He let go, only to have the puppy move in and grab it. "Tex!" Rowan shouted, and gave chase as the puppy romped away. Sanderson headed for the benches then, and Paula followed.

When they were sitting, he asked, "You look funny. What did she say to you? "

"Nothing much." He seemed to accept that. That was something she really liked about Sanderson—he let her have her space.

Paula wondered whether she should be uneasy about what the old woman had said, but she felt strangely calm. The events of six months ago were fading and the old life was falling away from her and Rowan. The last threads had been cut when they'd sold her mother's place and Sanderson's too. He had said he wasn't sad to let it go, although she had worried about that.

Every morning Paula now woke up in their new house, with Sanderson beside her and her daughter down the hall. Both Rowan and Paula were in school, and they made their lunches in the morning side by side. The worst thing that happened to them these days was the puppy having an accident in the house and Sanderson stepping in pee with bare feet. He seemed surprised whenever it happened. "Goddamned dog," he said, every time.

Sameness. For the first time in many years, she and Rowan had sameness and security. It was glorious.

Recently she'd even begun talking to Marla again. Marla, who was painfully sorry, whose family had survived that horrible night and now had to make their way in the world without . . . help. She didn't want to see Marla yet, and might never want to see her. But she was Rowan's aunt. Time would heal or it wouldn't. They'd have to wait.

"Wanna do takeout tonight?" Sanderson asked.

She nodded and leaned happily into his shoulder as they watched Rowan with the dogs. Paula's hand was on her belly. She thought about the old woman again. She hadn't said anything to Sanderson yet. But the woman was right. She also thought it would be a boy.

As they drove away from the park, both dogs lay flopped on the floor of the van in the back, tuckered out. Rowan, who no longer wore her school blazer everywhere—mostly because she didn't go to that school anymore—felt around in the pocket of her hoodie and found the pink crucifix. She wrapped her fingers around it.

She'd never told that lady her name, or anything about Old Tex. But somehow she wasn't freaked out. She'd liked her.

"So, burgers or fish and chips?" Paula asked.

"Fish and chips," Sanderson said. "The Kooby place—"

"Burgers," Rowan said. "Come on—burgers!"

"We had burgers last time," Paula said. "But we can compromise. Tacos?"

"Burgers," Rowan tried once more.

"Come on, Ro," Paula said. And she shot her daughter a look.

"Hmmm . . ." Rowan said. Then she looked out the window. As she did, she drew little circles in the palm of her hand, her eyes angled sideways at her mother. "I want," she whispered, too low for her to hear.

"What did you say?" Paula asked.

Rowan raised her index finger and flicked something invisible at her mother. And then towards Sanderson in the back seat. He was her dad now. The dead boy who had made her with her mother was hardly real to her, no matter how much was explained. She loved Sanderson.

She repeated the spell, drawing circles in her palm and flicking her desire at each of her parents. *I want.*

Paula half-turned to her. "I can't hear you, Ro."

"Nothing," Rowan said.

"Okay, then." Sanderson rubbed the back of his head. "Burgers. Where should we go?"

"How about Burgerland, at Fenton and Garvis?" Paula said.

Rowan clapped her hands with excitement. "My favourite!"

Burgerland it was.

ACKNOWLEDGEMENTS

There are witches and warlocks in my life who kept me upright with their potions and passion. So thank you to Michael, Josh and Jackie, Vern, Dawn. The enchanting Donna Carreiro read the book too many times to count, which makes her a saint. She also kept me well watered and fed. The bewitching John Hudson provided escape and relief, inside and out, from the big city. The entrancing Richard Wagner let me talk and talk and talk about witches and never looked bored. Magical Ryan Shymko let me finish up at his place, like the gentleman he always is. Joanne Kelly graciously offered her whole home when all I needed was a desk. My partner, Vern Thiessen, has me under his spell. He read it and loved it, which was magically just what I needed to hear. Most of all, I want to thank the surely supernatural Anne Collins, who edits with elegance and respect, and whose patience and dedication really wrote this book.

SUSIE MOLONEY is the bestselling author of *Bastion Falls*, *A Dry Spell* and *The Dwelling*. She has been published in numerous countries and assorted languages. She divides her time between the wild prairies of Manitoba and the wild world of New York City.